FIRESTORM

A PROSECUTION FORCE THRILLER

LOGAN RYLES

SEVERN ⚓ RIVER
PUBLISHING

Severn River Publishing
SevernRiverBooks.com

ISBN: 978-1-64875-581-1 (Paperback)

ALSO BY LOGAN RYLES

The Prosecution Force Series

Brink of War

First Strike

Election Day

Failed State

Firestorm

White Alert

The Reed Montgomery Series

Overwatch

Hunt to Kill

Total War

Smoke and Mirrors

Survivor

Death Cycle

Sundown

To find out more about Logan Ryles and his books, visit

severnriverbooks.com

For Melissa — Maggie Trousdale's biggest fan.

1

The earthquake struck at 3:32 a.m., local time. A forty-three-second burst of ground-shaking mayhem, registering 8.7 on the Richter scale and ripping through the heart of Port-au-Prince like a nuclear blast. As buildings collapsed and concrete dust mushroomed into the sky, nobody heard the screams of the dead and dying. Only the incessant rumble of the earth, bringing the Haitian capital to its knees for the second time in just over a decade—decimating thousands of buildings, wreaking nearly twenty billion dollars' worth of damage, and silencing the lives of a quarter million people.

All in less than a minute.

As the dust settled and wails rose above the sudden stillness, the Western Hemisphere remained fast asleep, heedless of the agony and heartbreak erupting only a few hundred miles away.

But on the other side of the globe, eight time zones removed from the island of Hispaniola, somebody had been waiting for this moment. Sheltered in a dusty hut, baking deep in the heart of desert desolation, Abdel Ibrahim remained riveted to his satellite TV as the news broke. Hours dragged into days while the men outside waited in silence, and Ibrahim watched the news reels.

CNN. The BBC. MSNBC. Regional networks out of Saudi Arabia and the UAE—all reporting on the Haitian tragedy in stunned disbelief. Displaying footage of the pancaked apartment buildings and collapsed office towers across Port-au-Prince. The fields of body bags and the clouds of flies descending on the city even as international aid groups scrambled to provide basic necessities to the reeling nation.

But hope was a forgotten word in Haiti. The baking hot Caribbean sun poured insult onto injury, leaving people exposed to the elements without any place to shelter. The initial efforts of first responders were complicated by the presence of heavily armed, roving Haitian gangs who exploited the chaos to loot retail stores and homes, opening fire on anyone who stood in their way.

Each day the death toll climbed higher, crossing three hundred thousand by the end of the first week. The world stood by in shock and awe, repeating the same dazed questions over and over.

How could this happen?

Ibrahim didn't know, and what was more, he didn't care. The questions of the media crackled through his aged TV set and he ignored them, waiting patiently for the inevitable. The moment he'd waited nearly three years for.

Because one man's tragedy is another man's opportunity.

One man's earthquake is another man's wide open door.

After eight days of international scrambling, that door finally opened. It began in New York City, with an emergency session of the United Nations. A resolution signed by all 193 member states called for two billion dollars of emergency aid to be poured without delay into Port-au-Prince—fresh water, food, shelter, medical supplies, and two hundred heavily armed coalition peacekeepers to ward off the gangs while those precious supplies were dispersed.

The Americans would manage the operation. The Port of Savannah, the third busiest port in the United States, would serve as the logistical hub of all international aid shipments. Initial aid would reach Port-au-Prince within a week, though the operation would continue for up to four months.

A coordinated international effort. A bright spark in the darkness of an often war-torn and hostile planet. A moment of belief, the journalists called it. A candle of solidarity for Haiti.

But for Abdel Ibrahim, the moment represented something else. As the news reels switched from the smashed desolation of Port-au-Prince to helicopter footage recorded from high above the Port of Savannah, he watched the ships gather. He observed the inevitable havoc as two dozen nations rushed to outdo one other's generosity, pouring precious resources into the city. Cramming them aboard a score of ships. Urging them south.

It was a mess. Just like he had known it would be. And for the first time in three years, a smile crossed Ibrahim's face. His prayers had been answered. Allah had provided him with an opportunity.

The time had finally come.

2

"Is that all you've got? My *grandmother* could do better, and she's rotting in a casket. *Push harder!*"

The concrete floor was stained dark with sweat, lined with grunting bodies, cooled by a giant fan mounted high in the wall. The parking lot out front was packed tight with two dozen black and silver vehicles, none of them worth less than sixty grand. Mercedes and Porches, Maseratis and Teslas.

So many Teslas.

Reed stood in the doorway, guzzling water while he watched Turk march down the line of overweight white men, stretched out in push-up formation, shaking like leaves in the wind as they fought to press out "just one more."

Turk wore ACU pants, combat boots, and no shirt. His muscled chest gleamed with sweat and his face twisted into an ugly snarl as he descended into a crouch and screamed into the face of the fifty-year-old businessman flopped out on his stomach.

"What are you doing?" Turk bellowed. "Why are you lying on my concrete? *Why? Why? Why?* Do you freaking hear me? Are you deaf? Do you not have arms?"

The guy shook and fought to get back onto his palms. Turk pressed his face to within inches of the guy's cheek and kept up the hail of questions. Reed couldn't resist a smirk as he watched, but the look in the businessman's eye told him Turk had gone too far. The "motivation" was not being well received.

Reaching to the wall, Reed mashed a button on the built-in timer, and a loud buzzer went off. In unison, every man across the room hit their chests in an exhausted heap as Turk looked up in confusion.

"Too far," Reed mouthed.

Turk raised a middle finger and headed for his water bottle, leaving Reed to reach the end of the pushup line and clap his hands together.

"Great job, everybody. We'll see you tomorrow."

The grimy pile of men pulled themselves slowly to their feet, groaning and staggering to the water fountains, trading curses and shooting dark glares at Turk.

But concealing grins, also. Puffing out their chests. Elbowing each other with smug remarks and confident tilts of their chins.

Just like a bunch of Marine recruits, fresh off an hours-long beatdown that failed to break them. Reed had seen it before. He remembered what it felt like. There was a strange magic to bludgeoning men as a unit. Individually, they all hated it. But that misery soon formed a bond. A codependency of survival that could quickly blossom into brotherhood.

So long as you didn't single one of them out and drive him into the mud, anyway. The guy Turk had been screaming at marched straight for Reed, breath whistling through clenched teeth.

"I want my money back!"

Reed took a calm swig from his water bottle, looking the man over. He was in his early fifties, a little flabby, a lot indignant. His accent said Chicago. Yet another transplant to Middle Tennessee.

"I'm sorry, sir. Was something wrong with your workout?"

"That wasn't a workout, that was torture! I paid to be trained, not to be screamed out while—"

"What's the problem here?" Turk appeared out of nowhere, all bowed up, face blazing. Chicago whirled on him, jabbing a finger into his face.

"I've never been treated that way in my life! What's wrong with you? You think this is boot camp?"

Turk snorted. "If it was, you'd be a washout."

Chicago's eyes bulged. *"Excuse me?"*

Reed cut between them, raising a hand before the confrontation drew any further attention.

"Look, we're sorry. This style of workout isn't for everybody. We'll be happy to refund you."

Turk ground his teeth. Reed kicked him in the shin to keep him quiet, then guided Chicago into the makeshift office built near the bathroom. It took fifteen minutes to calm him down and return his money. The guy continued to bark about bad service and abuse, promising a hailstorm of Google reviews and complaints to the Better Business Bureau. By the time Reed got him out of the building, most of the early morning group class had departed, and private clients had begun to arrive. Reed mopped sweat off his face and met Turk near the water cooler, glancing up at the block wall and the painted logo sprayed across it. Turk's new bride, Sinju, had done the painting. She had talent with a brush. The mural of a glowering Marine drill instructor was sufficiently intimidating and paired perfectly with the gym's name and slogan: *Jarhead Fitness—No Motards Allowed.*

"You gotta calm down, bro," Reed said. "That's the third one this week. You're gonna kill our client base."

Turk snorted. "Or weed out the wimps. I was going easy on him. Don't they come here to be screamed at?"

"They come here to have an *'authentic experience.'"* Reed made air quotes with his fingers. "These aren't soldiers, and this isn't Parris Island. Seriously, you gotta chill."

Turk rolled his eyes. His gaze darted across the gym to settle on a shirtless sixty-something guy walk in, a gym bag slung over one shoulder. The man was hairy. Very hairy. He wore Bulgari sunglasses and grinned as he waltzed in, shoulders back like he owned the place.

"Great," Turk growled. "Carpetbag is back."

"I'll take him," Reed sighed. "You clean up."

"It's my turn," Turk's voice was hesitant, as though he knew he had to say it, but really didn't want to.

"Yeah, well, you're not in a tip-maximizing mood. And in case you hadn't noticed the light bill, we could use a big tip."

Turk didn't answer. Reed grunted knowingly. "They may be wimps, but they're wimps with deep pockets. Get with the program, Jarhead."

He met Carpetbag—real name Richard Barclay III—near the warm-up mat. The guy was in his early sixties, chunky but not fat, a transplant from Boston. Or maybe it was Providence. Reed couldn't care less. Barclay was a machine-gun conversationalist, spewing unsolicited details about his stock trading fortune two or three times a week whenever he was in town, which was only about half the time.

He liked to be shouted at, sometimes. He liked to be pushed—but not really. Mostly he liked to be seen and heard. He liked to be appreciated. He liked to be asked questions about his financial expertise and his business acumen.

Now and then, he even liked to work out.

"What's good, Richie?" Reed met him next to the bench press where Barclay was already warming up with a convoluted sequence of '90s workout video stretches.

"Aw, you know. Just got back into town." Barclay's voice crackled with a New England edge. He gave Reed a fist bump. "Barbados, two weeks. Kinda tough to leave the office that long, but I gotta get that R&R somehow, right? I don't have to tell you that. You know!"

Barclay laughed and smacked Reed on the stomach before continuing with the stretches. Reed tried not to check his watch.

When he and Turk had founded the gym ten months prior, Reed knew it would be a lot of work. A lot of early mornings. A lot of sacrifice. But he never expected the therapy sessions. The endless dronings of ultra-rich transplants prattling on about the burdens of their business empires. The ceaseless biting of his tongue.

Maybe that was why Turk had become the de facto drill instructor of the gym. Most of these guys—and they were almost all guys—made you want to scream.

"Just bought a new plane!" Barclay chirped as he stretched out beneath the bench press. "King Air 360. Twin engine, eleven seats. Eighteen hundred nautical mile range. Brand new, of course." He spread his hands along the bar and shot Reed a mischievous grin. "Eight *million* dollars. Crazy, right?"

"That's crazy," Reed agreed.

Barclay pumped the bar. Ten reps, low weight, a lot of hissing and gritting his teeth. Already the shag carpet covering his bare chest glistened with sweat. The bar hit the cradle again, and Richie let out an aggressive growl.

"Yeah! That'll do it. Say, load me up, will ya? Let's break a personal best!"

Reed reached for more plates while Barclay rambled on.

"Been flying since I was a kid. Used to take my old man's Piper up for a spin. What a crap bucket that was. A poor man's plane! But you gotta start somewhere, am I right?"

"Right." Reed loaded the bar. Richie heaved and hissed, arms bulging. Teeth clenched. Dripping like a wet mop.

The bar hit the cradle again, and he sat up to twist his back and grunt some more. Reed shot Turk a glare.

"I don't have to tell you about planes, though. You were Air Force, right?"

"Marines," Reed said.

"Oh, sure. Well, the Marines got planes. You fly a lot?"

"Not in a while."

"You should join me sometime! Bring your wife. I'll take you up."

"That's kind of you."

"Ah, it's no problem! I mean, you know me. I always like helping people out. I like what you're doing here, Reece. A business man! I like a business man."

"It's Reed."

"Say what?"

"My name's Reed."

"Right! Reece. Anyway, I keep her parked down at Leiper's Fork. New private airfield. Not cheap, let me tell ya! Ten grand a year, and that's just for the hangar. Sheesh. Freaking Californians driving all the prices up, am I right?"

"Right," Reed sighed. He stepped behind the bar as Barclay settled beneath it again. His sweaty face grinned up at Reed, flashing whitened teeth as he placed both hands on the bar.

"Okay. Personal best. Spot me, Reece."

3

The warehouse walls were still marked with the rising lion coat of arms, the now forgotten symbol of the People's Republic of Bulgaria. Not technically a member of the Soviet Union, but so closely aligned with the Evil Empire during those long frigid decades of the Cold War that it was sometimes called the Sixteenth Soviet State.

Back then, the warehouse had been an arms depot. A storage facility to house the hundreds of thousands of small arms and munitions necessary to confront the encroachment of Western imperialism. Twenty thousand square meters of storage space, featuring rolling doors wide enough to admit a Soviet T-72 main battle tank.

A weapons cache of a dictator's wet dreams. The fighting strength of an entire nation, ready for war.

That was then. Before 1990. Before *the People's Republic* became simply *the Republic*. Before the USSR crumbled, the Cold War melted, and decades of easy peace rocked Bulgaria to sleep. The warehouse was emptied, the outdated arsenal sold off to warlords in Africa and freedom fighters in the Middle East. The windows cracked, the cobwebs multiplied.

The building eight kilometers outside of Pleven was forgotten, just like hundreds of its twins across Eastern Europe. And that made it the perfect place for a man like Wolfgang Pierce to be reborn.

None of the scattered farms or distant villages were close enough to hear the gunshots. The splitting cracks of the 10mm echoed against block walls and rattled windows while brass rained across the concrete. Wolfgang's shoulders slammed against a stack of moldy crates stamped with the Soviet hammer and sickle as he slammed a fresh magazine into his piping hot Glock 20. He racked the heavy slide and breathed evenly, shoulders loose, body relaxed. Vague phantom pain radiated up his right leg—the leg that didn't exist from just above the knee down—but his mind had already blocked it out. A thumping heart and a surplus of adrenaline kept him alert as he swung out of cover and entered the narrow hallway.

A metal shipping container on his right, more crates on his left. Target, ten o'clock, six feet off the ground. The Glock cracked twice, and the target went down in a shower of sparks. Wolfgang broke into a jog, reaching the end of the container and orbiting right. Two more tangos greeted him, only yards away, protected by chest plates too thick for even a 10mm to penetrate. Wolfgang made headshots instead—not thinking, not waiting, not even aiming. It was all instinct. One and then two, a pair of brass casings dropping to the floor as he hurtled down the next alleyway between empty oil drums.

His heart rate was up now. He was losing control of it, but that was okay. He could still fight. He could still make shots out to sixty yards with ease. A flash of white caught his eye from the top of an oil drum and he yanked the Glock to match his line of sight, shoulders still loose. Finger resting over the trigger.

It was a rat, not a tango. As big as a house cat, but not the enemy.

Wolfgang moved on, advancing to the end of the alleyway. He slipped behind an oil drum, conscious that he had obtained concealment but not cover. The position disguised his location, but it offered little protection against a heavy 7.62mm slug spat from the mouth of an AK-47.

He couldn't stop here.

Dropping into a crouch, Wolfgang lunged across a gap between the barrels, moving for shelter behind the next shipping container. A burst of automatic gunfire ripped across the warehouse from fifty yards away. Bullets skipped over the concrete, one of them kissing the heel of his prosthetic foot. Wolfgang rolled in behind the crate as the next burst pinged off the shipping container. An AK round whirred like a hornet as it whizzed overhead. Wolfgang checked his hip. Only one more fully loaded magazine of 10mm remained.

Back on his feet, Wolfgang turned down the length of the container. Rushing around the next corner, he unloaded on the three targets standing there. Headshot, headshot, double-tap to the chest. Three tangos down before the AK fire from across the room sent him sliding for cover again.

He could see it now—the red balloon at the end of the building. Inflated to about ten inches in size, like a child's birthday party decoration. Still a hundred yards away, but within reach of the Glock given a calm and steady shot. He rotated toward it and raised the muzzle. Rested with his finger over the trigger.

No.

Not this way.

Wolfgang returned to his feet and ran. Between the barrels, crates, and containers. Beneath a heavy metal shelving unit once stacked with hundreds of metal ammunition tins. The thunder of the AK resumed, angry and incessant. Slugs pinged off the shelving unit and skipped across the concrete. Two more tangos confronted him halfway to the balloon. He gunned them down like the first eight.

A bullet whistled over his head and another cut his sleeve, close enough to break skin and draw blood. The voice of the AK drew closer, now. Much closer, only a couple dozen meters away. The Glock locked back on empty and Wolfgang dove for cover. As he pushed off against his prosthetic leg, the straps holding it to the stump of his thigh shifted, and he lost his balance.

He hit the floor with a pained grunt, the Glock sliding out of his hand and skittering across the floor. Wolfgang rolled, shoulders slamming into concrete. He came to rest on his back and spotted the shadow of a tall, burly man moving in from behind a row of oil drums. Armed with the AK.

The Glock lay yards away. Wolfgang abandoned it, twisting instead to the right to reach for the carbon fiber shell of his prosthetic leg. He gave a trained smack to the side of his fake calf, popping open a concealed, spring-loaded door. The shadowy man reached the end of the oil drums and pivoted toward him. Wolfgang could make out the profile of the AK now, a familiar slanted muzzle break joined by a rising front sight post.

Wolfgang reached inside the hidden compartment of his prosthetic and touched hard polymer. He wrapped his fingers around the grip of another Glock—this one a G29. The little brother to his G20, housing only ten plus one rounds of 10mm instead of fifteen. Already locked and loaded. Sliding free of the prosthetic and raising to aim even as the AK swung toward him. The burly man dropped his finger over the rifle's trigger. The world stood still. Wolfgang wrenched the G29 up, twisting his shoulder.

Pressing the trigger.

The G29 barked, spitting fire and a heavy 180-grain hollow point.

The AK stiffened.

The red balloon shattered.

Wolfgang exhaled and slumped back against the concrete, heart pounding. The burly man with the AK stood motionless in the shadows, then slowly lowered the rifle. He stepped forward, illuminated by the late afternoon sunlight that streaked through a broken window. His brow wrinkled into a disapproving frown. Raising his left wrist, he checked his watch.

Then he spat across the concrete.

"Three minutes, fourteen seconds." Ivan Sidorov spoke in a heavy Russian accent, his thick face crinkling with age, his crooked nose twitching as he cradled the AK under one arm.

Wolfgang dragged the back of one hand across his brow, hauling himself into a seated position. "Not bad," he panted. "Ten seconds shaved."

"Not bad?" Ivan barely concealed his disgust. "You lost your weapon!"

"My prosthetic shifted. I tripped. That's what backups are for."

Ivan snorted. "You should have taken the shot when you had it. From over there! Why come all this way?"

"Because I wanted to."

"Oh, you *wanted to*?" Ivan mimicked Wolfgang's American accent. "This is stupid reason to risk life. I could have shot you."

"Yeah, about that. Explain this!" Wolfgang pulled at his sleeve, exposing the cut on his arm. Ivan shrugged.

"Scratch."

"*Scratch?* If I had twitched, that could have blown my arm off."

This time Ivan grinned, slinging the AK over one shoulder. "So don't twitch."

The big Russian sauntered off across the warehouse, calling something over his shoulder about more balloons. Wolfgang hauled himself upright. He didn't feel the phantom pain when he stood. He didn't feel anything other than the marriage of metal and carbon fiber to his stump of a leg. But that wasn't unusual. Sometimes the pain would come when he was training, but usually it came during meals, or in the shower, or late at night. All the dumbest, most inconvenient times.

He retrieved the fallen G20 on his way back through the obstacle course, stopping along the way to inspect the grouping of his shots through the various wood and cardboard "tangos" Ivan had erected for him to engage. Most of the shots were dead-on. Not as perfect as Wolfgang used to shoot, but very close. And getting better.

By the time he returned to the makeshift living quarters at the end of the warehouse—a table, two cots, a couple of ice chests, and a stack of bottled water—he had collected all of his spent brass and fallen magazines. He lined them on the table and proceeded directly to reload the magazines from a bucket of target rounds. Ivan was outside, standing in the high grass of the rolling Bulgarian field that surrounded the abandoned warehouse, talking on a satellite phone in Russian.

It had been this way for nearly two weeks. Wolfgang had left New York and flown to Europe after finally receiving an invitation from Ivan to join him on an operation—an unsanctioned, private mission. Ivan Sidorov was a former Russian SVR agent who'd recently been forced into retirement after uncovering hints of deep corruption within the Kremlin. Wolfgang Pierce was a recently *un*retired professional assassin. The two had met a decade prior, in Paris, when rival government missions put them at odds in an art gallery bathroom. That was where Ivan had received his crooked nose.

Years of combat and espionage had brought their paths—and priorities

—into alignment on a number of occasions, eventually leading Wolfgang and Ivan to Bulgaria, where they were working directly alongside one another for the first time.

Ivan had invited Wolfgang to Bulgaria for one reason: arms dealers. Russian arms dealers, specifically. The kind who, ten months earlier, had supplied weapons and mercenaries to Venezuela at the behest of a disgraced Russian oligarch who had attempted to turn the South American country into his crude oil powerhouse. Ivan and Wolfgang both suspected that the oligarch hadn't been working alone, but was acting at the behest of Russian President Makar Nikitin, serving as one piece in a larger puzzle of Russian aggression.

But without proof, such speculations were just that. Speculations. Locating the arms dealers who facilitated the mercenaries in Venezuela could be the path to establishing such proof.

That was why the two men were here, in middle-of-nowhere Europe, eating canned tuna, sleeping on cots, and training for hours at a time while they waited for Ivan's contacts in the European criminal underworld to deliver. After thirteen days, Wolfgang was beginning to wonder if he would be better off eating canned tuna in the comfort of his upstate New York home.

He laid the G29 on the table and stripped down the G20. The target ammo was cheap and dirty. He liked to clean his weapons after each use.

Outside the warehouse, Ivan's phone call rambled on. Wolfgang didn't speak Russian and wasn't interested in learning. Ivan made a couple of phone calls a day, cautiously probing his contacts for leads on the arms dealers they were looking for. His escape from Moscow had been a nearly mortal one, and the Kremlin was still looking for him. A misplaced word to the wrong person could bring the hellfire of the motherland down on his head—and Wolfgang's with it.

So the process was both cautious and painfully slow.

Wolfgang reassembled the G20 and rammed in a fresh mag. He chambered and holstered the weapon, then moved to the G29. The smaller pistol was still a chunky block of hard plastic, but Wolfgang liked that. It felt solid in his hands.

A dependable tool.

Ivan stepped in through the door, feet crunching on the concrete.

"Let me guess," Wolfgang said. "No news yet, be patient."

Ivan didn't answer. Wolfgang looked up. The big Russian was framed by the door, his lips lifted into a sadistic smile. Wolfgang had seen it before, but it never failed to chill him.

"What?"

"We have them," Ivan said.

4

The White House
Washington, DC

"Center mass. Drive with your hips." White House Special Advisor James O'Dell spoke calmly, his voice a syrupy Cajun drawl as thick and strong as good New Orleans gumbo. He stood behind the heavy bag, biceps bulging as he braced himself for the next strike.

President Margaret Trousdale brought it, twisting at the hips and driving the mass of her one hundred and twenty pounds through the open-fingered MMA glove and into the bag. Sweat sprayed from her lips as she exhaled, keeping the left glove up, palm turned protectively over her face. She danced back, transferring weight to her right leg and moving left. Then a one-two combo hard enough to break ribs.

At least, it felt that hard. Maggie staggered back, wheezing, and O'Dell grinned from behind the bag.

"Very nice! You're getting stronger."

Maggie mopped dirty blonde hair away from her forehead and collapsed into a chair at the back of the White House gym. She gulped water, still gasping for air. Her right side burned like hellfire, the mass of inflamed pain concentrated just above her pelvis. Just in front of her still-regenerating liver.

Right where the assassin's bullet had blasted through flesh, bone, and organ barely twelve months prior. If she closed her eyes she could still hear the shot—which was an ironic trick of her mind, because she had never heard the shot. She just felt the force of the truck-like slug slamming into her gut, and then everything had gone black.

Maggie wiped her lip with the back of one glove. O'Dell was prattling on about her progress, talking her up like some kind of fitness coach—a role that suited him no better than that of White House advisor. Maggie wasn't listening. Her attention was drawn to the TV mounted in one corner of the gym, and the live White House press conference it displayed. Maggie's press secretary, Farah Rahman, fielded questions from a dense crowd of correspondents. Rahman maintained perfect composure, shifting between dismissive smiles and intense, engaging nods, but Maggie could see the tension in her eyes.

The discussion was heating up.

Maggie reached for the remote and ran the volume up. She recognized the voice of Matt Crusher, a reporter who worked for some independent news blog and made it his daily goal to harass Rahman into a mental breakdown.

". . . to be clear, you *don't* feel that the president's obsessive prosecution of the American business sector is an irrational witch hunt?"

Rahman flashed that *are you kidding me?* smile. Her voice—smooth with a second-generation Iraqi accent—remained calm.

"Matt, we discussed this yesterday. Questions about the DOJ should be directed to the DOJ. The extent of the president's involvement in the legal proceedings you reference is to support Attorney General Thomas. Any direct interference from the executive branch would be an abuse of power. We studied this in fifth grade."

Rahman's jab earned her a couple of chuckles from the crowd. Crusher didn't back down.

"You keep spitting that canned answer, Farah, but you're dodging the question. You've stated previously that President Trousdale requested the FBI investigation into Cunningham Enterprises following her attempted assassination. It's beyond question that the president has a personal interest in bringing the American business sector to its knees. Can you not simply admit that—"

"That's a dramatic mischaracterization, Matt, and you know it. The president requested the investigation, yes. Vice President Stratton has been designated as White House liaison for the DOJ. But that's a purely practical arrangement. The idea that the Trousdale administration is driving some manner of witch hunt against the American business sector—"

"But you *are*," Crusher cut her off, voice rising. "The DOJ has filed over four *hundred* indictments against wealthy Americans in the energy sector, each alleging international corruption in the oil trade. Meanwhile, your boss seems all too eager to facilitate international drilling in Venezuela in partnership with the Rivas regime—a regime we *know* to be corrupt. How can you explain this blatant hypocrisy? And speaking of the president, where is she? It's been nearly five weeks since she's made a public appearance. Is Muddy Maggie a lame duck?"

Rahman flushed. In the gym, Maggie gritted her teeth. She threw a towel over one shoulder and turned for the door.

"Where are you going?" O'Dell said.

"To make an appearance," Maggie snapped.

She barreled through the door and out into the hallway of the White House basement. It was a short elevator ride to the ground floor, followed by a corridor to the West Wing and the Briefing Room. Maggie speed-walked through the basement, still swigging water.

O'Dell rushed to follow. They reached the elevator and she punched the button, muttering a curse. She had no real issue with the media. It was an art—and sometimes a pain in the ass—to manage them, but free press was a cornerstone of democracy. She respected that.

Crusher and his antics were something else. The blog he worked for was little more than a weapon of chaos, dumping gasoline on whatever contentious fires it could find, often playing jump rope with political ideology. Neither right wing nor left wing, not conservative or progressive.

Just a pit of vitriol, with no apparent greater goal than to maximize ad revenue via increasingly hyperbolic headlines.

"Are you sure this is a good idea?" O'Dell kept his voice calm as Maggie entered the elevator.

"You heard the man," she snapped. "He wants an appearance."

"He wants a soundbite," O'Dell said. "He's just pushing buttons."

"I oughta have Farah revoke his credential. Grimy SOB."

"You can't do that and you know it. Even the moderates would turn on you."

O'Dell was right, per usual. Maggie didn't care. The elevator dinged and she turned for the West Wing. Aides and White House staff mumbled confused greetings as she marched by—visibly sweaty, still dressed in tennis shoes, gym shorts, and a pink tank top. By the time she neared the entrance of the Briefing Room, she could hear Crusher's demanding voice still barking at Rahman. They were cutting each other off. Rahman's tone grew sharp.

Maggie paused at the door and passed O'Dell the water bottle and the towel. She reached for the straps of her gloves, then stopped, remembering Crusher's comment about her health.

Lame duck my ass. Let's have some theatrics.

She left the boxing gloves on and pushed through the door, driving straight into a blast of TV lights. Rahman pivoted toward her, a hint of desperation in her eyes. Crusher broke off mid-sentence, and a soft gasp echoed around the packed room.

"Good morning, Farah!" Maggie said brightly. "I'll take it from here."

Rahman slid seamlessly into introductory mode, gesturing to Maggie as she took the podium.

"Ladies and gentlemen, the president of the United States."

Maggie peeled the Velcro straps off the fighting gloves, flashing a fearless smile straight at Crusher.

"Good morning, everyone! I apologize for my attire. Caught me in the middle of a workout. Now, what was your question, Mr. Crusher?"

Matt Crusher closed his mouth abruptly. Maggie laid the gloves neatly on the podium, still smiling.

Go ahead, dingbat. I dare you.

Crusher found his courage. "Good morning, Madam President. I was just discussing your administration's investigation of the American business sector—"

"The DOJ," Maggie cut him off.

"Ma'am?"

"The DOJ's investigation. There are three branches of government, Mr. Crusher. The Department of Justice is working in partnership with the judicial branch to bring the investigations you reference to trial."

"Right," Crusher's cheeks flushed. "But you do admit to sponsoring those investigations?"

"I do my job, yes."

A muted chuckle sounded from somewhere amid the reporters. Crusher shifted.

"Your question?" Maggie prompted.

"My question, Madam President, is how do you justify this witch hunt of honest American entrepreneurs while eagerly supporting the corrupt Rivas regime in Venezuela?"

"Easily." That earned her another anonymous chuckle. "Because it's not a witch hunt, and the Rivas regime isn't corrupt. I appreciate your attempt to play lawyer for the Cunninghams and their chums, Mr. Crusher, but you should really stick to writing hit pieces on my lame duck administration."

The smile didn't break, even as she poured on the fuel. Everyone in the room stiffened. Maggie kept going.

"From the day I announced my campaign, I have made my anti-corruption agenda clear. Energy production is a cornerstone of our economy that has too long been ensnared by corporate misconduct and oppressive greed. Honest Americans are punished at the pump because men like Harold Cunningham are in bed with corrupt foreign interests, more eager to fuel the economies of our enemies than secure our own energy markets. I won't waste time working down the laundry list of indictments the DOJ has brought against Cunningham Enterprises. You can google those. What I can tell you is that due to my administration's partnership with the new democratic government in Venezuela, fuel prices are down twenty-six percent over this time last year, and the trend is building. We're becoming less dependent on OPEC by the day while supporting the rebuilding of the Venezuelan economy. Nothing is perfect. The corruption of the Moreno regime was systemic, and it'll take time to fully heal Venezuela. But this administration stands behind its allies. Next question?"

Maggie deliberately turned away from Crusher. He might have pressed Rahman for a follow-up, but she knew he was at least smart enough to not pressure her. A correspondent from the *Los Angeles Times* was the next to raise her hand.

"Thank you for joining us, Madam President. I hope you're feeling well this morning."

"Never better." Maggie grinned. Crusher glowered.

"I'd like to pivot our conversation to the crisis in Haiti," the correspondent continued. "The *Los Angeles Times* reported this morning that while unprecedented international aid has been raised on Haiti's behalf, many of those resources are bottlenecking at the Port of Savannah, mired in red tape and logistical turmoil. Meanwhile, the situation on the ground is worse than ever. United Nations peacekeepers are facing an uphill battle to distribute aid while repelling the attacks of heavily armed Haitian gangs. What update can you give us on your administration's efforts to combat these challenges?"

Maggie allowed her grin to melt naturally over the course of the question. It wasn't a softball, but she appreciated the pivot.

"As I've stated from day one, the situation in Haiti isn't a Haitian disaster. It's a human disaster. I've spoken with Governor Grier of Georgia and he is actively engaged with authorities in Savannah to accelerate aid shipments and clear up any bottlenecks. Meanwhile, I have personally authorized the Department of Defense to deploy an additional fifty United States Marines and related equipment into Port-au-Prince to assist the United Nations peacekeeping mission. We won't stop working until the Haitian people are fed, clothed, and secured."

"I'm glad you mentioned Haiti, Madam President." Crusher broke into the conversation, chin jutting toward her like a battering ram. "My sources inform me that FEMA's disaster relief fund has been pilfered to provide Haitian aid. With hurricane season bearing down on us, how can you justify raiding our limited emergency resources to—"

"As easily as you justify that haircut, Mr. Crusher. Hurricanes are a possibility. Sunbaked, starving Haitian children oppressed by violent gangs are a reality. We can bicker about allocations later. Congress has always been generous in funding disaster relief. I don't see why they should stop now simply because the disaster struck Black people."

Crusher's eyes bulged. "Madam President, I resent the implication that—"

"Thank you all very much," Maggie said, flashing another smile at the press corps. "I think I need a shower."

She ducked through the side door, back into the hall. Rahman and O'Dell followed. The press secretary was babbling before the door even closed.

"Madam President, I'm so sorry. I let Crusher get out of control—"

"Suspend his credential," Maggie said, turning toward the residence.

"I'm sorry?"

"You heard me," Maggie said.

"Ma'am . . . I can't do that."

Maggie stopped. She faced Rahman for the first time.

"Farah. Do you know why I hired you?"

Rahman hesitated. She closed her mouth, and didn't answer.

"Because you're *good*, Farah. You're a woman of integrity in a pit full of vipers. I need that. But I also need somebody to manage the circus. Do you understand?"

Rahman nodded slowly.

"Suspend his credential. Have one of your aides leak a comment to a friendly reporter—Crusher was combative with the president and spoke over one of his colleagues. The Trousdale administration doesn't tolerate unprofessional behavior. Crusher will be reinstated after a public apology. Understand?"

Rahman nodded again. "Yes, ma'am."

Maggie turned back toward the residence, tucking the boxing gloves under one arm. "When somebody screws with you, Farah, you screw back. Hard."

5

The drive out of rural Williamson County was picturesque, but Reed was already sick of it. Piled in behind the wood-trimmed steering wheel of his battered 1969 Camaro Z/28, he barely noticed the open expanse of the Tennessee summer sky. He just saw the knots of expensive cars, the clusters of multimillion-dollar homes, and the growing developments of luxury apartments packed with young professionals from the West Coast.

Located forty minutes south of downtown Nashville, Williamson County was—according to Forbes—the nineteenth-wealthiest county in America, which made it filthy rich by any standard. Luxuries were available in spades: fine wine dealers, preppy restaurants, a Tesla dealership, and, yes ... a gym run by former Marines who would scream at you on demand. An *authentic* military experience, programmed for people who never came close to serving.

It was Turk's idea to build the gym in Williamson County. He and Sinju had lived in Middle Tennessee for over a year when Reed disbanded the Prosecution Force—the team of elite, off-the-books operators Reed had commanded for nearly two years. The idea was to cut loose from the operator lifestyle. To embrace suburbia. To be with family, to make some friends, to bulk up a retirement account and develop some hobbies.

To live the American dream. After so many years of fighting to defend the country's freedom, it seemed like the logical next step. To savor some of that freedom for themselves. What better way to begin than to open a business? What better clientele to serve than cash-flush wannabe tough guys?

That was the idea. Six months in, the reality had become something else entirely. It turned out that cash-flush wannabe tough guys were flaky customers under the best of circumstances. They paid their membership dues without question, but would often disappear for weeks on end, taking their tips with them. Even when they showed, they didn't always respond well to the "Parris Island training program" they had signed on for. Sometimes they got butthurt. Sometimes they shouted back.

Sometimes they demanded six months' worth of membership dues to be refunded.

And then there was the commute. The house in the hills Reed had dreamed of had evaporated quickly into a pricey and outdated two-bedroom apartment situated in southeast Nashville—one of the less desirable parts of town. Crowded, congested, rife with growing crime, and without a rolling hill in sight. An hour's drive from the gym on a good day.

It was everything he didn't want in a home address, but he hadn't come to Nashville just for the dream of a country home. He'd come to Nashville for the sake of Banks, his wife of three years, the mother of his two-year-old son. The love of his life. He knew it had been miserable for her, being married while Reed was constantly on deployment. Banks often felt neglected and alone, her own dreams of becoming a singer-songwriter put on indefinite hold.

Reed knew turnabout was fair play. He'd pushed Banks to the point where he almost lost her, and she was the one thing he couldn't give up, no matter what. Even if the "what" was her pursuing a shot at fame in the heart of a big city overrun by talented people all fighting for the same thing. She was worth it.

Reed rolled down the Camaro's window and ran a hand over his face to mop the sweat away. A blazing sun beat down on the car as he squeaked to a stop at yet another red light. The motor dropped into a rough idle, and the smell of raw gasoline leaked through heat vents built beneath the dash. The engine was running rich—it needed a tune, badly. Or better yet, a garage and a full restoration.

Not like Reed had the time or money for either.

The light turned green, but the little blonde girl in the Mercedes convertible ahead of him didn't move. She giggled and stared at her phone as Reed hit the horn. No sound came from beneath the Camaro's rattling hood.

So that's broken, also.

"Hey! Let's go!" Reed shouted.

The girl didn't hear him. He dropped his foot off the brake, left toe still clamped down on the clutch, and mashed the gas pedal. The V8 roared like a jungle cat, and the girl finally looked up. She shot him a surly glare and wrinkled her nose, then finally looked to the light.

It was yellow by the time she raced through, and red before Reed reached the line. He stopped and gritted his teeth as the Camaro coughed, then quit. A fresh wave of brutal Tennessee heat washed through the open cabin, and he reached for the key.

"Come on, I don't have time for this."

The motor turned over, but didn't start. It sounded flooded. Reed held the accelerator down to drain the carburetor and scrubbed at his face again. He knew it wasn't just the heat making him irritable. Not just the promise of another forty minutes of stop-and-go traffic making him contemplate an act of vehicular terrorism.

It was the whole package. The whole existence. The pressure of a round hole cramping down over a square peg.

His phone buzzed, and Reed glanced down to see Banks's smiling face illuminate the screen. It was a picture he'd taken two months earlier—a snapshot of Banks performing solo on Broadway at one of the honky-tonks.

It was a great picture.

"Hey, sweetie," Reed kept his voice calm as he depressed the clutch and tried the ignition again. This time the Camaro acted like it wanted to start, coughing three times. It failed to get over the hump.

"Where are you?" Banks's voice was all stress, popping at him like an AK-47.

"Franklin," Reed said. "I had to work a little late. I'm on my—"

"Reed. I need to leave in *twenty minutes!* It's Wednesday night. Don't you remember?"

Reed clamped his eyes closed. *Wednesday.* He thought it was Tuesday.

"The auditions. Right. I'll get there soon—"

"I can't be late again!" Banks's voice descended into a semi-sob. "What am I supposed to do with Davy?"

The light flicked to green. The blare of a horn pounded through the roof of the Camaro. Reed double-tapped the gas and tried the ignition again.

"Come on, baby . . ." he whispered.

"What?" Banks said.

The Camaro whined and choked. The horn behind him blared. The light flicked to yellow.

"Reed, are you hearing me? I have to leave! What am—"

Again with the horn. The Camaro quit entirely.

"*I hear you!*" Reed shouted over his shoulder. He twisted the key again, and the aged brass broke off in his hand. His thumb scraped over the jagged metal and tore. Blood streamed over his palm and another curse erupted from his mouth before he could stop it. Banks's confused voice garbled through the speaker. A heavy car door slammed shut and a fat guy in a business suit marched forward. Reed saw his angry face concealed behind designer sunglasses, distorted by the dirty rearview mirror. Before he could stop himself, Reed dropped the phone and threw the door open. The fat guy was halfway down the length of the Camaro, spraying curses, his finger jabbing at Reed like a knife.

Reed's hand tightened into a fist and he closed the distance between them. Already cocking. Already aiming. Ready to smash a two-thousand-dollar pair of ugly shades into the uglier face behind them.

Then he saw the Camaro move. They both did—he and the rich guy. The heavy muscle car rolled backward as Reed passed the rear wheel, sliding down the low incline toward the Maserati SUV parked behind it. Reed threw himself left and caught the door pillar, planting his boots into the baking hot pavement.

It was too little, too late. The solid steel of the Camaro's rear bumper smashed into the Maserati in a crunch of busting plastic and contorting metal. Reed skidded to a stop as the rich guy stood dumbfounded, his mouth dropping open. He pointed at his car and spluttered. Reed looked, and his shoulders simply dropped. The guy went to cursing again, screaming and tearing his sunglasses off, but this time Reed barely heard him.

He just stood under the sun, glistening with sweat, ready to drop. While the rich guy phoned the police, Reed found his phone in the floorboard. He rolled it over and looked for the picture of Banks standing behind a microphone.

Banks was gone. She'd already hung up.

It was long past dark before Reed clambered out of the Uber. He'd texted Banks to inform her of the accident. She'd asked if he was okay, but hadn't texted since. The Camaro still wouldn't start, so he pushed it into an outlet store parking lot and locked the doors.

A problem for the next day.

The rich guy was already threatening to sue. Franklin police told Reed the accident report would be available in seven days, and advised him to contact his insurance. He walked a mile to a grocery store for fresh flowers before calling the ride share to take him home.

Thirty bucks, one way. Welcome to the big city.

Reed's back ached as he exited the compact car. Banks's race-red Volkswagen SUV sat in the parking lot, local music venue stickers adorning the back glass. Reed stared at it for a moment, remembering how much better it had looked sitting in a driveway instead of a shared parking lot—even if it had been a rental home driveway. Living in the grimy apartment felt like a step in the wrong direction. Like moving backward in life.

Why was everything such a fight? His entire life had felt this way. One crummy, angry situation after another. He'd served his country. Paid for his mistakes, and then some. Spilt blood and sacrificed for years . . . for this?

He slung his backpack over one shoulder and started up the concrete steps. The bouquet of flowers was still wrapped in a grocery store bag. He knew it wouldn't make up for Banks missing the audition, but maybe it would help. Maybe it would let her know that he still believed in her. Keep her from asking about his day, or the gym, or any of the two dozen things he absolutely didn't want to discuss.

Reed fumbled with his key and turned the lock. He almost fell over Davy's strewn toys as he entered the undersized apartment, but he didn't see his son. He didn't see Banks either. Dim lights illuminated the living area, dirty dishes on the table.

"Banks?"

No answer. Reed pushed the door shut, dropping his backpack on the couch. His faithful English bulldog, Baxter—a companion that dated back to the years before he even knew Banks—slept on the couch with his pudgy face propped up on a pillow, drool running from his lips in twin ropes as it dripped onto the carpet. He awoke with a snort as the backpack landed, shooting Reed an irate glare.

"Sorry, boy," Reed said. He leaned down to scratch his old friend behind one wrinkled ear, then called again across the living room. "I'm home!"

Banks appeared from the kitchen, phone pressed to her ear, holding up a finger.

Reed waited, exhaustion descending on him like a ton of bricks.

"Yes, sir . . . uh-huh . . ."

Banks's face was pointed at the carpet, loose blonde hair falling over her shoulders. She wore a tank top and sweatpants, a fresh tattoo of the Nashville city skyline rising from the neck of an acoustic guitar on her left forearm. Reed had bought her the tattoo for her birthday, saying he never wanted her to forget this time of her life.

Her time.

Looking at it now, the thoughts of the gym, the wrecked Maserati, and the broken-down Camaro faded from Reed's mind. He only saw his wife. His gorgeous, talented wife.

"Yes, sir," Banks whispered into the phone, her voice catching. "That . . . that would be amazing."

She mumbled twice more. Then hung up. Reed waited by the couch, arms down, eyebrows raised.

"Who was that?" He asked.

"Joe Carpenter," Banks said.

Reed didn't recognize the name. "He is . . . ?"

"The organizer for the Tennessee Summer Music Fest, down in Rutherford County."

"Oh."

Reed recognized that name. He'd seen the billboards. It was a big deal
—a massive, outdoor music festival featuring folk and country artists. Lots
of big names. Lots of midsized names. Not something he'd really cared
about.

"What did he want?"

Banks began to cry, large tears slipping down smooth cheeks. But she
smiled.

"When I couldn't make the audition, I emailed them a demo. He heard
it, and . . ."

"And?" Reed took a step forward.

"And one of the artists had to cancel. She has the flu. They want *me* to
play at the festival . . . *this weekend*."

Banks's face exploded into a broad grin, and Reed ran forward. He
dropped the flowers on the cheap carpet and swept his wife off her feet. She
wrapped him in a hug and he held her close. Banks giggled, and Reed
pressed his face into her hair.

That sound—that joyous laugh. It made it all worth it.

6

Savannah, Georgia

Abdel Ibrahim watched the conclusion of President Trousdale's press conference from the seventh floor of the Marriott Savannah Riverfront. With the shades drawn to block out the blaze of the morning sun, the room was mercifully cool. He stood shirtless in front of the TV as the camera cut back to the two news anchors at some green-screened desk in some big city on the East Coast. The man whistled softly, and the woman's eyes widened as she fanned her face with one hand.

"Was it just me, Greg, or did that get a little heated?"

"You aren't kidding, Cindy. Safe to say the president took the gloves off with LibertyWire's Matt Crusher."

"No pun intended, right?"

Both anchors laughed. Ibrahim flicked the TV off and tossed the remote onto the bed. If anyone were around, he might have made a snide comment about America choosing a woman as president. Blasphemy, to the prophet. He might have commented on how she dressed like a hooker, or how he'd like to bend her over backward before cutting her throat.

But truth be told, Ibrahim didn't care who led the Great Satan. He didn't even care that it was a woman. There was nothing America could do now that would surprise him—nothing that would more perfectly cement in his mind the justice of the damnation that was rolling in from the east like a sandstorm. He didn't need a young man's bravado to fuel the fire already rushing in his chest. Memories of detonating American bombs and raking Western gunfire kept that blaze white hot. He'd seen it so many times—the same sad, endless story played on repeat in desolate lands.

Iraq. Afghanistan. Syria. Yemen.

American had wantonly spilled blood from one corner of the old world to the other. Had drenched herself in it. Had starved young mothers and scorched children alive.

No—it didn't matter that a woman stood at the helm. That was the least of the infidel nation's sins.

Ibrahim moved away from the TV to the little table built next to it. Bottled water, bread and cheese, a roast chicken, half consumed from its plastic container. All purchased at a local supermarket near the hotel.

And one document. Stapled at the corner, printed with a bold red-and-black logo at the top, displaying the name of a prominent American rental company. Ibrahim scanned slowly down the page, double-checking each detail. Confirming that all-important note printed at the bottom.

Payment method: Cash.

The rental period was for ten days. Far longer than Ibrahim needed. But the excess time would ensure that nobody would miss the truck or come looking for it until it was far too late.

The last item on the table was a folded short-sleeved shirt. Thick cotton, with double-stitched sleeves. Plenty rugged and durable for intense outdoor exposure. Royal blue, bright enough to be recognized at a distance.

Familiar to all the worst, most broken places in the world.

Ibrahim put his hand on the shirt, but before he could unfold it the keycard reader in the door behind him clicked, and two men entered. Both short, ordinary-looking guys of Middle Eastern descent. Clean haircuts and no beards. Western clothes. Bahir and Mahmoud were their names. Both Syrian nationals. But Ibrahim knew enough about American culture to know that appearance was more valuable than a U.S. passport. If you looked like an American, dressed like an American, and walked like an American . . .

Nobody would question you.

Bahir closed the door, one hand clutching a brass keychain with a dangling red-and-black tag. He was the younger of the two men. The more zealous and violent, on any given day. Mahmoud was older, the hair at his temples graying. A friend of Ibrahim's for many years, and no longer strong enough to execute this mission on his own, but every bit as dedicated as his younger counterpart.

"We are fueled and ready," Mahmoud announced in Arabic, his native tongue.

"And the pickup?" Ibrahim replied in the same language.

"No problems. The crate was right where it was supposed to be. We double-checked everything. It's loaded now."

Ibrahim nodded slowly. Noted Bahir rubbing one thumb against the rental tag, an eager light in his eyes—the anticipation of a true believer, amped up and ready to go. Enthusiastic to spill blood by the gallon.

And if Bahir somehow lost that nerve? Somehow faltered at the last moment?

Well. That was why Mahmoud carried a gun.

"Allah be praised," Ibrahim said.

Both men ducked their heads in respectful agreement. Ibrahim took the shirt from the table, unfolding it to reveal bold white letters printed across the shoulder blades.

UN VOLUNTEERS

He slid the shirt on, then he approached the two men and rested an arm on each of their shoulders, pulling them into a circle. Speaking calmly.

"Remember what they have done, my brothers. We must not waver now."

The edgy light in Bahir's eyes intensified.

Mahmoud simply nodded. "*Allahu Akbar.*"

Ibrahim lifted his chin. "*Subhan Allah.* Death to the infidels."

7

The shipping facility sat alongside the Danube river. Flowing southeast out of the Black Forest of Germany, the Danube was the second-longest river in Europe, passing through ten countries and numerous major cities before eventually discharging into the Black Sea.

The bulk of Rousse, Bulgaria, was three miles removed from the aged concrete docks and battered metal buildings, so the warehouse's surroundings were relatively quiet. Only one paved road provided access for incoming trucks, but that was because the river served as the facility's primary highway.

Romania lay a thousand yards to the north, across the water.

Once the frontier border of the Roman Empire, now a major source of hydropower for mainland Europe, the river was also the perfect highway for shipping all manner of things from Vienna to Bratislava to Budapest to Belgrade. All manner of things, including illegal small arms.

Thousands of them.

From the bluffs south of the river, just a few hundred yards inside Bulgaria, Wolfgang overlooked the shipping compound with a pair of night vision–equipped binoculars, an expensive gadget Ivan had provided. Only a few security lights marked the property, gleaming as hot white marks amid his otherwise lime-green view. He marked the semitruck as it parked at the loading dock just after 2:00 a.m. One man climbed out and smoked for half an hour before entering, and the next vehicle didn't arrive until nearly three. It was a Saab, a dinky little sedan with dim yellow headlights. It parked near the end of the warehouse facility and three men got out, all dressed in black. Two entered the building. The third remained at the door, smoking a cigarette and barely concealing the MP5 submachine gun hanging from a sling beneath his trench coat.

"Old school," Wolfgang whispered.

Ivan's breath whistled between his teeth as he joined the surveillance with a matching pair of binos.

"In this part of the world, Amerikos, old school is the only school. You must not underestimate it."

Wolfgang continued his surveillance, noting no other visible vehicles or personnel. But from a gap between two warehouses he detected the outline of the river freighter tied off to the dock. It was mostly invisible behind the facility, but from time to time he made out the passage of a forklift—illuminated by dim headlights, always laden down with a heavy pallet.

"Three confirmed occupants," Wolfgang said. "One exterior guard, plus whatever kind of digital surveillance is present."

Ivan snorted, resting his binoculars on the ground and cracking open a small tin of sardines. The little fish stank, and Wolfgang curled his nose.

"Something funny?" he said.

"You think like American."

"I am an American."

"This is true, but you are not *in* America, are you?"

"I don't follow."

"There is no digital surveillance. No cameras. No invisible laser trip wires."

"How can you be sure?"

Ivan slurped down a sardine and shot him an incredulous look. "Are you really asking me this?"

"I literally am."

Ivan sighed theatrically. "Sometimes I forget what a child you are.

When you see cameras in America, you think of safety. You think police are watching, and they will help you if bad things happen. This is not the way in Eastern Europe. Here, cameras are bad thing. They mean police state. Overwatch. Oppression, you may say."

"You're starting to sound like a modern man," Wolfgang said.

"Hardly. I am only a realist. These people in this warehouse are hardened criminals. They use guns for security. They want no risk of being detected by the government. There will be no cameras."

"You're sure?"

Ivan shrugged. Rocked the sardine can back and sucked down the grimy juice. Wolfgang grimaced.

"Mostly sure," Ivan said. "If I am wrong, you will die, and I will apologize."

"Well, that's a comfort."

Wolfgang scanned the facility one more time. Despite Ivan's shoddy intelligence, a warmth of anticipation crept into his gut. He could feel it rising to his chest, priming his body for the dump of adrenaline.

It had been a long time. Too long.

He laid the binos down and flicked his finger across the smartphone resting next to him. The screen was set to dim, and it displayed a single photograph. A middle-aged Caucasian man with short-cropped gray hair and dark eyes. Five foot ten or eleven. Average build. A scorpion tattoo on his neck.

Oleksiy Melnyk. Ukrainian-born international arms dealer. The target.

"You're sure this is him?"

Ivan grunted. "As sure as winter in Moscow is cold."

"All right, then. Let's grab this sucker."

8

Ivan took the battered Mercedes delivery van around the hill and down to the road, a headset affixed to his skull for clear communication.

Wolfgang took the hill, sliding into the shadows dressed in all black, a Glock 20 strapped to his hip alongside extra mags, the G29 encased inside the carbon fiber calf. Riding in his hands was a brand new APC10 Pro by B&T—a 10mm submachine gun with an Aimpoint Micro T-2 red dot sight. More gifts from Ivan. The APC accepted the same fifteen-round magazines used by the Glock 20, which limited him somewhat in total firepower, but Wolfgang enjoyed the interchangeability.

He enjoyed launching 180-grain slugs at over thirteen hundred feet per second even more.

By the time Wolfgang reached the bottom of the hill, he was jogging easily. Not breathing hard, but his heart rate was up. He'd tightened his prosthetic to prevent any further shifts, and the ground felt solid beneath his boots. Solid enough for him to risk a slide behind a dumpster a hundred yards from the first warehouse.

The loading dock was open now. Somebody had raised a rolling metal door to provide access for the forklift into the back of the semitruck, but even through the sprawling gap in the wall, Wolfgang could make out none of the interior. There were no lights—the forklift relied solely on its head-lamps as it transferred pallets marked as automotive parts onto the truck.

Wolfgang seriously doubted whether more than a few alternators and brake pads lay inside. Ammunition was more likely. Magazines and small arms, lifted out of the war zones of Ukraine and carried upriver before being transferred onto the trucks. Next, those weapons would be driven across the Balkan Peninsula to Albania, or perhaps Montenegro, where they would be loaded onto ships and pointed south.

Warlords in Africa might purchase them, eventually. Militias in the Middle East, perhaps.

Or maybe they would be bought by mercenary units based in mainland Europe—heavily armed private militaries on standby to serve the needs of a corrupt Russian president hell-bent on dangling the entire globe from puppet strings. That was the theory, anyway. Capturing Oleksiy Melnyk—and having an extensive *conversation* with him—would provide the proof.

Wolfgang raised the APC and scanned the facility. The Aimpoint's red dot contrasted perfectly with the subdued landscape, providing a constant focus point as he kept both eyes open. He marked the progress of the forklift, passing across the open rolling metal door every hundred or so seconds with a fresh pallet. He couldn't see the driver, and the guy with the MP5 was four hundred yards away at the western end of the facility.

That left the eastern end—and the unguarded door there—as a perfect intrusion point.

Wolfgang timed the forklift for a full five cycles, then sprinted from the shadows and made for the door. His stride still felt awkward, but months of intensive training with the prosthetic leg had worked out most of the insta-bility and slowly rebuilt his speed. As a plus, he could be shot in the leg and just keep on chugging. Like Arnold Schwarzenegger's Terminator.

At the door, Wolfgang slid close to the building and pressed his back against the metal. He cradled the APC and hummed briefly to engage his throat mic.

"East end of the building, ready for intrusion."

"In position for extraction." Ivan's Russian accent rumbled through Wolfgang's single earpiece. "Proceed at will."

Wolfgang placed a gloved hand on the doorknob. He twisted. It was unlocked.

Keeping the APC pressed into his shoulder and his finger just above the trigger, he eased the door open. It groaned on aged hinges, and he froze. He could hear the rumble of the forklift from deep inside the warehouse—a clang of metal on metal, a grind of forks against concrete, the whir of the propane-powered motor. Voices joined the mix, grumbling orders in some Slavic language.

Nobody responded to the groaning hinges. Wolfgang slipped inside the warehouse.

Darkness encased him. Tall columns of shrink-wrapped pallets stood three and four units high on metal shelves, marked in half a dozen languages with bold black letters. AGRICULTURAL FERTILIZER, the English label read. Truckloads of it, probably waiting for a fleet of legitimate semi-trucks to dispense it south across Bulgaria.

The enterprise Melnyk and his crew were engaged in, hours before sunrise, was much less legitimate. They would be long gone by the time the work day started and the facility returned to its sanctioned purpose.

Wolfgang crept between the pallets, moving on the balls of his feet, the APC held at eye level. The earpiece crackled now and again as Ivan opened another can of sardines and set off his throat mic with irregular chewing. Wolfgang wanted to berate him to shut up, but couldn't risk breaking his own silence. He kept his head down as he moved, checking every intersection of forklift paths crisscrossing between the pallets.

He could see light now, illuminating the warehouse floor from a single overhead bulb that marked the path between the dock and the semitruck. The closer he moved, the louder the voices became. He could make out clear words, but they were meaningless to him. Multiple gruff male voices, mixed with the occasional creak of wood and clink of metal.

Wolfgang reached the end of the fertilizer pallets and peered around the corner. The open space in the middle of the warehouse was occupied by four men, all dressed in leather jackets and strapped up with visible handguns. Crates of "automotive parts" lay scattered around them, many of the lids pried off to expose interiors packed with sawdust . . . and rifles.

American rifles. Gifted by Washington to reinforce the broken Ukrainian government, no doubt. M4 carbines and a collection of Beretta M9 hand-guns recently retired by the U.S. Army.

Great.

Wolfgang crouched close to a pallet and leaned out far enough to survey the men. He located Melnyk almost immediately. Average size, average height. A bold scorpion tattoo on his neck. With a quick press of the APC's trigger, Wolfgang could take out the other three men and catch the forklift driver on his next passage. Put Melnyk at gunpoint, and haul him out by his ear.

But there was a wildcard waiting at the western end of the warehouse. The guy with the MP5. And how many men were aboard the river freighter?

"Amerikos! Our friend at the door is speaking on a radio . . . he's running now. Around the building."

Wolfgang looked impulsively over his shoulder, back the way he'd come. The door was shut. Then he heard a stir from the crowd of men gathered around the open crates. A radio chirped. Voices shouted, and then one of the men looked straight at him and raised an arm.

"Intrus!"

Wolfgang opened fire. A short burst from the APC brought the man down with a checker pattern of 10mm holes drilled through his chest. The other three dove for cover behind the crates, handguns flashing out, the warehouse descending into a cacophony of cracking gunshots and splintering crates. A fertilizer pallet ruptured above Wolfgang, granulated red powder spilling over his back as he scrambled for cover. The back door burst open, and he turned in time to see the guy with the MP5 rushing in.

The man never reached his trigger. He took four 10mm slugs to center mass and collapsed. Wolfgang dropped his magazine and slammed in a fresh one. Then he was on his feet, rushing across the width of the warehouse, down an alleyway between stacked pallets.

"Tangos down!" he called into his mic. "Standby. I'm going for Melnyk!"

On the other side of the pallets, men shouted and feet pounded. Amid the chaos Wolfgang couldn't determine which direction they were headed. But he could guess. Neither the semi nor the dated Saab was any sort of escape vehicle. Even if they tried, Ivan could cut them off farther up the road.

If Wolfgang was in Melnyk's shoes, he would go for the river. Even a small boat, taken north to the Romanian shore, would be a better means of escape than hitting the road.

Wolfgang reached the end of the pallets and spun left, already reaching for his trigger. The first thing he saw was the forklift. It had stopped just inside the massive rolling door on the dock side of the warehouse, the engine still running. The driver was gone, but as Wolfgang pivoted around the fertilizer pallets a handgun appeared from the back end of the forklift, and muzzle flash lit the warehouse.

Wolfgang dove behind the pallet and counted the shots. A string of four, then a pause. Ramming the APC around the pallets, he clamped down on the trigger. Automatic gunfire pinged off the forklift at random, shredding the seat and ricocheting off the roll cage.

The staccato of bullets striking metal was broken by a rushing hiss. Wolfgang smelled gas. The propane fuel cylinder mounted to the back of the forklift had been hit. He released the trigger just as the man with the pistol fired again.

Then the warehouse convulsed with a thunderclap of detonated gas. Wolfgang twisted and covered his head as ruptured fertilizer bags cascaded in a dusty red avalanche. Hot fire reached for the ceiling, come and gone in a split second as shards of metal rained across the concrete.

He choked and clawed for a fresh mag. His ears rang too loudly to hear anything, but he still could make out shadows rushing amid the dust. A figure charged, pistol raised. Wolfgang abandoned the APC to dangle on its sling and snatched his G20. Thunderclaps of 10mm split the air and the guy convulsed. Wolfgang threw his body to the side and wrenched his prosthetic leg free of a pile of fertilizer. He could barely see. Barely breathe.

He fought his way through the mess to the fire-blasted hulk of the forklift and the roasted body that lay next to it. The air was rife with the stench of scalded human flesh. Wolfgang didn't see Melnyk.

But he could hear again, and what he heard was a boat engine, the telltale revs of a big motor warming quickly out of gear. Wolfgang leapt past the burned body and hit the concrete, rushing through the rolling doors to the dockside.

More gunshots flashed from the side of a two-hundred-foot river freighter. Wolfgang engaged with the G20 and brought the shooter down. The body flipped over the gunwales and crashed into the black water.

Then he saw the boat. A small powerboat, outlined by a dim moon as the motor raced. Melnyk stood behind the wheel. One of his guys turned to engage Wolfgang, lifting an American M4. Wolfgang took cover behind an industrial dock pylon. 5.56mm slugs pinged off the metal, and Wolfgang twisted to bring the Glock to bear.

It was too late. The powerboat was already two hundred yards away, then three hundred. White wake marked its path all the way to the Romanian shore.

Wolfgang slumped, breathing hard, and dropped the pistol's mag. He slammed in a replacement and checked over his shoulder.

The warehouse was a flame-blasted mess.

"Ready for evac," Wolfgang said quietly.

"Do you have him?" Ivan's voice carried excitement for the first time that night.

"Negative. Melnyk took a boat . . . we lost him."

9

"Nationals fans! On your feet—it's time for the *waaaaaave!*"

From the beefy speakers mounted around the circumference of the forty-one-thousand-seat baseball park, the announcer's voice boomed like thunder. Arms and beer mugs shot into the air in a slowly moving surge of drunken revelry through the suffocating August night. It was the bottom half of the sixth inning, and the Washington Nationals were up two over their rival Atlanta Braves.

The air itself felt sticky. The players moved a little slower across the field. The pitches came a little farther apart. The game dragged along with the methodical temperament of an accountants' softball league.

Maggie had never been a fan of baseball. She had nothing against it— she just didn't get the appeal. Without an MLB team in the entire state of Louisiana, and with both college and pro-level football teams ready and willing to enrapture the sporting lusts of the Pelican State, she'd simply never made time to learn the nuances of the older, slower sport. In fact, this was actually the first MLB game she'd ever attended.

Even nestled inside an air-conditioned box lined by bulletproof glass, kicked back in a plush leather chair with a cool drink close to hand, she found herself hoping it would be the *only* MLB game she ever attended.

Heaven save me if this goes to overtime.

A pair of Secret Service agents stood guard behind her, but the leather seats to her right and left were empty. Maggie alone had made the journey from the White House to Nationals Park, her media team going out of their way to announce her impromptu outing. Following her collision with Matt Crusher in the briefing room the day prior, Jill Easterling—Maggie's chief of staff—suggested it would be a good idea for her to make a public appearance. Something fun, and normal. Something that said she *wasn't* a lame duck.

Maggie was nearly two years into her term as president, and that meant her staff was already considering her reelection bid. If they had any hope of overcoming the growing opposition to her controversial position as an independent, they needed to recapture the Americana image of a wholesome swamp girl from Louisiana. Simple and honest. Somebody the voters could identify with.

That meant showing up at baseball games, hair in a ponytail, waving to the camera whenever her face appeared on the Jumbotron.

Joy.

Halfway through the top of the sixth inning, Vice President Jordan Stratton strutted into the suite dressed in a pristine black suit and an open-collared shirt. Maggie suspected it was meant to be a casual look, but Stratton had been born with a silver spoon in his mouth much too large for him to ever truly understand the meaning of the term *casual*. He probably had the shirt freshly pressed before taking his limousine to the baseball park.

Maggie motioned to the seat on her right. Stratton's dark gaze flicked across the scoreboard as he sat, the hint of a smile breaking across his mouth. He applauded the next pitch and spat some statistic about the Puerto Rican pitcher.

Of course he'd like baseball, Maggie thought.

"O'Dell not make it?" Stratton asked.

Maggie didn't answer, making a fuss of rearranging the ice in the bottom of her branded Nationals stadium cup. Stratton caught her eye, but he had the good sense not to press. Maggie was grateful.

O'Dell, in fact, wasn't even on the East Coast. Shortly after their workout the previous morning, her pseudo-advisor and undercover boyfriend had announced his desire to fly to Texas and spend some extended time with Holly, his daughter. Maggie hadn't objected, of course, but she couldn't shake the gnawing feeling in her gut that O'Dell's sudden travel agenda was linked to the perpetuated awkwardness that had developed between them over the last ten months.

Their romance had been a spontaneous one. O'Dell's loyalty and affections were as genuine as they came. But the jump from longtime bodyguard to would-be lover simply wasn't working. They could spend all day hitting the gym and managing meetings and sharing lunch, only to sit quietly around the dinner table at night and have nothing to say.

Maybe O'Dell simply needed a break. Maybe Maggie needed a break, too.

"I saw your press conference," Stratton said, jarring her out of her thoughts. "Way to cut Crusher off at the knees. I freaking hate that prick."

"I had Farah pull his credential," Maggie said. "It's a short-term win, but maybe it will send a message."

"Are you sure she's the right face for your press corps?" Stratton's voice was calm, but Maggie detected the subtext of it. The words were more a suggestion than a question.

"What does that mean?" Maggie asked.

Stratton shrugged.

"Spit it out, Jordan."

"I just wonder if she projects a strong enough image. It's bad enough to be yanked around by the press on a *good* day. Right now ..."

He trailed off, and this time Maggie didn't need him to finish. She knew what point he was making, and the point was valid.

Right now we look weak, she finished. *Right now I've been invisible for too long and our enemies are making hay.*

"Give her time," Maggie said. "Yesterday was an anomaly. With Crusher on suspension, the reporters should calm down. I appreciate Farah's ability to stay on message. We need that."

Stratton grunted, and Maggie knew he wasn't sold. But he didn't contradict her.

"What's the update from Thomas?" Maggie asked.

Attorney General Greg Thomas had been a member of Maggie's cabinet since the moment she stepped into office under the Twenty-fifth Amendment. He was a calm, convicted leader. A bit of a stick in the mud sometimes. Not as flexible as she would like. But when Maggie had thrown him the Cunningham lead, he'd run with it like a hunting dog on a blood trail. She appreciated that.

"Greg expects to announce two or three dozen more indictments against Cunningham's pals next week. It's a bit of a deluge at this point. He's got some hungry young FBI guys on the trail. The more they dig, the more they find."

"Good," Maggie said. "Tell them to dig until they reach China. I want everything."

Stratton didn't answer, and Maggie glanced sideways. He was still looking at the field, but he didn't so much as flinch when the Atlanta batter hit a home run.

"You have something to say?" Maggie prompted.

Stratton drummed one finger on the arm of his chair, but still didn't answer.

"Good grief, Jordan. Are we past this or not? If you've got something to say, say it."

"I don't want you to question my loyalty."

Stratton faced her. For a moment the park faded out and it was just the two of them. Maggie thought back to a moment ten months prior, during the Venezuela fiasco. When Stratton first brought her evidence of Harold Cunningham's potential involvement in her attempted assassination, and his certain involvement with corrupt practices in the international oil sector.

She'd questioned Stratton then. Doubted him. But Stratton had proven himself, driving her doubts into remission, if not into the grave.

"I don't, Jordan," Maggie said simply.

Stratton faced the field again as the next batter took the field.

"I think you should scale back the investigation," he said.

"Are you serious?"

"I am."

"Why on earth?"

Stratton didn't answer immediately. He cracked open a water bottle and drank half of it first.

"You've opened a Pandora's box, Madam President. It had to be opened. But the deeper you dig, the worse it's going to get. The thing you have to understand about these people"—he faced her—"*my* people, is that the corruption never ends. Billionaire businessmen don't become billionaire businessmen by keeping their noses clean. Some are worse than others. Cunningham may not be as bad as it gets. But if we continue down this path of declaring war on America's elite, it will consume your presidency. You'll win a few points with the working class while completely alienating the corporate sphere—and the corporate sphere is where the money is. Long before next election, they'll throw enough funding at our opponents to drown us. We'll be dead by the primaries."

Maggie pursed her lips. The raw pragmatism in Stratton's argument should have upset the idealist in her, but it had been years since her inner idealist had been naive to the realities of politics.

"I ran on an anti-corruption platform," Maggie retorted. "This is what I promised the American people."

"Yes. And you delivered. You got Cunningham. That fish alone is fat enough to make a meal out of for the rest of the year. But if you keep throwing out the net, I'm concerned that we'll snag a whale, and then be pulled overboard."

So this is politics, Maggie thought. She wanted to be disgusted, but she couldn't deny the logic in Stratton's argument. Since ascending to the Oval Office, her life had become a whirlwind. Very little of her presidency had anything to do with the sort of idealistic reforms she'd hoped to achieve as the leader of the Free World. Her job felt more like that of a fireman—rushing from one blaze to the next, fighting to keep the country from descending into ashes.

Unleashing the DOJ on Cunningham felt like the first meaningful thing she'd accomplished to date.

"I'm not scared of these people," Maggie said.

"You should be. They're some of the pettiest, most vengeful people on the planet. And they'll band together, if backed into a corner. This could get ugly very quickly, and the worst of it is, there's no real virtue in staying the course."

"What does that mean?"

"It means you've already mined as much political capital out of this situation as you're going to get. It's a game of diminishing returns now. Some Americans will applaud you for hunting down billionaire crooks, but most will get bored. They'll be more concerned about inflation and the economy than the latest handcuffed WASP you parade in front of the cameras. And that's reasonable."

"The economy is fine," Maggie retorted. "With oil flowing out of Venezuela, the price of gas is plummeting. That will bring inflation in check. The Fed will lower rates again. It's only a matter of time."

Stratton nodded. "I agree, which is why I think you should be talking about *that* and not about Cunningham. Tell Greg to back his people down. Let's phase this investigation into the background and focus our efforts on more vulnerable topics."

"Such as?"

"Well, Venezuela, for one. Crusher might be a pig, but he's not wrong about President Rivas. I spoke with Lisa yesterday—the state department is receiving some unsettling reports from Caracas. Rivas is cracking down on his people, leveraging the national police to enforce curfews and secure private businesses. The situation has the flavor of the last guy, and that's precisely what we *don't* want."

Maggie knew Stratton was right. She had dismissed Crusher offhand when he raised concerns about the new Venezuelan government—mostly because she didn't want to engage on that subject. The oil was flowing again. The old regime and all of its corruption were problems of the past.

Those were the talking points, anyway. Rivas's heavy-handed approach to establishing stability in a city so long ravaged by chaos was making it difficult to sell that story.

"I'll speak to Lisa," Maggie said, referring to her secretary of state. "We'll lean on Rivas, make him calm down."

Stratton nodded. "I think you should. And in the meantime, let's talk more about Haiti. That's a no-lose situation for you. An easy win."

Maggie didn't like the idea of couching the deaths of three hundred thousand as an "easy win," but she knew what Stratton meant.

"I agree."

The scoreboard slid into the bottom of the seventh inning, and Stratton rested both palms on his knees. She thought he would get up. He didn't.

"Something else?" Maggie asked.

"Just one thing." Stratton's tone dropped in volume. He faced her. "We need to . . . secure loose ends."

"Say what?"

"You've made some enemies going after Cunningham. They're going to dig. Find anything they can to throw at you."

"There's nothing," Maggie said, too quickly.

Stratton raised an eyebrow. Maggie looked away.

Oh, there was something, all right. A lot of somethings, actually. Stretching all the way back to her tenure as governor of Louisiana. A series of questionably legal, often heavy-handed power moves and shortcuts all designed to bring her enemies to their knees.

Those decisions hadn't been made in the interest of political power. There was always a greater good at stake. But still, lines had been crossed. Questionable decision made. And right at the heart of that mess, intertwined in her rise from political obscurity to political stardom, was Reed Montgomery and his Prosecution Force. The disgraced former Marine turned black ops warrior.

A man who was as pragmatic and ruthless as they came.

"I've heard nothing since they retired," Maggie said. "We've distanced ourselves."

"We need to keep it that way," Stratton said. "Have Jill and O'Dell scrub any records of Montgomery or his team. And if they reach out for any reason . . . let me know."

Maggie caught his eye. There was something cold behind the exhaustion and focus. Something deadly.

Stratton stood, buttoning his jacket, and his voice returned to its normal volume. "Thank you for the invite, Madam President. Enjoy the ball game!"

10

From a cloudless sky the summer sun blasted the fifty-acre field with the full wrath of August, spiking the thermometer to ninety-eight degrees without wind or shade to break the torment. Reed stood back from the crowd with his two-year-old son propped on one hip, sweat gluing his T-shirt to his chest and doubtlessly printing over the brand new SIG SAUER P365-XMACRO concealed just above his belt buckle.

Reed didn't care. He guzzled lukewarm water from a plastic bottle that would have been a dollar at the supermarket. Eight bucks at the music festival, and he was already on his fourth. Somebody was making an unholy fortune off life's most basic necessity. Over thirty thousand people had packed the field, toweling away sweat as they clustered around vendor booths and music stages, cheering the onset of every new act.

It wasn't fun. At least, not to Reed. He'd never understood why people enjoyed cramming themselves together to experience B-grade music blared from overpowering speakers while drowning in their own sweat. It was a bizarre obsession to him.

But this was Banks's world, so there was nowhere else he'd rather be.

"Reed! You've got to keep him covered. My lord, son."

Sharon O'Hara—formerly Sharon Morccelli, in a life long gone— appeared like a witch on a broom from Reed's blind side, adjusting little Davy's hat to protect his face from the sun and producing a bottle of child-friendly sunscreen to slather over his bare arms. Reed remained stoically silent while his mother-in-law squawked and scolded about his slip-shot parenting skills, going out of her way to call him "son" and boil the most basic attributes of human survival into third-grade-level lessons.

By the time Sharon finished with the sunscreen, Davy looked more like a snowman than a human child. His skin was caked with the stuff, little globs of it sticking to his eyelashes. His cheeks puckered as he looked desperately to Reed for help.

"Put the lotion away, Sharon. He's fine."

Sharon's hawkish little eyes bulged. She snapped the sunscreen tube closed, shoving it back into a designer diaper bag filled with designer child-care accessories.

Everything was designer with Sharon. Her family was about as drenched in Texas oil wealth as a person could be without choking to death, and her ceaseless efforts to refer to Reed as her own child did little to overcome the obvious reality that she couldn't stand him.

The feeling was mutual.

Reed ignored Sharon as she continued to mutter beneath her breath, fishing through the diaper bag. He shifted Davy to his opposite hip and took his place in line for a nearby hot dog stand. Banks would take the stage in thirty minutes. Time for lunch and another bottle of water.

"You want a juice box?"

Davy looked up with wide blue eyes—Banks's eyes. Crystal clear and as deep as the ocean. It made Reed smile just seeing him.

"Yeah, let's get you a juice box. It's hot out here, ain't it? But don't worry. If I can keep myself alive in Iraq, I can keep the pair of us healthy in Tennessee."

Reed lost Sharon in the line and purchased lunch for Davy and himself. Then he found welcome shade beneath the branches of a pecan tree and fed Davy bite-sized bits of hot dog. His son smiled when he tasted ketchup, but he made no sound. Even at twenty-five months old, Davy almost never spoke more than single-word sentences. It worried Banks, and it drove Sharon to something close to panic.

Reed wasn't concerned. Montgomery men had never been big talkers. He figured that when Davy had something to say, he'd say it.

"Sheesh, it's hot out here."

Turk appeared like the headliner of a circus, sweat-soaked military green tank top clashing magnificently with the polka-dot pink baby back-pack slung on one shoulder. Sinju, Turk's new bride and the mother of his two-month-old daughter, followed just behind, pushing a baby stroller with one hand and sucking on a slurpy drink cradled in the other. The stroller was a massive thing, built with all-terrain tires and enough extendable awnings to drive the sun into irrelevance. Reed even heard an electronic buzz, soon identified as the whir of a fan mounted to the inside of the sunshades.

Little Liberty Seoul lay encased in a star-studded blue dress with red and white striped bloomers poking from beneath. Her face was an elegant blend of Sinju's olive-skinned Korean heritage and Turk's Tennessee-born, corn-fed look. She gurgled happily from within the mega-stroller.

"You buy that thing at the Porsche dealer?" Reed jabbed.

"Shut up," Turk said. "You're just jealous you can fit."

Sinju parked the stroller and rolled the sun shades back. Liberty appeared in her arms as a happy red blob, mouth spread in a grin. Sinju tickled her and giggled. "You like the sun? Huh? You like the music? Take a selfie with Mommy!"

Liberty grinned as if on cue, and Sinju made a duck face for the picture. Reed watched out of the corner of one eye, noting the way Turk stood with his hands jammed into his pockets, staring slack-jawed at his family. There was a warm glow in his eyes that Reed had only ever seen at the prospect of a brand new Jeep, or the sound of a Marine Viper helicopter rushing in to unleash judgment.

Except this was deeper. A lot deeper.

"Hey dummy. You find the stage?" Reed asked.

"Back that way," Turk jabbed a thumb over one shoulder. "Near the fence. Kind of a long walk. We should probably get going."

Reed passed him the rest of the hot dog and scrubbed ketchup off

Davy's face. Then Sharon reappeared like a bad stomach flu, bustling in with Goldfish crackers and a sippy cup full of Kool-Aid. Davy held his hands out for the drink, flashing baby teeth.

"Who's Grammy's good little boy? Can you say *please?* Tell Grammy please for the drink," Sharon crooned.

"Pweeze."

"That's a good boy!" She ruffled his head, still clucking at him. Reed restrained an exhausted sigh.

"Turk, meet Sharon. Banks's mom. Sharon, this is Turk and Sinju."

Sharon swept a scathing glance over the pair, forcing a polite smile. It was only a little less transparent than her designer sunglasses.

"A pleasure, sir. Did you say *Sujin?* Is that Indian?" Sharon spoke slowly to Sinju, overenunciating each syllable.

Sinju didn't miss it. Nor did she waste a moment in pouncing.

"Is *Kor-eee-an!*" Sinju raised her voice and dragged the word out. "I from Korea. No speak a good English like white people."

Sharon flushed scarlet, turning away to busy herself with Davy. Reed passed him off and shot Turk a glare. Turk only smirked and wrapped his arm around Sinju.

"She's got jokes."

"I'm laughing my ass off," Reed said, stone-faced. "Come on, Banks is on in twenty."

11

The wrath of the blazing American sun felt like the wrath of Allah himself—
and that gave Bahir strength. He didn't mind the way the utility uniform clung
to his sweat-soaked skin as he piloted the rental van up the rutted, red dirt road.
Hardwood trees and rolling hills filled his windows on every side, leafy green
trees withered by the heat. There was no water in the ditch. The tires kicked up
dry dust that clouded his rearview and misted over the back windows.

In a strange way, Tennessee felt a little like Syria. It didn't look like
Syria, or really have much in common with Syria other than being unrea-
sonably hot. But the bad road and the rural landscape felt right for war.

It felt right for jihad, the holy war Bahir had thirsted for his entire adult
life.

Applying the brakes, Bahir slowed the van as the line of cars headed to
a Y-shaped split in the road. The left leg led to a grass parking lot. The right
leg was blocked by a cattle gate and an attendant dressed in khaki cargo
pants and a black T-shirt. That shirt read "Security" across the shoulder
blades, but as far as Bahir could tell the man was unarmed and only semi-
engaged with the environment around him.

His phone took precedence. That would make this easy.

Bahir cast a sidelong look at Mahmoud. His companion nodded once. Bahir pulled right at the Y and stopped at the gate. The security guard took his time pocketing the phone and approaching the driver's side window. It was already down.

"Where you headed?" he drawled.

Bahir smelled sour cigarettes on his breath. He wore a University of Tennessee ball cap. He sounded like a local.

"Lot Fourteen," Bahir said, muting his Syrian accent and offering a gentle smile. "Replacement drum set for one of the bands. The heat must have damaged theirs."

He passed a crinkled document through the window. It was nothing more than a purchase order for a new drum set, with a fake music shop listed at the heading. Ibrahim had provided it. Bahir and Mahmoud's fearless leader had designed the entire thing for free using a software he found online. He ran a Google search for drum sets to select an appropriate price, then added a $50 fee for delivery. The logo was from another free software. The document was folded and crumpled, as though it had ridden in his pocket.

A very basic ruse, really. But that was part of Ibrahim's genius. He knew how to make things only complex enough to get the job done, minimizing the risk of failure. It was one of the many things Bahir admired most about Ibrahim. One of the many reasons he so willingly volunteered his own life for this mission.

Ibrahim wasn't like the scores of other wannabe holy war generals to be found scattered across the Middle East. He'd tasted combat. He'd faced the enemy before.

He knew how to bring them to their knees in their own land.

"Mind if I see in back?" the security guy asked.

Bahir shrugged. "Help yourself."

He sat calmly while the security guy opened the rear door. Mahmoud's dark eyes flicked sideways to the mirror to watch him, but neither man moved while the guy looked inside.

The interior of the van was full of boxes. All cardboard. All large enough to house a drum set. The rear box was printed with the name of a prominent musical instrument manufacturer.

The security guy scanned the cargo, shifting a wad of chewing tobacco in his mouth and taking his time. Ibrahim's heart accelerated as the guy squinted at a box, sucking his teeth and slurping tobacco-laced saliva.

Then the security guy grunted, and slammed both doors. He reached the driver's window again.

"You know where to go?" he asked.

"We do," Bahir said.

The guy returned the purchase order, then walked without comment to the gate and dragged it open. He shot Bahir and Mahmoud a two-finger salute as they passed. Bahir offered a smile.

"Watch out for the ruts," the security guy said. "Wouldn't want to bust that new drum set."

Bahir rolled the window up. He did watch out for the ruts, steering the rental van carefully around them. But not because there was a drum set housed beneath that pile of carefully constructed boxes. Not a musical set, anyway. These drums were made of metal, welded together long ago in a Soviet weapons factory on the other side of the globe. Still emblazoned with the hammer and sickle emblem. Designed to be triggered by the boot of an American foot soldier.

But now repurposed. Wired together into an orchestra of death powerful enough to turn the whole moving van into one giant fragmentation grenade. A symphony of slaughter.

Even at the edge of the festival grounds, Bahir could already hear the music.

12

Rutherford County, Tennessee

"Ladies and gentlemen, from small-town Mississippi, by way of Nashville, Tennessee, please give a warm welcome to *Banks Montgomery!*"

The crowd gathering in front of the stage wasn't large—just a few dozen people, with more drifting in every few minutes carrying sodas and popsicles. But they cheered enthusiastically as Banks took the stage, trotting out in a flowing white sundress and cowboy boots. An elegant straw hat was perched on her head, cocked back enough to expose a radiant smile as she stepped behind the mic.

The band was small—just a drummer and a single guitarist, neither of them exceptionally talented—but their hourly rate had still managed to consume the bulk of Banks's performance fee. Reed knew she didn't care, and neither did he. As the guitarist struck a riff and the drummer found the beat, Banks swung straight into her opener—a cover of an obscure 1980s pop song that she felt best warmed a crowd.

Reed had to agree. The song was hooky, and it matched her vocal range perfectly. Within seconds the polite cheers became more enthusiastic. Reed stood near the back with Davy on his hip, lifting his son's pudgy arm to wave at his mother.

Banks saw them and grinned, but she didn't break focus. She finished the song and delivered a bow to the crowd. It had doubled in size. Over a hundred people, most of them probably there to see the popular country artist Banks was opening for. But with an eight-song set, that rising star didn't matter. This was Banks's moment, for as long as she owned it. Her cheeks flushed as her second track was rewarded with an enthusiastic ovation. Reed settled into the grass, crossing his legs and cradling Davy. Sinju and Turk sat nearby—Turk cradling baby Liberty, Sinju whooping. Reed wasn't sure where Sharon had gone, and he wasn't in a hurry to find her.

"Thank you all for coming out today," Banks half-giggled at the crowd. Some brute of a guy from left of stage whooped and whistled, and she flashed an innocent smile. Reed was surprised to feel a flush of heat in his chest, and he focused on adjusting Davy into a better position on his knee.

"This is my first time playing a music festival. You guys having a good time?"

An enthusiastic cheer. Banks brushed hair behind one ear.

"Me too!"

More people had streamed in now. It was becoming difficult for Reed to see the stage. He twisted in the grass just as the brute to his left shouted again at Banks.

"Show us your jugs!"

The flush of heat returned. He reached his feet and looked in that direction. He couldn't see the guy, but apparently Banks had either not heard him or was choosing to ignore him. She was already giving an intro to her new song, slinging a guitar over her shoulder while she gave background on the lyrics. Not far from the stage Reed observed a line of college-aged boys drinking from unmarked water bottles. They were drunk—that much was evident.

He rolled his eyes and looked away. Then he stopped, and looked back.

It wasn't the frat boys who caught his eye. It was the vehicle—a moving van with a prominent rental company logo sprayed across the rear doors. Even from a hundred yards away, he recognized the simple black and white of a Texas license plate. The van was backed in alongside the stage, and two men were getting out. Both dressed in deep-blue utility uniforms. Dark hair. Olive complexion.

None of that was particularly unusual. There were lots of rental vans scattered around the festival. Lots of guys in utility uniforms unloading production equipment and oversized speakers.

It was the position of the van that threw him off. The back of it was pushed all the way to the waist-high metal fence that outlined the crowd-space in front of the stage, much too close to allow the rear doors to swing open. Likewise, the sliding cargo door on the righthand side of the van was positioned too close to the stage itself for any cargo to be loaded to unloaded. As Reed watched, the two men standing outside the van loitered near their open doors. The one on the right lit a cigarette and looked toward the stage. He seemed to be enjoying the music. Seemed to be thinking.

Then he checked his watch, and a cold claw closed around Reed's stomach. He watched the guy turn. Reach into the van. Bend over out of sight, just for a minute. Saw both men step away and slam the front doors. Turn away from the van and break into a fast walk.

Reed was on his feet. He thrust Davy into Sinju's arms and wrenched her upright by one arm.

"Go! Get out of here!" He shoved Turk by the shoulder. "Get Liberty out of here!"

Turk found his feet. Momentary confusion was quickly extinguished by understanding.

"Van!" Reed pointed. "Get them out!"

Turk followed his line of sight to the rental. Gathering Sinju and the two children under his arms he pushed them toward the open back of the metal corral. Reed turned for the stage, his gaze snapping to Banks where she stood behind the mic, strumming the guitar and breaking into the chorus. The drummer slammed his sticks across symbols and the snare. The speakers blared music.

Reed broke into a run, shoving people aside and fighting his way toward the stage. He screamed for Banks, and somebody caught his arm.

"Hey bro! Watch where you're going!"

"Get out!" Reed shouted. "There's a bomb! Get away from the stage!"

He made it another three yards, fighting through the pack of bodies. Entering the spontaneous mosh pit that had formed twenty yards from Banks. Pushing the bodies aside. Screaming. Waving his arm.

Banks saw him, and confusion crossed her face. Then momentary panic.

Then anger.

She shook her head once and stumbled over a line in the song. Reed hurled himself forward, back hand dropping instinctively toward his stomach where the SIG was concealed.

And then hell burst open. The earth split with a blinding thunderclap —a rushing red flash of nuclear heat. An upheaval of dirt and stage and fence and flying bodies all in the space of an instant.

Reed hit the ground face-first, and everything turned black.

13

Forty thousand feet above north Georgia

The aircraft's four General Electric engines produced nearly 227,000 pounds of jet thrust, but from inside the insulated cabin of Air Force One, they were almost silent. Maggie sat near a window in a private office situated alongside her executive cabin and watched the Appalachian mountains unfold far below.

Dense forests and rolling fields. Mountain peaks and bright green valleys. It was all very serene, but it paled in comparison to her anticipation of a much muddier, much less picturesque landscape lying just an hour away—the swamplands of lower Louisiana.

Since accepting the vice presidency and moving to Washington, Maggie had often found it easier to have her family visit *her* rather than the other way around. The double-wide trailer her parents called home was little more than a shack, and it was buried way out in the sticks nearly five miles from the closest paved road. Her brother Larry's place was a palace by comparison—a ranch-style brick house on the outskirts of Chackbay, boasting both an asphalt driveway and easy access to a Dollar General. In the opinion of the cousins, Larry had "made it."

None of the simplicity or borderline poverty bothered Maggie. She'd never been ashamed of her roots, and nothing about the White House or her international spotlight could change that. It was simply a matter of logistics. The Secret Service hated planning trips to Louisiana. All the aforementioned cousins turned up in droves, bringing stacks of uninspected casseroles and slow-cooked gator meat, not to mention guns. Loads of guns. More by accident than intention. Maggie's family simply owned a lot of firearms, and they often forgot where they put them. Add to that the sprawling swamplands and the near impossibility of securing them, and it was little wonder the Secret Service went out of their way to facilitate family get-togethers in Washington.

But once in a while, Maggie pushed back. Once in a while the pressures and pretensions of the nation's capital overwhelmed her, and she insisted on a flight south. This was such an occasion. The Nationals game of three nights prior had been her last straw. She needed a break from the spotlight. She needed mudbug gumbo and a low country boil that brought cousins from miles.

She needed home.

Relaxing against her headrest, Maggie wanted to reach for O'Dell's hand, but the seat next to her was empty. O'Dell was still in Texas, still visiting family. He hadn't responded to any of her texts in nearly two days. Someplace in her gut, Maggie knew that wasn't a good thing. Knew it probably meant she was right about the unidentifiable barricade standing between them. She was simply too overworked to begin unraveling the mystery.

Maybe this was the wrong time for a relationship. Maybe she should focus on work. On her presidency. On resolving the Cunningham investigations and establishing some sort of a legislative agenda. On her physical recovery.

But if not now . . . when?

Maggie pushed the racing thoughts away, reminding herself to be a grown-up. Her mother would have prepared a family dinner. Larry had four kids now. They were all young and rowdy. She should rest on the flight. Not worry about O'Dell.

She reached for the window shade to block out the Appalachian landscape. Then Maggie's stomach lifted toward her chest, and the air raced from her lungs. Pressure descended on her shoulders, not severe but sudden. She swallowed hard and grabbed the seat. Outside, the mountaintops rotated toward her as the right wing dropped. Air Force One was banking—hard.

The phone next to Maggie chimed. She snatched it up as the Boeing pulled out of the turn and leveled out. Her stomach still flipped. Her head spun.

But her mind remained sharp. She already knew the right question to ask.

"What happened?"

"Bomb, ma'am. Near Nashville. We don't have details, yet, but we're diverting from Louisiana just to be safe. We'll keep you posted."

Maggie hung up and instinctively peered out of the window, forward of the right wing. In the general direction of where she thought Nashville lay.

Of course she didn't see anything. No smoke, no fire. No flashing emergency lights. Only the endless green of those Appalachian forests, stretching to the horizon.

Dark foreboding seeped into Maggie's gut. It was a familiar feeling—a feeling that hallmarked her presidency more than her youth, gender, or political independence ever had. A dull horror.

As if on cue, pain flashed into her side, and Maggie dropped a hand over the scar tissue massed over her stomach. The bullet wound. She cocked her head toward the window again, and this time she did see something. Not fire, smoke, or emergency lights.

Jet trails. Two of them. Streaking in from directly ahead, a glimmer of light glistening over polycarbonate canopies. That glimmer grew into a racing orange glow, then the two streaks split and swung into wide circles—back and around.

Thirty seconds later a gunmetal gray F-35 slid into position barely a hundred yards off Air Force One's righthand wing, so close she could see the helmet of the pilot turning toward her. She couldn't see the sidewinder missiles housed within the jet's concealed weapons bay, but she knew they were there. Whispering death, a trigger-pull away from deployment.

The pilot lifted two fingers in a stiff salute. Maggie raised two fingers in return, even though she doubted whether the pilot could see her. She withdrew from the window, the knot in her stomach boiling into a flash of hot rage.

A bomb. In Nashville.

Maggie snatched up the phone and waited for the operator.

"Yes, ma'am?"

"Connect me with the vice president. ASAP."

14

Rutherford County, Tennessee

Reed tasted death. It was the first sensation he recognized as his vision returned, and the macabre flavor brought with it a flood of programmed responses overtaking his brain in practiced automation.

Obtain cover. Retain weapon. Control environment.

Reed reached for the SIG tucked into his belt, and his fingers found something hot and sticky instead. Blood and raw flesh—the realization sent a bolt of lightning through his body and he rolled sideways and kicked.

It wasn't his blood—it wasn't his shredded flesh. He lay on the ground, surrounded by falling ash and dense smoke. A body lay over his legs. Or, rather . . . part of a body. An arm and half of a ribcage, still semi-clothed in a folk band T-shirt. Reed kicked it away and found the SIG. The weapon slid from his belt in a rush, the Trijicon RMR red dot optic mounted to the slide glowing in the smoky haze. Reed thrashed to his knees, sweeping the gun left.

Toward the stage.

He couldn't see the structure. He couldn't see anything. Everything was a haze of gray, laden with the stench of burned flesh and blast fumes. He couldn't hear anything, either—just a dull ringing in both ears. The sun blazed down but failed to illuminate a path ahead.

"Banks!" Reed screamed into the haze, but his voice was barely audible over the ringing in his ears. He stumbled over something heavy and thick. Bringing the nose of the SIG down, he flicked the power switch on the rail-mounted light and unleashed a six-hundred-lumen LED beam.

Bodies. It was like something out of a nightmare—the bottom of a foxhole in an R-rated war film. Detached limbs and torsos blown in half, many of them laced with little round holes. Most of the faces weren't even recognizable. Gallons of blood drenched the ground and stained his pant legs.

Reed blocked it all out. He ignored the gore and the ringing in his ears and settled in behind the SIG, using the LED beam to cut through the smoke.

"*Banks!*"

No answer. Only more ringing. Reed fought through the carnage and choked on the smoke. His eyes ran with tears, chest heaving. Then a hand closed around his arm. Firm fingers gripped once. Reed whirled, leading with the SIG, finger dropping over the trigger.

Turk caught him by the forearm and stopped the pivot, shaking his arm.

"Reed! Can you hear me?"

Reed could hear. Turk's voice sounded like it was coming through a fish tank, but it was there. Strong features and a stronger grip, both smeared by smoke.

"Davy?" Reed shouted, a new edge of panic breaking through the controlled calm of his mind. "Liberty?"

"They're secure!" Turk pushed him forward. "You take left."

Turk's own weapon appeared in a flash—a Glock 17, concealed on his giant frame like a child's toy. The two of them moved in tandem through the field of bodies, and then Reed knew his hearing was returning.

Ripping screams joined the ringing in his ears. Sirens in the distance. Agony all around him.

Reed didn't stop, and neither did Turk. As the smoke began to clear, Reed saw a tangled mass of the metal fence that blocked the crowd from the stage. It was already cleared out of their path, blasted by the thunder of the bomb. The weapon light on Reed's SIG cast an LED glow over the shattered edge of the stage, sprayed by blood and burning in one corner. Fresh black smoke clouded his face, and then he reached the stage.

Turk dropped to one knee automatically and interlaced his fingers. Reed ran and jumped, launching off Turk's hand and landing on his knees over the stage.

Landing on a body.

Reed's stomach flipped. He swept the SIG down, blazing light over the face.

It wasn't Banks—it was the guitarist. Most of his neck was gone, his face riddled with little round holes as though he had caught the edge of a buckshot pattern. There was no doubt he was dead. Already his face was gray and his body limp.

Reed clawed his way to his feet and turned left—toward the last place he remembered the mic standing. He almost tripped and looked down to find the shattered remnants of Banks's guitar. Turk reached the stage and closed behind him. They both tore through the debris.

Then Reed saw her. A leg, first. Then the shadowy outline of a body. His heart spiked and blind panic broke through the practiced calm of his mind. He slid to his knees next to a crater in the stage. Collapsed plywood and shards of 2x4s opened a hole over the ground below, and Banks lay halfway slid down it. The weapon light flashed across her face, and Reed saw ashen white skin and closed eyes. Blood ran from the corner of her mouth. The sundress was a torn, wadded mass, gathered around her hips to expose a field of red dots across her stomach and pelvis.

Buckshot holes, like the others. A dozen or more.

Reed abandoned the gun on the broken stage and dropped into the hole. He found her left arm and searched for a pulse—he felt nothing. Banks's skin was both soft and cold, and when he pressed a hand under her nose he couldn't feel the breath.

Reed didn't scream. He didn't panic. The temporary desperation that had overtaken his mind had been driven back. He was back in control. He scooped his hands beneath her body and pulled her close. Banks was soaked with blood. More of it streamed from two dozen wounds.

Turk shouted from the stage. "I got you!"

He extended a hand into the hole and Reed hauled himself out. He could still barely see, but now it was only because his eyes had blurred with so many protective tears. The smoke itself was thinning out. He could taste fresh air, only it wasn't really fresh. It was still laden with the horrid flavor of death.

Turk pulled him out of the hole and led him down a collapsed portion of the stage, away from the bomb crater. They crossed the edge of the field of bodies and Reed glanced right, just once.

Not dozens. Hundreds of corpses, torn and shattered. A landscape of death.

His stomach convulsed despite himself, but there was no time to wait. No time to think. Turk pushed him around the edge of the stage, toward the open field beyond. The screams were desperate, now. Thousands of them, people surging everywhere. Sirens blaring and a fire engine rushing in. Police ran with weapons drawn while unarmed security officers shouted and gestured, as lost as anyone else.

Reed blocked it all out and searched for one thing—an ambulance. He couldn't see one amid the fire engines. Most of the first responders who ran past him were either cops or dressed in fire retardant uniforms—probably a crew on standby ready to fight an accidental fire. They unrolled long hoses and ran to combat the burning stage, but the flames there were the least of their concerns.

"Ambulance!" Reed shouted at them. "Where are the ambulances?"

No answer. Only dazed faces and rushing humans. Turk caught the attention of a sheriff's deputy with a Glock in his hand, but when the man saw Banks his face went ashen. He stumbled back, choking. Unable to speak.

When he turned away to puke, Reed ran past him. He thought he heard something else, now. Something very familiar. The thumping, pounding beat of a helicopter's rotor blades.

"There!" Turk pointed, and Reed saw the medevac. No, not a medevac. The civilian equivalent. A blue-and-white Bell helicopter equipped for air medical services, landing slowly at a cleared portion of the field two hundred yards away. The doors ripped open and paramedics and nurses dressed in hospital scrubs spilled out.

Reed hurtled toward the chopper, Turk at his elbow. Shallow depressions and abandoned camping chairs left a field of obstacles, but Reed bulled through them all. The two of them reached the helicopter in time for the last paramedic to bail out, dragging a bag full of emergency supplies behind him. Turk reached for the door and the pilot shouted over his shoulder.

"Stand back! This isn't an ambulance."

"It is now!" Turk screamed.

Reed lunged in, dragging Banks with him. She hung limp in his arms. He still couldn't find a pulse.

"Get us to a hospital!" Turk called, cramming in alongside Reed.

"I can't do that, sir! I've got orders to ferry in more paramedics. Please exit the—"

Turk rammed his Glock 17 over the pilot's seat, muzzle meeting helmet with a snap.

"*Fly!*"

The pilot's hands found the controls, and the engines howled. Reed knelt on the steel floor as one of the paramedics leapt aboard and went to work on Banks from his backpack. The chopper lifted off with the grace of a jetliner, then spun in the air.

Hot wind ripped through the open doors, and Reed tuned it all out. He clutched Banks's hand.

And just prayed.

15

The helicopter ripped through the sky like a rocket, nose down, max speed. The pilot appeared more pissed than frightened by Turk's violent threat, but he remained professionally calm in the cockpit, ignoring the passengers behind him and working his radio to obtain clearance for a hospital landing.

Even with the rotor thundering overhead and hot wind rushing by, everything descended into slow motion for Reed. He watched the paramedic work, his vision still blurring every couple of seconds. An IV found Banks's arms and the paramedic conducted modified CPR to avoid pressing on her chest wounds.

The little round holes were everywhere, like a shotgun pattern from fifty yards—a wide, chaotic spray.

"Clear for landing at Vanderbilt!" the pilot shouted. "Six minutes!"

Six minutes. The figure sounded like a gauntlet to Reed—like six blocks of an ISIL-held city deep in Iraq. A desperate, final hurdle.

The chopper's nose dropped further. Reed clung on to Banks, grasping her shoulder as her body shifted. Turk hit his knees across from him and wrapped one of his giant hands around her shoulder. The floor shook. The paramedic produced a syringe and thumped it, pressing out the air bubbles with practiced ease. Perfectly calm.

But Reed could see the urgency in his eyes.

The chopper slowed. Reed looked through the open door to see Nashville racing by beneath—long highways packed with cars. Tall apartment buildings and lots of trees. He saw downtown and the chopper banked left. The tail swung out. The altitude bled away.

The pilot spoke in an abrupt bark into his radio. A helipad appeared, and a flash of hope ignited in Reed's chest as a knot of hospital staff surged onto the roof.

The helicopter dropped rapidly as the pilot managed the controls with ease, head up, shoulders loose. The wheels touched with a snap, then everything became a blur again. Reed stumbled out. A stretcher rolled against the side of the chopper and the paramedic helped to shift Banks onto it. Reed moved alongside her, fighting to find her hand.

A nurse pushed him away. "Sir! You need to back up."

Behind him the chopper spun to life again. Reed looked over his shoulder to see Turk waving him on from inside the open door.

"I've got Davy! You go!"

The little wheels of the stretcher rattled. Reed rushed to catch up. Hospital doors clapped, and blurry white hallways opened ahead. Reed ran with one hand clasping the edge of the stretcher. His heart thundered. Head buzzed. White and green scrubs closed around him, men and women already wearing surgical caps and masks pressing in close. The stretcher pivoted left toward a set of double doors.

A strong hand grabbed Reed's shoulder and pulled him back.

The stretcher ripped out of his hands. Reed cocked a fist and whirled, swinging straight for whoever stood behind him. His fist met a massive meaty palm, closing easily over his fingers and shoving him back. An immense Black man stood there, dressed in nurse's scrubs, holding him firm.

"Breathe, brother. You can't go back there. They've got her."

Reed shook. He made a feeble attempt to yank himself free, but the nurse held him firm. He looked back just in time to watch the surgery doors smack shut.

Banks was gone.

16

The surgery waiting room was small, situated down the hall from the double doors Reed had been locked out of. He found his way to a chair and sat until he couldn't be still. Then he paced. Every thirty seconds, he checked his watch. He checked his phone.

Banks's surgery dragged on. The waiting room crowded with anxious loved ones as more helicopters made emergency landings on the roof—and more victims were rushed in on stretchers, hanging to life by a thread.

A few of the distressed people packed in the waiting room, noticing Reed's bloody and smoke-stained clothes, asked him if he had been at the blast. If he was hurt. If he knew what happened.

Reed flatly ignored them all, pacing around the room until his feet hurt. Barely thinking about the blast, fixating instead on his last image of Banks. Standing behind the mic, turning confused and angry eyes on him as he shouted for her to take cover. That beautiful sundress and bright blonde hair.

Would that be his final memory of his wife? Was this the end?

No. Life was just getting started. He and Banks had barely gotten their feet wet in this ocean of domestic bliss. Sure, there had been hurdles. Hiccups. He was struggling to adapt to suburban life. He didn't like the city. But he was trying. He was working day and night.

And in a quiet, subtle way . . . he *was* happy. He had a son. He had a family. This *couldn't* be the end.

The waiting room door groaned open, and Sinju appeared. The sunglasses were gone and her dark eyes swept the crowd before landing on Reed. She was sweaty and smoke-blackened, but unharmed. She rushed to him and extended her arms for a hug. Reed accepted it awkwardly, his chin dropping onto her narrow shoulder.

"I'm so sorry," Sinju whispered. "Any word from the doctors?"

"No," Reed shook his head.

Sinju wiped her eyes and sniffed.

"Where's Davy?" Reed asked. "Is Liberty okay?"

"They're fine—both fine. Your mother-in-law is looking after them. They're at hotel."

Reed nodded dumbly, strangely grateful that Sharon had enough sense to take Davy to her boutique Nashville hotel instead of joining the crowd at the hospital. Maybe she wasn't a complete idiot.

"Turk?"

"He's helping the first responders," Sinju said. "I couldn't make him leave."

No, Reed thought. *I bet you couldn't.*

"Hey!" A stranger's voice broke across the room. Reed looked up to see a man pointing at the TV mounted to the wall. The volume was down, but it had been playing news reels accompanied by subtitles for the last hour. All reports of the blast. All replaying the same facts over and over again without any real substance or context.

But now there was something. A fresh headline, outlined in red with the backdrop "BREAKING NEWS" printed behind. The headline read: *Terrorist Claims Responsibility for Nashville Attack.*

"Turn that up!" The man called. Somebody found the remote and obliged. A female voice crackled through the cheap speakers, easily reaching Reed's ringing ears across the breathless room.

"We've just received an update from our breaking news room in Atlanta. Sources now inform us that an international terrorist cell is claiming credit for the Nashville bombing. Now we . . . hold on . . . okay . . . okay. My producers tell me that a video posted to a private website has been referred to us by an anonymous tip. We can't make the video available to you here, but my producers are reviewing it now and they tell me that . . . yes. A man claiming to the be the representative of a radical Islamic terror network say he was the author of the Nashville attack. I don't have many details just yet . . ."

Reed turned away from the TV and dug into his pocket. He found the web browser on his phone and retreated to the quietest corner of the room while everyone else remained fixated on the TV. It wasn't difficult to find the video. A couple of quick Google searches produced a news article from an independent media outlet who was willing to share the link.

The website consisted of a black page. No header. No logo or navigation pane. Only a single video pasted right in the middle. Reed tapped the play button and Sinju leaned close. A simple white wall appeared, with a single chair sitting in the center of it. As Reed watched, an olive-skinned man dressed in white robes with a trimmed beard took the chair. When the man spoke his voice was smooth, rustling with a Middle Eastern accent, but easily understandable.

"To the people of the United States, and the evil American empire. I speak on behalf of true Muslims, believers in the prophet, servants of Allah, and victims of your tyranny around the globe. My name is not important. But who I am is the leader of the Islamic Caliphate Army—an organization birthed to declare war against the evils of western tyranny. We are not politicians. We are not revolutionaries. We are true believers and soldiers of Allah—blessed be his name."

Reed kept the phone's volume low to prevent anyone else in the room from overhearing and crowding in. The man in the chair lifted his chin.

"For decades, the tyranny of western immorality has cost the lives of many thousands of Muslims. Your unfettered greed and lust for what is not yours has led the Muslim world into ceaseless wars and constant tumult. While our children starve, their schools blown to ashes by American bombs, our cities ravaged and laid to waste, our precious natural resources pillaged and pirated by soldiers with American flags on their sleeves . . . we are told that *we* are the enemy. That our faith, and our very way of life, is a blight on the face of the planet. That we are radicals, terrorists, savages. That your ideals of freedom may only be purchased with the blood of our sons and daughters. And this is a small price for you, only that your oil may be cheap and your homeland secure. But it is not your security which has been in jeopardy—not for these many decades. It is ours. Our children have been burned. Our young men gunned down. Our fathers and mothers crushed under collapsing buildings while your bombs rain from the sky. And to you, this is just business."

The man's face grew very cold. His tone dropped.

"It is the holy mission of the Islamic Caliphate Army to bring this battle across the oceans and into your own homes. This jihad, as commanded by the Prophet, will bring the enemies of Allah's people into the grave. The attack today in Tennessee was only the first of many to come. The Americans that met judgment today will be joined by tens of thousands more, very soon. We will stack the bodies of infidels both day and night until the blood of our brethren has been avenged—no matter how long it takes. This is our mission. This is our conviction. This is the will of Allah."

The man stood slowly, pushing the chair back. The camera rose with him, matching his face and holding steady atop a tripod. He spoke through his teeth.

"Allahu Akbar! Death to the infidels."

17

"Allahu Akbar! Death to the infidels."

The clip ended, and Maggie simply stared at the laptop. The smooth-speaking man standing in front of the chair finished the video with a slight curl of his upper lip. Just a small gesture. Easily missed.

But Maggie could feel the rage in it. A very dark, very sinister wrath. There wasn't a doubt in her mind that he was legit—and that he'd just topped the FBI's Most Wanted list.

"Stratton, did you finish it?" she spoke into the speakerphone.

"Yes," Stratton's voice was clipped and focused. He had entered his battle stations mode—all business, no drama. It was one of the things she appreciated most about him.

"What the hell, Mr. Director? Who are these people?"

The next question was directed at another member of the joint conference call, CIA Director Victor O'Brien. White House Chief of Staff Jill O'Brien and Secretary of Defense Steven Kline were also dialed in. The emergency response team—on deck yet again.

But O'Brien didn't answer right away. Maggie waited, teeth clenched as she hit the refresh button on the terrorist's website. The page reloaded, and the view counter built beneath the video doubled in volume.

Five million hits in less than fifteen minutes.

"Did you hear me, Victor?" Maggie snapped.

"We're researching now, ma'am."

"Researching? What does that mean? You don't have a file on these people?"

Another long pause. O'Brien cleared his throat.

"No ma'am. We don't."

Maggie lifted the handset and pressed it to her ear. "What are you telling me? The Agency has never heard of them?"

"Like I said, ma'am. We're still researching. But . . . no. I've never heard of this 'Islamic Caliphate Army.'"

"How is that possible?" It was Stratton who spoke next, thrusting into the conversation. "You're telling us there's an entire network of extremists capable of striking our homeland, and you never—"

"There's a difference between launching an attack and taking credit for it, Mr. Vice President." Now it was O'Brien who snapped, his voice turning loud in a way Maggie had seldom heard it. "For all we know, this is just some pissed-off radical with a video camera. We have no *idea* who perpetrated this attack. That's why we're researching. I'm sorry, Madam President. I have to go."

The phone beeped. The operator came online to notify Maggie that the director had left the call. Maggie flushed, her fingers clinching around the phone. She smacked the refresh button and watched the views multiply again. Eleven million.

"Steven, what's the situation on the ground?"

"Early reports indicate at least one hundred fatalities," The SecDef said. "Likely, many more. Twice as many injured. I just spoke with Governor Jeffreys and he's already deployed a unit of the Tennessee National Guard to secure the site and protect the crime scene. Director Purcell has deployed a unit of the FBI's Joint Terrorism Task Force. We'll have answers soon, ma'am."

"What about the video?"

Slight pause. "We're not sure. I'll need to speak with Director Purcell about that. I would guess the website is hosted internationally, probably out of China or India. One of the big international servers with a lot less security and oversight than our own."

"I want it blocked," Maggie said. "Whatever you have to do. Save a copy, then tear it down. I don't want America watching this."

"That may be difficult, ma'am. We don't really have a system in place to limit public access. Unless we can locate the server and have them take the video down, our options would be limited."

"Then *locate the server*. I'm not asking, Steven. I want it *down*."

"Yes, ma'am."

"You're dismissed."

Kline left the call, and Maggie chewed her lip. The view counter now edged past twenty million. The video had hit Facebook. Twitter. Minor news outlets. All the major media conglomerates still had sense enough not to share the link, but that wouldn't matter in another hour. Most of America would have seen it.

And then the terrorist would have won. He would have spread fear to the furthest corners of the nation.

"Would you like me to speak with Director O'Brien, ma'am?" Jill Easterling spoke for the first time. Her tiny voice squeaked, but there was edge behind it. Maggie's mind flicked back to O'Brien, and she thought quickly.

"Give him two hours to come up with something," she said. "Then hound his ass until he does. I want names and I want locations. Make contact with General Yellin and have him prep a JSOC team. Keep me posted."

"Yes ma'am."

Easterling left the call. Only Stratton remained.

"Where are you?" Maggie demanded.

"Chicago," Stratton said. "But I can be back in DC by dinner."

"No. I need you in Nashville."

"Nashville?"

"This won't be like 9/11, Jordan. We're not watching markets tumble and people panic. Get Jeffreys on the phone and have him meet you at the airport. As soon as the FBI clears the scene, I want your boots on the ground. Notify the media. Put on your angry eyes. We're not scared of these people."

Long pause. "Don't you think ... that should be you?"

"I need to be in the West Wing calling shots. You're the better face in front of a camera. This isn't a contest."

In her gut, Maggie knew she was making a political mistake—handing her VP the visibility and making him the face of a strong nation while she was already under attack for being unavailable and weak. But the pragmatic side of her understood the value of letting him manage perception while she managed the response. It made the most sense.

"I understand," Stratton said. "I'll take care of it."

Maggie hung up the phone, then immediately hit the speed-dial for Air Force One's cockpit. The first officer—an Air Force major known as the Deputy Presidential Pilot—answered immediately.

"Yes, Madam President?"

"We're going back to DC. Burn a trail, Major. I'm not worried about fuel economy."

"Understood, ma'am."

The call ended. The Boeing banked again, pivoting north. Then all four of the giant General Electric engines thundered into max thrust, and the jet raced for Washington.

18

Pleven, Bulgaria

The target-laden obstacle course inside the Cold War warehouse lay forgotten as Wolfgang bent over a table strewn with computer drives and captured cell phones. They were all things he had taken from the riverside warehouse—one laptop found near the crates of automatic weapons, and a cell phone from each of the men he had killed. Plus two thumb drives he found in their pockets.

All of it was passcode protected. Ivan had roared in to extract Wolfgang even as sirens rang from Rousse. Apparently somebody had heard the gunfire, or maybe the propane explosion. There wasn't time to fully inspect the bodies, or use thumbprints and faces to gain access to phones. Only time enough to snatch the tech and hit the road before Bulgarian police infiltrated the facility.

Wolfgang took a little satisfaction in the fact that those police had captured a sizable arms shipment. Between the truck, the boat, and what open crates lay in the warehouse, it was safe to assume that Oleksiy Melnyk would never again be able to use Rousse as an offloading point for his arms shipments. The Danube itself might no longer be a safe highway for him. The Bulgarian government would launch an investigation. INTERPOL might be involved. Romania at the least would be notified. Melnyk's operation might be in real jeopardy.

But even if it was, Wolfgang couldn't declare *mission accomplished*. He hadn't come to Bulgaria to shut Melnyk down. He'd come to Bulgaria to capture the man and have an extensive conversation—the kind of conversation that resulted in details of a much larger, much more consequential operation with much higher stakes.

Wolfgang slammed a cell phone down. After inputting another bad passcode, the screen had yet again notified him of a twenty-minute lockout. He'd used a blacklight to detect fingerprints on the screen, recorded the spots where the most finger oil had been deposited, and correlated them to the keypad numbers that lay beneath. Then it was just a matter of arranging and rearranging those numbers into various four- and six-digit combinations, trying patterns and dates, sequences and random scrambles.

It was little better than throwing spaghetti at the wall, but it was something. Something to focus on. To keep him moving. To keep the darkness and the demons at bay.

Wolfgang moved on to the next phone, flipping the page in his notepad. He crafted a new combination and input the code. No dice. He scratched the number off on the pad, and moved to the next.

No dice.

From across the darkened warehouse, boots shifted on the concrete. Wolfgang wasn't sure if Ivan had slept or not. The big Russian had driven into Pleven for groceries, and come back with something smelly and unappetizing in a Styrofoam soup carton. Wolfgang declined to eat, focusing instead on his work.

"Amerikos," Ivan's voice rustled from between the stacked oil drums. Wolfgang ignored him, and tried a fourth code. He was down to two more tries, then this phone would lock him out for another twenty minutes.

Ivan stepped to the table, heavy boots thumping on the concrete. Wolfgang could smell him before he saw him—he smelled like whatever had been in that Styrofoam container, mixed with vodka and sweat. He was also shirtless.

"You must see this." Ivan extended an iPad toward him. Wolfgang ignored him and attempted the final code. The phone buzzed and the screen turned black.

Lockout.

Wolfgang ground the pen through the last of the attempted codes. This was worse than throwing spaghetti at the wall. It was like throwing air.

"Amerikos," Ivan's voice carried an edge.

"*What?*"

Wolfgang took the iPad. He scanned the screen, then stopped and scanned again from the top. It was a news article from CNN. Bold print and a single, horrific photo.

Nashville Music Festival Target of Terrorist Bombing—More than a Hundred Believed Dead.

Wolfgang's gaze flicked to the article itself, his stomach twisting into cold, angry knots. Then he set the iPad down and moved to the computer. The black light trick had worked with the keyboard also, but it hadn't really given him anything. The most frequently used keys were the same ones he might have found on any keyboard, simply the most frequently used letters of the alphabet. A couple of emails would be enough to disrupt any finger oil pattern left by a password input.

"Do your friends not live in Nashville?" Ivan asked.

"Yes," Wolfgang said simply.

"You should call them. Make certain they are safe."

"They're safe."

Wolfgang attempted a password. The computer rejected it. He ground another line across the pad.

"Amerikos," Ivan said. His voice dropped. Wolfgang ignored him.

Then a heavy hand dropped over his shoulder, and Ivan wrenched the swivel chair around. Wolfgang grabbed the man's bear-like arm and fought to dislocate it. Ivan's skin was slick with sweat and taut with muscle.

"*Look at me*," Ivan snapped. "You must take breather. You have done this work for too long. We need to make a plan."

"We *had* a plan, jackass. If you'd held up your end and covered my back, that plan would have worked."

He threw Ivan's hand off. The big Russian crossed his arms.

"I am not God. I do not see everything. Now we must make the best of it."

Wolfgang punched another attempt into the computer. The screen flashed a rejection, and a lockout timer kicked on. Wolfgang slammed the laptop closed.

"We should be sure your friends are safe," Ivan said slowly. "And then you should sleep."

"I don't have time to sleep. I've got an arms dealer to catch."

Wolfgang reached for another phone. Ivan's hand shot out like a striking snake. He slammed the phone back onto the table.

"*Listen to me*," Ivan's voice descended into a growl. "You are a young man. Full of piss and vinegar. I remember what this is like. But I am old man. I fight these wars against madness my entire life. I learn lessons, sometimes. And this," Ivan pointed to the table at large, "This is not new. This arms dealer is not new, either. Always we will fight these problems. But not always will we have our friends. So . . ."

Ivan reached into one of his gargantuan pockets and produced a satellite phone. He shoved it into Wolfgang's hand.

"Call your comrades. Be sure they are safe. And then sleep. This is not option. Tomorrow, we go back to work."

Ivan retreated to his cot without another word. Wolfgang sat in the shadows, his chest tight as a drum, his stomach knotted. He looked at the field of electronics. Most of the devices were on lockout. He'd had no better luck with the flash drives.

Standing slowly, he moved deeper into the warehouse. Then he lifted the phone and dialed.

19

"Mr. Montgomery? The surgeon can see you, now."

A tired nurse in stained scrubs led Reed out of the waiting room and through the double doors. He smelled blood on the air as he passed multiple operating rooms, nurses and surgery assistants bustling in and out. Reed wanted to push his guide from behind, forcing her to accelerate beyond a weary walk. A burning urgency had entered his gut and was slowly consuming him, one thought on replay in his mind.

Is she alive?

The nurse finally stopped at the door to a small washroom, where a surgeon stood at a stainless steel sink scrubbing his hands. A mask dangled from around his neck and soiled surgical gloves were jammed into a biomedical disposal bolted to the wall. He looked just as tired as the nurse as he dried his hands with a paper towel and turned to Reed.

It had been nearly five hours since the medical chopper deposited Banks on Vanderbilt's roof. Reed figured the surgeon had a right to be exhausted.

"You're Mrs. Montgomery's husband?" the surgeon asked.

"That's right."

Reed's heartbeat accelerated as he spoke, his throat turning instantly dry. Every fiber of his being screamed for him to grab the man by the collar. To shove him against the wall and shake every detail out of him. But a few hundred high-stress situations had taught him the hard way that people respond best to cool heads. The surgeon was a professional, a soldier on a different sort of battlefield. Reed waited.

"Your wife is in very critical condition. We removed twenty-one projectiles from her torso and legs—small metal pellets, mostly, as well as some shrapnel. Many of these penetrated only a couple of inches, but a few entered her organs. Her liver is perforated and one kidney destroyed. Her stomach and intestines are the most damaged. This is a good thing in the short term, because those aren't vital organs. But over the next forty-eight hours, the risk of serious infection is very high. It would have been impossible to remove all the contamination from what entered her body. She's already taking heavy doses of antibiotics. Hopefully we can get ahead of any infection, but we still have concerns about the liver damage. Do you understand what I'm saying?"

Reed's mouth felt suddenly very dry. He didn't know what to say. He saw Banks on the stage, moments before the blast. So alive and full of passion. Glowing like the rising sun.

All snatched away in a split second.

"Is she going to live?" Reed's voice was toneless and dry. The question felt overly clinical, but he needed to know.

"I don't know," the surgeon said simply. "Right now, I would say her chances are fifty-fifty. That may be optimistic. We're doing everything we can for her. The best you can do now is pray."

Reed closed his mouth. It was still dry. He still couldn't speak. He glanced down to the doctor's hands, still damp from the sink. There was a small tattoo on the inside of his wrist. A cross, with a Bible reference. Psalm 41:3.

Reed nodded once. The surgeon didn't leave. He stood awkwardly next to the sink, hesitating. Opening his mouth, then closing it.

"What?" Reed asked.

The surgeon cleared his throat. "Was there . . . anything else you wanted to know?"

Reed frowned. Licked his lips with a dry tongue. The question hit him wrong, but he couldn't make sense of why. His mind was still fogged. All he could see was Banks on stage. Singing. Playing the guitar. Leaning into the mic.

Then the blast . . .

Reed shook his head. The surgeon offered a small smile. Then he was gone, headed back toward the operating rooms. Back into surgery. Locked into an endless carousel of bodies, each barely clinging to life.

Reed stood next to the sink as the tired nurse approached from behind. He stared at the floor, and the tiles blurred out of focus. The woman put a hand on his arm.

"Sir? We have a chapel, if you'd like someplace quiet. I can have a counselor or a minister speak with you . . ."

Reed ignored her, simply scrubbing his hand across his face before turning back the way he came. As he exited back into the hallway, Sinju met him. The question on her face cut Reed like a bullet. He simply shook his head.

"We don't know yet."

Sinju wrapped him into a hug and pressed her face into his arm, crying softly. Reed remained motionless, his eyes so dry they hurt when he blinked. He saw the floor, he saw the walls, he saw hospital workers passing by . . . but none of it registered. He couldn't process a clear thought. He couldn't move. He just sat with a brick in his stomach, imagining the thunderclap over and over again. The flash of brutal heat. The conclusive blast that drove him to the ground. That instant stench of death—boiled blood and scalded flesh.

Reed's hands shook. He clenched his fingers into a fist, and knew something was missing.

Where's my gun?

A vibration in Reed's pocket sounded like distant artillery shells. Sinju pulled her face away from his shoulder and said something. He didn't hear her. He didn't even see her.

The bland beige wall opposite him had become a movie screen. Fire and wrath. And the buzzing continued.

"Reed . . . your phone."

Sinju produced the phone from his cargo pocket. A *Hidden Caller* number crossed the screen. Reed saw it, but didn't really register. He simply shook his head. Sinju sent the call to voicemail.

"It will be okay, Reed. We'll pray for her. Okay?"

Sinju ducked her head and closed her eyes. She didn't speak out loud, or maybe she did and he simply couldn't hear her. His ears still rang. Her lips moved, and she squeezed his arm. Reed just watched the movie on the wall.

The phone buzzed again—shorter this time. From the waiting room behind them, a stir resounded through the walls. Agitated voices and growing alarm. Reed's phone dinged, sharply. The signal of an incoming text message.

The ding was finally enough to break him out of his mental deadlock. He looked down to the phone in his hand and saw a new text message. It was from the same anonymous number that had just called him. Reed thumbed the message. It was short—only three words: Check your voicemail.

Reed tapped dumbly on the phone icon. He hit the play button and waited for the message to load while the stir in the waiting room behind him grew louder. A woman wailed.

Had somebody died?

Then the recording crackled through the tiny speakers, and Reed's blood ran cold. He recognized the voice. It was the same voice he'd heard only a few hours prior, on the video recording. The ICA terrorist.

"This is a message from the Islamic Caliphate Army. We are calling to say we know who you are. We have taken your loved one, and now we will come for you. There is no place you can hide. Your streets will run with blood before the week has ended. Praise be to Allah!"

The message ended. Reed blinked. A sudden dump of adrenaline drove back the fog in his mind. He pushed Sinju gently away, fixating on the phone. Then he looked through the security glass into the hospital waiting room. Saw the panicked faces, the phone screens flashing. Heard the same words from the same voice replaying from half a dozen voicemails.

"Reed?" Sinju's voice wavered next to him. "I just got the same call—"

Sinju's eyes watered as she looked up from her phone. Reed's mind spun. He flicked quickly back to his call log, reaching for the contact labeled *Hidden Caller.*

Then a new text message popped through. The same number. The same hidden caller. He tapped it quickly, and the cold in his blood turned to ice.

Hello, Prosecutor.

20

The White House

The Situation Room beneath the West Wing was already packed with aides and cabinet members when Maggie arrived. Everyone stood as she entered, including O'Dell. He wore jeans and a maroon shirt, unbuttoned at the collar. Hair a little disheveled. But he was there.

"I caught a flight as soon as I saw the news," he said. "What do you need?"

O'Dell's hand brushed her arm, and Maggie felt a flood of warmth through the cold pain in her gut. She knew she should feel selfish for tearing O'Dell away from Holly. He barely ever saw his daughter as it was. But there was something reassuring about having him here. It felt like stability.

"Just stay close," she whispered, heading for her seat halfway down the righthand side of the table. She slid into the high-backed leather chair and immediately addressed the room.

"What do we know?"

Easterling spoke first—a practiced rhythm developed over a series of crises. Everyone used to speak at once, talking over one another and descending into chaos. Maggie had stamped that habit out with the heel of her metaphorically muddy boot.

"Governor Jeffreys has deployed Tennessee Guardsmen to the site of the blast. All civilians have been evacuated and the injured relocated to local hospitals. The dead are still being removed."

"What's the body count?" Maggie's voice was clipped and cold. No use for emotions now.

"One hundred and forty-two," Easterling said, her voice just as flat. "But we expect that number to rise. Many of the wounded are barely hanging on. The crowd was packed pretty near to the bomb. It was . . ." Easterling broke for the first time. She swallowed. "Like fish in a barrel."

"Who's on the ground investigating?" Maggie said.

"FBI Joint Terrorism. I've got Director Purcell on the line now. Mr. Director?"

Easterling spoke to the oversized speakerphone situated in the middle of the table. Purcell's edgy voice filled the silence on cue.

"I've got forty agents on the ground now, with specialists on the way. We'll have details over the next few days, but preliminarily the facts are pretty clear. The weapon was a bomb—specifically, a vehicle bomb. The chassis of a small moving van was found in the blast crater. We located a VIN and have already traced it back to a rental dealership in Macon, Georgia. I've deployed agents to speak with the rental office. I'll update you."

The screens installed along either wall of the Situation Room flashed, displaying images of the blast site from FBI field photographers. Maggie's stomach twisted, but she fought to suppress the reaction.

It was ghastly. Like something from a war zone. A bomb crater twenty feet across, tearing up the Tennessee soil and sending black scorch marks ripping across the grass beyond. The stage next to the blast was mangled and shattered, half the pavilion standing over it collapsing toward the ground.

And the bodies . . . dozens of bodies. Twisted and mangled. Blown apart. Articles of clothing burned away. Blood everywhere, joined by hundreds of small, glittering objects.

"What's the shiny stuff?" Maggie asked.

"Projectiles," Purcell said. "Metal ball bearings, we think. The bomb was packed with them. It was designed to kill anyone in its path."

The bitter reality of it all sank over the room like a dark cloud. Maggie could feel it—not just in the muttered curses and reddened eyes, but in her chest. It sank like a weight.

"A few moments for the dead," Maggie said, softly.

The Situation Room went perfectly silent. Maggie imagined the bomb blast in her head—the mangled bodies and mutilated flesh. The scorch marks. The chaos.

They were sons and daughters, wives and husbands. Children. College students. Newlyweds. Soldiers home from deployment, maybe. War had been visited on them in their own homeland. A place that should have been safe.

It was her responsibility to make it safe again.

"Keep us posted, Mr. Director," Maggie said. "You're dismissed."

Purcell left the call and Maggie pivoted directly to O'Brien. He sat three chairs down across the table, owl eyes fixed on her behind round glasses. Braced, because he knew what was coming.

"Mr. Director, what does the CIA know about the Islamic Caliphate Army?"

O'Brien didn't waffle this time. He dove right in.

"Very little, Madam President. This is the first we've heard of them. We know something about the man in the video, however."

O'Brien went to work on his own laptop. The screens returned to life, displaying a Middle Eastern man. Dark hair and cold, lethal eyes. Mid-thirties, perhaps. The same face Maggie had seen in the video.

"Fakir Ibrahim," O'Brien said. "Syrian national and Sunni radical. Born in 1990, Ibrahim grew up in Damascus, sharing close relationships with a number of persons we now know were members of al-Qaeda. He disappeared in 2009 and didn't resurface again until 2014, by which time he had developed an advanced skillset with explosives. Specifically the improvised kind. We can't be sure, but our best guess is that he left Syria to flee the civil war, and wound up studying abroad. He learned English and French, but maintained his radical connections in the Middle East. From 2014 through 2018 he popped up all over the region—Iraq, Syria, Lebanon,

Jordan, Yemen. Even Dubai, at one point. He found employment with every Islamic terror cell known to man—he wasn't picky. He built some of the best IEDs in the region. Locals called him *Mawt Khabir* . . . the Death Master."

"The kind who could build that?" Maggie jabbed a finger at the blast crater still on screen.

"Yes," O'Brien said. "In theory. But he didn't."

"How can you be sure?"

"Because he's dead," O'Brian said simply. "He died in 2019."

Maggie's gaze flicked to the picture of Ibrahim. She frowned, inspecting the face again. Looking very closely. Remembering the video. The man certainly *looked* the same.

"How do we know he's dead?"

No answer. Maggie narrowed her eyes. "Did you kill him?"

"All I can tell you, ma'am, is that we're one hundred percent certain of his death."

So, yes. You killed him.

Maggie could have pressed the point, but really, it was off topic. The facts at hand remained.

"Somebody made that video, Mr. Director. Recently. Dead or otherwise, I want to know who."

O'Brien nodded once. Maggie pivoted to the SecDef, sitting two chairs down.

"And speaking of the video, where are we with taking the website down?"

"I've spoken with the FBI and they're working to trace the server," Kline said. "We still don't have a precise lead. It's certainly international. We're looking for options to block it, but it's already gone viral. There's a download option on the website, so it's now spreading to other servers. Blogs, small media outlets. To be honest, ma'am, even if we found the server in the next ten minutes, it's too late to suppress this thing."

It wasn't the assessment Maggie wanted, but she recognized the inevitability of the situation. They'd moved too slowly. Things were spinning out of control.

ICA—or whoever was behind this—*knew* what they were doing.

A phone rang next to Easterling's chair. She accepted it, listening only for a moment before turning back to Maggie.

"I have Director Purcell back on the line. There's been a development."

Maggie motioned to the speakerphone and Easterling made the transfer.

"What's happening, Bill?"

"I'm not sure how to explain this, ma'am. I think you'd better hear it for yourself."

The speaker crackled. Then a beep was followed by a smooth, rolling voice. Low and strong. Maggie recognized it instantly as the voice from the video.

"This is a message from the Islamic Caliphate Army. We are calling to say we know who you are. We have taken your loved one, and now we will come for you. There is no place you can hide. Your streets will run with blood before the week has ended. Praise be to Allah!"

The beep sounded again. Maggie sat frozen.

"That was a voicemail," Purcell said. "We're receiving hundreds of reports. Family members of the victims are receiving robocalls with that message on replay until they hang up."

"*What?*" Maggie didn't hide the shock in her voice. Everyone around the table sat in rapt silence, awaiting Purcell's next words.

"We don't know how they got the numbers," Purcell said. "I'm looking at one hundred and seventy reports, and every one of them is from a friend or family member of a victim."

"Back trace the number," Maggie said. "Put everything you have on it, and keep me posted."

"Yes ma'am. I'll call in a couple hours."

Purcell hung up. From across the table, Easterling already had a copy of the voicemail, emailed to her from the FBI. She played it on the overhead speakers, then on Maggie's direction she switched to a copy of the terrorist's video found online.

The voices matched. Perfectly.

Maggie looked to O'Brien. "Fakir Ibrahim?"

"He's dead," O'Brien repeated.

"He sounds pretty alive to me, Director."

21

The White House

O'Dell bumped the first four calls. They came in rapid succession, buzzing in his pocket until he silenced the phone. By the time he checked again, twenty minutes deeper into the emergency cabinet meeting, there were eight calls in total.

All from the same number. It wasn't saved in his phone, but he recognized it. The area code was 205. Birmingham, Alabama. Although he knew the caller no longer lived in Birmingham.

Switching to his text messages, O'Dell found only one from the 205 area code. It was as abrupt and cold as the person who sent it.

Call me. Emergency.

O'Dell scanned the room. Maggie was now playing referee to an intense disagreement between SecDef Kline and Secretary of Transportation Stacey Pilcher. Kline wanted to shut down all major highways surrounding the bomb site and establish immediate search and seizure. Pilcher argued that such a strategy was logistically impossible and would send the transportation sector into a tailspin.

Easterling was concerned about widespread panic. Secretary of State Lisa Gorman wanted to discuss an international statement. Some cultural aide was already voicing concerns about racial backlash against Americans of Middle Eastern descent.

The storm was here, and there was little O'Dell could contribute. He slid out of his chair without comment and stepped through a door into the hallway. The 205 number picked up on the first ring.

"O'Dell, it's Montgomery. I got a call."

"What?" O'Dell squinted in the dimness, keeping his voice low. Montgomery sounded terrible—ragged and desperate. Even more raw than usual.

"I got a *call*," Montgomery repeated. "From the terrorists. They left me a voicemail, and then there was a text. I need to speak to Maggie."

O'Dell's mind raced. Then he hit an obvious conclusion—a cold brick wall.

"You were *there*?"

"Yes. We all were. Banks . . ."

Montgomery stopped. His voice choked. "Banks was on stage. She's just coming out of surgery."

The brick wall crumbled over O'Dell's shoulders. In an instant he was transported away from DC, away from America. Back in time to roughly two years prior, in the middle of nowhere Honduras, where he'd been sent by the president to locate Montgomery. O'Dell had found him hiding out in a village, his pregnant wife in tow. Banks Morccelli. Or Banks Montgomery, he guessed. O'Dell had no idea that Banks was a singer. He couldn't actually remember ever exchanging a word with the woman.

He only remembered that she was very pretty, gave off a kind aura, and that Montgomery probably didn't deserve her. Certainly, no woman deserved him.

"I'm very sorry," O'Dell said. They were empty words, but they were the only words he knew to say.

"I need to speak with Maggie," Montgomery repeated.

O'Dell pursed his lips together and didn't immediately answer. It wasn't because he didn't know what to say—there was only one thing to say. *No.* He just had to think of a way to say it that would shut Montgomery down. Close that door permanently. It wasn't an easy thing to do. Not with Montgomery, anyway. The man gave the term *relentless* an entirely new meaning. But it had to be done.

Two nights prior, O'Dell had received a phone call from Vice President Stratton—a rare thing, to say the least. Stratton detailed a conversation he'd shared with the president regarding the Prosecution Force. How they needed to be isolated. How they were becoming a liability for the administration.

For Maggie.

O'Dell didn't need to be told twice. Not only because he put more stock in the VP's opinion than most, but because O'Dell himself had never liked nor trusted Montgomery. The former Marine was bullish, thick-skulled, and worst of all, he didn't respect Maggie. O'Dell had been waiting for an excuse to run him off from day one.

"You no longer have access to the president," O'Dell said simply. "You're retired."

A brief hitch of breathing. Montgomery's voice dropped. "This isn't about that. This is about the terrorist. *They know who I am.*"

"What?"

"The voicemail—"

"Lots of people received that voicemail, Montgomery. The FBI is taking hundreds of reports."

"Not with names," Reed snapped.

"What do you mean?"

"They texted me. They *named* me. They know who I am."

O'Dell stopped. Momentary indecision flooded his mind. His phone buzzed and he pulled it away from his ear to check an incoming text. It was from Montgomery—a screenshot of a text message thread. There were two messages from the incoming number.

Check your voicemail.

And then: Hello, Prosecutor.

A chill ran down O'Dell's spine. He scanned the rest of the screenshot, but all the remaining texts were from Montgomery.

Who are you?

Pick up the phone.

I'm going to kill you.

O'Dell returned to the call. "That's from the same number?"

"The same one that left the voicemail," Montgomery said. "Now get Maggie on the phone."

O'Dell glanced toward the Situation Room. He thought of the crowded conference table. The competing voices. The overwhelmed cabinet.

And he thought of Maggie—mitigating yet another crisis. Fighting to keep the Free World from toppling into the abyss. Fighting to restore her own health after an attempted assassination that still kept her up at night.

He still didn't know what to do with the awkward tension that had developed between them over the course of the secret romance that had flourished so quickly and then floundered so suddenly. But he cared about Maggie more than anybody he'd ever worked for. He was still loyal. And that meant there wasn't a chance he was putting her on line with Montgomery. If the terrorists did indeed know Montgomery's call sign, and this wasn't just some ruse Montgomery had cooked up to obtain access to the president, that could only mean that his identity as a black ops weapon had been compromised.

And if that was the case, he was a far greater liability than Stratton thought. Maggie needed *more* distance from Montgomery, not less.

"You're retired," O'Dell repeated. "Look after your family. The President doesn't need you any longer."

Then O'Dell hung up before the man they called The Prosecutor could say another word.

22

O'Dell hung up, leaving Reed staring dumbly at the cell phone in his hand. He smashed the call back button.

O'Dell sent him straight to voicemail.

Reed slammed his open hand against the hospital wall. His palm left a dent against the sheetrock, and he struck again. The edges of his vision blurred. He saw Banks on the stage. Saw the flash of red fire.

Imagined O'Dell hanging up on him.

He wanted to wrap his fingers around that Cajun's throat and squeeze until his vertebrae collapsed. He wanted to choke the life right out of him.

"Sir? Are you okay? Somebody call security!"

Reed was only vaguely aware of the voice to his left—rising in alarm and joined by the chirp of a radio. He stumbled back from the wall and swayed on his feet. The hospital hall faded around him, and his legs felt suddenly very heavy, his head very light. He wiped his mouth with the back of one hand and looked down the hall. Two bulky men in blue security uniforms were closing toward him. One of them rested a hand on his sidearm while the other took the lead, cradling pepper spray.

Reed's fist closed. He planted one foot against the tile, already falling into a fighting stance.

Then another voice broke down the hallway.

"Hold up! It's okay. I'm his brother. Don't draw that gun!"

Turk appeared behind Reed, placing a heavy hand on his cocked fist and pulling him back. The security officers paused, still tense and ready for action. Turk placed his free hand on Reed's shoulder and squeezed.

"Breathe, Reed. You're okay."

Reed's shoulders relaxed a little. His vision blurred. He swallowed hard, and opened his fist. Looking down at his hand, he noted a tremor in his fingers. The knuckles were still white from being clenched.

"Come on. Let's get a smoke."

Reed didn't fight. Turk led him by the shoulder, pivoting away from the security officers. He stumbled to an elevator, rode two floors down, and then they were pushing through a glass door into a concrete courtyard.

It was growing dark outside, but still sticky hot. A cloud of humidity closed over Reed's head as he collapsed onto a bench. Turk thumbed a cigarette out of a paper pack and held out a lighter. Reed sucked down hard, flooding his chest with a cloud of nicotine. He burned through the entire cigarette without comment, exhausting it in mere minutes.

Turk handed him another, then lit up one of his own. Reed's body began to loosen, and he slumped against the dirty brick wall behind him. His vision still blurred at the edges, but his hand had stopped trembling. He didn't want to put his fist through any sheetrock, or any security officers.

For the first time, his gaze switched to Turk. The big Tennessean looked like an actor in a war film. Every part of him was smeared with blood and dirt. His face was sweaty and strained, his skin still blackened by bomb smoke. Red-rimmed eyes and bruised hands were shrouded by a cloud of cigarette smoke. Tangled, sweaty hair poked from beneath a stained University of Tennessee hat.

He looked awful.

"How is she?" Turk pumped smoke through his nose.

"On the edge," Reed said. His own voice rasped. Dry and distant, as though somebody else were speaking. His mind raced, switching from the bomb to the hospital to the text messages. And O'Dell.

Then he looked at Turk and thought of something else—something obscure, but suddenly very important.

"Why aren't you in jail?"

Turk blinked blankly. Reed held his hand like a gun and pressed his index finger against the side of his head. A weak grin flashed across Turk's dirty face.

"Oh. That. Turns out the guy was an Army vet. Flew OH-58s in Iraq. Caught a little action. I owe him a case of beer."

Lucky sucker.

Reed owed the helicopter pilot a lot more than beer.

"How does it look?" Reed's voice was dry again. He didn't have to specify what he was asking.

"It's bad. We did what we could. There . . ." Turk swallowed. The cigarette trembled in his fingers. "There were children."

The red Reed saw while pounding the hospital wall crept in again. He gritted his teeth. "You hear about the phone calls?"

Turk nodded. Reed dug his cell phone out and flicked to the message stream. He handed the device off and Turk scanned it. The tears dried. The red eyes turned cold.

"Are you kidding me?"

"I already called O'Dell," Reed said. "He's blocking us from Maggie. They're cutting us loose."

Turk thumbed through the messages. Reed's increasingly violent demands for contact had all been ignored. Only two messages from the terrorists had come through.

Check your voicemail.

Hello, Prosecutor.

Turk returned the cigarette to his lips. Reed knew what he was thinking —the same things Reed had thought. The same path of questions and logical conclusions.

Who would know to call him *Prosecutor*?

In truth, there were hundreds of people who knew Reed by that name. Dating back to his days as a contract killer, and leading up to his tenure as Muddy Maggie Trousdale's secret weapon. Reed had made a lot of enemies in his career. A few dozen people might hate him enough to want him dead.

Many of them might be Middle Eastern—old enemies from his years as a Marine scout sniper.

But none of those particular enemies would know him as *Prosecutor*. The moniker was something he picked up after leaving the Marine Corps, and he'd fought in the Middle East only one time since, while recovering the flight recorder from the ashes of an Air Force One wreck.

So . . .

"I have no idea," Reed said.

Turk sucked on the cigarette. It burned down to the filter and he ground it beneath his boot. He looked to Reed.

"We can't deal with this right now. You need to focus on Banks. Sinju and I will look after Davy. After Banks is on the mend we'll circle back. Okay?"

It wasn't the answer Reed wanted to hear. It probably wasn't the answer Turk wanted to suggest. But it made the most sense.

Reed opened and closed his hands a few times. They felt empty. Like he was missing something.

"I've got your gun," Turk said quietly. "It's in my truck."

Reed nodded. Probably just as well. So long as he was in a mental state to declare war on drywall, he probably shouldn't be armed.

The door to the hospital squeaked open, and a nurse poked her head into the courtyard. She was young, but looked like she'd aged a decade in the last ten hours. Lines ran through her face, and black bags joined her eyes.

"Mr. Montgomery?" she called.

Reed stood up quickly. "Yes?"

"We've moved your wife into an ICU bed. You can see her now."

Turk handed the phone back to Reed. "Go."

Reed followed the nurse down corridors and hallways, up stairs and through double doors. He found Banks in a curtained-off bay of the intensive care unit, wired to half a dozen machines. A heart monitor blipped. An oxygen mask was pressed against an ashen face.

Reed stepped through the curtain, and it was like the bomb was detonating all over again, driving molten metal right through his gut. Banks's face was puffy. Her eyes closed. Her chest rising and falling under the assistance of a ventilator. Hair matted on one side, shaved on the other. Stitches running across her forehead, down her neck, and beneath her hospital gown. One arm was wrapped in a cast, the other bruised and dark. A mass of thick bandages lay beneath the blanket, making her look pregnant.

Reed didn't move. He swallowed back the dry feeling in his throat and touched her fingers softly, tracing past chipped nail polish and slipping his hand into hers.

The heart monitor beeped, and the rage returned. Not like a creeping fire, this time. More like a Cat 5 hurricane, closing on a coastal city at full speed. Wind and water and unbridled fury. Reed's jaw locked and he wanted to punch something again, but he didn't move. He just stared at Banks until the nurse reappeared, a clipboard in one hand. She approached the bed and stood across from Reed.

"I'm very sorry to bother you, Mr. Montgomery. There's just a few forms I need you to sign. Permission slips, disclosures, just standard procedure. . ."

She trailed off. Reed ignored her. He stared at his wife until the nurse lowered the clipboard.

"I guess . . . it can wait." She shifted back toward the curtain. "I'm so sorry for your loss."

Reed's heart skipped a beat, and his gaze flicked to the heart monitor. It was still beeping.

"What?" He pivoted toward the nurse.

She looked confused, meeting his gaze, then looking quickly away. Her face flushed.

"She's still alive," Reed said. "Right? She's still breathing!"

"Of course." The nurse swallowed, then teared up. Suddenly, she didn't look old anymore. She looked very young, and very over her head. "I meant . . ."

She trailed off, and something black descended over Reed's mind. Like a thundercloud, driven forward by the hurricane in his chest to drench him in dread. Reed released Banks's hand and moved quickly around the bed. The nurse recoiled and held up a defensive hand. Reed ignored her and snatched the clipboard out of her hand. He tore past the HIPAA disclosures and insurance requests until he located Banks's ER file near the bottom.

Twenty-six-year-old female. 5'6". Blue eyes. Blonde hair.

And then a box near the bottom. A single question, with a yes or no option.

Pregnant. The POSITIVE box was checked.

Reed's fingers went numb. The clipboard slipped from his hands and crashed over the floor. The room faded away. He looked back to Banks, and the wad of bandages piled beneath the blanket. The ashen gray of her face. The beep of the heart monitor.

He remembered the hail of ball bearings tearing through her stomach and pelvis like a shotgun blast.

And just like that, the hurricane made landfall.

23

Maggie was on her fourth cup of coffee, the bulk of a Cobb salad untouched on the table next to her. The last five hours had passed in a flurry of activity—aides and cabinet members moving at will in and out of the Situation Room as updates poured in from the Joint Terrorism Task Force investigators on site in Tennessee.

Most of the information served as a mere confirmation of what the FBI already knew or suspected. The rental van had been built into a bomb, Timothy McVeigh style. Likely, most of the rear cargo area had been packed with explosives that turned the sheet metal of the van walls into shreds of ripping shrapnel.

The ball bearings were a mix of lead, steel, and various dirty metals. Nothing you'd make an actual ball bearing out of, which was the FBI's first clue that the little projectiles hadn't been repurposed into a weapon, but were likely cast as bomb projectiles from the start. The explosive residue recovered at the blast sight and analyzed in FBI crime labs appeared to be a basic mix of TNT, but not a domestic one. Purcell rattled through a list of technical specifications about the compound before Maggie eventually cut him off and demanded the bottom line.

The TNT was Russian, Purcell said. And not recently mixed. The FBI suspected Soviet anti-personnel mines, wired together into one giant blast. That suspicion was confirmed when technicians on site in Tennessee uncovered a scrap of stamped steel with the Soviet hammer and sickle logo still pressed into it.

Maggie wanted to know how Soviet land mines had found their way into the United States. Purcell didn't know, but the weapon's origins were not his primary interest. He was more preoccupied with the complexity of converting relatively small land mines into a weapon of this magnitude. It wouldn't be easy work, he explained. Not something you could research on Google. To improvise an explosive device such as this without accidentally blowing yourself up, you'd need advanced skills.

You'd need to be an expert bomb maker. A master of death, like Fakir Ibrahim.

Maggie's next line of questioning shifted immediately to the rental van. Who had rented it, and where. Purcell's investigators were already digging into that lead, but he wasn't optimistic about uncovering anything helpful. Any terrorist with brains enough to build a bomb in the first place should be smart enough to cover his tracks, but the van was still the most logical next step.

Using the vehicle identification number recovered from the scene, the FBI contacted the rental company who owned the van and traced the rental transaction to a rental franchise built into a storage unit center outside of Macon, Georgia. It was a small city just off Interstate 16, about halfway between Atlanta and Savannah. The clerk at the center was an elderly woman in her seventies with bad eyesight. The ID on file was quickly determined to be a fraud, the name and address blatantly bogus.

John Johnson. 135 Freedom Lane, Macon.

A person who didn't exist, living on a street that didn't exist. But his fake Georgia driver's license passed muster for the aging clerk, and she could remember very little about her interaction with the customer in question.

Video cameras? There were no video cameras. The franchise owner had read Orwell's *1984* and knew about police states. He wasn't about to play into that dark future.

"The rental office was handpicked," Purcell said. "I'd imagine they spent weeks scoping out the right one, which meant they probably visited several. We'll canvass the region and obtain security footage from other rental franchises. We might get lucky."

Maggie sipped water and stared at the speakerphone. Purcell was still working from the Hoover building. He probably wouldn't leave for the foreseeable future.

"Keep pushing," Maggie said. "I've already spoken with Governor Grier. Georgia stands ready to assist you in any capacity. I want all collected evidence to be forwarded immediately to the CIA. We expect this fight to be carried overseas."

"Of course, ma'am."

Maggie checked her notes. Over the past few hours her handwriting had deteriorated into chicken scratch, but she could still read the most important points.

"Any update on the robocalls?"

Purcell's phone rattled against his ear. "I actually have one thing, ma'am. We received a tip from a Georgia woman who bought tickets to the music festival, but had car trouble and never made it. She still received a call. Our working theory is that the terrorists somehow hacked the ticketing vendor used by the music festival and obtained phone numbers from their sales records. We recovered a couple of working cell phones from deceased victims, and they received phone calls also. We think the terrorists simply made a list and blasted them all."

Maggie muttered a curse. It was a logical enough theory. Much of the news media had reported calls "blanketing the families of victims," but Purcell had already informed her that every call seemed to be directed at somebody who was actually present at the music festival.

Still, that number totaled nearly thirty thousand people. More than enough to trigger significant panic.

"I'd like you to prepare a statement as soon as you're able. We need to calm people down."

"I'd rather wait, ma'am. I don't want to risk tipping our hand to anything. If the video is to be believed, there's another storm coming."

Maggie thought back to the violent promises made by Ibrahim in the video. Purcell had a point.

"Just keep me posted, Director."

The call terminated. Maggie ran a hand over her face and tried not to sigh. Demonstrating exhaustion would only add to the tension in the room. Pretty soon she'd retire to the residence for a couple hours. Grab a shower and a few hours of sleep.

Then start all over again.

"Madam President, can I have a moment?"

Maggie looked down the table. Victor O'Brien stood near the door, an iPad in one hand. His bald head glistened beneath the fluorescents, but he looked as prim and proper as ever. Unfazed.

Maggie waded around a bustling knot of aides and met O'Brien at the door. He closed it gently behind them. The hallway outside was narrow, and quiet. O'Brien extended the iPad without a word.

"What's this?" Maggie said.

"Just have a look, ma'am."

Maggie dropped her gaze to the screen, and her stomach tightened.

It was a body—or a photograph of a body, rather. A middle-aged male with light brown skin and dark hair. He was laid out on an army-green cot with his arms dangling off the sides. His shirt was stained with blood, his chest riddled by bullet holes.

"What the hell is this?" Maggie said.

"There's more," O'Brien said. "Swipe left."

Maggie swiped. The next picture was a close-up of the dead man's face. Pale and ghastly, blood speckling his forehead. Eyes closed in death.

It was Fakir Ibrahim. No doubt about it. The likeness was impossible to deny.

"When was this taken?" Maggie demanded.

"June, 2019. Damascus, Syria."

"When you killed him?" Maggie prompted.

O'Brien's blinked once but didn't answer.

Maggie looked back to the image. She chewed her lip, recalling the video. The voice on the phone.

"You asked for proof," O'Brien said, at last. "Fakir Ibrahim is dead."

"Then who did I see on that video?" Maggie demanded. "You saw the face, Director."

"I did. And I grant you, it's problematic. Could be an AI deepfake. An attempt to throw us off."

"Is that actually possible?"

O'Brien's lips twitched in a semi-condescending smirk. Maggie switched the iPad off. She thrust it back at him.

"Look. I don't care who the man is. I don't care what his club is called. I don't care what he's faking or where he's hiding. *Find him*, Mr. Director. Find them all. Do whatever you have to do. No more Americans are dying —period."

24

Resting in the Caribbean darkness 128 miles due north of Port-au-Prince, the coastal city of Cap-Haïtien had sustained a fraction of the earthquake damage wreaked on Haiti's capital city but still looked like a war zone. Slouching buildings and busted roads were joined by streets clogged with heavy trucks and blaring horns. The sun had set three hours earlier, but the intensity of activity packing into the port and spilling through the shantytown suburbs only grew by the hour.

Tens of thousands of refugees from the shattered lower half of the country had fled north to the coast in search of food, incoming relief supplies, and shelter. They rode in the backs of battered pickups and clung two and three at a time to underpowered motorbikes. Some walked. Some collapsed alongside the road, baking beneath the brutal summer sun, dehydrated and fainting.

Some died. Others pillaged the bodies. Gunfire broke out next to a UN aide tent as a local gang fought to seize a precious supply of clean water. UN peacekeepers from Europe and America fought back. The body count spiked by another dozen.

And the chaos was really just beginning.

Abdel Ibrahim had seen it all before. In Iraq, then Syria, and most recently in Yemen. Starvation, desperation. War and famine. Turmoil and the endless *clack-clack-clack* of Kalashnikov rifles wielded by some of the planet's most desperate people. Politicians pointed fingers and journalists pontificated about justice and the survival of the human race, but for Ibrahim the only relevant questions were simple: Who was the guilty party? Who made the mess? And who was profiting from it?

The answer wasn't an earthquake. It wasn't a hurricane, or a tsunami, or disease, or even a local dictator drunk on oil money. The universal problems of power and abuse were much simpler than that. The world was divided into two opposing classes: the powerful, and the weak. The domineering and the dominated.

Haiti was a study in that philosophy. If you wanted to understand why twelve million wretched souls were trapped in this hellhole, locked in a perpetual cycle of poverty and desperation, you need look no further than the abuses of France. White, Western, and evil. The French had colonized Haiti with slaves, sucked her sugar wealth dry, and then when those slaves had the nerve to launch a successful revolution, France demanded a blood payment that kept the Haitians impoverished for over a century, eventually leading to a complete collapse of their society.

It was a story as old as time, so commonplace in the Middle East that Ibrahim barely appreciated its gravity. But the monster in Iraq, Syria, and Yemen wasn't a French monster. It was an American monster, wielding the power of the greatest military the world had ever known.

Delivering freedom at gunpoint.

Ibrahim sipped cool water from an insulated bottle as he watched two of his men, Hamid and Kadeem, load the truck. It was a UN vehicle—or, at least, it was *painted* like a UN vehicle. White with a blue emblem. The truck was a military style deuce-and-a-half. A retired American army vehicle, actually. What a twist of irony.

The three massive crates that offloaded from the shady Albanian frigate were unmarked. The captain didn't care what they contained. He was paid in cash not to ask questions—a lot of cash. All American dollars, of course.

The ironies really never ceased.

A forklift loaded each of the three crates aboard the deuce-and-a-half. Ibrahim watched from a distance, conscious of the fact that he wasn't standing nearly far enough away should one of those crates topple off its pallet and burst over the concrete pier. Should the straps break, every man within a hundred yards would be dead.

Not immediately, of course. But soon enough. After a lot of retching and pleading.

The straps didn't break. The pallets and their crated cargo reached the bed of the truck, and Ibrahim's men strapped them down. Already they were peeling adhesive labels from their paper backings and pressing them against the crate walls. The labels were printed in English and—more irony —*French*. Still an official language of Haiti.

They read MEDICAL SUPPLIES in both languages, and were also printed with the UN logo.

Ibrahim gulped more water to replenish the fluids his body was dumping under the baking heat, and approached the forklift operator. He passed the man a one-hundred-dollar bill—almost a month's income in Haiti. The man accepted it with a toothless smile, and Ibrahim took the driver's seat of the truck. Hamid and Kadeem packed in next to him, wiping sweat and not speaking. He could feel the tension in their bodies—a warranted tension. Death was riding behind them. That was why Ibrahim would drive. The 128 miles to Port-au-Prince would be rough ones, passing along unpaved roads and through the mountains. There would be ruts, potholes, and ravines running right alongside narrow mountain tracks. One misstep would be death.

On a normal day, the journey would take six or seven hours. With logjams of disaster relief supplies slowing traffic to a crawl, it would likely take a lot longer than that.

Ibrahim lifted the St. Louis Cardinals hat from his head and ran a hand through his sweaty hair. The truck's heavy transmission ground and barked as he fought it into gear. The heavy diesel growled, and Ibrahim wondered how many times he'd heard that sound before and reached for a Kalashnikov himself.

The provisions of Allah were poetic, indeed. As was the fear currently gripping the United States. The reports from Bahir and Mahmoud in Tennessee were golden. The nation was unraveling. The phone blast was working—escalating panic and confusion.

Chumming the waters for the next shark attack.

The truck left the port and rattled along the busted roads, past slouched and damaged homes. Ibrahim reached a UN checkpoint at the southern edge of town and squealed to a stop as a white soldier wearing a baby-blue UN helmet approached. He carried an M4 carbine over his chest. There was an American flag patch on his arm.

He was twenty or twenty-one at the most, but still older than many of the true believers waging jihad on the other side of the globe.

"Good evening, sir. What are you hauling?"

Ibrahim put on a disarming smile, dropping his left arm through the open door of the truck the way he'd seen United States Marines do it. He kept his tone relaxed, remembering his Western education. How Americans liked slang, and the pretense of camaraderie.

"Good evening, brother. I'm hauling medical supplies for some of the mountain villages. You can check in back, if you want."

Ibrahim passed him a shipping manifest. The American scanned it, squinting under the glare of a flashlight. He called to another soldier, and the truck shifted as somebody climbed in back.

He remained relaxed. So did his companions.

"Where are you from, my friend?" Ibrahim asked. Still easy-going. Still personable, like strangers in an American bar, watching baseball.

Ibrahim knew something about baseball.

"Ohio," the American said, flashing a smile. "Columbus."

Ibrahim returned the grin. "*The* Ohio State University," he quipped.

"That's right! You a Buckeye?"

Ibrahim shook his head, lowering his voice conspiratorially. "Go Blue."

"Oh hell no!" The American shoved the papers back. The truck shifted again, and boots hit the ground. The cargo inspection was complete.

"Get out of here, Wolverine," the American said.

He shot Ibrahim a sloppy salute. Ibrahim lifted two fingers.

Then the deuce-and-a-half ground through the checkpoint. Aged head-lights pointed the way south, deep into the mountains.

But Ibrahim wasn't headed for mountain villages. He was headed a lot farther.

Maybe all the way to Ohio.

25

Working for Maggie Trousdale was like living with your ex-wife. At least, that's what Victor O'Brien had decided, and it was a qualified opinion. He'd served as director of the nation's chief intelligence agency from day one of Trousdale's administration, and knew all about her compulsive, demanding, impetuous ways.

He had some experience with ex-wives, also. At least one of them. The endless court battles, custody disputes, and constant demands for *more, more, more*. More money. More time. More attention for the kids.

Trousdale's demands hit on a similar cadence. More information. More details. More results. It was exactly the sort of amateur song and dance O'Brien would expect from a woman who had literally never set foot in Washington, DC prior to being tapped for vice president. She didn't understand how the system worked. She didn't understand what reasonable expectations and results looked like.

She didn't understand that O'Brien had clawed his way up from the very bottom, over decades of dedicated service and cutthroat sacrifice. That he knew the CIA like the back of his own hand, loved it more than his own children, and ran it better than any of his predecessors ever dreamed. In his

Firestorm 115

own humble opinion, of course. For Victor O'Brien, the CIA was more than just a job. It was his family. His hobby. His social network. His religion. If he wasn't at home sleeping, he was at work.

Sometimes he cut out the middleman and simply slept on the couch in his office.

So, yes. He was offended when Trousdale questioned him about Ibrahim. He had a right to be. O'Brien himself had signed off on the targeted kill operation that brought down Fakir Ibrahim in 2019. He'd overseen the hunt for the Death Master for nearly half a decade. It was something of a pet project. For Trousdale to question the accuracy of his intelligence felt like a fifth grader questioning Einstein about basic mathematics.

It was infuriating. And the worst part? This wasn't the first time. Far from it. Since the moment Air Force One went down in flames and Trousdale had ascended into the Oval Office, it had been an endless stream of this crap. Demands. Questions. Intrusions. Trousdale treated the CIA like her personal search engine. Leveraging their resources and disregarding his advice. Even using the agency's Special Activities Center as a concierge for her own private black ops team.

It was unthinkable. Unprecedented. Impossible to swallow.

Ignorant redneck.

O'Brien fumed as his limousine reached the private entrance of the George Bush Center for Intelligence. He took the elevator to his executive office, snapping for his secretary to have Dr. Sarah Aimes, CIA deputy director of operations, join him. He settled behind his plush desk chair and mashed the intercom, barking again at the secretary for fresh coffee. Lots of it.

His narrow fingers rattled over the keyboard. He input a password and scanned his palm print. Aimes pushed through the door thirty seconds later, carrying the coffee.

O'Brien didn't have time for romance, and he almost never thought about women. But he had to admit, Aimes was a looker. Tall and poised, collected and calm, she was an anomaly of the female species in his opinion. She kept herself together. Contained her emotions. And best of all, she knew when to shut up.

"Sit," O'Brien snapped.

Aimes sat. O'Brien rocked his cup back and took a gulp. The coffee was boiling hot, and it scalded his throat. He cursed and smacked the intercom.

"Dammit, Phyllis. This is hot enough to boil eggs!"

"I put an ice cube in it for you, sir. Like always."

O'Brien scowled at the cup. Aimes flicked her lid off and grunted.

"Huh. I thought this was cool."

O'Brien exchanged cups with Aimes. He input a search into one of the CIA's databases and called up an image of Fakir Ibrahim. The monitor swung on a swivel to face Aimes.

"That's our man."

"Fakir Ibrahim. I know. I saw the report. But—"

"But he's *dead*," O'Brien finished. "I already informed the president."

Aimes waited. O'Brien tapped a finger on the polished desk, teeth clenched. It wasn't like him to lose his cool. He prided himself on being icy chill and resolved at all times. Never letting his emotions spill over. Until very recently, he was known in Washington to be the coldest man in town. The ultimate, classic spook.

But then *Trousdale*. The woman was worse than his ex-wife. Dumber, louder, and more insistent. After nearly thirty months of dealing with her, O'Brien was ready to put his fist through a wall.

"The president wants results," O'Brien said, forcing his voice into a monotone. "It's our job to secure them."

"Results on . . ."

"On *him*," O'Brien jabbed a finger at the screen. Aimes's face remained impassive, but he could still see the wheels turning behind her eyes. She was smarter than the average skirt, no doubt. Another anomaly.

"Could be a deepfake," Aimes said. "Or a look-alike. We're running vocal analysis from the voicemails and the videos, now. I can already tell you they match, but I could run them against recordings we have on file of Ibrahim, also. Most of those recordings are in Arabic, if I remember correctly. If we got a match . . ."

"He's *dead*," O'Brien said.

Aimes sipped coffee. "I know."

O'Brien stared at the photo of the dead Ibrahim. He fumed and clicked through the body images. He'd selected the most graphic for Trousdale to see. He wanted her stomach to turn. He wanted her to experience a little of the *real world* that he dealt with on the daily.

Might do her some good.

"I think we may be asking the wrong question," Aimes said.

"What does that mean?" O'Brien's gaze snapped toward her. Aimes remained calm.

"We know Ibrahim is dead. How these terrorists managed to replicate his voice and appearance, I'm not sure it matters. The better question is *why?* Why would they want us to think this is coming from Ibrahim?"

O'Brien tapped one finger against his desk. Still looking at photographs of the body. And pondering.

It was a really good question.

"I've got analysts working the Islamic Caliphate Army angle," Aimes continued. "No results, so far. That name has literally never crossed our radar."

"That's because *they don't exist.*"

"Maybe. Or maybe they do, and they've recently changed their name."

O'Brien shook his head. "No. We would have known."

Aimes scratched one polished fingernail against her paper cup. It was an irritating, skin-crawling sound. Like crickets chirping in a field. O'Brien hated crickets.

"*What?*" he demanded.

Aimes shrugged. "We've been blindsided before."

"Not since *I* took over." O'Brien smacked the escape key, closing out of Ibrahim's file. He pivoted the monitor to face him again. "Have our people on the ground in the Middle East and Africa go to work. Whoever these people are, their weaknesses will be predictable. One of the frontline soldiers will brag to somebody, and word will leak. We're dealing with a usual suspect hiding under a new name. Al-Shabaab, maybe. The Islamic State. Hezbollah. We know the players. Contact the NSA and have them go to work on the phone numbers—the voicemails and calls. Backtrack and spiderweb. Find a connection. Something will break."

Aimes took her coffee with her, stopping halfway to the door.

"If I may . . ."

"What?" O'Brien's voice snapped.

"We should cover all bases. This is the worst terrorist attack on American soil since 9/11. Whoever these people are, they know what they're doing. And they're promising more of it."

"Then we better *stop them*."

"Of course. I'm just saying . . . we shouldn't assume anything."

O'Brien said nothing. Aimes dipped her head and pushed through the door, heels clicking. His jaw clenched, and he looked back to the monitor with a disgusted shake of his head.

Women.

26

The red wouldn't leave. It fogged Reed's mind, creeping in on the edges of his vision and sending fresh tremors down his arm. He felt it in his bones. In his gut.

He'd felt it before—blind rage. Absolute hate. Not just at the scum who had set off the bomb, but at himself. *He* had let this happen. He'd stood in the crowd, watched the van close in. Watched the men walk away.

Watched the whole thing play out in front of him like a movie scene. And acted too late.

He wouldn't have made that mistake in Iraq. Under the blaze of the desert sun, Reed knew what to look for. He knew all the red flags. He was constantly on the alert for dead animals alongside the road. Patches of freshly disturbed dirt. Vehicles that hadn't been there the night before. Abandoned bags and children walking to school with chalky white faces.

He had been in a war zone. He *knew* what death looked like. Had he lost his edge?

This was his fault. Half of the beautiful things in his life had been on that stage, and he'd watched them vanish into a cloud of black smoke.

Half the beautiful things . . . and a beautiful thing yet to be born.

Metal doors exploded on their hinges as Reed barreled out of the ICU and back into the hallway. Turk waited there, leaning against the wall with a Coke dripping condensation over his hand. He straightened as Reed plowed for the elevator. Reed smashed his thumb against the down button and dug for his phone. Turk fell in alongside him but had the good sense to keep his mouth shut.

Reed dialed O'Dell. The phone rang and rang—no voicemail. Maggie's old bodyguard had blocked him.

"Give me your phone," Reed snapped his fingers as the doors rolled open. A weary nurse in stained scrubs stumbled out. Reed and Turk shoved in.

The wallpaper of Turk's phone was a picture of Sinju on the beach. A spring getaway to Fort Lauderdale. She wore a swimsuit printed in the stars and stripes with baby Liberty cradled in her arms—also dressed in stars and stripes.

The beauty and untarnished happiness made Reed's stomach turn. He found O'Dell's contact in Turk's phone and dialed.

Three rings, then to voicemail. O'Dell had bumped him. The Cajun's cold voice rumbled through the speaker, inviting the caller to leave a message. Reed obliged.

"Listen, you swamp rat. Tell your boss to call me—ASAP. There's a job to do. If you don't get involved, I'll do it myself."

Reed hung up and tossed the phone back. Turk caught it deftly, but still didn't say anything. The elevator reached the ground floor and Reed turned automatically for the courtyard again, stopping halfway when his gaze fell across black clouds and pouring rain.

Figures.

He turned for a waiting room instead. Larger than the one upstairs, but still packed. He found a corner and extended a hand. Turk passed him the Coke, and he guzzled half.

"How is she?" Turk said.

"Hanging on."

Reed wrapped his fingers around the bottle until the plastic constricted into a series of shallow dimples. The label crackled. And he focused.

Not on the blast. Not even on the faces outside the van, or the face on the video.

He focused on the text message.

"How did they know, Turk?"

Turk folded his arms. He didn't answer immediately.

"Somebody told them," he drawled at last. A simple answer, but Reed knew it was probably the correct one. Most truth was simple.

Somebody. But who? And more importantly—*why?*

"O'Dell won't call back," Turk said. "Trousdale is making distance. We're a liability."

Reed snorted. Not because he disagreed, but because he'd always known this day would come. He'd known Muddy Maggie Trousdale for what felt like forever, even if it had really only been a few years. She had a lot of great qualities, no doubt. She was smart as a whip, and stubborn as an ox. She would throw her own body on the tracks to derail a train.

But she was also a politician, even if she pretended otherwise. And Reed had never encountered a politician who wouldn't sell out their own mother if push came to shove. It was only a matter of time before the Prosecution Force outlived its usefulness and became a liability.

Reed wouldn't fault Trousdale for that, if only she had outlived her own usefulness to him first.

"We need intel," Reed said. "Did you ever get any contact information from O'Brien?"

Turk wrinkled his nose. "What do you think?"

Reed guzzled more Coke. He focused on the faded pattern in the carpet —beige, purple, and burgundy. Like that combination had ever been a good idea.

"Reed . . ." Turk's voice softened. He rested a large hand on Reed's shoulder.

"What?" Reed's voice snapped, maybe more than he meant it to. His chest was still tight. All he could think of was Banks laid up in that hospital bed, wrapped in bandages and unconscious. He'd held her hand before he left. Cried a little. Whispered to her and kissed her forehead.

But none of that meant anything. Not if he couldn't protect her.

"You should go home," Turk said. "Take a shower. Get something to eat and sleep a while. I'll stay here until you get back."

"I'm not leaving this hospital unless I'm headed to hunt terrorists." Reed knocked Turk's hand off his shoulder. He finished the Coke and tossed the empty bottle into a nearby trashcan, hard enough to make plastic ring against metal.

Turk folded his arms. "That's not on the table, Reed. There's nobody to hunt. You need to think about Banks, right now. About Davy."

"I *am* thinking about them. That's all I'm freaking thinking about!"

His voice rose into a dull shout, drawing the attention of weary men and women seated in the nearest row of chairs. They looked exhausted and grief-stricken. Many had tears in their eyes.

Turk put up a hand in a calming motion. "I know. I just mean, there's nothing else we can do right now. We don't have a target. Okay? We don't have a way to get one. We have to be *here* right now. Right? With family. You hear me?"

Reed wasn't listening. His mind was spinning. The caffeine from the Coke was hitting him hard. His right hand trembled again. He wanted a cigarette. He wanted intel.

He wanted a target.

"You hear from Wolfgang?" Reed said.

"Huh?"

"Wolfgang. You still got his phone number?"

Turk pinched his lips together. Reed waited.

"*Well?*"

"He called a few hours ago," Turk said. "Just to check in. First I've heard from him in months."

"He still in New York?"

"I have no idea. The connection was weak. Sounded like he was overseas."

"Give me your phone."

Turk didn't reach for the phone. Reed extended a hand.

"Wolfgang can't help you, Reed. You've got to find a way to be still. That's all you can do."

"*Give me the phone*," Reed's voice dropped to an ice-cold snarl. Turk's jaw locked, and for a moment Reed thought he might have to take it by force. Not an ideal prospect.

Then Turk handed him the phone with a resigned sigh. "Third number down."

Reed scrolled through the call log and located the number. It was fifteen digits long with an 881 prefix—an Iridium satellite phone. Wolfgang could be anywhere.

Reed dialed, and the phone rang. A lot. Reed waited it out, knowing that if the phone was on, it would chime. It might take Wolfgang a moment to reach it. Maybe it was dark, wherever he was. Maybe he was asleep.

Eventually, the speaker crackled. Then the man they called The Wolf answered in a groggy voice. If he ever touched the stuff, Reed might have thought he was drunk.

"Hello?"

"Wolf, it's Montgomery."

The phone crackled in his ear, and Reed heard a slight echo of his own words in the speaker. It took a split second for the sound waves to transmit.

"How is she?" Wolfgang cut straight to the chase. Reed appreciated that. Wolfgang hadn't always been that way.

"Hanging on. Listen, I need help. We're looking for a target."

This time the pause was protracted. Longer than it should be. Wolfgang was stalling.

"I'm not in a position to help," Wolfgang said. "I'm sorry."

"I don't need your peg-legged muscle, I need your network. You still in contact with that Russian?"

"What Russian?"

"Exactly. We need intel—anything you can find about this Islamic Caliphate Army. Known associates. Any shelter countries. Any hotbeds here in the United States. Whatever—"

"Reed. That's not what I do. It's not what my contacts do, either. I'm working on something else. You should call Trousdale."

Reed turned his face to the corner of the room and lowered his voice.

"That's not an option. She cut us off. Blackballed us."

"So she's finally wised up. Good for her."

"You son of—"

"Calm down, Reed. I'm not taking shots. Your arrangement with Trousdale was always paper thin. And besides, I thought you retired."

"My *wife* is clinging to life by a thread," Reed snarled.

"So be with her," Wolfgang said. "Look after your son. Let Trousdale figure this out. You're a civilian now, Reed. Civilians don't get to play Batman."

Reed's fingers tightened around the phone. He tried to think of something to say. He opened his mouth, but the words wouldn't come out.

He saw Banks in the hospital bed again, all pale and bandaged up. It turned his body rigid. Dropped his mind into a barrel of thick mud.

Slowed the world down around him.

"I'm very sorry about Banks," Wolfgang said. "Be well, Reed."

Wolfgang hung up. Reed shoved the phone back to Turk. Suddenly his body felt weak. His arms very heavy. Exhaustion was setting in. Turk put a hand on his shoulder and squeezed. Reed closed his eyes.

He wanted to see blackness, but all he saw was fire.

"*. . . and say this to the murderous cowards who have extinguished so many innocent lives.*"

Sudden calm settled over the waiting room. The murmur of voices and rustle of shifting clothes against sagging seats evaporated, and a familiar voice reached Reed's ears. He pivoted toward the sound.

It was her. Trousdale. On the TV mounted in the top corner of the waiting room, surrounded by a protective plexiglass shield. She stood behind a podium, shoulders squared, chin held high.

Eyes blazing unbridled rage.

"There is nowhere you can hide. No place you can run. We will find you. Your friends will become our enemies. Your allies our first targets. We will root you out of your hole and bring you to certain and absolute justice. No matter the cost. No matter how long it takes. You have committed an act of absolute evil, and your fate will be absolute destruction. America is coming for you."

Maggie exited off the stage. As she disappeared, Reed caught sight of O'Dell's bulky form falling into step next to her. Then they were gone.

Off to hunt terrorists.

But they wouldn't be the only ones.

27

The trip consumed almost twelve hours, but Ibrahim and his companions made it alive, without toppling off a mountainside or busting any of the three crates.

A miracle, perhaps. Or simply the provision of Allah.

They parked the truck ten miles outside the shattered outskirts of Port-au-Prince, and spread out their prayer rugs in time to face the rising sun and give thanks for their safe passage. Ibrahim bowed with his head generally pointed toward Mecca, but Mecca wasn't on his mind. The Middle East in general wasn't on his mind.

Only the next phase of his complex and difficult plan. The phase most likely to go very badly awry.

The three men shared a meal of crackers and halal canned tuna, washed down with lukewarm water. Then Ibrahim adjusted a handheld radio unit to obtain news reports about the road ahead, and the war zone of a city resting at the bottom of the mountain range, reaching out to the coast.

He found the news reports, but not before he stumbled across another report replayed out of America and broadcast from a Dominican station. It seemed to Ibrahim a brutal twist of irony that in a country so recently ravished by unbelievable pain and suffering, the radio waves would be consumed by America's relatively insignificant black eye.

But that was the way it always went wherever America was concerned. She was the fat dog on the porch, yelping at a horse fly while scrawny, starving little dogs shivered in the yard amid the pouring rain.

It disgusted him, but Ibrahim listened anyway, because he recognized the president's voice.

" . . . no matter the cost. No matter how long it takes. You have committed an act of absolute evil, and your fate will be absolute destruction. America is coming for you."

The president's voice faded, replaced by a radio anchor who spoke in Spanish. Ibrahim didn't speak Spanish, and he didn't care what the reporter said. He flicked the radio off, dry rage crackling someplace just beneath the surface of his practiced calm.

An act of absolute evil? Had the whore really *said that?*

"What is it, Abdel?"

Kadeem addressed him in smooth Arabic. Ibrahim looked up, fingers still clenched around the radio. Both men stood motionless next to him, waiting. Neither man spoke English. Both men could detect the rage boiling in his blood.

Act of absolute evil.

"It is the Americans," Ibrahim said. "They are declaring war."

Hamid perked up. He raised an eyebrow. "Damascus?" he asked.

Ibrahim looked toward the rising sun. The bill of his Cardinals hat blocked the glare so that he could appreciate the rolling horizon of Haitian mountains. A calming vista to focus on while he calculated. Damascus wasn't a card he really intended to play. It wasn't even his idea. His ally had cooked it up—just like the voicemails and text messages. A psychological thing.

But after listening to Trousdale's vitriol spewing through the speaker, he was coming to like the idea. It was poetry, like everything else. A vicious sonnet.

"Yes," he said. "Damascus. Make the call."

28

Rif Dimashq Governorate, Syria
27 kilometers outside Damascus

The house sat alone, sandblasted and baked by decades of brutal desert sun. Surrounded by a sprawling, dusty yard. There was a fenced paddock for goats, and an open parking garage for small vehicles. The two-story structure featured a flat roof, and on calm nights when the air was clear, you could see the lights of Damascus illuminating the horizon.

Technically a member of the greater Damascus metro, the house sat amid the suburbs of Syria's capital city, but the nearest home was nearly fifteen hundred meters away. This was more of an estate—a rich man's home with a view.

Or it had been, anyway. Before the war. Before the ceaseless carnage. Before the brutal death lock of the Rif Dimashq Governorate campaign had left bullet holes in the walls and dead children in the yard. For years since then the house had lain abandoned, an unsafe location for any family. A forgotten relic of a more peaceful time.

Except it wasn't completely abandoned. During the baking hot summer of 2019, it had served as the epicenter of a very critical mission conducted by the CIA's Special Activities Center. Agency assets working in war-torn

Syria had traced the Death Master—Fakir Ibrahim—to this home three weeks earlier, eventually establishing the property as his primary residence.

In June of that year, a team had been deployed from an Iraqi black site, just across the border. Not a wing of helicopters loaded with battle-hardened Navy Seals. Just four men in an SUV, a few small arms at the ready.

The mission was simple. The result satisfactory. Fakir Ibrahim met his fate just before lunchtime. His body was photographed prior to being dumped in the desert, where the wildlife would quickly consume it without leaving a trace. The Death Master was no more.

Mission accomplished.

Or had it been?

When agency field asset Mark Patton received instructions to check the house for Ibrahim's presence, he thought Langley had lost their minds. He wasn't on site in 2019 when Ibrahim bit the dust, but he'd been briefed on that mission. He'd seen the photographs. Certainly the facial similarities between the very dead Ibrahim and the very much *not* dead leader of the so-called Islamic Caliphate Army were undeniable, but that didn't mean Ibrahim had been resurrected.

Even if he was alive, why on earth would he return to the last place he called home? A dusty, shattered hulk of a building he most certainly knew to be compromised?

Sometimes Patton wondered what the agency was coming to. He'd served as a field operator since leaving the Army in 2012, and seen more than his share of drama and chaos as the agency's presence ballooned in size, compliments of a bottomless budget and an insatiable desire of the American people to be safe. Whatever the cost.

Patton knew the world didn't work that way. Freedom and safety were a seesaw, and always would be. When one end rose, the other must drop. But he wasn't paid to be a philosopher. He was paid to secure black sites, to protect analysts, to "interview" terror suspects, and, on rare occasion, to go check out long abandoned houses.

So he drove his Toyota Hilux to a mountain ridge a full kilometer from the property, hid it in a shallow ditch, propped himself up just beneath the horizon, and took a look.

Swarovski binoculars magnified his view. A floppy hat provided shade. He scoped out the broken windows, guzzled water, and thought about the twenty-something analyst from San Francisco perched behind a laptop back at base. She wasn't hot—not really. A six, maybe a seven in San Fran. But in Iraq? In a baking hot block building packed with military has-beens and nerdy guys who never wore enough deodorant? She was a ten all day long. Easy.

He'd played a round of poker with the guys to win the rights to hit on her first. If HR ever found out about it, he'd be buried under a sand dune. For now, he just needed to practice his desert pickup lines.

"So you're the reason it's so hot here."

"Girl, are you sure you're American? Because you're Syria-sly looking good."

"Is your name Sahara? 'Cuz being around you makes me thirsty."

Okay. Maybe pickup lines weren't his greatest talent. Neither was frying like an egg in a pan looking for a dead man haunting his last known—

Patton's train of thought collided with a block wall. He squinted, then adjusted the binoculars. Focused on the door. Saw what he thought was a shadow forming into a hard outline. And then moving.

It was a man. Passing through the garage, carrying a bag over one shoulder. Wiping sweat from his face. Moving to a cabinet . . .

Patton only made out a profile. Five-nine, maybe five-ten, based on the height of the garage roof. A hundred and sixty pounds, give or take. A little stocky.

He glanced down from the binos to the iPad resting between his elbows. It displayed a series of pictures and a brief bio. Height, weight, physical attributes. Basic stuff.

He returned to the binoculars. Steadied his breathing to stabilize his view. Two thousand meters was a long ways, even under ten times magnification.

The figure in the garage squatted next to a box on the floor, showing Patton his back. He dug for a moment. Then he stood, rotating toward the door. Exposing his face for the first time.

Patton's heart almost stopped.

29

Langley, Virginia

The report hit Dr. Sarah Aimes's desk first. As Deputy Director of Operations, it was her responsibility to manage the sprawling, ever-growing network of CIA field officers, case officers, and assets that fed the agency with a steady diet of intelligence.

It sounded like an exciting job. In reality, it was a lot of office work. A lot of conference calls. A lot of reports and emails and headaches.

And every once in a while ... a picture of a man who should be dead.

Aimes received report from the unofficial CIA field office in Damascus just before lunch, all but ensuring that the chicken Caesar wrap in her office fridge would remain there yet another day. The image was grainy. The field agent—some guy named Patton—was still on site, hoping for a better shot with the super telephoto zoom lens locked into his DSLR camera. But even despite the pixelation, the likeness was uncanny, and the location was unbelievable.

Aimes transferred the report to her agency iPad and proceeded directly to O'Brien's office, heels snapping and lunch forgotten. She plowed through the heavy double doors and into the executive suit, finding O'Brian halfway through his own lunch of stale chicken fingers from the agency cafeteria.

Honey mustard dripped from his lip as his head snapped up. Instant indignation and irritation flushed his cheeks, but Aimes didn't give him a chance to speak.

"We've got something."

Aimes jabbed the iPad across O'Brien's desk. The director swabbed his face with a napkin and accepted it. He squinted at the screen, then flicked to the next image. There were four in total, all taken from different angles as the target maneuvered inside the home's attached garage. Only one was very clear.

O'Brien's lips tensed. He shook his head. "Not possible."

Aimes took a seat across from him, smoothing her skirt. "Photographs are forty minutes old. The asset is still on site."

"What site?" O'Brien prompted.

"That's the wild part. It's the house."

O'Brien frowned, still not understanding. Aimes waited. O'Brien made the leap.

"You can't be serious . . ."

"Keep flipping."

O'Brien swiped to the end of the report. The last image was a satellite view, taken from a CIA intelligence satellite orbiting high above Syria, snapping live photos of the sunbaked landscape. Twenty-seven kilometers outside of Damascus. A weathered estate with a flat roof and a collapsed goat pen, nearly fifteen hundred meters away from the nearest residential structure.

"Somebody decided to double-check the kill site," Aimes said. "It wasn't my idea. But we hit pay dirt. Doesn't that look like Ibrahim?"

Aimes waited while O'Brien's owl eyes fixated on the screen. She could see the wheels and gears turning behind them. Thoughts clipping along at ninety miles per hour. O'Brien was a smart man. Prejudiced, maybe. Sexist, certainly. Pigheaded on days that ended with Y.

But nobody's fool.

If there was one thing Aimes could appreciate, it was the tactical brilliance that had made him director in the first place.

"Contact the DOD and supply them with a full report," O'Brien said. "Hold your asset on standby and have the Damascus field office run surveillance around the target. Advice of any militant assets in the region or potential military threats."

Aimes frowned. "Wait . . . you're not thinking of *striking?*"

O'Brien flicked the iPad off and shoved it across the table. "Of course I am. What else would we do? The president wants a target, and we found one."

Aimes sat stunned for half a second. Then her own mind went to work. The grind of wheels and gears similar to O'Brien's. The thought patterns of a practiced spook.

"Sir. With all due respect, we are nowhere *near* ready to launch a strike. I'd need another twelve hours just to survey the site and get an idea who might be inside. I'd want to deploy additional assets to obtain better photographs. Put ears on the ground in Damascus and see what we could learn about present occupants of the property. Cross check intelligence with SIS and Mossad—"

"By which time he could be *gone,*" O'Brien snapped. "Leave logistical concerns to JSOC. We found their man. It's their problem how they take him out."

Aimes sat forward. "Mr. Director, I'm sorry. I can't green light that. Literally all we have is a picture. A bad picture, at that. Reason for further investigation, but hardly any reason to assume that Fakir Ibrahim—"

"Fakir Ibrahim is *dead,*" O'Brien snapped.

"All the more reason to proceed with caution. We don't know what we're looking at."

"So we find out." O'Brien folded his arms, settling into the seat. Uncharacteristic venom laced his tone, his lips pinched into an angry pucker.

This wasn't like him. As long as Aimes had worked for Victor O'Brien, she'd never considered him impulsive or irrational. If anything, he could be overly cautious. This change felt mercurial. Almost bipolar.

"Give me eight hours," Aimes said. "Let me move additional assets to the region. At least touch base with Mossad. We—"

"Two things we know for certain, Deputy," O'Brien cut her off. "First, Fakir Ibrahim is dead. And second, these thugs want us to think otherwise. I don't know how they're faking his face. I really couldn't care less. We'll figure it out over time, but in the meanwhile, the *president* demands answers. She wants a lead. So we're gonna give her one. Understood?"

Aimes didn't like the way O'Brien spat the word *president* like sour chewing gum. She lifted her chin.

"What are your orders, sir?"

"Refer the report to the DOD, and keep your man on site. If the president wants to strike, that's on her."

O'Brien turned back to his computer. Aimes sat stoically for a moment, collecting herself. Still thrown off guard. Then she took the iPad and turned for the door, the gnawing uncertainty in her gut erupting into a storm.

30

Wolfgang couldn't sleep. He lay shirtless on one of the cots in the warehouse, staring at the ceiling high above and fighting back the dreams.

They weren't nightmares. To qualify as a nightmare, he would need to feel fear. Wolfgang hadn't felt fear in a very long time. The dreams were more like . . . horrorscapes. The worst things he'd ever witnessed in his lengthy career of bloodshed and violence, all twisted into a cocktail of visceral pain.

People he'd killed. People he'd failed. People he'd lost.

Staring at the moonlight that leaked through the fractured roof, a part of him wondered why the dreams visited him now. After so many years, he'd experienced cold sweats and shaking hands and all the usual manifestations of a guilty conscience, but never the dreams. Maybe it was because the last shred of meaning in his life had left him when his baby sister died, ten months prior. There was nothing else to hide behind. No further pretense for his chosen career.

He used to kill in the name of something. Now . . .

"Amerikos!"

Ivan was still awake. For the last three hours he had sat at the desk littered with Oleksiy Melnyk's captured electronics, using one of their own computers and the satellite internet connection to catch up on international news. Ivan had a ritual about international news. Every night he pored over reports from news companies in Washington, Moscow, London, Tokyo, Beijing, Dubai. Wolfgang didn't understand it. All the news was bad.

"But it is all the same story," Ivan had said. Whatever that meant.

"Come here!" Ivan called.

Wolfgang sighed and placed his bare feet on the floor. He hauled himself up with a grunt and left his shirt and shoes next to the cot. He found a bottle of water on the way to the table, where Ivan was also shirtless. Sweat glimmered on his skin, his back so covered in coarse black-and-gray hair that he looked like a gorilla.

"Look at this," Ivan said. He pointed to the screen.

Wolfgang didn't have to lean in to read the headline. It was in English. Bold, oversized letters, paired with the still frame of a video.

It was about the bombing. All the news was about the bombing.

Ivan hit the play button, then sat back and folded his arms. It was a video from a cell phone. Somebody was filming a music stage, people packed in close. Wolfgang recognized Banks singing into the mic, head thrown back, body tensed as she hit the high note. The crowd cheered and the drums thumped.

Banks sounded good. Wolfgang wouldn't deny it. She looked good, too. Healthier than when he last saw her. He wondered if her Lyme disease was in remission. It had to be.

"Here," Ivan marked the left side of the screen with his tree trunk of a trigger finger. Wolfgang followed his gaze to the moving van.

Not a moving truck. Just a regular panel van, sheet metal printed in the bright logo of a popular rental company. The vehicle rocked and glass flashed as a door shut. Wolfgang's stomach tightened, knowing what came next.

Seconds ticked by. Banks hit the chorus again. She moved to the edge of the stage, mic in one hand, sweaty hair rippling in the breeze of a box fan. The cymbals clashed. Somebody shouted a curse, and the crowd parted. A big man was barging his way toward the stage, arms up. Shouting. Waving.

Banks turned toward him.

Then the bomb detonated. Fire and fury. Flying metal. Instant chaos. The camera toppled to the ground.

Wolfgang swallowed. Ivan smacked the spacebar to stop the video.

"Did you see it?"

"See what?"

Ivan grunted irritably. He rewound the video, back to the split second the bomb detonated. Before the smoke clouded the camera lens. Before whoever was holding the phone was sent hurtling to the ground.

Ivan paused the video again.

"Do you see it now?"

Wolfgang peered at the screen. Studied the bomb blast as the van buckled and shards of metal ripped outward. Fingers of fire and hot smoke reaching for the sky.

"I see a bomb," Wolfgang said. He turned away, back to the table full of computers. After six hours of steady work, he'd managed to crack only one. A cell phone. The combination was six zeros—how original. There were no messages or phone calls on record. Just a stack of emails, mostly in languages other than English. He was still working through them.

"I forget." Disgust tainted Ivan's tone. "You were never soldier. Look again."

Wolfgang looked once more. This time Ivan lifted a stylus and marked the core of the blast with a digital circle. Fingers of fire shooting out in a star pattern . . . and this time, Wolfgang did notice something. A thousand little glimmering dots, like flecks of platinum.

"What's that?"

"Ball bearings," Ivan said.

"Little steel pellets?"

"Da. Or iron. Whatever."

"What's your point?"

"This is not homemade bomb. These ball bearings are used in anti-personnel weapons. Very common in Russia. And this blast signature—notice how all the force is directed up and out. Not down. If you look at news photos, you will see that the chassis of the van survived the blast while the roof and walls are completely destroyed. This is calibrated weapon."

"So, what it is?" Wolfgang still didn't see the point.

"Land mine," Ivan said simply.

Wolfgang froze. His gaze flicked from the screen to Ivan. "What?"

"Land mine. Or many land mines. I see this once before, in Chechnya. The Chechens wired land mines together, to make one bigger bomb, then placed it inside a church as they retreated. Russian soldiers took shelter in the church ... and *boom*. It killed dozens."

"So this—" Wolfgang pointed to the laptop. "These are *Russian* land mines?"

Ivan shrugged. "Impossible to say. Many countries use this design. Perhaps if I had better video ..."

Wolfgang ignored him, turning back to the pile of captured electronics. He fished out the single phone he'd managed to unlock. He flicked quickly to the email application and ran down the list of messages he'd already perused.

Searching for something—something he'd seen before. Something that had been meaningless at the time.

He found the message near the bottom. Written in abrupt, simplistic English. A sales order from Oleksiy Melnyk's arms operation, directed to an anonymous buyer.

An order for two dozen high-explosive land mines, dated for three weeks prior. The brief correspondence that followed detailed pricing and delivery. There was even a shipping address, listed in Cap-Haïtien, Haiti.

"You believe in coincidences, Ivan?"

Ivan took the phone. Squinted at the screen, reverse-pinching it to zoom in on the text for his aging eyes. Read it slowly. Then he looked up, both eyebrows raised.

"Neither do I," Wolfgang said, and reached for the satellite phone.

31

The White House Situation Room
Washington, DC

"The structure sits about four hundred yards from the nearest home. Concrete walls and wood doors—two floors, with an open living room on the ground level and bedrooms upstairs. About two thousand square feet in size."

From the end of the table, CIA Director O'Brien used a laser pointer to highlight spots on the display of satellite and ground images stretching across the Situation Room screens. They depicted a house in the Syrian desert, bleak in the truest sense of the word—lonely and sandblasted by the wrath of a loveless environment. There was an open-faced garage with a Toyota Land Cruiser visible inside. A lone dog wandered across the yard, so skinny his ribs were visible under the powerful magnification of a zoom lens.

There were no people. No signs of Fakir Ibrahim.

Maggie followed O'Brien's presentation in perfect silence. To her left, O'Dell was joined by SecDef Kline and General John David Yellin, chairman of the Joint Chiefs. On her right, Jill Easterling sipped coffee while Secretary of State Lisa Gorman rotated a pen slowly in one hand.

O'Brien was joined by his righthand woman, the deputy director of operations, Dr. Sarah Aimes.

All these faces had visited the Situation Room so many times they felt like permanent fixtures to Maggie, but one face was new. A slender man with gentle gray hair and intense, dark eyes. He wore a dark blue Navy dress uniform, heavy with ribbons and pressed perfectly smooth against his chest.

Vice Admiral Garret Price. Commander, Joint Special Operations Command.

General Yellin had introduced Price only six weeks prior when he was promoted to command JSOC, and Maggie had liked him from their first interaction. Price was quiet and soft-spoken. He only opened his mouth when he had something truly important to say. He was competent and sharp as a whip.

But despite all that, she hated seeing the man. His presence was indicative of a problem too large to be solved by diplomacy and political maneuvering alone.

"How certain are you that our target is inside?" Maggie asked. She avoided using Ibrahim's name. There was still some debate over whether Ibrahim was alive. How could he be? She'd seen the pictures.

But as Aimes pressed a key on her laptop and the image switched to a high-resolution, zoomed photograph of the man in the garage, Maggie's stomach tightened. It wasn't like the grainy snapshot that had first triggered this emergency meeting. The clarity of this shot was much better.

And the face was unmistakable.

"We don't know who we're looking at," O'Brien said. "It's not Ibrahim, obviously, but it may be his imposter. Agency psychologists are currently developing a theory that a man who looks like Ibrahim—perhaps a relative —could have developed a deep psychological attachment to him, and is now acting in his shoes. Living out of his house, presenting himself on camera as Ibrahim. Committing terrorism in his memory."

"The man in the video never claimed to be Ibrahim," Easterling pointed out.

"That's true. We won't know for sure unless and until the target is brought in for questioning. But that's really outside our area of expertise."

Yellin snorted from halfway down the table. His bulldog shoulders bulged, and the twin medals pinned to his chest clinked as he sat forward. "You want JSOC to plan a snatch and grab."

O'Brien's owl eyes blinked. He didn't smile. "Well that would be up to you, General. I'm just here to bring you the facts."

Yellin's lips pursed. He thought for a moment. "We do have assets in the Mediterranean. Damascus is well within helicopter range. We'd have to fly across Lebanon, but—"

"Wait." Secretary Gorman held up a hand, and Maggie restrained a frustrated sigh.

Right on schedule.

"You can't just fly a kidnapping mission through international airspace. Terrorist or no terrorist, there are protocols to consider. We'd need to notify the Lebanese—"

"Like we notified the Pakistanis?" Yellin cut Gorman off.

"Let me finish, General. We'd need to notify the Lebanese of impending action in the region. It wouldn't need to be specific. They'd just need to know we'd have helicopters flying across their borders."

"Any sort of international notification could alert the target," O'Brien warned. "Not to mention the delay of processing that notification. We need to move *quickly*, while the target is static. This window of opportunity could close at any minute."

Gorman rested her hand on the table. She pivoted away from O'Brien, as did Yellin. Everyone turned to their boss.

Maggie ran a hand through freshly washed hair, her skin still warm from the shower. It was well past dinner time, and she'd just completed an extensive cardio workout, leaving her drained and aching.

Physical therapy was not her friend.

"Let's say we do it," Maggie said, pivoting toward Yellin. "What would that look like?"

Yellin passed the question on to Price with a grunt. The vice admiral took his time answering, but Maggie was used to that. He'd have something worth listening to when he was ready.

"Our quickest option would be to deploy a platoon of SEAL Team 8 from the Sixth Fleet. Probably two, maybe three birds in total. Total time of mission . . . about two hours, maybe two hours fifteen. It's a lot of flight time over the Mediterranean, but flight time over Lebanon and Syria would be minimal. It's workable, ma'am."

Maggie fixated on the satellite image of the house. It was daylight in Syria. A blazing sun illuminated the property, making her feel hot and sticky just looking at it.

A simple target. Overwhelming force. The best soldiers in the world.

Yet something in her gut felt off. It felt . . . simple. Maybe too simple.

Maggie glanced to Deputy Director Aimes, noting for the first time that Aimes had yet to speak. Like Price, Aimes was a quieter figure, biding her time and hand-picking her words. Maggie had less face time with her than almost anyone else in the room, including Price. But she'd never known Aimes *not* to contribute. Especially on something this critical.

"Deputy Director . . . do you have any thoughts?"

Aimes pinched her lips together. Opened them. Then stopped. Maggie noted O'Brian's eyes flicking sideways behind his glasses, turning suddenly hard.

"Honestly, ma'am . . ." Aimes trailed off. Her gaze met O'Brien's, and something sparked. She looked back to Maggie. "I'm unconvinced. The target appears to match the suspect in the video, but my gut tells me there's no logical reason for him to be present at this house. In my entire tenure with the agency, I've never located a target so quickly and with such positive ID. It feels . . . off."

O'Brien bristled, and once again he and Aimes locked eyes. Then he resumed the practiced calm Maggie had so often witnessed, pushing his glasses up his nose.

"You asked me for a lead, Madam President," he said. "Here's your lead."

Maggie nodded slowly. She still felt a trace of uneasiness, but maybe this wasn't simplicity. Maybe this was luck. It had been so long since Maggie had experienced luck that she no longer felt safe trusting it.

"Admiral Price, have your people draft a mission plan. Lisa, you'll coordinate with JSOC on the timing of our statement to the Lebanese. Let's give them as little notice as we can get away with—I don't want to risk any American lives needlessly. Victor, have your assets maintain constant surveillance of the target and keep us updated. If anything—and I mean *anything*—should change, I want to know immediately. Barring that, I'm prepared to green light a mission the moment JSOC is ready to move. Everybody good?"

Maggie stood. The room stood with her. She ducked her head and followed O'Dell out of the room.

Carrying that uneasiness with her.

Deputy Directory Aimes followed her boss back into the corridors of the West Wing. A single flight of stairs led the way to the ground level, where O'Brien's limousine waited to cart him back to Langley. Aimes, who had ridden with him to the White House, moved automatically toward the entrance of the stairs. O'Brien always preferred the stairs, and Aimes assumed it was an impatience thing. He didn't like waiting for doors to open—or waiting for anything, generally.

But this time, O'Brien mashed the button for the elevator. Aimes stalled behind him, unsure. The doors rolled open, and O'Brien stepped in. Aimes followed. A White House aide moved to join them.

O'Brien blocked the aide's path with an outstretched arm and a cold smile. "Grab the next one."

The aide retreated. The doors closed, and the motor hummed. Aimes tensed, sensing the storm brewing in her boss's chest like the tremors of an impending earthquake. She'd felt that brewing rage ever since contradicting him in the Situation Room. It was something she'd never done before—not publicly. Aimes wasn't military, but she believed in the chain of command. She believed in respect, and in protocol.

She wasn't sure why she'd stepped out of line this time. Already she was regretting it.

Stupid, Sarah. What are you doing?

The elevator slowed. O'Brien's lips were pressed into a hard line, his round glasses perched on his nose in perfect balance.

The doors rolled open, but O'Brien didn't move. He faced Aimes.

"If you ever sabotage me again, I'll cut your throat. Am I clear?"

Aimes stiffened. Her lips parted, but she didn't know what to say. She just stood like a fool in the corner of the elevator, her face turning hot.

O'Brien marched across a field of maroon carpet to the double glass doors that hissed open automatically. The limousine waited, the door already open.

O'Brien ducked in without looking back. The door closed, and the car rolled off.

Leaving Aimes to find her own way back to Langley.

32

Reed still wouldn't leave the hospital, so Turk drove to his apartment and brought back a change of clothes and some toiletries.

"Hit the head, you smell like ass," Turk said.

Reed complied, finding a restroom to change in. He dumped his soiled and bloody clothes straight into the trash and washed his face in the sink before applying fresh deodorant and brushing his teeth. It didn't help much. He really did need a shower.

But he couldn't leave. Not until he knew she would be okay . . . or he knew who to kill.

Back in the waiting room, Sinju had brought Subway sandwiches—a footlong for Reed, and two for Turk. Reed looked pointedly at Turk's gut as the big man unwrapped the second sandwich, and Turk shot him the finger. Reed already knew the perfect six-pack was gone. It was more like a four-pack now, drifting dangerously close to something less.

Love was treating Turk well, as was fatherhood. Reed might have been happy if he could have torn his mind away from Banks, lying broken in the ICU. The nurses wouldn't let him in to see her again for another hour.

"I'll see you tomorrow." Sinju kissed Reed on the cheek and Turk on the lips—for a little too long—before she left for the elevator. Reed forced the food down his throat, dry bread sticking to the roof of his mouth. Stomach twisting.

"I'm going to call O'Dell again," Turk said. "Maybe he'll talk to me."

Reed already knew the Cajun wouldn't answer Turk's call. He'd probably already blocked the number. Trousdale had iced them. But he only nodded as Turk dialed.

He felt numb, deep in his bones. Worse than he could ever remember. Just sort of shut off. He didn't know what to do with himself, locked in a holding pattern. He couldn't fight for Banks's life. He couldn't throttle the men who had choked her out.

He couldn't do anything except sit like a fool and wait . . . and wait.

"I'm going to find them," Reed muttered. His own voice sounded dead in his ears. Toneless. Turk didn't answer. He lowered the phone, and Reed glanced sideways.

"We're going to *find them*," Reed repeated. "Every last one of them."

Turk simply nodded, and Reed extended his hand for Turk's cup of Dr Pepper. He was sucking air bubbles through the straw when Turk's phone buzzed from his pocket. Turk clawed it out and flipped it over. A frown passed across his face like a thundercloud.

"It's Wolfgang."

Reed dropped the cup on the floor and reached for the phone. Instead of relinquishing it, Turk motioned Reed to the door. They stepped out into the same courtyard they had smoked in earlier that day. It was dark now. The air was heavy with humidity, the concrete gleaming with rainwater.

Turk put the call on speakerphone. "Wolf?"

"Turk, you with Reed?"

"I'm right here," Reed said. "What've you got?"

Reed didn't fight to suppress the anticipation in his tone. The thirst. Wolfgang's voice was still distorted by distance, but Reed detected an energy that had been lacking before.

"The blast at the music festival—did either of you get a look at the aftermath?"

Reed looked automatically to Turk. Everything he remembered about the bomb was a blur—his only focus had been recovering Banks. But Turk had returned to help the first responders.

"I did," Turk said. "Why?"

"Describe the blast site," Wolfgang said.

Turk took a moment to consider. "It was a moving van—like a panel van. The bomb was loaded in the back. It blew out the walls and the roof. Shrapnel everywhere. And, of course, the ball bearings. Thousands of those."

"What did the chassis look like?" Wolfgang asked.

"The chassis of what? The van?"

"Right. Did it remain intact?"

Turk scratched one cheek. Then he nodded slowly. "Yeah . . . it did, actually."

"All the force blew up and out," Wolfgang said.

"A shaped charge?" Reed joined the conversation.

"No," Wolfgang said. "Land mines. A lot of them. All rigged to blast together, directing the ball bearings straight into the crowd. Like a giant shotgun."

Reed squinted. "Wait. How do you know that?"

"Because I found the sales receipt."

Reed's heart rate quickened. He and Turk closed on a quiet corner of the courtyard, away from a chain smoker blazing through Marlboros. Reed lowered his voice.

"What are you talking about?"

"This isn't a secured line, so I'll keep it high level," Wolfgang said. "Do you remember that friend of ours? The one who told us about the coffee merchant in Venezuela?"

Reed remembered. Ivan Sidorov hadn't been a friend, exactly, and he hadn't told them about coffee merchants. He'd told them about a disgraced Russian oligarch in hiding, and where to find him . . . in Venezuela.

"Right," Reed said.

"He and I have been hanging out," Wolfgang said. "We've been . . . looking for other merchants."

"What kind of merchants?"

"The kind who supply land mines."

"And?" Reed pressed.

"Two dozen anti-personnel mines were sold three weeks ago to an anonymous purchaser working under the pseudonym *Abraham*. This Abraham paid via wire transfer. The mines were delivered a week ago."

"You know that for sure?" Reed pressed.

"I know that I have emails," Wolfgang said simply.

"That blast was too big for anti-personnel mines," Turk said. "Usually those are small. They take your leg off. They don't turn vehicles into fragmentation grenades."

"Our friend says these are probably old Soviet mines," Wolfgang continued. "Circa 1970s. What the USSR would have used to secure Eastern Europe. Packed with TNT and ball bearings . . . plenty to turn a vehicle into a fragmentation grenade."

Reed and Turk exchanged a glance. Reed wasn't quite sold, but this was a better lead than anything he'd had ten minutes prior.

"Thanks for the intel," Turk said at last. "I'm not sure what we're supposed to do with it."

"Call Trousdale," Wolfgang said. "Update her people. I'm happy to transmit the emails I found, just don't tell her where you got them."

"Not an option," Reed said. "I told you, she's iced us. No contact at all. We're done."

Wolfgang snorted. "So what did you want from me, then?"

Reed shook his head and stepped away. Turk kept his voice calm as he asked for additional details. Reed just crossed his arms and looked back through the window into the ground level waiting room. Families gathered in tight knots, holding one another and stared red-eyed at the carpet. Mothers zoned out. Fathers fought to stay awake. Children curled up on blankets on the floor, sleeping.

Reed wondered how many of these families were here because of the bomb. He looked to the flashing TV mounted to the wall, and saw yet another replay of the blast. This one had been taken from the cell phone camera of somebody filming Banks from the crowd. Fire flashed, and smoke ripped across the screen.

The woman went down, and with her a crushing weight descended over Reed's shoulders. Why hadn't he moved faster? Why hadn't he drawn the SIG and opened fire on the two men exiting the van?

Behind him, Turk pressed for more details about the mines. Wolfgang's garbled reply was irritated and clipped. Reed barely listened as his eyes blurred over. The TV on the wall had switched news reports, now displaying endless reels of helicopter footage, high over the broken city of Port-au-Prince, Haiti. Amid the shock and horror of the terror attack, the Haitian earthquake already felt like a distant memory. Reed and Turk had both donated money to the recovery. Banks had wanted to go down and volunteer. Reed wouldn't allow that. He'd been to places like Haiti before, many times. Chaotic disaster zones controlled by whoever had the most guns and the least conscience. It was no place for his little family.

"I still don't understand," Turk said. "If the mines were Russian, how did they get here? That's not something you slide through customs."

"You're not listening. They didn't ship them to the U.S. The delivery address is for some town called Cap-Haïtien."

"Cap what?" Turk said.

"Cap-Haïtien!" Wolfgang snapped. "It's in Haiti."

Reed's heart thudded. The fog closing over his mind ripped back like a curtain, and he wheeled on Turk.

"What did he say?"

Turk looked up, confused. Reed closed the distance between them and snatched the phone.

"Wolfgang, it's Reed. You said Haiti?'"

"Right," Wolfgang sighed. "Cap-Haïtien. It's a port town on the north side of the island. The mines were delivered there."

Reed looked back to the TV. It was blurry through the misted glass, but he could still make out the news report. Helicopter reels had switched to ground footage now, dockside in Port-au-Prince. Long lines of starving, sun-blasted Haitians converged on a massive row of UN aid tents. The back-sides of those tents were stacked with tall columns of pallets, all loaded with dry foods and fresh water. Medicine and camping tents. All the things a million homeless, destitute souls needed to survive.

As the camera panned out, Reed saw ships. Dozens of them. Big freighters from all around the world, delivering those desperately needed supplies.

Not from the countries that donated them—not according to the news report. No. The supplies were being staged in Savannah, Georgia. The ships were making regular trips.

In and out. Back and forth.

Down to Haiti with a fresh load. Back to Georgia . . . empty.

"Why would they ship mines to Haiti?" Turk said. "How did they get them *here?*"

"That's how," Reed said.

He pointed to a ship churning out of the harbor. A French flag flapped from her stern as she steamed north, bound for America. A few hundred shipping containers were stacked on her decks.

All presumed empty.

33

Maggie green lit the mission at 8:42 that evening. It was full dark in Washington, and she was dressed in her customary night attire of gray sweatpants and a dark blue sweatshirt with the presidential seal embroidered on the chest. She and O'Dell shared a quick meal of pastrami sandwiches from the White House kitchen before they joined her war team in the Situation Room.

Yellin was back, as were Price and Gorman. Kline and O'Brien connected via video link. Aimes wasn't available.

From the end of the table nearest the display screens, Admiral Price walked Maggie through the proceedings. He spoke with the same gentle calm she'd come to expect, raising his voice just loud enough to be heard over the hum of the air conditioner.

"We've positioned a portion of Task Force 61 fifty miles off the coast of Lebanon, including the USS *Kearsarge*. She's a *Wasp*-class amphibious assault ship—like a small aircraft carrier. Two squads of SEALs from SEAL Team 8 will fly aboard MH-60M Black Hawks, compliments of the Army's Night Stalker regiment."

Maggie raised an eyebrow.

"Special ops pilots, ma'am," Yellin clarified. "The best we have."

"The Night Stalkers will keep it stealthy moving in," Price continued. "They'll take the house by opposing angles and deploy their SEALs outside the northeast and southwest corners of the property."

A graphic of the blockhouse appeared on the display screen. Price marked it with a red laser pointer.

"Half the force will remain outside to secure a perimeter while the other eight men will infiltrate the building and secure any occupants. They'll also search for any valuable sources of intel on site. Computers, cell phones, hard drives, notebooks. That kind of thing."

"When do they launch?" Maggie asked.

"They're already in the air, ma'am. Once they cross into Syria we'll have live camera and audio feed."

Maggie looked to Secretary Gorman. "Lebanon?"

"I'll place the call when the choppers are ten minutes out from the coast," Gorman said. "The Lebanese will be pissed, but they won't be able to claim we didn't notify them."

Maggie nodded silently. The screen now displayed a giant map. Lebanon and Syria were marked in light tan on the righthand side. To the left, a baby blue expanse represented the Mediterranean Sea. A gold dot marked the location of the warships, with a red line traced all the way through Lebanon, terminating at a red star just east of Damascus. Most of the line was dashed, but beginning at the warships and moving gradually eastward, a pulsating dot slowly paved the dashed portion of the line into a solid red highway. Marking the path of the choppers.

"Can I get you anything?" O'Dell spoke softly at Maggie's elbow. She shook her head impulsively, wincing as a fresh flash of pain ignited in her liver. The pain always seemed to accompany escalated stress—which meant she was always in pain. Tonight it was worse than usual. She craved more of the prescription painkillers O'Dell kept in his pocket for emergency situations, but the last thing she needed was for her war team to witness her popping pills.

She simply shook her head, not meeting O'Dell's gaze. The pastrami sandwich dinner had been a quiet one. They had barely spoken since

O'Dell returned to Washington. Whatever had felt off before had escalated into the proverbial elephant in the room, and she couldn't afford to be distracted by that. The nation needed her to be at one hundred percent.

Maggie focused on the pulsating dot and tried to picture two black helicopters, each loaded with young American men dressed in dark uniforms with night vision optics mounted to their helmets. According to the clock displayed in one corner of the screen, it was nearing four a.m. in Syria. Admiral Price had reinforced for her the necessity of completing the mission at night. The odds of success, he claimed, dramatically decreased after sunrise.

"My men own the night," he'd said.

Maggie glanced toward the admiral now as Gorman retreated to one corner of the room to place her diplomatic phone call. Price focused on his laptop, a headset wrapped around his skull. He took calls now and then, speaking softly and keeping his words to a minimum. Alongside him Yellin watched the same blipping dot as Maggie, his bulldog shoulders now housed beneath a simple black golf shirt with a U.S. Army logo on the chest.

Everyone was dressed down for this. Everyone was focused. Maggie wondered if they felt the same uneasiness that now burrowed deep in her own stomach, impossible to shake.

There was no reason to question Price, she told herself. No reason to doubt the plan. It was a good one.

Right?

"Crossing into Lebanese airspace," Price said. Maggie imagined the two black choppers racing high over beaches, someplace north of Saida and south of Beirut. Price had explained that there were mountains, here. The choppers rode low to the water to fly beneath radar while over the Mediterranean, but the mountains would force them to climb, increasing the risk of exposure.

Maggie scratched one thumbnail against the edge of the table. She watched the dot creep across the middle of the small Arabic country, and willed it to hurry.

The sooner they arrived, the sooner they could leave. The sooner she could shake this uncertainty.

"Approaching Syria," Price said. "If you're ready, ma'am, we'll switch to cameras."

Maggie nodded. Price made a call, and the screen flickered. It went very dark, then dull green light illuminated the shadowy interior of a small space. Speakers crackled on in the ceiling above, bringing the instant whine of a jet engine and by the thunder of rotor blades.

Faces appeared in the dark. Big men wearing black helmets, bearded faces shrouded by the green glow. The camera shook as whatever—or whoever—it was mounted to twitched. Then she heard voices.

"Carter! Lock and load, jerkoff. Four minutes!"

"Kiss my sweaty ass, Gordon."

Price's face flushed. "My apologies ma'am."

Maggie suppressed a smile. "It's fine."

The whine of the jet engine shrieked louder. Maggie's smile faded as the camera twisted, panning over the interior of the chopper. She saw two men sitting next to each other, one chewing gum, the other adjusting something on his chest rig. Neither man looked older than twenty-five. Both wore camouflage paint and the same black helmets, night vision goggles rotated down. Rifles hung over their chests.

Headed straight into the storm.

"Two minutes!" somebody shouted.

The screen blinked again, and the camera feed shrank to one side, opening space for a second feed to appear. The new picture was black-and-white, with crosshairs near the middle and tiny numbers in the bottom corners. A bird's-eye view of the house.

"Drone feed," Price explained.

Nobody else spoke. A breathless tension had descended over the small room. Maggie could feel it in her chest. Her mouth went dry, but she didn't reach for the water bottle resting next to her. She remained riveted to the screen as O'Dell scratched one finger absently over his chin.

She remembered what O'Dell once told her about his background. About how he came to work for the Louisiana State Troopers after washing out of BUDs. He'd been a SEAL candidate who couldn't make the cut. She knew it was a scar he would never outlive.

"Sixty seconds!"

The video feed tilted as the chopper banked. The SEAL carrying the camera moved into position near one of the Black Hawk's doors and crouched. His hand moved as he signaled to the men behind him. Weapons rattled. Wind roared. Black desert raced by, far below.

Then the two birds appeared on the drone feed. Racing in like striking snakes, they hit the compound from opposing corners and dropped straight for the ground, desert sand rising in a dense cloud.

"Go! Go! Go!"

Men appeared on the ground. The camera feed bounced. Maggie could hear the SEAL breathing. The house appeared ahead of him, both the front door and the garage door closed. The SEAL ran straight for an outside corner. His weapon rose with him, and a green laser streaked through the darkness. He crouched and hissed an order.

Another SEAL approached the front door. Maggie's gaze flicked between the camera feed and the drone feed as she traced his progress. He slapped the door with one arm. More machine-gun communication. Short, snapping words. The guy pulled back and knelt against the wall.

Then the breaching charge detonated in a cloud of gray. Half the SEALs moved at once, rushing for the door with weapons sweeping the path ahead and the windows above. The other half remained behind, dug in near the choppers, rifles trained on the house.

Maggie focused on the camera feed. Doors burst and feet pounded. Her heart rate quickened, and the uneasiness returned.

The house was almost empty. The SEALs moved with practiced ease from room to room, calling "Clear!" as they swept each one. It didn't take long—there was no furniture. No kitchen appliances or shelves along the walls. The place was stripped bare.

Maggie's stomach tightened. She placed a hand on the table and leaned in until the edge of it bit into her stomach.

The SEALs navigated toward the garage. Hissed orders were joined by green lasers darting across the walls. Weapons rattled. They reached the kitchen and ran headlong into another door—bolted shut.

Maggie's view was obstructed by broad shoulders and chest rigs. Another breaching charge was slapped in place. A snapping bang, and more "Go! Go!"

She suddenly realized she'd quit breathing, the air frozen in her throat. Clouds of gray obscured her view. The SEAL with the camera took two steps forward. The view opened across the interior of a garage.

Maggie blinked, unable to make sense of what she was seeing. The room was only half as large as it should have been. A tall, broad partition cut right down the middle. Was it a . . . projector screen?

"*Wait!*" The command came from the SEAL taking point. He held up a fist, then spun on his heel and jerked his hand toward the door. "Back out! Back out! Back—"

The camera feed went black the same moment a flash of white consumed the drone feed. Fire and smoke exploded toward the sky as the house detonated, shockwaves ripping across the desert and driving one Black Hawk onto its side. The drone shuddered and Maggie lurched to her feet. Half a sob escaped from her lips as she clutched the edge of the table. Her eyes blurred and she blinked through it.

Begging. Praying. Pleading.

She couldn't have seen what she thought she saw. It wasn't possible. It had to be a dream.

But it wasn't. The house was gone.

The SEALs were gone.

Everything was smoke and flame.

34

O'Dell had blocked Turk's phone number. Reed tried again, but it simply rang and rang. No voicemail. No answer.

Reed terminated the call and shoved the phone back into Turk's hand, then he turned directly for the doors leading back into the hospital. Turk ground his cigarette out and followed him to the elevator. Reed jammed his thumb against the call button as a familiar dump of adrenaline reached his bloodstream. A feeling he'd experienced a thousand times before—a practiced biological prelude to impending action.

The elevator closed around him and the car accelerated back toward the ICU. Reed stared at his reflection in the stainless steel, thinking quickly.

All the pieces were there. The image was clear. It was freaking brilliant, if you were a terrorist. A golden opportunity.

"I'll call the CIA," Turk said. "Remind them of North Korea. Something that will get us on the phone with O'Brien."

Reed shook his head. "That jerkwad won't talk to us. He wanted us burned from day one."

"Okay. FBI, then. Or the White House. We'll get Maggie on the line somehow."

Reed ran a tongue over his lips. He tasted grit and grime—Tennessee dirt, probably. From the blast. He was filthy. He didn't even care.

The door rolled open and he marched straight for the ICU. Catching the secure access door as a nurse passed through, he ignored her demands for him to halt and proceeded straight for the row of beds. Turk lagged a moment to talk the desk nurse out of calling security.

Reed reached Bank's bay and pulled the curtain back. His pace slowed as he reached her bedside. She was still unconscious—probably in an induced coma. The doctor had explained her condition in advanced medical terminology that Reed didn't understand nor care to learn. He was a simple man. Just the facts. Was she going to live, or not?

The doctor still didn't know.

As Reed put his hand on Banks's arm, his fingers trembled. He blinked back sudden hot tears and focused on her face. Puffy cheeks, washed pale. Gorgeous blonde hair tangled around her skull. That mass of bandages around her stomach where the doctors had . . .

Reed closed his eyes. He clamped his mouth shut. He saw the little apartment in southeast Nashville, Davy's toys scattered around the floor. Davy liked cars and trucks—because of course he did. He was a Montgomery, after all. He had good taste.

But when Reed imagined the plastic muscle cars and bright yellow construction toys, he saw something else. A baby doll. Soft pink, with brown curls. A bassinet with a frilly blanket covering a sleeping child.

Bright, rosy cheeks. Soft blonde hair. Her mother's nose.

Reed wasn't sure how he knew the child was a girl. Maybe he didn't know—maybe he just envisioned her that way. But he knew she was *real*. She'd been real. She'd been his.

Turk opened the curtain. There was a security officer standing behind him, hands on his hips, indignation in the irate lift of his chin.

"Just two minutes. Okay?" Turk addressed the guard. The guard opened his mouth.

Turk's jaw locked. The guard recalibrated his confrontation calculus and reached a new answer.

"Two minutes. That's all."

Turk shut the curtain. He stood quietly in the corner and put his hands in his pockets. Reed squeezed Banks's hand and listened to the steady whir of her ventilator. He bowed his head and asked himself the question he already knew the answer to. The question he could never escape.

Then he faced Turk. "We're going. Assemble what gear you have. I'll arrange transport. We leave ASAP."

Turk held his gaze a long moment, lips pressed tightly together. And then he nodded, because he knew. The ugliest reality a soldier could face was helplessness. Worse than death, worse than watching your buddies die, was watching it happen without a thing to do about it.

It was unacceptable.

"Give me a couple hours to get back to the house," Turk said. "I've got us covered on gear."

Turk left the room, and Reed descended to his knees. He leaned close to Banks and pressed his open hand against her side, searching for warmth. The beat of her heart.

Cold skin was joined by the faintest pulse. Life hanging by a thread.

It was a battle Banks could only face alone, and if Reed knew anything about his wife, he knew she was more than up for the challenge. For himself, there were other battles to face.

He kissed her cheek, long and slow. Then he squeezed her hand as he whispered into her ear.

"I'm going to get them. I'm going to get them all."

35

The graveyard shift at the headquarters of Britain's Secret Intelligence Service boasted all of the energy and excitement of . . . well. A graveyard.

Suits and office dresses were replaced by blue jeans and T-shirts. Most of the men hadn't shaved. Most of the women wore only traces of makeup. A hint of body odor hung in the air, and everyone typed a little slower than their dayshift counterparts. Calls were allowed to ring a few times before being answered. Somebody had a replay of a Newcastle match going. Work drummed along almost lackadaisically, even as analysts and technicians of a dozen different specialties monitored the events unfolding in America with growing concern for their international impact.

Right in the middle of it all, packed into a tiny cubical, SIS analyst Kirsten Corbyn sat slouched behind her computer and fought to keep her eyes open. Spread across her twin monitors were a combined five hundred pages of intelligence reports written by field agents in South America, all reporting on the ongoing instability in Venezuela and its ripple effect across the region. Corbyn knew the story behind the recent regime change in Caracas better than most. Not just because she'd been parked here at this desk "analyzing" intelligence reports for the past eight months, but because she'd been there when Cesar Moreno, Venezuela's late dictator, was shot to death in Palacio de Miraflores. She'd flown the chopper that extracted the black ops crew that infiltrated that compound. In fact, the chopper in question was Moreno's personal transport, and she wasn't supposed to be flying it. She wasn't even supposed to be in Caracas.

Corbyn had . . . colored outside the lines a little. Okay. She'd colored outside the lines a *lot*. Enough to earn her a one-way ticket out of the field life she craved and into this miserable hole surrounded by thirty-five-year-old nerds covered in acne. It was pure misery. Ever since the day her Royal Air Force Chinook had gone down in Iraq, breaking multiple bones and shattering her future as a military aviator, Corbyn had fought tooth and nail to get back into action. *Any* action—she wasn't picky. She just wanted to be out there, with the wind in her face and adrenaline in her blood, crashing headlong into the danger zone.

To be fair, it was that obsession with action and adventure that had led her to screw up her job as a South American field agent in the first place. When Reed Montgomery and his scrappy team of American operators pitched her a plan to steal a despot's chopper and fly like a madwoman over riot-torn Caracas, it was too juicy a slice to refuse. And hadn't it been justified? Wasn't it her *duty* to support His Majesty's allies?

Her superiors hadn't thought so. Her superiors had wanted her hung from Tower Bridge. She counted her blessings when they transferred her to Vauxhall Cross instead of terminating her altogether. Eight months later, she was beginning to think their mercy was really cruelty in disguise. She was about ready to blow her own brains out, working all night and sleeping all day. It had been so long since she'd felt the wind on her face, danger creeping at the corners of her mind, that she was ready to go insane.

Maybe she'd buy that motorcycle. She'd stopped by the dealership to test drive it, where the salesman explained that her credit was poor and the payment would be astronomical. Corbyn had always been more interested in the heat of the moment than any long-term priority, which hadn't been a strong financial strategy.

But screw it, didn't she *deserve* some fun? The monster Triumph Rocket

3 sported a 2,500 CC engine. Enough power to launch her straight into the stratosphere. It couldn't replace the glory of flight, not really. But maybe she'd take it up to Scotland. Find a twisty mountain road. Roast her own demons under the piping hot exhaust of that gargantuan engine.

Corbyn's desk phone rang, jarring her out of her daydream. She blinked the haze away and cradled it against her shoulder, slurping an energy drink as she answered.

"Latin American ops, this is Corbyn."

"Hello, Brit."

Corbyn blinked. The voice was male, American, and sounded ragged. But more than that, it was familiar. *Very* familiar.

"Montgomery? Is that you?"

"Bingo."

Corbyn sat up, fully awake now. A flash of energy mixed with a hint of anger. Both crept into the tone of her next question. "How the bloody hell did you get this number?"

Reed Montgomery snorted. "Stop kidding yourself, Corbyn. You're not that big a fish. I called SIS directory."

Directory. Was he kidding?

Montgomery didn't give her time to consider.

"I need your help. Can you fly fixed-wing?"

Corbyn's mind skipped. She squinted in temporary mental deadlock, her mind racing back to Venezuela. To Caracas. To the battered American warrior asking her a similar question: *"You can fly a chopper?"*

Corbyn's face flushed. "You've got a lot of nerve calling me up to ask a question like that. Do you have any idea what your last favor cost me? I'm riding a bloody desk, now. Got paperwork up to my neck—"

"Can you fly fixed-wing or not?" Montgomery's voice snapped.

Corbyn sat back in her chair, arms folded. The hot indignation was settling quickly into a deeper, more irate sense of frustration. This yank really didn't take a hint.

"Of course I can fly fixed-wing. Got my private license after I left the army. A cheaper fix for an aviation addict than whirly birds. What's that got—"

"Can you fly a King Air 360?"

Corbyn hesitated, caught off guard. It was a strangely specific question, but easy enough to answer. She could indeed fly a King Air 360. She'd trained to fly King Airs as part of her brief tenure as an SIS field agent. They were terrific little aircraft with respectable flight ranges and cruising speed. Excellent for working across rural South America.

"I can," Corbyn said.

"Great. How soon can you get to Tennessee? I'm headed to Haiti. I need a pilot."

"Say what? Have you lost your marbles?"

This time, Montgomery hesitated. She detected a hitch in his breathing. Corbyn narrowed her eyes.

"You saw the news?" Montgomery asked.

"About the bombing? I saw it. Terrible thing. I don't know how you Yanks keep letting—"

"My wife was on stage," Montgomery cut her off.

Corbyn's heart dropped. She detected the ragged pain in Montgomery's tone, and her mouth went dry. She didn't know what to say. She shifted in her chair.

"I'm so sorry. Is she . . ."

"She's hanging on," Montgomery said. "That's not why I'm calling. The terrorists used Russian land mines, strung together in sequence. I have documentation proving that those mines were shipped from an arms dealer in Ukraine to Haiti a week ago. I think the terrorists smuggled them aboard aid ships returning to Georgia, and then drove them to Tennessee."

"Wait. They what?"

"There's more coming," Montgomery continued as if she hadn't spoken. "Another attack. You saw their video. I'm going to Haiti to hunt them down. I need a pilot."

Corbyn raced to follow Montgomery's trail of thought, almost tripping over the logical leaps he skipped over like mud puddles. Russian mines? Aid ships? *What* was he talking about?

"Where are you getting this?" She said. "The Agency?"

"I don't work for Washington anymore. I have my own sources. Look, none of that matters. There are no flights into Haiti right now. I need to bring guns anyway, so I have to fly private. I've already got a plane lined up. You fly me, and I'll make it worth your while."

Corbyn's mouth opened. She glanced quickly over the top of the cubical to see if any of the aforementioned thirty-five-year-old nerds with acne had drifted nearby. Had anyone overhead this?

"Look, I don't know what you think I am, but you're looney if you think I'm an Uber. You need to call your government and—"

"I've tried. They've got their heads so far up their ass they don't know what daylight is. Stop telling me what I already know. Can you help or not?"

"Of course I can't help! If you were standing here now, I'd smack the daylights out of you. I lost field work, thanks to you. I almost lost everything. You must be insane if you think—"

"My mistake," Montgomery snapped. "I mistook you for somebody with balls."

Montgomery hung up. Corbyn's face turned red-hot as the dial tone rang in her ear.

Had he really just said that? Sexist son of a—

She mashed redial before she knew what she was doing. The phone buzzed. It took time to connect overseas. Montgomery answered.

"I'll buy you a ticket—"

"Now you listen here, you backwoods trailer trash. I've worked too hard and accomplished too much to be demeaned like that. You'd have lost your own balls in Caracas if I hadn't flown your ass out of there. You ought to be thanking me. You ought to be begging my forgiveness. You ought to be—"

"Heathrow to Nashville?" Montgomery cut her off.

"That's fine," Corbyn snapped.

"I'll have your ticket waiting at the desk."

"See that you do." Corbyn hung up, hard. She sat fuming for a moment, breathing like an enraged bull. Still growling through her teeth.

Inbred redneck tosser.

Her boss stood with a cup of coffee steaming in one hand in the entrance of her cubical, acne-scarred cheeks glistening with sweat. He raised both eyebrows.

Corbyn rolled her eyes and smacked the lock button on her keyboard. She grabbed her purse and barreled past him.

"Where are you going?" he demanded. "You can't just leave. You're only halfway through your shift."

"Yeah?" Corbyn stopped at the end of the aisle. She looked back, well aware that most of the office was now eavesdropping on the confrontation. "Well how about this. I quit!"

Corbyn pressed her thumb against her nose and waggled her fingers, sticking her tongue out and blasting spit toward her boss.

Then she turned for the door and didn't look back.

36

The Midwest Addiction Recovery Center sounded like a hospital to Lucy, but in practice it was something closer to a summer camp. Constructed of a few dozen log cabins situated in the middle of nowhere alongside a twenty-acre lake, the retreat featured everything a person might need to support their war against the clutch of narcotics.

Therapy centers. Long walking trails. Group classrooms, and benches overlooking the lake. A shared mess hall and enough daily activities to "busy the mind and nurture the body"—core tenants of addiction recovery, according to MARC. It was a truly beautiful place, but the peace and serenity projected by the landscape was little more than an unloaded gun in the face of an attack helicopter.

The angry grip of opioids had taken almost everything from Lucy Byrne. They'd stolen her health, her identity. Consumed her financial stability and her self-image with it. They'd turned her once toned and shapely body into a rail-skinny shell of her former self, leaving her homeless and starving on dark city streets from Bangkok to Tampa.

She was almost ready to call it quits when an old friend extended a hand. Reed Montgomery had been something of a colleague in her days as a professional assassin. Their relationship wasn't a close one, but he picked her up off the street when nobody else would. He put a roof over her head, and offered her a way forward.

He'd even reached for his own checkbook to send her to MARC.

It all seemed like a dream come true when she first arrived. Onsite medical professionals oversaw her detox process, easing her slowly off the painkillers while ensuring that her heart didn't stop. A soft bed and balanced meals aided her rest and recovery. She gained weight. She made it thirty days sober.

And then the real misery began. Not just the withdrawals and the cravings, but the nightmares. The cold sweats. The memories. Over a decade of trauma crashing through the barriers of her weakened mind. Lucy saw every body, every target. Every gory moment of every long, bloody year she'd spent so deep in the criminal underworld that she'd forgotten what her conscience felt like.

It was more than guilt. More than a psychotic breakdown. It was Lucy coming face to face with Lucy, and not liking what she saw. Not remembering how she got there.

But knowing beyond any doubt that she couldn't continue.

She slipped out of her bed late one night beneath the cool touch of a full moon and escaped through her window. She found her way to the lake and kicked her off her shoes.

It didn't take long for the water to reach her chin. She kept walking until her feet slid out from under her. Until she leaned back and let the lake close over her face. Until the oxygen left her lungs, and the darkness closed in. The pain in her chest subsided. Her heartbeat began to slow. She was slipping away—eager to let go.

And then . . . she met God.

It wasn't like a movie. There was no bright light or window into heaven. There was just love. As corny as it sounded to say, she felt it in her soul. That somebody was there, very near. Warmth enveloped her like a blanket, lifting her out of the depths. She saw a shadow, silhouetted by morning sun. A crucifix on a hill, bloody but empty. And then a hand, soft but strong, cradled her body, and lifted her up.

When Lucy opened her eyes she floated on her back in the lake. It was still dark, but the moon had set. She was ice cold, but her heart still thumped. She still saw the cross on the hill. The sunrise behind.

And the warmth in her mind remained, despite her shivering body.

She left the lake and returned to her bed. The next day, she attended chapel for the first time. The minister was called Brother Matthew, and he taught from the Christian Bible. His lessons were about love, and forgiveness. Responsibility, and repentance. Lucy went every day for a month, crying sometimes. Other times, just staring at the floor. Not understanding most of what he said, but somehow knowing the answers she needed would be found in that room.

It wasn't until summer that she gave in, praying alongside Brother Matthew and relinquishing her life. The crushing weight of guilt had become too much. She couldn't handle it any longer.

Lucy broke. And Lucy found healing.

When her time at MARC wound to a close, Lucy wasn't ready to leave. She didn't have any place to be. Brother Matthew helped her negotiate long-term residency with the recovery center in exchange for work as a janitor, cook, and groundskeeper. Lucy learned how to cut grass and trim hedges. How to fry eggs and clean windows. It was menial, sometimes tedious work, but Lucy didn't mind. She'd take peace and a toilet brush any day over the alternative.

And if the pain ever returned, she had an answer. She would sneak out of her room. Strip down to her underwear and take midnight swims in the lake until the pain evaporated, or the sun crested the horizon.

This night, she'd bested the pain. Her auburn hair still dripped as she found her way back inside, padding on bare feet and crossing the main lobby, headed toward her bunk. She shared a room with two other recovering addicts. One of them had nightmares, also. Lucy would pray with her until she could sleep again.

"Lucy?"

Brother Matthew called to her from his office as she passed. It was still dark outside, but it wasn't unusual for the minister to arrive early. Sometimes Lucy wondered what demons of his own might be keeping him awake.

"It's just me," Lucy said, lifting a hand. "I couldn't sleep."

She turned for the hall. Brother Matthew called after her.

"The front office asked me to give you a message. Somebody called half an hour ago."

Lucy stopped. A frown crossed her face. She looked over one shoulder. "Who?"

"He didn't say. He just asked to leave a message. Sounded important."

Lucy ducked into the office, still dripping. Momentary confusion was soon muted by rationalization. Almost nobody knew where she was. In fact, almost nobody knew she existed. Lucy didn't have family and she had precious few friends.

Really, she could think of only one person who might call. The man who had pulled her from the gutter and sent her to MARC in the first place. The man she literally owed her life to.

Brother Matthew slid a yellow legal pad across his desk. The message was brief. Only one complete word—thirteen characters in total.

Nashville. 911. R.

Lucy's heart accelerated. She dropped the sopping towel to the floor and bent to pull her shoes on. Already her mind had left the lake, left MARC. Left Ohio.

Without comment she hurried back into the hallway, through a metal door, and into a small employees-only locker room. She spun the dial on her assigned locker, exposing a small pile of personal effects. An Ohio state ID rubber-banded to a roll of two thousand dollars in cash, and a leather bound New Testament, worn by extensive reading and many long nights spent beneath her pillow. It was all she owned in the world—and all she needed.

Lucy turned for the door.

"Lucy. What's going on?" Brother Matthew's voice edged with concern as he appeared in the hallway.

Lucy stopped at the front entrance, looking over one shoulder. "Tell the others I'll be back when I can."

Brother Matthew cocked his head, arms folded as he leaned against the doorframe. For a moment she thought he might protest. Might demand more details.

Instead, he only nodded. "God be with you, Lucy. Live in the light."

"Live in the light." Lucy returned the smile.

Then she pushed through the door and headed straight for the drive. It was two miles to the little gas station at the crossroads. If she couldn't hitch a ride there, she'd have to walk another ten to the nearest town.

She'd walk all night, if needed. Because she owed Reed Montgomery her life, and Lucy Byrne had learned to appreciate just what a gift that was.

37

Ibrahim's men loaded the three crates aboard an empty, rust-red shipping container. They put them right in the middle, then strapped them down a dozen different ways to avoid any shift in transit.

The container was marked in three different languages—English, Spanish, and French. That made it an aid shipment from Spain, probably. Printed in Spanish for the government officials who originally assembled the medical supplies and dry foods housed within. Marked in English, because that was the international language used by the UN officials coordinating the aid. Then marked again in French, because that was what the Haitians would understand.

What a convoluted mess, Ibrahim thought. So many do-gooder politicians falling over themselves to get in front of the camera first. To send the most aid. To claim the greatest amount of generosity. To puff out their chests and brag about their dedication to saving helpless little brown people.

It made him sick. Not because he felt any malice toward the Haitians—quite the opposite. Because Ibrahim *knew* what it was like to be destitute. Crushed and obliterated, lying in a dust bowl of shattered dreams and broken homes. It was an absolute level of pain and desperation that the Western world had never experienced—couldn't possibly understand or respect.

Their inflated promises to pull Haiti from the mire of her misery rang hollow to Ibrahim. Not just because he saw through their obvious double standards and empty empathy, but because he understood who was really responsible for the misery of the third world in the first place. It was the first world. The so-called "Free World."

The world that had crushed the Middle East. Left it every bit as broken and destitute as Haiti. And then abandoned it.

Where were the press conferences and aid shipments for Syria? For South Sudan? For Yemen? Where were the teary-eyed politicians and pledges of rescue then? Where were the celebrities prattling on Instagram about the greater good and the unity of one human race?

No. None of those people cared, then. And it wasn't because they were ignorant . . . it was because they were the *authors* of that devastation. Having raped and pillaged the Middle East of her wealth at every available opportunity, exploiting and enflaming wars at every turn, the Western world and its armies of enlightened leaders and movie stars were only too quick to ignore the fallout of that greed and corruption.

Yemen? Yemen what? Was that even a real country?

Ibrahim double-checked each strap inside the shipping container, pushing on the crates to ensure their security. He couldn't hear the slosh of death from within. It was too well sealed, thanks be to Allah. Protected, until the proper time of retribution.

And what a sweet, sweet retribution that would be.

Ibrahim closed the crate and applied a metal security tie to the latch. It was a perfect replication of the security tie he and his men had cut to gain access to the container in the first place. The tie signaled to dock workers that the container was empty, ready to be returned to America aboard one of the massive freighters before being reloaded with aid.

Ibrahim wasn't concerned about the weight of the three barrels. The sixty-five-ton cranes erected on rails near Port-au-Prince's harbor were so powerful that the addition of a thousand pounds inside a supposedly empty container wouldn't be noticed. Ibrahim just hoped they didn't drop the container by accident.

If they did, they wouldn't survive to tell the tale.

Backing away from the door, Ibrahim looked down the long columns of dozens of similar containers, reaching all the way to the edge of the water. They were battered and muddy, many of them dinted and dinged by unskilled crane operators shifting them off of freighters and onto shore. The dockside was a mess. A disaster zone. Chaos, from the moment the sun rose and the volunteers arrived.

A golden opportunity.

Ibrahim breathed a prayer to Allah for the safe passage of the container, then slid inside the Toyota Land Cruiser waiting nearby and watched the container fade in his rearview as Kadeem drove out of the port.

Through the open window, Ibrahim could hear the strained and desperate voices of ten thousand displaced Haitians taking shelter at an emergency UN camp. The cries were joined by distant automatic gunfire someplace beyond the camp—another clash between UN peacekeepers and Haitian gangs eager to exploit the influx of precious food and supplies.

It was the soundtrack of Haiti, and it was visceral to Ibrahim. It sank knives into his stomach, unleashing fresh hatred for the infidels.

They hadn't caused the earthquake that had ripped through this land, but they had caused plenty of others. He imagined that the heartbroken, terrified voices of Haitians that he heard were really those of Americans.

Slowly dying. Wracked by terror. Screaming and writhing wherever they fell, boiling in their own blood as judgment finally descended upon them.

The thought eased the pain in his stomach, and brought a smile to his face.

From the back seat, Hamid took a call on a satellite phone. He spoke softly in Arabic, just a few clipped sentences. Then he hung up.

"That was Omar," Hamid said. "Damascus went perfectly. A complete success."

"And the video?" Ibrahim asked.

"Like an American movie. Omar is emailing it now, then he and Youssef are boarding a plane. They will meet us in Atlanta."

Ibrahim leaned back in the seat, pulling the St. Louis Cardinals baseball hat lower over his face. The bill blocked out the glare of passing security lights.

But it couldn't block out the widening smile on his face.

38

It was midnight by the time Maggie retreated out of the West Wing. A flurry of phone calls and panicked posturing followed the explosion of the house outside Damascus. O'Brien went offline almost immediately, claiming he needed to coordinate with his people—whatever that meant. Price's flawlessly calm demeanor flickered as he worked his computer to order a QRF team from USS *Kearsarge* to respond to the site. Yellin shouted into a phone. Gordon fielded calls from Lebanese officials, now objecting to further U.S. military flights across their airspace.

It was organized chaos, but Maggie didn't need answers. She already knew what had happened. The uneasiness in her gut mushroomed into sickening dread as she watched the continued drone feed displaying clearing smoke.

Both choppers were destroyed. The house was reduced to an ashen heap, blocks and fragments of metal roof slung as far as two hundred yards away.

And the bodies . . .

Maggie stumbled out of the elevator and returned to her presidential suite. She made it as far as the Private Sitting Room before crashing onto a sofa and staring blankly at the wall. The hot weight in her stomach was boiling into lava. She thought she might be sick. If she closed her eyes, all she saw was that white hot flash of sudden flame.

All she heard were the last words of SEAL Team 8. *"Back out! Back out! Back—"*

Maggie's hand trembled as she lifted a telephone handset from the decorative end table next to her. The operator transferred her to a White House steward. Maggie ordered whiskey. Whatever the kitchen staff had in stock.

Then she asked to be transferred to a member of Easterling's staff. Some aide with a squeaky New England accent picked up.

"Yes ma'am?"

"Have the Navy send me a list," Maggie mumbled. She didn't have to clarify what the list should contain.

The kitchen brought a bottle of Blanton's Black Label—some fancy stuff in a pineapple-shaped bottle. No doubt a selection from Stratton's private collection. The VP was a connoisseur of fine whiskeys. To Maggie's swamp pallet, they all tasted the same.

She dumped three fingers in a tumbler and knocked it all back at once. It hit her stomach like a cannonball. The edges of the room blurred, and she slumped back on the sofa. By the time an aide brought her the list, she was halfway through another three fingers and feeling the haze of inebriation closing around her mind.

She mumbled her thanks and nearly dropped the page. The aide left. Maggie set the list on the coffee table and took another swallow. The sheet was mostly blank. Only a tight column of text filled one side—eleven lines, top to bottom.

LCDR James Warner, USN. Little Rock, AR.

PO3 Francis Wainwright, USN. Lincoln, NE.

PO3 Bryce Carter, USN. Montpellier, VT.

CW2 Timothy Decker, USA. Biloxi, MS.

The remaining seven names blurred almost out of focus. Maggie rocked the glass back and almost dropped it. The page fluttered to the carpet instead, and she collapsed into a chair.

And sobbed.

Maggie wasn't a crier by nature. She'd almost never allowed herself to embrace the surge of emotions that often waylaid her as one catastrophe after another bombarded her presidency like lightning bolts striking the West Wing. But how much was enough? How much could she take?

How many storms could she wrestle the nation through by grit and determination alone?

This wasn't what she signed up for. Maybe one hurricane. Maybe two. But four? Five? Half a dozen?

"It's fragile."

The words of President William Brandt, Maggie's predecessor, echoed in her mind in the same tired, burdened voice she'd last heard on the tarmac of Joint Base Andrews before Brandt flew to his doom.

"The nation . . . the grand experiment. It's made of glass."

Maggie hadn't understood Brandt then. Not really. But she understood him now. The entire thing felt like a house of cards, erected on a paper-thin table resting over a fault line. Just waiting for the next tremor to send the whole thing exploding into the abyss.

Maggie finished the glass. She was already drunk. Her head already floating. Her gut churning. She fumbled for the Blanton's and knocked it off the table. Half of it spilled across the carpet. She watched it gurgle out, only semi-conscious of its value, and not really caring. The whiskey gushed over the page of fallen service members, staining their names like the blood that now stained the Syrian sand.

Another battle lost.

And it was *her* fault.

The door across the room opened, but Maggie didn't look up. She figured it was a White House steward, drawn by the crash of the bottle. But the footsteps were too solid to be those of a steward. The hand too firm as the door was pushed closed.

"Maggie."

It was O'Dell. He took the glass from her hand. She didn't fight him as he scooped the bottle up and checked the contents.

"How much of this did you drink?"

Maggie shrugged, wet lips feeling suddenly very thick and clumsy. Like she couldn't really control them.

O'Dell crouched alongside her and felt the carpet with one hand, mapping out the wet spot to determine how much liquor had spilled over the floor instead of down her throat. He found the page and peeled it free of the saturated carpet fibers. For a moment he just stared at it, and Maggie wondered what he was thinking.

Maybe that she was a murderer. A careless, reckless fiend. A soulless maniac who had just sent nearly a dozen of America's very best straight to their deaths. For what?

O'Dell said nothing. He simply laid the sheet on the table and smoothed it with his hands. Then he sat alongside her, the Blanton's bottle riding his knee. He tipped it back and took a long swallow.

When he faced her, Maggie saw something she'd never seen before. O'Dell's dark eyes were rimmed red. A single tear crept down his broad cheek.

"I killed them," Maggie whispered.

O'Dell looked at the bottle. His hand trembled. Then the bottle hit the table, and O'Dell's thick arms encased her. He pulled her into a bear hug, and she buried her face in his chest. The sobbing returned, and O'Dell didn't fight her. He pressed one hand over her back and clamped down until it felt like she was encased in protective concrete. A barricade to block out the storm. Just for a moment.

"They died heroes," O'Dell said. His voice rasped, thick with Louisiana mud and restrained emotion. "The best of us."

Maggie just kept sobbing. Even once the tears left and her throat went dry, she continued to shake. O'Dell gave her a few minutes, then he gently pushed her back. He lifted her chin with a strong finger.

His face was blurry, but Maggie saw kind eyes. The strongest, kindest man she'd ever known.

"You didn't kill them," O'Dell said. "The enemy did. And you're going to make it right."

The lump in Maggie's throat was so large she didn't know if she could speak. She tried, and it came out as a whisper.

"I can't do this, James."

"You can," O'Dell said. "And you have to. An entire nation is counting on you. You have no other choice."

"I have no answers."

"Then you *find* answers. You're Muddy Maggie Trousdale. This country elected a scrapper. It's time to get scrappy. Do you hear me?"

Something hot crept into Maggie's veins. Not like fire. Not even like sparks. More like slowly heating lava, creeping at first. Then beginning to roll.

"I can't do it alone," she whispered.

"You're not alone. You never were. You've got a whole nation standing behind you. And they want blood."

The lava reached her gut. It spilled over the whiskey and turned hot. The inebriation in her mind magnified the effect. She felt the anger. She saw the flash of white on the drone screen again. The blast of the land mines ripping through the crowd.

The smug face of Ibrahim. Promising more.

"I'm going to rain fire from the sky," Maggie said.

O'Dell nodded. "And bring our enemies to their knees."

39

Leiper's Fork, Tennessee

The airport was small and entirely pilot managed. Without any onsite staff, TSA, or control tower, it was a called an "uncontrolled field," which made it an ideal place to borrow an airplane without permission.

Reed had the Uber drop him off right at the gate and walked through, a backpack slung over one shoulder and a flashlight illuminating the path ahead. Long rows of metal hangars lined one side of the airfield, sitting quiet under the early morning darkness. The sun would rise in an hour. Staff for the little office building might arrive. Maybe pilots ready for an early morning flight to someplace quiet—someplace to get away from the news. Cabins in the mountains and condos by the beach.

Reed would be long gone by then. As would his makeshift strike team.

He began with the airport office, where a quick application of a lockpick kit provided access to the file room. A logbook disclosed the location of the Beechcraft King Air 360 owned by one Richard Barclay III. Hangar 31, near the end of the line. Fully enclosed and protected by a padlock. Reed dispatched the padlock with the same lockpicks, and the door rumbled open on steel wheels.

The aircraft was gorgeous. Reed didn't know much about planes and wasn't interested in learning, but even he had to pause a moment to admire the gentle curves and glistening gloss paint. Twin engines sported four blades each, the wings spanning nearly sixty feet from tip to tip with laminated glass protecting the cockpit. The door to the airplane opened with a click, hissing slowly down to expose a staircase that allowed access to a leather-clad interior.

The plane smelled like a brand new Mercedes. The carpet was clean and springy underfoot, the cockpit lined by LCD screens and polished controls. Reed had to bend at the waist to keep his head from colliding with the ceiling, but he knew Corbyn would have no problems. She was slender enough to slide right in behind the lefthand yoke. He only hoped she was also dumb—or smart—enough not to ask too many questions.

Reed's phone rang as he returned to the hangar. The contact screen displayed no picture, only two initials. *LB.*

"Hello?"

"I just landed." Lucy's voice was crisp and strong, a lot stronger than Reed remembered it the last time he'd seen the petite killer with scarlet hair. He'd given her a place to crash for a while, at his rental home in Birmingham. He'd secured her a paycheck from the CIA for the part she played in the investigation following Trousdale's attempted assassination. He'd located her a good rehab facility someplace in Ohio to help her work through the brutal clutch of opioid addiction.

And then he'd forgotten about her, truth be told. He wasn't a babysitter. But he was glad to hear Lucy sound more like the old LB he knew and respected. A trained killer. A lethal, cunning, and fiercely loyal soldier.

"She's still in the ICU," Reed said. "Stop by the patient lockers on your way in. Locker 334. The key is waiting for you at reception. You'll find cash to get you through. And the other stuff."

The "other stuff" was a razor-sharp KA-BAR BK7 Becker with a seven-inch blade, and a SIG SAUER P365 XL with three twelve-round magazines loaded with hollow point, +P 9mm cartridges. The knife wouldn't be Lucy's choice. She liked fancy, four and five hundred dollar blades with edges sharp enough to peel stone. But Reed spent money on guns, not knives, and as far as he was concerned the KA-BAR was good enough to kill anything that bled.

"I don't need the cash," Lucy said. "Thanks anyway. I'll stick close until you return."

Reed's throat felt suddenly thick, thinking of Banks lying alone in that hospital bed, fighting invisible demons in the dark. He didn't want her to wake up alone. And more than that, he couldn't leave her unprotected. With Lucy Byrne at her side, Banks would be at least as safe as Reed could make her.

"I owe you one," Reed said.

"You owe me nothing, Prosecutor. I've got your back. God be with you."

Reed squinted, thrown off guard by the last comment. He opened his mouth to reply, not really sure what to say, but just then headlights flashed across the row of hangars, signaling the arrival of a second Uber. Reed grunted awkward thanks and hung up quickly before fumbling for a cigarette. The Uber stopped at the entrance of the airport and two doors popped open. Turk unfolded himself from the compact car and dug into the trunk to produce a pair of backpacks and a pair of hard cases. The woman with him helped carry the luggage as the Uber driver raced away, probably eager to return to the city for early morning airport rides.

Probably not thinking about the strangers he'd just dropped at the airfield in the middle of nowhere, or what they carried inside those nondescript hard plastic cases. Musical instruments, probably. Or band gear. Wasn't everyone in Nashville a musician?

Reed lifted a hand to mark his position, and Turk appeared out of the shadows. The woman behind him was neither short nor tall. Well built, but not broad. A dark complexion someplace between Italian and Hispanic, with rich brown hair and eyes to match. She wore a sweater with an Arsenal Football Club logo printed across the chest.

Like it wasn't ninety-five degrees in Tennessee.

"Hello again, asshole," Corbyn said, dropping her backpack and one of the plastic cases.

Reed offered a reserved nod, unsure of what to say in way of apology for the manipulation he had employed over the phone. Maybe there was nothing to say.

"This the plane?" Corbyn's voice lifted with excitement as she pivoted toward the King Air, a hint of a smile crossing her lips.

"Yeah." Reed sucked on the cigarette and tapped another out of the pack for Turk. "Help yourself."

Corbyn didn't need a second invitation. She bounced across the tarmac and swung aboard, her bobbing brown head appearing behind the windshield a moment later. The hint of a smile had already blossomed into a full grin by the time she found her way into the pilot's chair.

"What did you tell her?" Reed asked.

Turk shrugged, cupping his hand to light the smoke. "Nothing."

"But?"

"But she may or may not be under the impression that the plane is a rental."

Rental. Yeah, sure.

Reed was one hundred percent certain that the very hairy Richie Barclay would pitch a royal fit and probably run straight to the police about the illegal use of his aircraft, but with any luck that wouldn't be a problem. Following his extended private fitness session earlier that week, Richie had said something about heading to Los Angeles for a weeklong business conference, compliments of his company. He'd bragged about the corporate charter jet. He said he hated to miss a week's worth of workouts. Maybe Reed could give him a discount.

The last thing on Reed's mind was the gym, or any of his clients. He only needed to have the King Air back inside Hangar 31, fueled and spotless, before Richie returned. Then nobody would have to know.

Reed lifted the case and the backpack Corbyn had dropped, and together he and Turk moved the gear to a table adjacent to the airplane. Metal clips popped, and the cases snapped open. Packed inside industrial-grade foam was a pair of Daniel Defense M4A1 rifles in jet black. 14.5" barrels were joined by quad rails, SureFire M300C Scout Lights, Trijicon MRO green dot optics, compact stocks and single-point slings. Beneath the rifles a row of ten Magpul PMAGS filled out each case, loaded with thirty rounds each of green-tipped 5.56mm ammunition.

Then came a heavy duffle bag packed with matching chest rigs, armor plates, and pistol holsters. A Glock 17 for Turk, a SIG P226 Legion for Reed. Five loaded mags for each. More KA-BAR Becker knives, canteens, binoculars, MREs, a medical pouch, night vision monoculars, a rubber-banded roll of American twenty dollar bills and . . . hand grenades?

"Where did you get these?" Reed lifted a frag grenade and rolled it butt-up in his hand. A familiar USMC stamp was pressed into the metal.

Turk shrugged innocently. "Buddy of a buddy."

Reed placed the grenade back into the bag and swept his gaze over the table full of death. Enough firepower to lay down fifty people.

"Good enough." He snapped the case closed as Corbyn appeared in the door of the King Air.

"You Yanks sure know how to pick out a plane, I'll give you that. She's all fueled and ready to go."

Reed thought of Richie, sweating on the mat, bragging about his plane.

"I always keep her fueled. Never know when the Bahamas might call, am I right?"

"I know," he said, scooping up the rifle case. In short order he and Turk had loaded the gear into the narrow aisle between the seats. Turk ran off to find the airport tractor, returning five minutes later with a modified lawn-mower fit with a custom-welded receiver hitch. There was a towing bar resting in the corner of the hangar. Corbyn instructed them on how to secure the King Air's front wheel, Turk dismissing her inquiries about his experience moving airplanes with a simple grunt before he backed the lawnmower up, dragging the airplane out of the hangar and onto the tarmac.

By the time the King Air was in position to taxi to the runway, the sky was already softening from deep black to gray. Reed and Turk clambered aboard the plane and packed themselves into plush but narrow leather seats surrounded by stacks of gear. Corbyn plopped into the pilot's chair and slipped on a Bose headset. She grinned as her fingers danced across the cockpit controls. LCD screens flashed to life, and she worked down a checklist of pre-flight inspections, flipping switches and pulling levers while she answered her own questions aloud.

Reed checked his watch, then glanced through a porthole window at the airport office. He didn't see anyone. Not yet. But as each minute slipped by, the sky grew brighter. He couldn't count on his pilot to get the job done if the sheriff's department turned up.

"We flying into downtown Port-au-Prince?" Corbyn called over her shoulder.

Reed tore his gaze away from the window, digging for his phone. "No. The earthquake smashed the airport. The UN has set up a temporary landing strip on a mountain plateau above the city."

"You got an airport code?"

"Right here." Reed handed her the phone. Corbyn went back to work punching at the dash, humming to herself like a happy housewife baking cookies. Reed looked out the window again, edgy nervousness building in his gut.

"Nashville departure, King Air November One Niner Two Lima Tango on the ground at Leiper's Fork, Kilo Lima Papa Foxtrot." Corbyn's voice was bright and chipper as she spoke into the mic. "Requesting IFR clearance to Port-au-Prince, Mike Tango Papa Charlie. Number one ready for departure holding short runway two-four."

A long pause. Corbyn continued to hum, fingers dancing across the iPad. After a moment she adjusted the mic and spoke again.

"November One Niner Two Lima Tango cleared as filed, heading one five zero entering controlled airspace. Maintain six thousand expecting two four zero, two seven two five, squawking two seven three five, hold for release."

Corbyn shot a thumbs-up over her shoulder, and rotated in the seat. Reed settled into his own seat and found the belt, somehow feeling the need to strap himself in.

A moment later the left engine coughed and turned over, then spun to life. The right joined it, aluminum blades shooting light vibrations through the fuselage as Corbyn worked the pedals to taxi the aircraft away from the hangars.

It was bright enough now to see the entire runway. Over a thousand yards of smooth concrete, painted with white dashes. The King Air roared as Corbyn touched the power levers. The grin on her face broadened to something approaching maniacal, and a dry chuckle left her throat.

"Big girl's got juice, doesn't she?"

Reed noted her flashing eyes, and the first hint of uncertainty rippled through his mind.

"You said you've flown this plane before, right?"

Corbyn shrugged. "Once or twice."

Reed shot Turk a look. Turk was already glaring at him. Corbyn put the brakes on and eased the power levers up. Both engines howled, the tremors through the fuselage leveling out to a steady buzz. Reed pressed himself into the seat, feet jammed against the rear wall of the cockpit for bracing as Corbyn continued to chatter into the microphone, still talking with Nashville departure.

Closing his eyes, he blocked out the whir of the airplane and thought instead of Banks. Of that horrible flash of fire. Of the gut-wrenching loss.

It was enough to focus him on the mission ahead, blocking out any concerns for Corbyn's piloting expertise.

"Montgomery," Turk's voice laced with tension from the seat next to him. Reed's gaze followed Turk's jutting chin.

There was now a white SUV parked just outside the door airport office. A tall guy in an official-looking uniform stood next to it, shielding his eyes as he stared at the King Air. Reed couldn't be sure, but he thought the man's face was twisted into a frown.

"Hey, Brit!" Reed called. "Let's go."

"Easy on, Yank. There's a procedure here."

More poking of the screen and jabbering into the mic. Reed watched the man in the uniform still shielding his eyes. He looked back to Corbyn, but Corbyn didn't seem to hear anything. The man in the uniform got back into his SUV, and the headlights flashed.

"That's it," Turk muttered.

Reed extracted himself from the seat. He bulled forward over the pile of bags and cases and into the cockpit. Before Corbyn could object he was in the righthand seat, twisting to block her view of the office building and the oncoming SUV.

Reed grabbed a headset off the dash and pulled it over his ears. The mic touched his lips, and he flicked the power on.

"Show me what you got, hotshot."

The devilish grin danced across Corbyn's face again. She reached for the power levers and pushed them up another half an inch. Then her left hand twisted, and the brakes released with a lurch.

The nose dropped. The engines roared. The white SUV slid to a stop alongside the runway, and the guy got out. Reed saw a smile on his face, and moderate relief washed across his mind. The guy waved cheerily, and the King Air raced by, roaring toward the end of the strip as Corbyn cut loose with a girlish squeal. Left hand on the yoke, right hand on the power levers. Both feet on the pedals. The nose bounced once, and Reed's stomach flipped.

"Easy there, girl," Corbyn chirped. "She's frisky!"

Then they raced skyward as Corbyn whooped like a drunk girl in a Nashville honky-tonk.

Pointed south. Headed for Haiti.

40

Deputy Director Dr. Sarah Aimes arrived at work at six a.m. sharp. She'd barely slept the night before. How could she when she'd been cut out of the loop at the eleventh hour of the White House's SOCOM strike into Syria?

It was O'Brien who sidelined her, and he wasn't shy about his rationale. Aimes still had doubts. Gnawing feelings deep in her gut that something about this mission didn't feel right. It was too easy. Too simple. Aimes didn't trust easy, and she didn't believe in simple. In her experience, anything worth knowing in the intelligence world was bought with time, sweat, and blood. Usually a lot of each.

Why Fakir Ibrahim, the supposed leader of the so-called Islamic Caliphate Army, would expose himself on the internet in the first place was beyond her. Why he would then return to the very place the CIA had last located him at the house outside of Damascus was more than a mystery. It felt like a riddle.

And where there was a riddle, there must be a riddler. A conniving SOB pulling strings and manipulating smoke among mirrors. Exactly the same kind of person who would craft a terrorist strike followed by a storm of automated phone calls the NSA was still struggling to back trace.

It was more than terror—it was a *game*, and Aimes couldn't shake the feeling that the house in Damascus was just another move on the chessboard.

Not checkmate for the CIA.

More like a trap.

Dropping her briefcase in her office, Aimes sucked down half her mug of coffee while her computer booted up. She was just loading her email when she suddenly realized how quiet the executive floor of the George Bush Center for Intelligence had fallen. Craning her neck over the monitor to look through her narrow window, she noted the receptionists avoiding her gaze. One of her aides was busy on a phone, hunched low in her seat. Two other lesser deputies were missing from their glass-faced offices.

Something felt wrong. Eerily so. Where was everybody?

Aimes's gaze flicked back to her email, and her stomach dropped. She didn't need to open the storm of messages. The subject lines were enough.

Smacking the lock button on her keyboard, she barreled out of the office. A left turn down the hall brought her to O'Brien's executive suite. The door was shut, the blinds drawn. O'Brien's secretary stood as she approached, lifting a hand.

"Ma'am, Director O'Brien asked not to be disturbed—"

Aimes ignored her, crashing right by. She plowed through the door, bursting into a darkened office populated by half a dozen men and women in sweat-stained dress shirts. All the blinds were lowered, blocking out the morning sun, but she spotted O'Brien immediately. He leaned over a conference table covered in computers, documents, and coffee mugs. Behind him a projector displayed satellite imagery. It was a desert scene. Sand and empty wasteland.

And one very large, very black crater, right in the middle.

Aimes's stomach fell someplace into her shoes, and the dread that kept her up all night descended over her like a wave. Crushing and dark. Absolute defeat. She couldn't look away from the screen.

"What happened?" she demanded.

O'Brien's gaze snapped up from the end of the table. His bald head glistened with sweat. His glasses were smudged. He looked like he hadn't slept either.

"Get out," Aimes snapped. "All of you."

Nobody moved. Deputy directors and aides exchanged uncertain glances. Technically, Aimes outranked them all, but O'Brien was the boss. It was a rock and a hard place.

Aimes put her foot on the rock, slamming her coffee mug onto the conference table. *"Out!"*

It was rare for Aimes to raise her voice. She doubted whether anybody in the room had ever heard her do so. But the black crater on the projector demanded answers, and she wasn't in the mood to ask nicely. Slowly, the deputies and aides filed out. The door shut. O'Brien still hadn't spoken. He stood at the end of the table, lips pressed into a tight line as Aimes just stared at the screen.

Her voice flatlined. "What happened?"

O'Brien tore his glasses off and threw them onto the table. Pinched fingers wiped sweat from his eyes. He swallowed coffee.

"What does it look like?" he snapped.

Aimes raised a finger at the screen. "Damascus?"

O'Brien crashed into a chair, face lifted to the screen. Lips pinched. He tapped his glasses against the mahogany tabletop and didn't answer.

Aimes closed around the table, pulling a chair back across from her boss. She sat without comment, waiting for O'Brien to put the inevitable into words. But the director didn't speak. He just stared at the crater.

"How many?" Aimes's voice was little better than a growl.

"What?"

"How many *men* did we kill?" Aimes knew her tone was sliding dangerously close to belligerent, but it was all she could do not to scream. O'Brien had shut her *out* of the Situation Room. Benched her, right in the middle of the most critical counterterrorism operation since bin Laden. As deputy director of operations, it was her job to manage missions precisely like this. Her responsibility. A mandate she took extremely seriously.

She should have fought him. Should have pushed back. Should have—

"Eleven," O'Brien's teeth flashed. Aimes's chin dropped. She couldn't help it. She felt every one of those bodies descending on her shoulders.

She shook her head. "I *told* you."

"Excuse me?" O'Brien's tone turned petulant.

"I *told* you we weren't ready. I told you I needed more time. That the intel wasn't verified. That this was too easy!"

"Watch your tone, Deputy," O'Brien snapped. "You forget your place."

"My place is director of operations, Mr. Director. My place is to *manage* these sorts of missions. You sidelined me. You deliberately cut me out of mission prep, and now *eleven soldiers*—"

"Are dead!" O'Brien shouted, flying to his feet. The chair rocketed back behind him. "You don't think I know that? You don't think I've got the White House breathing down my neck?"

Aimes snorted in disbelief. "Eleven lives, Mr. Director. I would think the White House should be the least of your concerns."

O'Brian snatched his glasses off the table and marched to his desk. A keyboard rattled. O'Brien placed his hand on a biometric security device to gain access. Aimes met him at the desk.

She was still furious, but the anger would have to wait. The terrorists were still out there. There was work to be done.

"I'll reach out to our field offices in the region," she said. "If Damascus was a trap, somebody had to be there to set it. We might get lucky."

O'Brien shook his head. "Negative. You're done with this investigation. Mitch Costner is taking over until further notice."

"*What?*" Aimes couldn't believe her ears. "I'm the *deputy director of operations.* You can't just put me in a closet."

"I can and I will." O'Brien's face snapped over the computer screen. "You're on thin ice, Aimes. Like you said yourself, missions like these are *your* responsibility." He jabbed a thumb at the screen. Aimes looked that way. Her mouth fell open.

"You can't be serious . . ."

O'Brien didn't blink.

"I wasn't even *here*," Aimes said. "I told you—"

"To green light the mission," O'Brien interrupted. "That your intel was rock solid. That this was a sure thing."

"That's a *lie.*"

O'Brien shrugged. "We'll see what the oversight committee thinks. Although, I have to warn you . . . congressmen tend to side with the guy who buys their breakfast twice a month."

O'Brien folded his arms. His face was cherry red. The owl eyes had turned dark. Aimes had never seen him this way before.

He looked like an animal.

"It's a boys' world, Aimes. No matter who is in the White House. You'd be wise to accept that."

Aimes inhaled sharply, so caught off guard she didn't know what to say. Then she laughed, because O'Brien's statement was that absurd. "A boys' world, huh? You'd be lost as a ball in high weeds without me, Mr. Director, and you know it."

"That may be," O'Brien said. "Which is why your directorate will be co-managed by Mitch Costner until further notice. Consider yourself on *soft* suspension. One more step out of line, one *word* of any of this to anyone . . . and you're more than done. I'll freaking *bury* you."

O'Brien's voice turned absolutely lethal, so cold Aimes couldn't help but swallow. His wide, animal eyes locked on her from across the table, and her palms turned sticky.

"Am I understood, Deputy?" O'Brian snarled.

Aimes chin lifted. She fought to keep her fingers from closing into a fist. Every biological impulse in her brain screamed at her to launch herself across the desk.

But she didn't. She forced a single nod.

"Excellent," O'Brian chirped. The murderous tone evaporated in an instant from his voice, and he pivoted to his computer. "Support Mitch in whatever he needs. You'll take no further operational action without direct approval from his office and from mine. And you'll make absolutely no statements to the media, or to anybody outside this building. Clear?"

"Crystal," Aimes snapped.

"Great. You're dismissed."

Aimes marched out of the room without another word, her cheeks red-hot. She felt all eyes on her as she proceeded to her office, but she didn't care who saw her, or what office rumors might be triggered. She didn't care about O'Brien's threats or what became of her career.

Eleven people were dead, and the director of America's chief intelligence service wanted to cover it up. Aimes had pushed ethical boundaries before, but this wouldn't be one of them.

O'Brien had barked up the wrong tree.

41

"I have him!" Wolfgang slammed a hand against the tabletop. It rattled, dumping a paper cup of water over the floor alongside a tangle of phone chargers and empty soup cans. "I *have him!*"

Ivan appeared from around the stack of oil drums, still shirtless. Still glistening like a wet grizzly bear.

"Calm down, Amerikos! What have you got?"

"Melnyk. I've got Melnyk!"

"How?" Ivan set a coffee mug on the counter. Whatever swirled in the bottom wasn't coffee—it wasn't even brown. Wolfgang barely noticed. He jabbed a finger at the screen.

"The *cell phone*."

"What about it?"

"I could only crack one of them. The one with the emails. I think Melnyk cycles through phones pretty quickly, using pseudonyms to register each one."

"This is not unusual," Ivan said.

"No. It's not. But it seems our Ukrainian friend has a particular affinity for Apple products."

"So?"

"So, Apple products require the use of an Apple ID. An email address and password associated with Apple's core service package. You can't use an iPhone without one."

"So?" Ivan repeated.

"So one of those core service features is an app called Find My. You know, so you don't lose all your fancy gadgets. It tracks every item, including devices newly registered with your Apple ID."

Ivan snorted. "This is amateur, Amerikos. A man like Melnyk would not enable such a feature."

"It's automatic," Wolfgang said.

"He would turn it off."

Wolfgang grinned. "You'd think, wouldn't you?"

He lifted the cell phone from the table, pivoting the device toward Ivan. The screen displayed a map with a list of devices fifteen or twenty units strong stacked beneath. Most were listed as *location not found*, but two displayed active beacons on the map.

One in a warehouse outside of Pleven, Bulgaria. The one in Wolfgang's hand.

And the other? A brand new device, only recently associated with the Apple ID in question. Pinging out of Thessaloniki, Greece. Barely three hundred miles south.

"No." Ivan shook his head. "Melnyk is smarter than this."

"Not smart enough to pick a better passcode than six zeroes, apparently. There's smart and then there's cocky, Ivan. A guy like Melnyk, trouncing around Eastern Europe for nearly two decades, selling to the highest bidder, a plethora of politicians and Interpol officers bought and paid for . . . he's cocky. He's *real* cocky. And it's gonna cost him."

Wolfgang pocketed the phone and left the rest of the electronics. He grabbed his pistol belt and bag on his way past the cots, headed for the door.

"Wait," Ivan said. "Where are you going?"

"Where do you think? To Thessaloniki. You coming or not?"

Ivan scratched the underside of a tangled beard. He belched, and even from fifteen feet away, Wolfgang smelled vodka. Ivan drained the mug, then flipped it over his shoulder. It shattered on the concrete.

"Why not?" The big Russian sighed. "Gyros are good with vodka."

Wolfgang's lips parted in another grin. He turned for the door. "Get your shirt. I'm not riding all the way to Greece next to a sweaty Sasquatch."

42

The flight from Middle Tennessee to the island of Hispaniola took just under five hours, with only one change in time zones. After the momentary stress of a rowdy takeoff, Reed returned to the back seat and settled again into the plush leather chair while Corbyn busied herself in the cockpit, flipping through the plane's operator's manual and experimenting with every bell and whistle on the complex dash. She had the King Air on autopilot, speaking occasionally into the mic on her headset as they traveled over Georgia, eventually orbiting around the outskirts of Jacksonville, Florida before streaking out over the Atlantic. They crossed the Bahamas, a myriad of little islands all marked by white sand beaches and crystal water, beautiful in the mid-morning sun. Reed gazed lifelessly out the window as though he were watching paint dry.

He couldn't sleep. He couldn't get comfortable in the tight compartment. He couldn't calm the dark energy in his mind.

He could only think of Banks. The blast. And more than anything, he thought of his daughter.

Reed still wasn't sure why he believed his murdered child to be a girl. The doctors said there was no way to be sure. Maybe Reed assumed daughter by default, because thinking of his child in terms of gender felt more personal, and he already had a son.

Or maybe it was something deeper than that. Something more instinctual. Maybe Reed felt a connection with his unborn child that defied science or logic. Maybe he knew she was a girl just because he *knew*, and there didn't need to be a reason.

Banks hadn't told him she was pregnant, but she had to have known. He wondered what distance between them could have driven her to keep the secret. He'd worked hard since their move to Nashville to support her dreams and give her the home she deserved. Sure, he was tired a lot. Grumpy sometimes. He probably drank too much. But surely she was going to tell him. Maybe after the festival. Maybe she was worried that if he knew she was pregnant, he wouldn't have wanted her out in so much heat and stress.

Would he have stopped her? Could he have known?

Hello Prosecutor.

The text message flashed across his mind again, and for the ten thousandth time since it first arrived, he wondered. How could the terrorists possibly have known? Who could have told them? And why?

It put an edge in his resolve to choke them out with his bare hands. This wasn't just a casualty of circumstance or bad luck. These people *knew* him. They wanted him to hurt. But they had no idea what kind of hornet's nest they had kicked. With his knife buried in their guts, slowly ripping upward and shredding nerves by the thousands, he would learn the truth.

They would tell him how they knew.

"Hey, Yank!" Corbyn peeled one half of her headset off as she pivoted around the pilot's chair. "I'm chatting with authorities in Haiti. They say the airfields are closed except for aid-related flights . . . what do you want to do?"

"Tell them we're an aid flight," Reed said, as though the answer were obvious. "Tell them we're delivering heavy antibiotics to combat a cholera outbreak in Port-au-Prince."

"There's cholera in Port-au-Prince?" Corbyn's voice rose, just a notch.

Reed simply shrugged, still watching the deep blue water far below. Corbyn returned to her radio and rattled off the message. It worked, just like Reed knew it would. Whoever was managing air traffic control in Haiti wouldn't have details of every aid shipment. It wouldn't be possible. In a chaotic place like earthquake-shattered Haiti, emergency shipments would be racing in every direction. Trucks and helicopters, small boats and massive freighters. Containers painted in a trio of languages. Barrels with undefined contents, moving through so-called "security" checkpoints with only passing inspection.

The ATC couldn't be expected to verify every incoming aircraft. Just like port authority couldn't be expected to search every outgoing ship, and what each container actually contained.

It was what made earthquake-shattered Haiti the perfect portal to smuggle a terror-calibrated weapon right into the heart of the United States.

Reed leaned across the aisle and poked Turk. The big man sat up with a snort, wiping drool off his chin with the back of one hand.

"Final approach," Reed said.

The King Air banked, engines whirring as the nose dipped toward the field of clouds below. Reed unzipped the coffin-sized duffle bag on the floor and went to work with his chest rig. Heavy armor plates manufactured by AR500 slid into the slots, front and back, dragging the rig down over his shoulders. Straps cinched into place to pull those plates tight over his chest and back. Magazine slots were double-stacked with PMAGs. Reed was strapping the P226 to his hip when Turk breathed a subdued curse.

"What?"

Turk was fixated on the window. "Dude, you've got to see this."

Reed packed into the seat behind Turk and pressed his face close to the window. The King Air banked left, wing dipping as Corbyn began her approach. The wingtip dropped below Reed's line of sight, and the breath caught in his lungs.

The city of Port-au-Prince rested ten thousand feet below, stretching around the notched base of the Port-au-Prince Bay, packed tight all the way to the water. Gray concrete buildings and tin-roofed shantytowns, as far as the eye could see. Tens of thousands of structures.

All smashed. Completely. Reduced to collapsed rubble and twisted metal, piles of blocks and broken concrete slabs strewn over the streets and into the water. Black smoke rose from garbage piles, faint little dots moving here and there like ants. Chaos and carnage reached straight to the horizon —worse than Reed could have imagined by an order of magnitude.

And then the bay. Dozens of cargo freighters packed into the obliterated port, anchored close to temporary floating piers covered with sprawling white tents with the United Nations logo printed across the top. The ant-like dots that Reed had noted around the garbage piles and amid the rubble gathered into a tight, dark wave near the tents. Tens of thousands. No, *hundreds* of thousands of people, all surging desperately toward the incoming aid. Like a swarm of bees, moving slowly in a wave. Pressing in beneath the blistering wrath of the summer sun. Roasting alive. Desperate for any relief to be found.

Reed withdrew from the window and looked to Turk. He saw the pain in the bigger man's face. He thought about Iraq, Kurdistan, and North Korea. Venezuela, just a few months prior. All the places the two of them had traveled to witness some of the worst human suffering on the planet.

It never got easier to watch, and Reed hoped it never would. He never wanted to become the type of man who couldn't empathize with the pain of others.

"Buckle up, gents!"

The seatbelt light flashed on above Corbyn's cockpit door. Reed braced his feet against the floor, but he didn't reach for the seatbelt, buckling his gun belt instead. The SIG rode alongside his thigh, one in the pipe and fifteen in the mag. He thought again of the swarming chaos below him— those hundreds of thousands of bodies near the port. For the first time since hatching the harebrained scheme to fly to Haiti, he realized just how impossible this task would be.

How was he *possibly* going to locate a handful of unknown actors amid the writhing, starving bodies of nearly a million refugees?

The King Air's nose dipped another ten degrees, and Reed looked through the windshield to see an airstrip stretched out two miles ahead, closing rapidly.

And he knew—it didn't matter what the answer was. He simply had to do it.

43

Maggie awoke tangled in sweaty sheets, hungover and groggy. Even though the drapes were closed, she could see the hot sunlight cutting through the cracks, racing across the hardwood floor.

Her head thundered. Her stomach convulsed. She felt like she was going to vomit, but she didn't. She just lay very still and focused on the ceiling, waiting for her eyes to focus.

They didn't focus. The nausea didn't abate, either. She twisted her face to the nightstand to check the clock, and found it was nearly ten a.m. Panic overcame the fog in her mind, and her vision finally focused. She fought to wrench herself upright, then gagged on a dry throat. Her stomach convulsed, and she rolled to the right side of the bed.

A trash can waited there. She only just managed to align her face with its mouth before spewing bile and Blanton's like a geyser. She choked and heaved, then vomited again. When she sat up, her head spun so violently she wanted to collapse.

She didn't. She braced herself on the bed and pivoted toward the door as the knob clicked.

"One moment ple—"

O'Dell appeared before she could complete the sentence. His broad shoulders were housed beneath the tight black fabric of a fresh suit. A silver tray rested in one hand, a glass of water and a small pile of multicolored pills riding it.

"Good morning, ma'am."

The hint of a sarcastic lilt crept into O'Dell's Cajun drawl. Maggie wanted to punch him, but she was too embarrassed at the trails of bile dripping down her chin to say anything. She flushed red-hot and looked quickly away, using the corner of the sheet to scrub her face. O'Dell set the tray on the table next to her and settled directly into the wing-backed chair situated alongside it. He went to work sorting the pills, pushing the water glass toward her without comment.

Maggie drank half of it. The flavor of acidic bile remained behind her teeth.

"Get any sleep?" O'Dell's tone softened. He scooped two yellow capsules off the tray and extended his hand. Maggie shook her head.

"Tylenol. Extra strength."

"No can do. I already spoke with the White House physician. It seems acetaminophen is incompatible with your existing drug habit."

Maggie shot him the bird. She didn't mind the joke—the assortment of daily medications she was forced to consume to aid her liver recovery certainly qualified as a drug habit. She just minded the headache, which was moving rapidly from uncomfortable to unbearable.

She took the yellow capsules and washed them down, avoiding O'Dell's gaze as she fixated on the bedside rug. She wasn't thinking about medication anymore. Or even the headache, bad as it was.

She was thinking again about that flash of white fire. The dirt exploding into the sky. The unthinkable dread that descended over her mind the moment she realized what had happened.

"What's the update?" Maggie didn't need to clarify what she was asking. O'Dell's position as White House advisor was a flimsy cover for their fly-by-night romance, but he took the job seriously. He kept up with the activities of her administration with lethal efficiency, befriending Easterling and becoming something of a deputy chief of staff.

"I told Jill you were under the weather," O'Dell said. "She's managing the fallout in Syria. Thus far we've kept it under wraps, but you'll have to make a statement eventually. General Yellin phoned an hour ago to report a full evac. They got the survivors out. And the bodies."

Maggie didn't answer. Her mind felt like it was locked in a mud bog. Everything moved in slow motion, even basic thoughts requiring superhuman focus.

What's wrong with me? I can't do this. I can't be like this.

"If you need a few more hours . . ." O'Dell's voice turned gentle. She met his gaze, and saw concern there. Kindness. No anger at all.

And that confused her. Hadn't he just abandoned her for five days with barely any communication? Hadn't there been a barrier between them that she couldn't ram through, no matter how hard she tried? Hadn't he refused to share her room, refused to open up about his own life, refused . . .

No. She didn't have time for this. Not right now. She had a job to do, and she had been asleep at the wheel long enough.

"I'm good," Maggie said. The blaze of the headache blurred her vision, but she ignored it. She felt the anger now. Not just at the blast and whoever had authored it. But at herself. She had to get it together.

"Just give me twenty minutes. Have Jill meet me at breakfast. You too. We're going to hammer this out."

A glint of respect passed across O'Dell's gaze. He rose and started for the door.

"Eggs and bacon?" he asked.

"Biscuits," Maggie said. "And a ton of gravy."

By the time Maggie finished a cold shower and dressed in a simple pantsuit, Easterling, O'Dell, and her breakfast were waiting in the presidential dining room. She didn't have an appetite. It was all she could do not to puke as she pulled her hair back into a trademark ponytail. But she knew if she ate, the nausea would subside. The brain fog would recede.

And then she could *work.*

"Good morning, ma'am." Easterling rose as Maggie pushed through the doors. Her chief of staff wore a customary pencil skirt and conservative blouse, narrow glasses pressed close to her mousy face. Maggie glanced at the clock on the wall and saw the hour hand closing rapidly on eleven o'clock. Morning was almost gone.

"Good morning, Jill. Have you eaten?"

"Yes, ma'am."

"Great. Go ahead and brief me while I get something down."

A plate of fresh, flaky biscuits greeted her, paired with sausage gravy and black coffee. Plenty of all three. Maggie shoveled the food down, barley tasting as Easterling outlined details of JSOC's rescue operation. They'd flown more choppers into Syria, blowing up the wrecked Black Hawks that lay alongside the bombed house. There was no definite intel yet on what had caused the explosion, but it didn't really matter. Clearly, the house had been a trap from the start, and their target had never actually been there. He had simply *appeared* to be there.

Based on the split second of video feed captured from inside the house's garage just before the bomb went off, the CIA had developed a working theory on how the trick had been conducted. The garage had been fitted with a wall-to-wall video screen. The man who looked like Fakir Ibrahim had been a video recording.

And we actually fell for that. Maggie could hardly believe it.

"What's the latest from O'Brien?" she said, chopping her biscuit into bite-sized chunks.

"They're working," Easterling said. "That's all he'll say."

Maggie raised an eyebrow. "They're *working?*"

Jill shrugged.

"I'm gonna need more than that. I need names. People. A plan of action. Call his office and let him know I expect a full brief by five o'clock this afternoon. His agency fell for a *video screen.* He's gonna make it right."

Easterling nodded, but she didn't answer. Maggie raised an eyebrow. "What?"

"I don't disagree with your assessment," Easterling said, carefully. "But we green lighted the mission. When news breaks, we're going to need a statement."

The aching pit returned to Maggie's stomach. She nodded slowly. "I know."

"You should suppress the details," O'Dell said. "There's no need for them to break. JSOC will have cleaned up the blast site. The Lebanese know we flew a mission, but the Syrians don't. There's nobody to tell the story, outside of the White House."

"You're saying I should lie?" Maggie said.

"Of course not. I'm saying you've got bigger fish to fry. Have the DOD withhold death notices for now. General Yellin can instruct the Navy to isolate the survivors. Just long enough to buy you a couple days. The focus right now should be intel. Getting on top of this thing."

Maggie looked to Easterling. Her chief of staff sipped green tea, pushing the glasses up her nose. Taking her time. Then she nodded.

"I agree. This isn't the fire you want to fight. Your next press conference should address the ongoing search for Ibrahim."

"I can't *conduct* a search without intelligence," Maggie snapped.

"I'll pay Langley a visit," O'Dell said. "Pour some gas on the fire."

"Tread carefully," Easterling warned. "Victor O'Brien is a proud man with a lot of power."

"Power vested in him by *me*," Maggie said.

"True. But playing that card may not advance his investigation. I recommend a light touch. Results should be our only focus."

"I'll be careful," O'Dell said.

Maggie turned back to Easterling. "Talk to me about this press conference. What did you have in mind?"

Easterling wasn't listening. The teacup rested on its saucer, her attention consumed by the smartphone in her grasp. As Maggie watched the rosy cheeks of her chief of staff washed pale, and then Easterling muttered a curse. She slammed the phone down and dug into the leather briefcase resting on the floor next to her.

"What is it?" Maggie said.

"CNN." Easterling's squeaky voice rose an octave as she produced a MacBook. She flipped the computer open and navigated directly for her email. Maggie recognized the name of one of Easterling's staff on the message. The email contained only a link.

Easterling smacked the trackpad and pivoted the screen. O'Dell moved quickly to join them. The connection loaded with lightning speed over secure White House Wi-Fi.

And then Maggie's heart plummeted to the floor.

Video: U.S. Military Operation in Syria Goes Down in Flames, ICA Claims Credit.

"Are you kidding me?" Maggie slammed the coffee mug against the table. "What the *hell*, Jill? Who freaking talked?"

Easterling scrolled. She reached a video, frozen into a blurry still frame. Even under distortion, Maggie recognized the deep gray of a pre-dawn sky. The empty expanse of the desert.

The sinking feeling in her chest opened into a canyon.

No.

Easterling hit the play button. The video shuddered under a blast of wind. Easterling turned the volume up and the thunder of helicopter rotors blasted through the speakers. Silhouetted against that gray sky, Maggie saw a black, blocky shape. Then the choppers appeared, racing in like diving dragons. Two jet-black Army MH-60Ms. They hit the desert floor on opposing corners of the house, and the men bailed out. Nearly two dozen of them.

Maggie closed her mouth. She wanted to look away. She wanted to tell Easterling to stop the video. She didn't want to live through this again.

But she said nothing. She watched as a portion of SEAL Team 8 disappeared inside, while a dozen others secured the perimeter. Watched as the choppers remained stationary, rotors still thundering, ready to take off at a moment's notice.

And then the blast. As sudden and horrifying as the moment Maggie witnessed it on the drone footage. The house went up in fire, the choppers were hurtled to the ground, the perimeter team flailed through the air and struck the desert floor.

Tears clouded Maggie's eyes, but she didn't look away as the camera rotated. She saw a face. Wrapped in both a turban and a scarf, exposing only dark eyes that seemed to sneer directly at her. The roar of the blast was still fading, but up close and personal, the voice was clear.

"Allahu Akbar! *Death to the infidels.*"

Maggie's hand shot across the table and she slammed the MacBook closed. Nobody moved. Nobody said anything. Maggie clamped her eyes closed and breathed hard. The headache still pounded, but she barely noticed anymore.

All she could see were those dark, hateful eyes. That angry, biting declaration spoken in accented but flawless English.

Death to the infidels.

"Get the cabinet on the phone," Maggie said. "Every one of them. Whatever they're doing, I want them to stop. *Everybody* works the terror case. State, Defense, Homeland, Interior. I want the freaking CDC hunting terrorists. Do you hear me? *Everybody on deck.*"

"Yes, ma'am. Of course."

"Where's Jordan?"

"Still in Tennessee. I think Nashville, today. Meeting with Governor Jeffreys."

"Get him back here, ASAP. I need him running the investigation."

"I'll make the call."

Easterling left the table, already drawing a cell phone. Maggie pivoted to O'Dell.

"Forget the light touch. I want your boot on O'Brien's neck. If he can't find these people, I'll find someone who can."

O'Dell was already on his feet. He gave Maggie's shoulder a squeeze as he turned for the door.

"I'll phone you with answers."

Maggie's gaze fell on the laptop. The heat in her blood turned up a notch, and she finished the coffee in a single gulp before turning for the door.

She was done being sorry. Done being sad.

There was one infidel in Washington who wouldn't accept death.

44

Corbyn parked the King Air on a cracked concrete pad alongside the mountaintop airport, and Reed and Turk hit the tarmac. The moment his boots struck Haitian soil, two things hit Reed in the face like boxing gloves.

The first was the heat—brutal heat, infinitely worse than Tennessee. It was tropical, thick like a cloud. Humidity so dense it suffocated him. The broiling sun hung almost directly overhead, working to turn this place into a griddle.

The second was the chaos. He could feel the tone of desperation and disorder even from just outside the airplane. Across the airstrip Reed saw a pair of U.S. Air Force C-130 Hercules cargo planes baking in the glare, soldiers of a half dozen different nationalities clad in United Nations uniforms working to offload crates of dry goods and emergency stores. Reed could tell by the markings on the pallets that they were military supplies—probably MREs and medical kits for the United Nations peace-keepers stationed here, but none of the order and precision Reed was accustomed to expecting from a U.S. Air Force supply drop was present. What he saw instead was anarchy. A spilled pallet here, a forklift buried in the mud at the edge of the tarmac there. A woman shouting into a bullhorn while the soldiers blatantly ignored her. Air Force pilots seated on crates beneath one of the Hercules's sprawling wings. Other aircraft gathered in jumbles wherever parking space could be found.

It was mania. And they weren't even close to downtown Port-au-Prince.

"Bloody hell, it's hot out here!" Corbyn dropped out of the King Air with a pair of aviator sunglasses pressed over her face, already panting and scrubbing sweat away. Reed looked past her, scanning the airfield for something other than an aircraft. He located a small motor pool near a collection of mobile offices—Toyota SUVs, deuce-and-a-half military trucks that appeared two or three decades outdated, and a small number of Humvees painted in dingy white with UN inscribed on their doors.

Reed jabbed his chin toward the Humvees, and Turk nodded. "I'll get the gear."

"What now?" Corbyn asked.

"Find fuel," Reed said. "Then stand by."

Corbyn grunted. "For how long?"

Reed accepted a rifle case and a backpack from Turk. "For as long as it takes."

"That's not reassuring," Corbyn said.

"You having second thoughts, Top Gun?"

Corbyn shot Reed the finger. He tossed her a radio handset from the backpack.

"We'll keep you posted. Be ready to go wheels up, quickly."

Reed shouldered the backpack and scooped up the rifle case. Turk fell in beside him, and the two of them set off across the tarmac, boots squishing over the boiling hot asphalt. None of the UN soldiers who gathered around the fuel depot or the C-130s paid them any attention. Reed thought that the bulletproof vests and sidearms probably helped with that. There was no order in this place. No central command. No detachment of Marine MPs to regulate access or secure the area.

This wasn't a military base. It didn't even feel like a civilian airport. It had more in common with a war zone—and Reed knew all about war zones. As he and Turk crossed the center of the airstrip and made a beeline for the Humvees, a rush of déjà vu joined the waves of heat. Suddenly, the tall green foliage crowding in on the outskirts of the airfield vanished, replaced by glistening horizon. Flat desert, as far as the eye could see. The humidity relaxed, but the heat redoubled. Reed was no longer wearing a black chest rig and dark gray cargo pants. He wore desert ACUs with a Marine M40A5 rifle riding across his chest.

The man beside him was no longer just his best friend. He was his spotter, a heavy pack on his back, his face so blasted by the Iraqi sun it looked leathery.

Reed blinked hard, shaking his head to clear it. The wave of memories evaporated, and he realized he'd stopped in the middle of the airstrip. Turk looked over one shoulder.

"You good, man?"

Reed thought of Banks again. Imagining the thunderclap bomb blast brought his mind back into focus.

"Yeah. Let's move."

They marched into the motor pool as though they owned the place. Turk moved instinctively toward the third Humvee in line, which was exactly the one Reed would have picked. Of the five options, it appeared the least battered by heavy use and abuse. More important than the appearance of its paint, however, were the fresh tires and thick plate glass blocking the windows—bulletproof glass.

Always a good idea.

Turk took the driver's side automatically. Reed threw the rifle case into the back seat and slammed the heavy door.

"Asshole incoming," Turk warned.

Reed looked over his shoulder. The woman with the bullhorn was marching toward them, a hundred yards and closing. One arm waving, her jaw twitching in exaggerated jerks as she shouted at them to stop.

Reed took shotgun, reaching over his shoulder to drag one of the M4A1s from the rifle case into his lap. He loaded a mag and chambered a round while Turk flicked the Humvee's starter switch from ENG STOP to RUN. In the brutal Caribbean heat it took only a moment for the orange WAIT light to click off, signaling that the diesel's glow plugs were hot enough to start the motor.

The woman with the bullhorn was barely twenty yards away now, face flushing red with furry. She lifted the bullhorn.

"You can't take that! That is property of United Nations—"

Her German accent was cut short by the rumbling roar of the diesel. Turk released the handbrake and shifted the transmission selector to drive. He punched the accelerator just as the woman moved for the front bumper, as though she were going to stop three tons of solid steel with her petite body. The Humvee roared right past her, and Reed shot her the peace sign.

"Freaking Germans," Turk laughed.

Reed rested the rifle between his knees, double-checking the MRO optic for a bright green reticle. Then he scooped the cell phone from his pocket and glanced at the signal bars. He was running on international service—maybe emergency service erected to cover the UN's disaster response.

Checking his messages, he found only one text. It was from Lucy.

At the hospital. Doctor's report optimistic. Godspeed, Prosecutor.

Reed squinted at the text, again thrown off by the last line. What was up with Lucy? This didn't sound like her.

Shrugging the thought away, his mind switched to Banks. Bandaged up, still fighting for life. The thought poured fuel on his mental fire, and he opened his navigation app to scope out the busted roads leading down from the mountain into the shattered city.

A five-mile trek. It was time to work.

45

After so many years spent in so many warzones, Reed should have been prepared for what Haiti had to offer. He wasn't. Nothing could prepare him for the unique brand of Caribbean misery. As Turk powered the Humvee away from the airfield and onto an asphalt highway crisscrossed by deep ruts and collapsed sections of roadway, Reed began to wonder if even the heavy, all-terrain tires and four-wheel drive of the beast would be enough to bring them into the city.

The entire *country* was broken. Not just the people, not just the buildings. The land itself was torn and rent, with gullies ripping through the mountainsides and valleys where smooth meadows had lain only a few weeks prior. Piles of rocks and dirt heaped into mounds where the deluge of an avalanche had been cleared away by military bulldozers. Wrecked vehicles slid into ditches, homes collapsed into heaps of broken timbers and tumbled blocks, and water gushed freely through the roadbed where rivers blocked by the wrath of the earthquake had found new routes out of the mountains.

It was indescribable—and they hadn't even reached the outskirts of the city. Reed braced himself against the door while Turk kept both hands wrapped around the steering wheel, wrestling the Humvee down the mountain road. They passed other military vehicles on occasion, along with small farms lying in defeated heaps while indigenous villagers picked through the mess to locate what could be salvaged.

Reed's heart thudded as he surveyed the damage, but when Turk reached a curve in the road and Reed's window opened to a view of Haiti's capital city, several hundred yards below, the breath froze in his throat.

It was so much worse than it appeared from the air. The gray swaths of shanty homes that had looked like fields of concrete and tin from ten thousand feet now appeared as complex tangles of decimated homes and blocked streets. It was as though a giant had walked through the city pushing a steamroller. *Everything* was flattened, many multistory structures pancaking in on themselves as they simply imploded toward the ground. The air was thick with haze—a mix of concrete dust and humidity blanketing the city as tens of thousands of displaced residents wandered like zombies through the maze.

Reed saw rescue workers, also. UN soldiers and volunteers gathered around heavy trucks and more Humvees. As Turk hit the brakes and Reed stared, he noted a knot of blue-helmeted peacekeepers gathered around what looked to be a collapsed school. Before he could turn away, two of them rose from the fallen blocks. They carried a limp child, no more than ten years old. Tiny and black as night.

It was only then that Reed noted the other black dots speckling the cityscape, and the buzzards in the sky circling over the field of dead.

It wasn't just a disaster zone. It was a graveyard.

"My lord . . ." Turk whispered.

Reed looked away from the bulletproof window. He wiped sweat from his mouth and swallowed hard to suppress the surge of bile building in his stomach. Then he waved two fingers forward.

It was the only thing to do.

Neither of them spoke as they crossed out of the mountains and into the basin where Port-au-Prince lay. Here, many of the roads were cleared. Forest green and desert tan military bulldozers—several of them stamped with the black letters of the United States Army or Marine Corps—worked amid the concrete haze to push the rubble into manageable piles along a makeshift highway. Other vehicles joined the mix, moving in convoys toward the outskirts, carrying aid workers and the seal of the United

Nations. As Turk pointed the Humvee downtown, Reed was confronted again with the overwhelming reality of finding a person he didn't know in a hellscape like this.

He'd developed a theory since speaking to Wolfgang, the concept of a terrorist organization using the chaos of the Haitian disaster as a portal to smuggle a weapon into the United States. It seemed more plausible than ever now that his boots were on the ground. Other than the German woman with the bullhorn, nobody had accosted or even given a second glance to the UN Humvee and its pair of American occupants. Why should they? There were UN vehicles everywhere.

Vehicles painted with UN letters and logos, at least.

It would be a cakewalk to offload a crate full of Russian land mines in a place like this, drop it onto a truck with UN spray-painted on the side, and then smuggle it back aboard an "empty" freighter headed to the United States. There was no possible way to prevent it from happening.

It left Reed wondering what else the Islamic Caliphate Army may have worked to bring back into the United States. Their opportunities would only be limited by what sort of WMD they could get their hands on. In chaos this extreme, they could sneak a freaking nuke into the U.S., and nobody would be the wiser until a mushroom cloud blocked out the horizon.

It all made perfect sense, but none of that logic solved the core of his problem.

How do I find these people?

Not for the first time in his long career of engaging terrorists and psychopaths, Reed put himself in the boots of his enemy. He pictured the problems at hand, and asked himself what *he* would need if he were smuggling a fresh wave of death into the Land of the Free.

He'd need a place to set up shop, probably. A place to repackage the cargo before smuggling it aboard a shipping container. In a field of carnage this dramatic, there might be plenty of places to work in secret. Which of them would be most advantageous?

The answer was obvious. Someplace near the port. Accessible by road. Close enough to the mountains of red, blue, green, and yellow shipping containers Reed saw stacked alongside the docks several miles away.

"We've got to get to the water," Reed said, pointing. "Take the next right."

The maneuver was easier said than done. The next right was blocked by rubble, as were the two turns that followed it. Turk kept his foot on the gas and his head low, looking beneath the Humvee's roofline to scope out the path ahead. There were more vehicles now—dozens more. The makeshift highway was crowded. The demolished shantytown they passed through reminded Reed of the barrios of Venezuela—tight clusters of blockhouses built on top of each other, clinging to the mountainside. Except those blockhouses had collapsed. Falling over each other and crushing downward all the way to the valley floor.

The stench of death was unbearable. As bad as war, but different. The usual undertone of seared flesh from fire bombs and missile strikes was missing. Instead, the odor saturating the air was simply that of rotting flesh. Tens of thousands of pounds of it. Swarms of flies clouded around the obliterated neighborhood and descended upon the body trucks as aid workers fought to load the corpses.

When Reed glanced left, he saw tears in Turk's eyes. His own vision blurred, and he scrubbed the back of one hand over his face.

The road ahead split into a Y, and Turk piloted the Humvee right. The path ahead led downward, deeper into the city. They crossed out of the shantytown and into a slightly wealthier district of faded apartments and low-rise business complexes. Some of these had sustained the wrath of the earthquake better than the makeshift shacks of the shantytown. Windows were shattered and covered over by tarps. Some roofs slouched. A few homes had caved in. But mostly the road was clear, and Turk was able to accelerate.

Reed kept his eye on the horizon, marking the multicolored shipping containers. They fell out of sight now and then, but he kept Turk pointed in that general direction. As they closed another block, Reed leaned toward the door. Before he could speak, Turk beat him to the punch.

"You hear that?"

Reed pushed his door open two inches. As the heavy steel opened a gap into the cityscape beyond, his first instinct was confirmed. His heart rate accelerated.

Gunfire. Fully automatic, a couple thousand yards away. Reed recognized the rolling *clack-clack-clack* of an AK-47 accompanied by distant screams.

He slammed the door shut just as Turk hit the brakes. Directly ahead, a roadblock crossed the full width of the street—sawhorses and two UN Humvees guarded by peacekeepers with American flags on their arms. As they ground to a stop, one of the peacekeepers stepped forward with a gentle lift of his hand.

"Oh goodie," Turk muttered. Reed slid his M4 down to conceal it behind the Humvee's transmission shroud. He kept his shoulders loose as Turk opened his door and offered the peacekeeper a smile. Reed recognized sergeant patches on the man's arm. He was U.S. Army.

"Sorry guys, road's closed." The sergeant's voice was calm, carrying an accent someplace between Baltimore and Philadelphia.

Reed made eye contact beneath the roofline. "We're trying to reach the port. Is there another way?"

The sergeant shook his head. "Not through this neighborhood. Can't you hear that?"

"The gunfire?" Turk said.

"G9," the sergeant said simply, spitting tobacco juice sideways across the busted road.

"G9?" Turk asked. "What's that?"

"Are you serious?"

Neither Reed nor Turk answered. The guy laughed.

"Welcome to the party, guys. G9 is a federation of Haitian gangs. They basically run this place—or they did, before the earthquake. Now we're telling them to move over. They aren't playing along."

"How bad is it?" Reed asked.

"Been fighting them all week," the sergeant said with a shrug. "We've got most of them corralled near Cité Soleil, but they keep launching lightning strikes against aid caravans and relief shipments. This place is hell, bro. Part of me wonders why we even bother."

Reed looked toward the sound of gunfire, still clacking for a mile or so away. It reminded him of Iraq, of a time when he'd asked himself the same question. *Why do we bother?*

"We still gotta get to the port," Reed said. "What do you recommend?"

The sergeant squinted, his jaw working as he chewed the tobacco. Reed didn't understand how he could chew anything while the awful reek of death hung so thick on the air.

"You guys with the UN?" the sergeant said, the first hint of suspicion crossing into his tone. His finger dropped to just above the trigger guard of the M4 hanging across his chest. Out of the corner of his eye Reed noted two other peacekeepers fanning out to either side of the Humvee, weapons held muzzle-down but at the ready. These guys weren't amateurs.

"No," Reed said. "We're private security. Got some VIPs headed to the port later this week. People from the Vatican, here to bless the city or something. The UN loaned us the Humvee."

It was a plausible explanation. The sergeant bought it with a tired shake of his head.

"Blessing, huh? I'd like to be blessed with a half dozen Apache gunships and twice as many Bradleys."

"I hear you."

The sergeant stepped back and motioned up the hill. "Back the way you came, half a mile. Take a right at the collapsed school building. It's painted baby blue. Then ride all the way to the bottom of the mountain. You can reach the port that way. *Don't* turn north."

Turk shot him a salute. The sergeant returned it with a flick of his hand. The Humvee rumbled and tires ground as they pivoted in place on the road. Then they were pointed back the way they had come again, a fresh wave of the sickening death smell carrying dread with it.

"We might have bit off more than we can chew," Turk muttered.

But we're gonna chew it, Reed thought. *No other option.*

46

The drive from Bulgaria to the Greek district of Central Macedonia consumed six hours, conducted on a winding highway that led straight through the heart of the Rhodope Mountains. Seated in the leather-clad passenger seat of a Mercedes SUV, Wolfgang might have been impressed by the towering ridges and sweeping valleys, had he been able to see them. It had taken Ivan the better part of the afternoon to secure the Mercedes, meaning that it was full dark long before they reached the Greek border.

Wolfgang wasn't interested in topography, anyway. He sat with Melnyk's captured phone in his lap, monitoring the location of the Ukrainian arms dealer's latest Apple device. That location had moved a few times over the afternoon. It started in what Wolfgang judged to be an apartment building north of the city, after which Melnyk relocated to a restaurant near the harbor before the beacon ventured half a mile offshore. A boat, perhaps?

"For a guy I nearly shot, he's playing it cool," Wolfgang muttered.

Ivan sat slouched behind the wheel, his grizzly bear forearms consuming the armrests as he piloted them southward. Wolfgang wasn't sure what the mph equivalent of 150 kilometers per hour was, but he knew it was fast. The Russian drove like he owned the country.

"These arms dealers are like old west cowboys," Ivan said. "They go where they please, do as they please. Interpol is scared of them."

He'll be scared of me *before the night's out*, Wolfgang thought.

They reached the Greek border at the Bulgarian village of Kulata, and breezed through the crossing station with all the ease of passing through a toll booth. A brief passport check was conducted. A friendly Greek woman with a bright smile thanked them for visiting her country.

Then Ivan punched the gas and the mountain elevation bled away as they approached the Greek coast. Wolfgang first saw Thessaloniki as little more than a bright yellow dot perched at the foot of the mountains with the Aegean Sea spread out beyond. As they reached the city's outskirts they were joined by thickening late night traffic and Ivan was forced to slow while the buildings around them grew ever taller.

Thessaloniki couldn't have been more different from Pleven. Gone were the muddy little cottages and rolling farmland. Northern Greece was all mountains and high rises, apartment towers built tightly together amid narrow, winding streets. Wolfgang remembered reading somewhere that this was an old city, but it didn't look it. The buildings were updated, the streets marked with modern lights and signs and paved in asphalt. Aesthetically unique, with lots of white stone and apartment towers painted in yellow and blue pastels, but structurally the city wasn't all that different from any other metropolis in Western Europe.

"He's still offshore," Wolfgang said, consulting the phone.

"Yacht," Ivan said with a disgusted shake of his head. "These people have no imagination."

Ivan used the Mercedes's built-in navigation software to lead them right down to the water, where a wide concrete walkway stretched for miles along the Thessaloniki Bay, lined by parks and cafes, small sailboat marinas and occasional high rises with water-facing balconies.

The picturesque beauty was lost on Wolfgang as Ivan parked the SUV and both men stepped out. Warm air flavored with salt and the smell of the sea greeted them. Wolfgang followed the sidewalks down to the waterfront, still cupping the phone in one hand. Melnyk hadn't moved in over an hour. The dot remained just offshore, southwest of the city. Wolfgang lifted a hand over his eyes to block out the glare of the streetlights.

He saw nothing. Only deep black water stretching to the horizon.

"He could be farther south," Ivan said. "The beacon could have lost signal."

Wolfgang zoomed the map out. He traced the Greek shoreline along either side of the Thessaloniki Bay, out to the Gulf of Thessaloniki, and finally to the Aegean Sea. For much of that twenty-mile stretch, the furthest a yacht could sail from shore was no more than three or four miles.

Melnyk hadn't escaped cell tower range. Not yet.

"He's there," Wolfgang said. "We need a boat."

Ivan found a powerboat rental company two kilometers up the bay. They were closed for the evening, but the owner was still busy scrubbing dirt and salt away from one of a trio of bowrider speed boats with outboard engines. They weren't very big, twenty or twenty-two feet.

Big enough.

Ivan approached the guy with an easygoing smile, addressing him first in French, then pivoting to English. The guy knew a little. Enough to rent boats to cash-flush American tourists, anyway. He explained that he was closed. Ivan produced a wad of American currency, slowly counting out hundred-dollar bills. When he reached six hundred, the guy flashed a smile.

He had just reopened.

Wolfgang slung his backpack into a speedboat and dropped in. The rental guy stuck a hose in the tank and topped them off. Ivan made small talk, still pretending to be French. By the time they finally got the motor started and pivoted toward open water, another half hour had passed. Ivan took the wheel and punched the accelerator. The bow reached for the sky as dark water flashed by. The vessel wasn't fast.

So long as Melnyk didn't move, that wouldn't matter.

"What's with the French?" Wolfgang shouted over the wind.

Ivan grunted. "Europeans don't like Russians. They mistrust us. Nobody fears the French."

That brought a dull smile to Wolfgang's lips, but he couldn't resist a jab. "You look about as French as I look Japanese."

"That is where your almighty dollar comes in. Enough Benjamins, and I *am* Japanese."

Wolfgang redirected his attention to the phone. Melnyk still hadn't moved. He was anchored just south of a little spit of land shooting westward from the Greek coast. There was a town there called Angelochori. The best Wolfgang could tell, the yacht lay about a mile offshore. If Ivan approached the yacht from the seaward side, the vessel would be silhouetted by the lights of the town, but the little speedboat would remain almost invisible. Just a black dot on a black body of water.

Wolfgang marked the spot with his finger, and Ivan nodded his understanding. The bow of the speedboat turned in a wide arc, tacking first westward before pivoting east for Angelochori. After another fifteen minutes of steady cruising, Ivan backed the throttle down, and Wolfgang dug into his pack for a pair of Vortex binoculars.

The horizon was perfectly dark on all sides except for a bright yellow dot right in the middle—the town. Wolfgang steadied himself in the bow of the boat and focused the binoculars. Ivan churned closer. Five minutes passed, and then Wolfgang finally saw it.

"There. One o'clock, two thousand yards."

Ivan took the binoculars and briefly inspected the horizon.

"I see it," he said, rotating the bow left, but keeping the throttle scaled back. Wolfgang monitored the location, holding up a fist when the distance was cut in half. Ivan killed the motor this time, and the boat rocked gently in the surge of its own wake.

Wolfgang could see the yacht clearly. It was a big one—no less than a hundred feet, and multi-decked. The light came from a window in the rear salon. A Panamanian flag draped from the stern, and the vessel tugged gently at an anchor chain. He couldn't see any people. He couldn't make out the name on the stern.

But there was a swim platform, with a ladder disappearing into the Greek water like a welcome mat.

Wolfgang returned to the duffel bag. There had been little time to properly prepare for a marine mission after leaving Bulgaria. Ivan had stopped briefly in Sofia on the drive down, but the landlocked Bulgarian capital wasn't known for its water sports, and the best gear they could find was a cheap pair of swim goggles and an even cheaper pair of fins that didn't really fit.

Wolfgang went to work strapping them on anyway, affixing the APC submachine gun to his chest with a two-point sling and cinching it tight using a quick-release adjustment. The weapon wouldn't move while he swam, but with a tug of the strap it would be ready for action. He left his Glock 20 in the bag, but kept the G29 tucked into his prosthetic calf.

Two extra mags for the APC in his belt. A Streamlight Polytac flashlight and a folding Benchmade Claymore. Too much weight, probably. But he was unwilling to deploy into a completely unknown environment with anything less.

Wolfgang stood in the stern and ran his hands through his hair. It was getting long again—almost down to his shoulders. A stark departure from the clean cut, carefully manicured style he maintained previously, the long hair was yet another reminder of how much had changed.

And how little he cared.

"Get me within three hundred yards," Wolfgang said. "I can swim that far."

Ivan stood still in the middle of the little speedboat, binoculars almost invisible inside his massive hands as he surveyed the yacht. Wolfgang waited another ten seconds, then punched him in the arm.

"Hey. Let's go."

Ivan lowered the binoculars. "I have bad feeling, Amerikos. I do not know about this."

"Know about what?" Wolfgang demanded.

Ivan gestured to the yacht. "All of this. The yacht, the big city. This is not an ideal place to hide for a man like Melnyk."

"He's not hiding. You said so yourself—he's a cowboy. He's not afraid."

"This is still true. But it is also true that he is not stupid. Why would he leave the location on his phone?"

Wolfgang shrugged. "How should I know? It's an automated feature. He forgot to turn it off. Are you seriously losing your stomach, right now? We just drove six freaking hours—"

Ivan held up a hand. "Take a *breath*, Amerikos. You wear me out."

The big Russian chewed his lip, still studying the yacht. Then he looked pointedly at Wolfgang's prosthetic leg, carbon fiber visible where an ankle should have been. He raised an eyebrow.

"I can swim," Wolfgang snapped, answering the obvious challenge. "Just get me close enough, and be ready to haul this sack of crap back to land."

Another protracted pause. Then a long sigh.

"Okay. But don't blame me if that thing goes up in flames and you are fish food."

47

The Aegean Sea

Ivan kept the throttle low and the resulting decibels to a minimum as they closed on the yacht. They approached from downwind, further assisting their stealth as the rumble of the motor was carried out to sea, away from Melnyk's pleasure cruiser.

Wolfgang double-checked all of his gear before sitting on the portside gunwales of the motorboat and flexing his foot inside the left fin. His right fin would be considerably less maneuverable, but that shouldn't matter. Wolfgang had swam laps at the YMCA in Buffalo. He knew he could keep himself afloat. Maybe not forever, but for a couple hundred yards he should manage. He was in excellent cardiac condition. The seas were calm. The tide was level.

Child's play.

At just inside three hundred yards, Ivan killed the motor. The wind was steady, and once the outboard went silent Wolfgang could hear gentle noises from the yacht's salon. Soft music, and laughter. The pop of a champagne cork.

"He isn't alone," Ivan said.

Wolfgang ignored him, sliding the goggles into place. They didn't cover his nose, but they didn't need to. He'd need to tilt his head for oxygen anyway. He did wish he had earplugs. Whenever Wolfgang swam, he always seemed to get water in his ears.

"There may be women," Ivan said, his voice trailing off.

Wolfgang tugged on the APC, ensuring it was firmly locked into place. Then he worked his hips backward across the gunwales until his butt hung over the water.

"Amerikos," Ivan said, his voice dropping a notch.

"*What?*"

"Be careful."

Wolfgang paused, taken off guard by the comment. He wasn't sure what to say, so he simply nodded. Then he placed one hand over his face, pinching off his nose. Sucked a deep breath through his teeth.

And flipped backward.

The water was warm. It closed around Wolfgang's head and shoulders like a gentle blanket. He dropped five or six feet beneath the surface, then rotated easily onto his stomach and stretched out with both hands. The light carbon fiber of his prosthetic kicked easily as he moved his thigh. His good leg felt strangely heavy, but it delivered more drive as he reached the surface and rotated his face to inhale.

He could see the yacht, a dark outline against a blackened sky. One hand scooped out, then the other. The goggles blocked the salty surge of the black water. Wolfgang's heart thumped evenly and he stretched forward, keeping his legs beneath the surface. Minimizing any splashing as the yards shrank slowly away.

He was halfway to the yacht before he knew he had dramatically miscalculated. Not about the distance—it was under three hundred yards. He had miscalculated his own physical endurance. The harder he stretched, the more his muscles burned. He found himself raising his face more frequently, sucking down more air. His heart beat faster and his shoulders burned.

He wasn't going to make it. Not at this pace. Wolfgang slowed and allowed himself to tread water whenever a gentle wave washed over him. Progress decreased to a crawl. The APC dragged against his shoulders like a leaden anchor. The belt held him down.

But Wolfgang kept going. Twenty minutes later, he finally orbited to the rear of the yacht and placed a hand on the swim ladder. He struggled not to gasp as he tread water behind the boat, listening carefully for any noises from the stern—footsteps, breathing. Low conversation or the puff of lungs on a cigarette.

He only heard gentle music—some kind of opera, he thought, paired with the occasional clink of glasses, and a woman's voice speaking something other than English. Greek, maybe.

Wolfgang didn't like the idea of innocent third parties caught in the crossfire—especially women. He'd never relished attacking women. It had been one of his rules as a contract killer. Ever since he watched his father beat his mother into a bloody pulp, he swore he would never be that man. No matter the cost.

But he couldn't help who was on the boat. He could only manage the outcome.

Wolfgang double-checked the APC, then slowly loosened the strap. He put one foot on the bottom rung of the ladder and eased upward. His clothes drained water, and he took his time. When he risked a glimpse onto the stern, he found only empty sunbathing chairs strapped to the deck.

No people.

Wolfgang rotated onto the platform and further released tension on the strap. The APC was fully deployed, now. He flicked the safety off. Checked the lockup on the mag.

Then he unstrapped the fins and allowed them to drop into the sea. He rose to his feet and stepped over the low stern of the craft, past a name spelled in gold letters beneath the Panamanian flag.

PRINCESS OF DANUBE

More like the warlord of Danube, Wolfgang thought. He navigated to an open back door. The salon ahead was paved in teak wood, glistening with polish. Silver rails ran along the walls below opulent works of art hung there. It looked more like a mansion than a yacht.

Wolfgang ignored the paintings. He smelled cigar smoke, faint but persistent. He eased through the door with the APC pressed into his shoulder, finger hovering over the trigger. The red reticle of the Aimpoint Micro T-2 glowed softly just beneath his line of sight.

Wolfgang took another two steps inside. Wet feet padded against the floor. He kept his breathing low. The music was much louder now, as was that soft female voice. The woman hadn't stopped speaking since Wolfgang had reached the boat.

Ahead, the hallway broke out into the salon. He saw leather couches and a wet bar with a granite countertop. A TV glowed to his right. He smelled salt air from the open window.

Two more steps, then he reached the end of the hall. Wolfgang pressed his back against the lefthand side of the hall and pivoted right, sweeping the APC toward the voice.

He saw no one. An empty couch with decorative pillows arranged across it. A cigar resting in an ashtray, smoldering softly. The woman's voice continued, but he couldn't see her.

Then he saw the speaker. A little Bluetooth thing, resting on the floor alongside the couch. Both the music and the voice flowed from it, followed by the pop of a champagne bottle. A man's laugh.

Wolfgang's heart thumped and he pivoted left—toward the next hallway. The APC rose and his finger dropped.

Then cold steel pressed against the base of his neck, and his body went rigid. The odor of cigar smoke intensified as clouds of it wafted around his face. And then a laugh.

"Welcome to Greece, my friend. So glad you could join us."

The voice was heavily accented—Eastern European of some sort, but Wolfgang assumed Ukrainian, because he assumed the identity of the speaker. He relaxed his body and released the APC, raising both hands. Hot rage rushed through his chest like a tsunami, but he didn't allow it to overcome him.

He remained loose as another man appeared from the hallway to the berths, and a third appeared from behind the wet bar. Both dressed in simple black clothes, both wielding MP5 submachine guns. Wolfgang recognized their faces from the warehouse in Rousse. He gritted his teeth.

"Search him," the voice behind him said.

One man closed in. The other stood back with his MP5 at the ready. Cold hands swept Wolfgang, tearing away the APC and the belt loaded with his flashlight, knife, and extra magazines. The hands continued beneath his shirt and down each leg. The searching man grunted, and said something in another language—Ukrainian, Wolfgang assumed.

The man with his gun pressed to Wolfgang's neck laughed. "You have fake leg? This is surprise. You move well for a gimp."

The searcher stood, tossing the mass of Wolfgang's gear onto a couch. Then the pistol prodded him in the neck.

"Won't you please sit, my gimpy friend?"

Wolfgang stumbled to the couch with the speaker next to it. The music still played. The woman still laughed.

Wolfgang sat facing his captor. He was unsurprised to find Oleksiy Melnyk looking back at him. In the flesh, a cigar clamped between his teeth, the scorpion tattoo on his neck glistening with a sheen of sweat. The weapon he pointed at Wolfgang was a nickel-plated 1911 chambered in gaping .45 caliber, such a cliché for a man of Melnyk's profession that Wolfgang almost laughed.

Melnyk kept his finger over the trigger, cocking his head. Studying Wolfgang. Thinking.

"You are American, no?"

Wolfgang didn't answer. Melnyk took a seat on the opposing couch next to Wolfgang's pile of sodden gear. He withdrew the cigar and exhaled smoke through his nose. A bona fide badass. Wolfgang wanted to blow his nuts off.

"You know, you cost me quite a lot of embarrassment in Rousse," Melnyk said. "Not so much money, this is easy to make. But reputation . . . reliability. These are things that take time to build, and are easily lost. My customers depend on me to deliver. To be reliable."

"My apologies," Wolfgang said, tone dripping with sarcasm.

Melnyk smiled. "Twenty years I have worked in the arms trade. Two long decades. In the early years, it was easy. It was like your Wild West back then. So many arms and ammunitions to be pirated from old Soviet Union. So many conflicts around the globe to sell to. I was like Robin Hood, yes? Steal from the rich, *arm the poor!* Ha."

Wolfgang squinted. "You're blending metaphors, Melnyk. Dumb it down for me."

Melnyk waved the cigar. "Yes, of course. I forget. You are dumb American. So, the point is this. Those were old days. These are new days. Business is more complicated. But for a man like me—a man with all this?" Melnyk waved his hand around the salon. "*Nobody* messes with me. I am now the Sheriff of Nothingham. Even governments are afraid. I am . . . invincible."

Wolfgang smirked. Melnyk cocked his head.

"This is funny to you?"

"It's Nottingham," Wolfgang said. "The Sheriff of *Nottingham*. But maybe your version is better."

Melnyk sank his teeth into the cigar. He leaned forward. "The point is this, you American prick. You are first one to interrupt my enterprises in these many years. You make grave mistake. I should have already blown your brains out. But a man like me, I have my weaknesses. One of them is curiosity. I am curious why you are here. I leave Find My iPhone on so that you would come. And now you have. So . . ."

Melnyk gestured to his men. One approached from Wolfgang's right, a fist full of zip ties clutched in one hand. The other accessed a closet and produced a tool bag. Wolfgang saw pliers, cable cutters, and a blowtorch.

He laughed, shaking his head slowly. "Wow. You really are one big fat cliché, aren't you?"

"Cliché?" Melnyk cocked his head.

"You have no imagination," Wolfgang clarified. "You're just a thug with too much money and not enough sense."

"I have sense enough to catch you!"

"But not sense enough to remember the boat driver."

"The what?"

Melnyk's question was cut short by the racing surge of an outboard motor. Wolfgang had heard it coming from two hundred yards away. Running soft and low, just a grumbling sound drifting in through the window directly behind him.

Melnyk and his men hadn't heard it. They'd been too busy posturing from the other side of the salon, the boat motor distorted by the continued music playing from the speaker. But the moment the sound drifted to Wolfgang's left, toward the stern of the yacht, he knew what was coming.

A roar of engine. A racing surge barely fifty yards away, closing fast.

Melnyk pivoted in that direction, leading with the nickel-plated 1911. Like it would do any good.

Ivan ran the powerboat right into the swim platform. The bow rocketed out of the water and broke across the yacht's stern as the momentum of the craft sent it hurtling toward the salon door. The yacht shook like an earthquake. Teak wood and fiberglass splintered. Glass shattered. Both of Melnyk's goons fell, scrambling for their weapons.

And Wolfgang reached for his prosthetic leg. He yanked his pant leg up. His right hand found the hidden compartment. The spring-loaded door snapped open even as the bow of the powerboat stopped in the mouth of the hallway. Wolfgang's fingers closed around the G29 and he pulled it free.

The first goon took two bullets to the chest and went down like a tree. Wolfgang hit his feet and pivoted left. The second guy's head detonated like a watermelon, spraying brains and blood over an art piece on the wall.

Melnyk's face washed with panic as he rotated toward Wolfgang. He raised the 1911.

He was much too slow. Wolfgang shot him in the kneecap, blasting the joint into a thousand tiny fragments and sending sudden, racing pain ripping into Melnyk's skull. The arms dealer dropped the 1911 and shrieked. He reached for his leg.

Wolfgang caught him by the throat and pinned him against the couch. The G29 found his temple, and Wolfgang rested a finger over the trigger.

"Now, Sheriff. We're going to have a little chat about what you've been up to in *Nothingham*."

48

Reed and Turk found the baby blue school, pancaked down on itself as though a giant had stepped on it. They turned right to merge into traffic headed toward the core of the city, and then progress slowed to a crawl.

There were *dozens* of heavy vehicles all moving toward the port—mostly empty trucks headed for a refill on relief supplies. The roads were still busted, rough paths bulldozed to allow snaking access around the rubble. Sometimes that path led off-road altogether, which might have been okay, but an hour into the drive it started raining.

Hard.

Sheets of water beat against the hood of the UN Humvee, running down the bulletproof windows and turning the already baking hot interior into a sauna. Turk kept his foot on the gas, punching where necessary to crash through bogs full of thigh-deep ruts.

Reed felt like he was in a video game. The carnage around them was too extreme for reality. It felt like a caricature of itself.

"We're never going to find anything in this soup," Turk muttered.

Reed had thought the same thing, but he wasn't ready to raise the white flag yet. They'd flown this far, committing a handful of felonies along the way. But more than that, every time he blocked out the turmoil around them he saw Banks. He saw the blast. He thought of red-hot Russian shrapnel tearing through her pelvis.

Tearing through his daughter.

"Keep it moving," he said.

It was late afternoon by the time they finally reached the port, and the rain hadn't stopped. It saturated Reed's clothes and filled the nylon compartments of his chest rig as he dropped out of the heavy vehicle and straight into hell.

The port was a war zone in every sense of the word. Throngs of blue-helmeted UN peacekeepers dressed in the uniforms of half a dozen militaries closed around a row of open metal containers, rifles pointed outward toward a wave of desperate Haitians. Containers of relief supplies—what looked like dry foods and camping tents—were being offloaded from the containers onto trucks to be dispersed across the city. The knot of three or four hundred rain-soaked Haitians must have missed the memo. They screamed and pushed against the low chain-link fence that barricaded the loading zone, arms up. Voices wailing at the sky.

More video game footage.

Reed had seen plenty of desperation in the Middle East, but nothing rivaled the sheer mass of ebony-skinned bodies, many of them emaciated and barely standing as they scrambled over one another for the truck. The rain worsened everything. The spot the Haitians had crowded into was thick with mud, and they floundered in it. While Reed watched, an old woman stumbled and two teenage boys scrambled right over her, driving her into the ground. A peacekeeper stepped in to help her, and caught a fist to the face. He stumbled back, and one of the teenagers grabbed for the AK-47 he wore across his chest. Two more peacekeepers stepped in. Somebody fired a rifle into the air.

Everybody screamed.

Reed spat rainwater from his mouth and turned back for the Humvee. Already his hair was dripping. Turk stood near the hood, watching the developing chaos in semi-disbelief, his M4 held at his side. Another peacekeeper appeared, a French flag sewn to the sleeve of his mottled green,

black, and tan uniform. Reed could see the rage in his mousy face long
before he opened his mouth to unleash it.

"You cannot park here!" the guy shouted. "You're blocking the trucks."

Reed barely glanced at the line of backed up deuce-and-a-halves buried
up to their axles in the disintegrating road. They weren't going anywhere in
a hurry.

"Who's in charge here?" Reed raised his voice to be heard over the chug
of diesel engines. The French guy held a hand to his ear.

"What?"

"Who's in charge?"

The peacekeeper pointed to a mobile office building resting on
cinderblocks two hundred yards away. Beyond it, an endless field of empty
shipping containers were stacked next to grinding cranes, multicolored
walls slick with rushing rainwater. A quick glance to the harbor confirmed
at least four freighters resting at anchor, and a fifth tied up at a temporary
floating dock.

Aide was pouring in by the billions of dollars, but it didn't seem to be
making much of a difference.

Reed left the French guy to deal with Turk, slinging his M4 over his
shoulder and marching for the command building. Thick mud sucked on
his boots, and the rain beating down on his bare head felt like it had been
microwaved on the way down, splashing hot against his exposed skin. For
the first time since leaving the Marine Corps, he actually missed his heavy
helmet.

Reed made it to the mobile building and reached for the doorknob. The
door opened as if by magic, and two men in USMC ACU uniforms barreled
out. Reed's quick eyes noted sergeant's and captain's patches, respectively.
Both men wore the baby blue helmets of the UN as they ran for a row of
offloading containers.

A third man appeared just behind them, bareheaded, also dressed in
USMC ACUs. A tight mustache ran across his upper lip, speckled with gray.
That mustache curled as he glowered at the devolving scene across the
dockside. Reed's gaze flicked down to his collar, noting a silver eagle
insignia. He was an O-6. A colonel.

Reed's hand lifted in a stiff salute, almost automatically. The colonel barely noticed him as he twisted to shut the door.

"You in charge here, Colonel?"

The guy stopped. His mustache dripped water as he surveyed Reed, his attention snagging on the uniform. Or, rather, the lack thereof.

"Who are you?"

"Montgomery, sir. I'm private security. I need a moment of your time."

The colonel turned back inside, grumbling darkly. "Of course you do."

Reed pushed through the open door without waiting for an invitation. The interior was just like any number of mobile combat command centers in the Middle East. Dusty DOD furniture, all outdated by two decades. A sagging floor and nothing on the walls. Dirt everywhere. Only one other person was present—another peacekeeper in a blue beret, a Canadian flag on her arm.

The colonel marched for a cooler and retrieved a bottle of water. He guzzled half before remembering that Reed stood behind him.

"You want a water?" he growled.

"No thank you."

The colonel found a seat with a weary sigh and mopped rain off his face. "Okay. What do you want?"

"I need to ask you about these containers," Reed said, gesturing generally toward the field of shipping containers lined alongside the doc.

"What about them?"

"I need to know what security measures are in place to prevent unauthorized cargo to be loaded onto returning aid ships. Who's in charge of that?"

The colonel snorted, shaking his head as he flicked the now empty water bottle toward a trash can. He missed. He didn't get up.

"Do I really have to answer that question, son?"

Reed pushed dark hair back over his scalp. It was just as hot inside the command center as anywhere else. Even beneath his saturated clothes, he could feel the sweat.

"I need to speak with whoever's in charge of reloading empty containers. I need to have a look at them."

"Why?"

"Because we're concerned about weapons being smuggled back into the United States via supposedly empty shipping containers. Specifically a crate load of Russian-built anti-personnel land mines."

Reed was deliberate in his use of the word *we*. He might be a lone wolf, but the colonel didn't need to know that.

"Who did you say you were?" the colonel asked, looking at him more closely.

"Security." Reed shrugged.

"Security for *who*?"

"A lot of people."

That bought him a long stare. Reed braced himself for an ID check, but a radio on the Canadian's desk crackled just then. The woman snatched it up and spoke into it. She wore a headset. Reed couldn't hear the answer.

The woman turned to the colonel.

"They want reinforcements at the containers. Civilians are choking off overwatch. They're worried about a gang attack."

The colonel snarled a curse and marched to a window. He held back the aluminum blinds and glowered outside.

"Radio McKnight. Have him send whoever he's got free."

"Yes, sir."

The colonel turned back to Reed with a disgusted shake of his head. "You come down here with a few billion dollars' worth of miracles, and they can't back up long enough to let you unload it."

"They're desperate," Reed said simply.

The colonel hesitated. Then he nodded. "That they are."

He gestured to the desk, and Reed approached. The colonel tore off a sheet of paper and wrote a name on it.

"I don't know anything about container security. That's under the jurisdiction of the Italians. They stack the containers over there until they run out of room, then they move a ship in to take them back on."

The colonel jabbed a finger over his shoulder. Then he handed Reed the torn-off paper slip. There was a name on it—some Italian name. Reed could barely read it.

"Where do the ships go from there?" Reed asked.

"Back to Savannah. To reload."

"They're not stopping midpoint to sweep the containers?"

The colonel snorted. "Are you serious? Look around you. This feel like a well-oiled operation to you?"

Reed didn't have time to answer. The Canadian's radio barked again, and the woman looked up from her desk, the color draining from her face. Her lips parted, but Reed knew what she was about to say long before she spoke.

He heard the pop and hiss—distant. More than a hundred yards, but audible through the beat of the rain. A sound he wouldn't forget if he lived to be a hundred.

"*RPG!*" Reed shouted. Then he drove himself forward, grabbing the Canadian by the collar and yanking her out of the chair as he landed chest-first against the colonel. Then rocket struck, and the whole building lifted off its mobile foundations with an ear-shattering blast.

49

Reed landed between the two soldiers as the flimsy metal walls ruptured and a storm of shrapnel whistled over their heads. Fire exploded to his left, and that ear immediately went deaf. Smoke and dust clouded the air, but already he felt rain on his neck. The rocket had struck near the roofline, blasting a Volkswagen-sized hole in the wall and sending shards of metal roof exploding into the sky.

Reed rolled over, choking and scrubbing his eyes free. The colonel coughed next to him, but the Canadian didn't move. Reed fumbled in the dark and found her arm.

It broke free of her body, blown away at the elbow. As the dust cleared he saw her face, and he knew she was dead. Her entire right side was laced with shards of the metal siding the building was clad in.

Like the blast of a land mine.

Reed fought to his feet. As he turned his right ear in the direction the rocket had flown, the rattling pop of gunfire broke through the ringing in his head. It was distorted by a blast of thunder and the continued pounding of rain, but his practiced ears picked out the rolling *clack-clack-clack* of AK-47s.

A lot of them.

"Stay here!" Reed shouted.

He swept the M4 beneath his arm and into his shoulder. His thumb found the safety. His eye found the green dot hovering inside the MRO. Then he was kicking through the door, back into the storm.

"Turk!"

"Over here!"

Reed traced his battle buddy's shout through a growing torrent of rain. Turk was dug in behind the Humvee, two USMC peacemakers crouched next to him as a storm of muzzle flash lit the rubble beyond the offloading shipping containers. Already the tight crowd of Haitian bodies had dispersed, but they left more than a few behind. Twisted in the mud, laced with bullet wounds. Two peacekeepers were dead. The rest dug in behind the containers, wielding French-made FAMAS assault rifles, but not returning fire.

Reed sprinted for the Humvee, sliding into cover behind the rear wheel just as another RPG tore through the air overhead. It struck the cabin of a parked deuce-and-a-half and detonated inside. Blood and shattered glass rained over the mud.

"What's going on?" Reed shouted over the ringing in his left ear. His headed still pounded from the blast. His chest rig was slick with the Canadian's blood.

"Haitian gangs!" That was the USMC captain. He wielded a SIG SAUER M18 sidearm, but no rifle. His companion—the sergeant clutching an M16 —lay on his stomach beneath the Humvee, aiming for the rubble and squeezing off slow, measured shots.

Just the way he was trained.

"They're coming for the aid," the captain continued. "We've been corralling them all week . . . some must have broken through."

Reed gritted his teeth. He popped around the rear bumper off the Humvee and pressed off a trio of shots. A tall Black man dug in behind a pile of toppled blocks with an AK took a round to the forehead and collapsed. Three more took his place, unleashing a storm of lead on the Humvee. Reed scrambled for cover again.

"I've got two, maybe three dozen on the ridge!" Reed shouted. "You guys got air support?"

The captain cursed. "What do you think?"

Turk scrambled through the mud, looking like a dog climbing out of a pit as he reached the hood of the Humvee and lifted his head for a look.

"RPG!"

All four of them hit the mud. The rocket whistled in, striking the dirt a couple yards short of the Humvee and detonating there. The sergeant let out a shriek and dropped his rifle. Reed scrambled back to his knees, semi-blinded by the rain. The water they knelt in was two inches deep now. It careened over the rutted ground, making it impossible to maintain strong footing.

He returned to the bumper and engaged the ridge—dumping a full magazine of green tips and dropping a trio of targets with head and chest shots before he ran dry.

"Changing mag!"

"I got you," Turk called.

Reed hit the mud behind the tire and swapped mags. His body was alive with adrenaline but his hands remained calm as he hit the bolt release. The Daniel Defense was as good as its price tag. The rifle was a tac driver inside three hundred yards.

Rocking to his right, Reed leaned under the Humvee to gain a sweeping view of the yard. A dozen bodies and twice as many wounded lay in the muddy basin where the Haitian refugees had swarmed only ten minutes prior. The French were still dug in behind the containers, their FAMAS rifles silent.

"Why aren't they shooting?" Reed demanded.

The captain swore again. "They're under standing orders not to engage unless mortally threatened."

"You don't call this mortal?"

"I'm not their boss!"

Reed looked beyond the containers to the endless rubble beyond. The tallest building standing couldn't be more than two stories. Bulldozed heaps of debris blocked his line of sight, leading as far inland as the base of the mountains. But crashing among those heaps, careening toward the offloading containers were a pair of heavy pickup trucks, their beds loaded with men wielding AK-47s. Amid the collapsed buildings further gunmen appeared like groundhogs, popping up to unleash short bursts of gunfire before vanishing again.

There were dozens. Maybe a hundred. The overwhelmed group of peacekeepers could never drive them back from a position of imperfect cover, even assuming the French deemed the situation mortal. The ground was against them.

Reed's gaze moved automatically up the sloping hillside, a quarter mile beyond the collapsed rubble of portside buildings, to a spot fifty or sixty feet above the containers. A spot with an open view of the unfolding chaos below.

It looked to be a church—or what was left of a church, anyway. Fallen walls and a collapsed roof. A position of high ground that spoke to his sniper soul.

"Hey!" Reed turned back to the captain. "You guys got an arms cache?"

The captain hesitated. His hand was wrapped around a radio, but nobody answered his calls. The only garbled responses he received were in another language. Italian, maybe.

"Arms depot!" Reed repeated. "Where is it?"

"Why?"

Reed ducked instinctively as another storm of fire pinged and ricocheted off the Humvee. The rounds were growing closer, as were the trucks.

"We're sitting ducks here! You need somebody in that church supplying cover fire. I need an M40 and two hundred rounds. Where are they?"

Another hesitation from the captain. Reed knew why.

"Force Recon sniper, 2nd Battalion. Three deployments. He was my spotter. You want our help or not?"

The captain's reluctance broke under the whoosh of yet another RPG, detonated inside the open mouth of a shipping container with an ear-shattering thunderclap.

He jerked his head toward the shattered command post. "This way, sniper."

50

The Marine weapons cache was little more than a miniature shipping container, lined by wooden crates and ammo cans. The weapon was an M40A6—a significant upgrade from the M40A5 Reed fought with in Iraq. Gone was the heavy fiberglass stock, replaced by a desert-tan modular system equipped with a folding stock, a bipod, and the same Schmidt & Bender M8541 optic Reed had used on his old A5.

A weapon of absolute judgment, in the right hands.

Turk grabbed a spotting scope on a tripod and a heavy can filled with loaded ten-round box magazines for the M40. Then they were off, rushing past the exploded command post and up the road. Gunfire from the shipping containers had redoubled in the past five minutes. The French had finally engaged, but they'd already given up too much ground to the closing gangsters. The two heavy pickup trucks were now rushing into the valley, rumbling right over the bodies of their slain countrymen as they moved to seize the aid shipments.

Reed took point, the M40 slung over his shoulder while his M4 remained at the ready. They tacked southward, away from the combat zone before circling left for the church. A muddy path opened the way for the first two hundred yards, but once Reed circled back for the high ground, he and Turk were forced to fight their way through the rubble. Collapsed blocks, sunken streets, and toppled light poles. The stench of rotting corpses had been somewhat reduced near the port, where the bodies had been removed to allow room for the aid workers to disperse supplies.

Now that stench returned. It sank into Reed's gut like a living thing, lacing his blood with a savage desire to overcome that he had only ever felt on the field of combat. A *kill or be killed* instinct. A primitive, irrefutable reality that if he didn't rise to face this evil, it would consume him.

Halfway up the hill Reed knew he was right about the building. It was a smashed church—a beautiful one, built with arches and decorative columns. The metal framework of a stained glass windowpane was still visible in what remained of the back wall—most of the glass gone, but a few fragments of orange and red clinging amid the bent and distorted iron. Just another brutal casualty of the earthquake's wrath.

"Lefthand wall," Reed said. "Alongside the columns!"

Turk followed him, dumping his gear and automatically sliding into a crouch while Reed descended into a makeshift shooting position. Prone was out of the question. The ground was a field of broken concrete and twisted rebar, fallen roof tiles and shattered church pews. The best Reed could manage was an awkward crouch, bipod braced against the bottom of a collapsed window frame. From that position he held a clear view of the port below, spread out at just under five hundred yards, the containers on his left, the surging Haitian gangsters to his right. A wide-open field of fire, well within the effective range of the M40.

"You want me to spot?" Turk called.

"Target rich," Reed replied. "Cover my six."

Turk turned his back to Reed, digging in behind a busted pew with his M4 at the ready. Reed slammed a loaded mag into the bottom of the rifle and worked the bolt. The scope covers flicked up. The safety clicked off.

And then the world went dark—tunneling out of reality. Closing off around him. In a split second the dust, the noise, even the relentless pounding of the rain ceased to matter. Reed lost himself in the scope. The vortex of crosshairs and mil dots consumed his attention and slowed time, just like it had thousands of times prior.

Absolute focus engulfed him. No outside noise. No thundering heart and thrashing desperation for survival. Only target acquired, target eliminated.

Reed breathed evenly. His finger found the trigger and he pivoted right. The surge of Haitian gangsters had now consumed the port. Half a dozen French peacekeepers lay dead. The interior of one shipping container burned. Two trucks raced for the final three containers, men wielding AKs firing into the air as they ground to a stop.

A target rich environment, indeed.

Reed pressed the trigger. The first guy went down with a tangerine-sized hole blown through his chest. The M40 was dead-on, as accurate as Reed could make it. His next target took a slug through the forehead. The third hit the ground with a geyser of blood surging from his neck, thrashing beneath the pound of the rain.

Reed worked the bolt with practiced ease, swapping the mag every ten rounds without removing his eye from the scope. Three hundred yards beneath him, the Marine captain dug in behind the Humvee, joined now by what remained of the French peacekeepers and a dozen riflemen wielding M4s. Both pickup trucks were stopped alongside the containers, sustaining an endless storm of small arms fire while the gangsters scrambled for cover. Reed rotated right, leaving the trucks to the peacekeepers while he orbited instead to the field of rubble beyond. The blink of hot red muzzle flash speckled the mounds of concrete and debris, unleashing automatic AK-47 fire on the peacekeeper's position. The rain beat down in sheets—even harder than before. So hard that Reed's view of his targets was blurred and obscured, some lying further than five hundred yards distant.

Reed remained relaxed. He rotated the elevation turret on the optic, using the mil dots to estimate distance and determine the correct number of clicks. It was complicated math, conducted quickly in his battle-hardened mind. A Haitian gangster rose above a rock and took a thirty-caliber slug to the face, flopping backward. Reed rammed a fresh cartridge into the chamber. His next shot skipped off the rubble, missing his target by mere inches. He worked the bolt and reacquired. Another gentle squeeze. The guy took the round right in his sternum, flailing as he tumbled from his perch and lost his rifle.

"Tangos at six! I got 'em."

Turk's shout was followed immediately by the thunder of his M4. Reed didn't break eye contact with his optic. It took time to find targets now. The gangsters were falling back, abandoning their trucks. Another UN Humvee had roared into position, the chugging thunder of a roof-mounted .50 BMG unleashing fresh wrath on behalf of the peacekeepers. Reed marked two more gangsters as they attempted last minute potshots at his position. They went down under targeted hits from the M40, rifles dropping to the ground while the last of their line descended into full retreat.

And then it was over. A flash of lightning was joined by a clap of thunder, marking a sudden ceasefire as though by divine intervention. Reed's shoulder relaxed, and he swept the battlefield one more time.

Dozens were dead—maybe a hundred. Peacekeepers, civilians, and a lot of Haitian gangsters. One truck smoked. Fire still belched from the burning supplies inside the lefthand container. The port looked as much like a war zone as ground zero of a natural disaster.

Humanity's worst impulses, on display.

Reed pulled the bolt and looked over his shoulder. Turk stood behind him, the M4 hanging in his arms, staring at the ground. Reed saw his face first—blackened by gun smoke, running slick with rain. But not just rain. Turk's eyes were rimmed red.

Reed fought his way to his feet, drawing the rifle with him. He pivoted toward the wrecked sanctuary of the church—and then he understood.

The tango at six o'clock lay spread-eagle across the floor, a fallen AK-47 resting on bloody concrete next to him, his chest riddled with a three-round burst from Turk's M4. He wore basketball shorts and a tank top. He was barefooted, and dark as midnight.

And he was no older than fourteen.

Reed's stomach twisted. He wiped rain from his forehead and scooped up his M4. Turk remained motionless, just staring at the kid.

"He never stood a chance," Turk said. "He just . . . ran right into me . . ."

Reed put a hand on his shoulder and squeezed once. Already the pound of the rain was washing away the kid's blood.

"Come on, Turk. The peacekeepers will get him."

"No." Turk shook his head. "I'm getting him."

Turk slung his M4 over his back, then gently knelt in the rubble. The kid slid into his arms, and Reed led the way back down the slope.

51

Ibrahim and Kadeem rendezvoused with Hamid a mile outside the mountaintop airport used by the United Nations to ship airborne aid into the shattered nation. The Dutch freighter carrying the shipping container marked in three languages had departed Port-au-Prince almost a day prior, and should now be somewhere north of the Bahamas, churning for Savannah.

Ibrahim could have left Haiti earlier that day, but Bahir and Mahmoud were already onsite in Georgia to prep a trio of moving trucks and whatever other miscellaneous equipment they would need once the Dutch freighter arrived. It would be better, Ibrahim thought, not to enter American airspace until the last possible moment.

His face was plastered all over the internet, after all. All over the FBI's and the CIA's field offices and computer systems. It would already be a trick to enter America at all. Better to wait until the last moment, when he could hit the ground running.

In the meantime, the chaos of Haiti made it an advantageous place to hide. He sent Hamid ahead to the airport to scope out possible transportation. He spent the afternoon in prayer and meditation even as the thunder of armed conflict ripped over the shattered hills from Port-au-Prince, another gun battle between the gangs and the host of would-be white saviors wielding automatic weapons.

Irony on top of irony.

As Kadeem pulled the same UN-labeled deuce-and-a-half they had used to transport the barrels into Port-au-Prince to the side of the road, Hamid appeared from beneath a sagging coconut palm tree, soaking wet and smoking, the motorbike he had been using covered in mud. Ibrahim scooted over to allow his companion room inside the truck, and the heavy door slammed. Hamid smelled of rainwater and rotting flesh.

Or maybe that was just Haiti.

"Well?" Ibrahim asked.

"There are options," Hamid grunted. "We shouldn't have a problem."

Ibrahim accepted the cigarette from Hamid and took a tug of his own. As he exhaled smoke through his nose he noted something amiss about his lieutenant's demeanor. The absent twitch of Hamid's lip. The way he gazed at the battered motorbike resting beneath the coconut palm without really seeing it.

Ibrahim had known Hamid for a long time. Almost as long as Mahmoud. Hamid and Kadeem both had spent most of the last decade assisting opposition forces in Syria. They were battle-hardened soldiers. Their instincts were honed and focused. Ibrahim could tell when something was off.

"What is it?"

Hamid grunted, shaking a soggy cigarette from the pack, but he didn't light it. He just rolled it between his fingers, still gazing at the motorbike.

"There was a plane at the airstrip," Hamid said. "A small one. Unmarked. It landed a few hours ago and offloaded two men. Both heavily armed—Americans, I think. Dressed in all black."

"And?" Ibrahim asked.

"They took a Humvee and went down the mountain. I didn't follow."

Ibrahim grunted. He finished the smoke and flicked it out of the window.

Soldiers in black. It probably meant nothing, but Ibrahim knew why Hamid was bothered. Black, nondescript uniforms were the favored wardrobe of white soldiers who operated outside the boundaries of traditional military service. Not only mercenaries and combat contractors who descended on the Middle East to wage war apart from any flag, but also of black ops killers working on behalf of the American CIA.

Soulless men. War dogs. Ibrahim, Kadeem, and Hamid had seen plenty of them, not only in Syria but all across Iraq and the greater Middle East.

"It is a coincidence," Ibrahim said calmly. "Nobody knows we are here."

Hamid nodded slowly. He put the cigarette in his mouth and lit up. It steamed and burned unevenly in the rain.

"All the same, I would feel better if we took precautions."

"What sort of precautions?" Ibrahim asked, knowing that Hamid would have an answer ready. He'd probably spent all afternoon contemplating this issue. He was a cunning warrior.

"We fly out tonight," Hamid said. "Before we go, we make contact with one of these Haitian gangs. Offer them payment in exchange for assaulting the airport."

"The airport?" Kadeem repeated, confusion lacing his tone. "Why not the single plane?"

"Because that would be obvious," Hamid said. "It would draw attention. This way, nobody is the wiser, and nobody can follow us."

Hamid gave up on the wet cigarette and dumped it out the open truck window. He faced Ibrahim, waiting. Ibrahim took his time contemplating, weighing his options. Considering exposure to a Haitian gang versus the risk of an American black ops team on his heels.

Hamid was right, he decided. The risks of anybody finding them were slim to none, but insurance in this instance was cheap.

"Do it," Ibrahim said. "But have them wait in the dark. Only attack if that plane should move."

Hamid wrenched the door open and piled back into the rain with a nod. He approached the motorbike and fired up the engine. Ibrahim shut the door and Kadeem ground the truck into gear.

"You really think it's a risk?" Kadeem asked.

"All of life is a risk," Ibrahim said. "Syria, Haiti, or America . . . there is no wrong place to kill an infidel."

52

Port-au-Prince, Haiti

The peacekeepers took the boy's body from Turk's arms while Reed rendezvoused with the Marine colonel at the bumper of a deuce-and-a-half. A makeshift awning had been erected there out of tent canvas, and a coffee maker was chugging along under the power of a generator.

The rain had finally slackened, but still fell in a steady spray. French and Italian peacekeepers were busy recovering the bodies. Film crews were at work documenting the carnage. Brass rifle casings glistened in the mud like hundreds of innocent yellow stars.

And the Haitian gangs were gone, driven back toward Cité Soleil where peacekeeping forces had yet to establish a foothold. Not that there was much there to take hold of—according to the Marine colonel, that part of the city held the worst slums in Haiti. It was a stronghold of G9, and a hotbed for suffering.

"Mark my words," the colonel growled, pouring piping hot coffee into a metal cup. "You'll be watching jarheads by the battalion take foot down here before this is over. This place is primed for nation building."

He shook his head in suppressed disgust and passed Reed the mug. Reed didn't really want a hot drink. The air was steamier than ever, thick on his lungs. But he'd learned long ago that when a man with an eagle on his collar hands you a drink, you take it.

Thank you very much, sir.

"I guess I'm behind on the local politics," Reed said, sipping carefully. The coffee was burnt, which was no less than he expected from a USMC standard-issue coffee maker. The colonel slurped from his own cup as he glowered across the port. He was still soaked to the bone, just like Reed.

And just like Reed, his uniform was stained with the Canadian soldier's blood.

"The Haitians assassinated their president a couple years back," the colonel said. "Since then, it's all been downhill. Port-au-Prince is effectively ruled by heavily armed gangs—G9 and their rivals. When the earthquake struck, the pinheads up in Washington thought it would be another 2010. Just a humanitarian crisis. I wish it were that simple."

Reed surveyed a truck backed up to the heart of the battlefield. Peacekeepers were busy loading bodies of slain refugees while a cable news crew stood by and filmed. It didn't look like a humanitarian crisis. At least, not a natural one.

It looked like Somalia. Iraq. Syria.

"It's never that simple," Reed said quietly.

The colonel grunted. "Corps?"

"Yes, sir. Three deployments."

"Scout sniper?"

"Recon sniper."

"Well that explains a lot. And now?"

Reed didn't answer. He met the colonel's eyes, and waited. Allowing him time to form his own conclusions, as people always do. It was a lesson Reed had learned over long years of working on the edges—or well beyond the edges—of the law. If a person liked you, there was no need to justify their own desire to be helpful. Just keep your mouth shut, and let them make their own justifications.

The colonel was no different. He finished his coffee, tossing the dregs into the mud. "So you're one of those. Fair enough. How can I be of service, Mr. Montgomery?"

"I'd still like to take a look at your container security. Whoever you have working there."

"Like I told you before, that's not under my jurisdiction. The Italians are managing all of that."

"The Italians then. Maybe you could make a phone call."

The colonel nodded slowly. His gaze had drifted across the port again. Across the bodies, and the bullet-ridden pair of pickup trucks. Standing here, it was difficult for Reed to believe he was only a few hundred miles south of the Florida coast. He felt like he was on the other side of the world.

"Sure, son," the colonel said. "I can make a call."

53

The White House
Washington, DC

O'Dell had never understood the term *hell in a handbasket,* but ever since joining Maggie in Washington he felt as though he had a front row seat to a never-ending play titled the same. It wasn't just one disaster. It was all of the disasters, everywhere, all at once. A house on fire, and Maggie was the fire chief, throwing just enough water to mitigate the blaze but never to extinguish it.

You couldn't extinguish it. The moment you salvaged one room, a fresh spark exploded into an inferno somewhere else. It was indeed hell in a handbasket.

Standing on the outside edge of the of the media briefing room, O'Dell was shielded from the cameras and the crowd of boisterous reporters gathered beyond them, but he could still see Maggie as she took the podium. She wore a conservative blue dress, and had let the makeup artists have their way with her for a change. The ponytail was gone. She'd even put on heels.

O'Dell barely recognized her, and for a split second he couldn't help but marvel at how much had changed since his years playing bodyguard in

Baton Rouge. Not just the circumstances that surrounded him, but the woman he worked next to. The woman he'd dedicated his life to serving, no matter where her career landed her.

She was changing, also. She had no choice. Little by little, the charm of her charisma was taking a beating in this basket. She was worn down. Exhausted. Frayed. O'Dell would have done anything to alleviate that burden, but there was really nothing he could offer her. And maybe that was the problem. Maybe that was why the spark of a romance that initially knocked him off his feet had so quickly turned cold.

Hell in any sort of basket was a poor incubator for love.

"Good evening, everyone. Please have a seat." Maggie held her chin up, shoulders squared as she began her address. She didn't use a teleprompter —she almost never used a teleprompter. But O'Dell knew the speech was carefully prepped and memorized ahead of time. Another hard lesson that Maggie had learned.

"I appreciate you all gathering on such short notice. I'd like to begin tonight's address by briefly commenting on a news story first published by CNN. Specifically, the video released by the so-called Islamic Caliphate Army, which alleges to have been filmed in Syria, and depicts the crash of American Black Hawk helicopters. I have tasked the FBI with launching a special investigation into the origins of this video. As that investigation develops you can expect updates, but at this time I will not comment further. Now, moving on—"

"Does that mean the Black Hawk crash was, in fact, the result of military action in the Damascus region?"

The question fired from the back of the audience, and O'Dell's blood boiled. He'd been present while Maggie, Easterling, and Stratton had debated the best response to the video. Everyone agreed that denial was off the table, but admission of a disastrous JSOC operation resulting in the deaths of eleven spec ops soldiers wasn't an option either. Maggie would ride the fence—for now. She would acknowledge without acknowledging.

That was the idea, anyway. The reality was doomed to be messy.

"As previously stated by the president, she will not be commenting further on this subject." It was Easterling who stepped in, speaking into an auxiliary microphone and shooting a death glare at the outspoken reporter. "Please hold all questions until the end of her address."

"Thank you, Jill." Maggie remained cool. "I'd like to offer updates on our continued efforts to track down the responsible parties behind the devastating Nashville bombing. In conjunction with joint task forces of the Department of Justice and in collaboration with the CIA, this administration..."

Maggie's words faded out for O'Dell as the phone buzzed in his pocket. He suppressed a weary sigh and stepped away from the press room, deeper into a darkened hallway. Flicking his finger across the screen to unlock the phone, he hoped to find a text message from Holly. Or maybe her mother. Vickie was a psychopath on a good day, and one of the worst mistakes he'd ever made in a relationship, but talking to her always brought the prospect of talking to Holly. And O'Dell would give anything for that.

The text message wasn't from Vickie. It was from an unknown number, and it wasn't a message at all. It was a picture. Black and white, blurred by rain or perhaps a cheap camera lens. O'Dell tapped on it, rotated his phone to expand the image, and zoomed.

Then his heart skipped. The image was of a muddy path between a stack of shipping containers. It looked like the picture had been taken at night. Tire ruts and wide puddles littered the path between the containers, and walking among them were two figures. Both average-sized men dressed in average clothes with baseball caps pulled down low over their ears. The man closest to the camera had his face turned down. His features weren't visible. But the second man walked tall, chin up. Not really facing the camera, but fully visible.

O'Dell zoomed in, focusing on the low cheekbones. The dark eyes. A narrow nose and bold, rounded chin.

It was Ibrahim. The man from the ICA video. He was sure of it.

O'Dell's phone buzzed again, and another message popped up.

Call me, asshole.

The skip in O'Dell's chest was instantly replaced by a flash of anger. He didn't recognize the number, but he knew who was texting. He could block a dozen numbers a day, but he could never shake Reed, not unless he changed his own number. That was an option he'd already begun to consider after the last blast of calls and messages.

The picture changed everything. O'Dell migrated away from the press room, deeper into the hall, and tapped to call the number. It rang only once, connecting quickly with the man they called The Prosecutor.

"Montgomery?" O'Dell barked.

"Nice of you to finally take a call."

The open hostility in Montgomery's voice dumped further irritation on the bonfire burning in O'Dell's chest. He kept his voice to a low growl.

"Where did you get the picture?"

"Haiti. At the port."

"*What?*"

"You should have taken my calls, swamp dog. I've accomplished more in the last twenty-four hours than the whole of the CIA, apparently."

"*Where did you get the picture?*" O'Dell repeated.

"I'll get to that. First I need to lay some groundwork, just in case you decide to ghost me again. I've got one of my friends in Europe running background on a Ukrainian arms dealer named Melnyk. My friend has uncovered evidence that the land mines used in the Nashville bombing were Russian-made, sold by Melnyk to ICA, and shipped to—"

"How did you know they were Russian land mines?" O'Dell cut him off.

"Because I was *there*, remember?"

O'Dell's mind flicked back to the last call they had shared, and how Banks was clinging to life in a hospital. It shouldn't have surprised him that Montgomery was willing to leave his wife in an ICU to run down her would-be murderers. That was how a killer like him operated. Destroy the enemy, whatever the cost.

"The land mines were shipped into a town called Cap-Haïtien. It's in northern Haiti. My working theory is that whoever these people are, they moved the mines south into Port-au-Prince, then smuggled them back into the States via a returning cargo ship."

"You put this together all by yourself?" O'Dell demanded.

"Pretty much. With some help from some intelligent people who know how to pick up a phone."

O'Dell wanted to snap back, but the leaden weight in his gut told him he didn't have the time. Maggie was taking questions now. The tone of her press conference was quickly becoming combative. He needed to get off the phone. But first he needed to know about the picture.

"Did you find Ibrahim?" O'Dell demanded.

"Is that what his name is? I didn't know. I saw him on the video released after the bombing, and I saw him again, on Italian security footage shot in Port-au-Prince. The still I sent you is from a camera mounted outside their temporary command center, near the depot where they stack empty shipping containers. The recording was shot last night."

A cold tingle ran up O'Dell's spine. He wasn't sure why. He wasn't even sure what the implications of Reed's intel would be. But he knew it meant something.

"You're telling me he's in Haiti?" O'Dell asked.

"I'm telling you he was, last night. And he was down by the empty containers. Most of those containers have now been loaded onto freighters headed back to Savannah. We have no way of knowing what he may have hidden onboard. But we do know he's promised further attacks. So it seems like something worth looking into, wouldn't you say?"

More biting sarcasm. Again, O'Dell ignored it. Already his mind was churning far beyond the nature of the information he'd been given, and struggling to decide what to do with it. He couldn't bring this to Maggie. She was embattled enough, and she still needed distance from the Prosecution Force—more than ever, in fact. Political liabilities were stacking up. He couldn't risk adding fuel to the fire.

But he couldn't ignore this, either. It was too blatant. Too logical. Reed had done a good job digging, even if O'Dell would never admit it.

"Send me the full video and everything else you have," O'Dell said. "I'll text you my email."

"What are you going to do?" Reed demanded.

O'Dell thought quickly. There was really only one thing *to* do, short of throwing it on Maggie.

"I'll touch base with the CIA," he said. "We'll let O'Brien have a look at it."

It was a reasonable plan. O'Dell knew Maggie was having difficulties with O'Brien, but no matter how crazy the old spook was, he couldn't ignore intel like this.

"Fine," Reed said.

"Where are you?" O'Dell asked. "Still in Haiti?"

"For the moment."

O'Dell thought again about liabilities. About what Reed was likely to do if he were left unattended. *Something*, that was for sure. He couldn't be counted on to sit still. The last thing Maggie needed was for there to be an international fiasco at the hands of an operator so closely linked to the White House.

Better to keep him within arm's reach.

"Get back to the States," O'Dell said. "I'll keep you in the loop."

"You better," Reed said. "Don't ghost me again, O'Dell."

Montgomery hung up before O'Dell could speak another word, leaving him standing alone in the hallway. Maggie was wrapping up her press conference early. It had turned ugly—no surprise.

O'Dell waited five minutes for the email to come in, then immediately forwarded it to O'Brien, taking his internal CIA email address from a curated list of contacts he kept in his phone, just in case.

Then he thought about Montgomery again. A loose cannon. A developing liability.

Something was going to have to be done to put The Prosecutor on ice before he burned down Maggie's entire administration.

54

"You sold land mines to a terrorist in Haiti. What was his name?"

Wolfgang's voice was barely above a growl, his gritted teeth pressed close to Melnyk's face. The Ukrainian arms dealer hung by his wrists from a rafter in the salon, his toes barely touching the ground. A bloody pair of pliers dangled from Wolfgang's left hand, the polished floorboards of the yacht littered by three molars and a left incisor. Melnyk's face was swollen with ruby welts. His lip bled.

But after nearly forty minutes of sustained pressure, he hadn't talked. Not once.

Wolfgang ran his hand behind Melnyk's neck and grabbed the back of his head by his hair. He yanked until Melnyk's line of sight met his own, then he raised the pliers and shook them an inch in front of his nose.

"You want another? I can go all day, you death-dealing worm! Which one you want to lose next? How about an apple-biter? You wanna be gap-toothed?

He jammed the pliers between Melnyk's teeth. Melnyk jerked and twisted, pulling his face away. Wolfgang's stomach churned. It was all he could do not to puke as the pliers crunched around teeth. He yanked without paying any particular attention to which tooth he had clamped around.

He pulled two. Melnyk thrashed and screamed, blood running down his chin. Wolfgang released him and turned away, taking a moment to steady himself against a table. After running the powerboat onto the stern of the big yacht, Ivan had taken the helm and turned them out to sea. They had run all ahead full for half an hour. They were now miles from shore, well outside the earshot of any nosy landlubbers. The seas had picked up, too, rocking the boat.

But it wasn't the waves that sent nausea through Wolfgang's stomach. Every time he walked through a blended puddle of piss and blood, stepping on teeth and listening to Melnyk's agonized whimpers, he wanted to puke. He wanted to throw himself overboard and drown in the warm sea.

He hated what he was doing. But he was also tired of asking nicely.

"I'll take them all, Melnyk," Wolfgang lifted the pliers. "You'll be toothless as a nurse shark before I'm done with you. Then I'll start on your fingers. You want that?"

Wolfgang jabbed with the pliers. Melnyk spat blood, still gasping. Then he laughed.

"There's nothing you can do to me . . . that's worse than what my clients would do . . . if I talked."

It took effort for Melnyk to get the sentence out. Wolfgang swept an open laptop off the salon tabletop. He shoved the laptop in Melnyk's face.

"You sure about that, smart guy? You wanna roll those dice? What's the password? Unlock the computer, Melnyk, or I swear I'll—"

"Enough already!" Ivan's baritone voice boomed from across the room. Wolfgang's gaze snapped over his shoulder to see the big Russian standing shirtless—again—in the doorway to the forward berths. He held an open bottle of Dom Pérignon in one hand. A plate full of fine cheeses and crackers in the other. A cigarette dangled from his lips.

"You are amateur at this, Amerikos. Have you tortured before?"

Wolfgang didn't answer. Melnyk offered a gap-toothed sneer.

Ivan guzzled from the champagne bottle, then slapped the cheese tray down on the table. He pushed Wolfgang out to the way.

"Step outside. Smoke a cigarette. I will deal with this."

"I don't smoke," Wolfgang growled.

"Then color a page!" Ivan snapped. "*Chyort voz'-mi!* You embarrass me."

Ivan grabbed the pliers from Wolfgang's hand and tossed them across the room. He took the laptop, then pointed to the door.

"*Out.*"

"We need him alive," Wolfgang said. "We need—"

"This is not my first rodeo, Amerikos. We will handle this problem the Russian way, like we should have from the start. Go now, and cover your ears."

Wolfgang turned for the door. He knew in his gut that he should argue with Ivan. That he should intercede on Melnyk's behalf. Whatever evil the big Russian was about to unleash, Wolfgang had no doubt it would be far worse than anything he himself could fathom.

Yes, he was an amateur. Yes, this was the first time he'd ever engaged in sustained torture. And he hated himself for it. It was against his rules.

As he squeezed past the nose of the powerboat, still jammed on the stern of the yacht like a personal watercraft parked by a drunk, he heard Ivan speaking to Melnyk. Not shouting, the way Wolfgang had. Ivan cooed, almost like a mother calming a newborn baby. He spoke in Russian, his words as soft and gentle as a kitten's cuddles.

But Wolfgang heard the knife snap open, the scream that followed was far sharper than any gurgling plea Melnyk had voiced while losing his teeth. It sounded like the dying screech of an animal, and it didn't stop. Ivan kept cooing, and Melnyk continued to scream. Wolfgang reached the stern and vomited into the black water, catching himself on a mutilated rail and wishing he was deaf. The horror track from inside the yacht didn't end. Wolfgang was sure it could be heard for miles. Melnyk gasped and shouted in Russian, his voice pleading. Ivan's tone remained calm, distorted now and then by swigs from the bottle.

And the sound of a smile. Wolfgang could picture the broad, toothy grin. The face of a madman.

He listened nearly ten minutes before finally turning back for the door. Melnyk's screams had fallen silent over the past thirty seconds, and somehow that was worse. Wolfgang couldn't stand not knowing. He forced his way past the nose of the powerboat and stepped over the fallen bodies of the dead goons.

Oleksiy Melnyk was dead. Wolfgang knew it the moment he crossed into the saloon. The arms dealer still hung from the rafters, but his chin drooped. His mouth hung open, his eyes wide and ghastly. His scorpion tattoo smeared with Ivan's bloody fingerprints.

And his stomach . . .

Ivan had eviscerated him. Pelvis to sternum. There was more lying outside Melnyk's open gut than in it.

"What did you do?" Wolfgang shouted.

Ivan sat at the table, bloody up to his arms. A pocket knife with a two-inch blade rested next to him, the bottle of Dom nearly empty as he rocked it back. The Russian belched, then wiped his face with the back of one hand.

"This you must learn about torture, my friend. It is all psychological. You must make them believe that you will really kill them. Eliminate all hope. Then they are easy as drunk college girl."

"But you *did* kill him!" Wolfgang shouted. "We needed him to talk, you fool!"

"He talked," Ivan said with a laugh. "Mostly to his mother, may she rest in peace. But I have password. Would you like to see?"

Ivan rotated the laptop. Wolfgang swallowed back a convulsing choke and turned away from the suspended body. Suddenly, he wanted to be off the boat. He wanted to be as far away as possible.

But instead, he moved to the table. Ivan passed him the computer, selecting a slice of gourmet cheese with still-bloody fingers. Wolfgang focused intently on the screen while the Russian chewed.

"Interrogation is art," Ivan mused. "Like good music. The ups and the downs, the beat and the crescendo. A perfect orchestra leads to a true story. Do they not teach you this in America?"

Wolfgang barely listened. The contents of Melnyk's computer were indeed unlocked, the keyboard stained with blood. There were emails, as before. But not just a few—hundreds. Purchase orders and supply shipments. Updates and invoices. More data than Wolfgang could sort through in a full workweek. He narrowed his search by filtering to the email address he'd found on the dead arms dealer's phone. That produced a slew of communication. Most of the discussions were in English, an apparent middle ground between Melnyk and his customer.

There was discussion of land mines. Coded discussions, anyway. But Wolfgang read between the lines. A certain quantity, a certain price. Delivered for cash on the barrel. American dollars.

And then . . .

Wolfgang squinted. The boiling nausea he'd felt all night turned suddenly very still. His joints went rigid. He scrolled quickly down the email, skipping through the broken English of Melnyk's messages paired with the slightly more fluent replies of his customers.

"Don't call it that," Melnyk had written. *"Speak in code."*

Wolfgang scanned back up the message, searching for whatever had prompted the rebuke. He passed over the email once, and didn't see it. He squinted, and his eyes caught a typo.

Then he realized it wasn't a typo, and the nausea in his gut froze over into solid ice.

55

Victor O'Brien took the call from the White House in his private office. All the staff were gone. Langley was winding down after another long and brutal day. Hundreds of intelligence specialists would remain through the night, of course. Monitoring overseas assets and analyzing reports from the darkest corners of an unstable planet.

O'Brien would stay, also. Partly because there was work to be done. Partly because there was nowhere else to be.

"O'Brien," he answered curtly, swallowing back the pills he'd just palmed into his mouth. They would land on an empty stomach, probably triggering acid reflux. O'Brien didn't care. He couldn't eat if he tried, and he needed the Xanax. His nerves were raw, stretched to the point of snapping altogether.

"Director, it's James O'Dell from the president's office."

O'Brien didn't need to be told who O'Dell was, and he certainly didn't need to be goaded with the reminder that O'Dell was a so-called "member" of the president's office. O'Brien knew what O'Dell really was. Why he was really in the building. He was nothing more than a glorified cop, landing in the right place at the right time.

Or rather, the right *bed* at the right time.

"What do you need, Mr. O'Dell?" O'Brien's voice was clipped. He intended it to be.

"I need to speak with you about something sensitive," O'Dell said. "Off the books."

O'Brien sat up. It wasn't like O'Dell to call him directly—he never remembered it happening before, but that wasn't what stirred his interest. It was the *off the record* bit. Off the record from whom? The president?

"What's on your mind?" O'Brien said.

O'Brien didn't interrupt as O'Dell spoke. The story was short, and barely halfway through it O'Brien's blood began to boil. Maddened frustration constricted his fingers around the phone until the plastic creaked.

The story was about Montgomery, the rogue operator. Because *of course it was*.

"He's in *Haiti?*" O'Brien snarled.

"Yes. But he's headed back. I thought it might be better that way. We need to insulate the president from this. I'm sure you understand, Mr. Director. The Prosecution Force has become a liability."

Oh, O'Brien understood. He'd understood from the start. Ever since Montgomery and his team went off script in North Korea, O'Brien had developed an increasing mistrust of the Prosecution Force. He'd worked to shut it down himself. Trousdale had overridden him, insisting on deploying the team into Venezuela.

Now things were getting out of hand. Montgomery had gone rogue. And like a good janitor, O'Dell expected the director of the CIA to clean it up.

But O'Brien was finished with that. He'd served as the president's private Google for far too long. He'd cleaned up enough messes. And this wasn't even the president—this was her lackey. Her bedtime plaything.

America was standing on the brink of complete chaos, and O'Dell *actually* had the nerve to call asking him to insulate the president?

O'Brien was done.

"Tell me something, Mr. O'Dell. What's it feel like to ring that bell?"

The phone went quiet, but O'Brien knew O'Dell had heard him. He detected a slight hitch in the man's breathing. A momentary hesitation, a sickening pause.

"What?" O'Dell said.

"The quitter's bell." O'Brien leaned back in his chair, a sly smile creeping across his face. Piloting his mouse across the desk, he pulled up a file on one of his expansive screens. It was a personnel file, complete with a background biography and even a DOD picture sporting a muscular Black man in a Navy uniform.

James O'Dell.

"You know," O'Brien said. "The one on Coronado. I heard you rang it so hard it cracked."

Another protracted delay. O'Brien grinned. He knew what O'Dell was thinking: *How does he know?*

"Whatever your differences with me, you need to listen to what I'm saying," O'Dell said, keeping his voice low. "Montgomery located Ibrahim in Haiti. *This week*. He sent pictures. Are you hearing me?"

"Fakir Ibrahim is *dead*," O'Brien snapped. "You were in the room. You watched eleven men who *didn't* ring the bell get blown away chasing this shadow. I don't have time to explain how the intelligence world works, Mr. O'Dell, but suffice it to say our enemy is toying with us, and I'm done taking my intelligence from washout wannabes on private crusades. You stick to shtupping the president. *I'll* handle the intelligence work."

O'Brien hung up with a slam, fingers trembling against the plastic. He blinked, and the phone blurred out of focus. Yanking open a desk drawer, he fished out the Xanax bottle and popped three more. Enough to numb his overworked mind into oblivion.

––––––––––

On the other side of the executive floor of the George Bush Center for Intelligence, Deputy Director Dr. Sarah Aimes listened to the plastic-on-plastic snap of the phone hanging up, followed by the buzz of a dial tone. She clicked her mouse to stop the recording, then cradled her own phone against her ear. She pressed the button to take the device off hold.

"That's it?"

"Y-yeah." The voice of the man on the other end of the line was strained and edgy, carrying a Cuban accent seasoned with South Florida sunshine. Roberto Fernández was the first of his parent's children to be born in the United States, and was likely recruited to the CIA for his direct connections inside the Republic of Cuba. Maybe the agency had wanted him as a case officer, or an eventual spy. His GPA at MIT was nearly perfect. He was exemplary in all subjects, something approaching a genius.

All subjects except girls, anyway. Or friends. Or social interactions of any kind. It turned out that Roberto suffered from crippling levels of social anxiety not at first apparent, which was why he had landed not inside of Aimes's own Directorate of Operations, but instead at the CIA's Directorate of Digital Innovation, a fancy term for an anthill full of tech wizards and computer nerds who supplied the Agency with every digital resource known to mankind.

And those not yet known.

Aimes had met Roberto in Langley's cafeteria two years prior. He'd almost spilled his chocolate milk when he approached her, fumbling and sweating, triggering a security officer to step in. Aimes waved the officer away and offered Roberto a seat, mostly because she hadn't left her office in nearly two weeks, and was starved for human interaction.

Roberto knew who she was. Roberto needed a favor. There was trouble in Cuba. Some of his family had crossed the wrong people inside the powerful Communist Party, and had since been labeled "enemies of the state." Roberto wanted Aimes to get them out. Aimes explained that she couldn't. It was well outside the scope of her authority, not to mention expertise. Family or otherwise, this was a matter of Cuban citizens inside Cuba.

Not something she could touch.

Maybe it was the heartbreak in Roberto's eyes, or the way his fingers trembled when he guzzled chocolate milk. A single tear trickled down his pudgy brown cheek as he stumbled off.

Whatever it was that tugged her heartstrings, Aimes returned to her office and called a friend who called a friend who called a ranking member of the State Department. Exceptions were made. Visas were issued.

Roberto's family made it to the Land of the Free aboard a rubber raft with a converted weed-whacker for a motor, and Aimes won a friend inside the DDI for life.

"When was this call placed?" Aimes asked.

Roberto kept his voice to barely above a whisper, still stuttering. "Tw-twenty minutes ago."

"From the White House?"

"I think so."

Aimes pursed her lips. She thought carefully, knowing that her next step could be her last if she misjudged the inky dark terrain surrounding her. Then again, the fact that she was spying on her boss's private communications in the first place was enough to imprison her under the Espionage Act.

Spying only makes you a hero if you turn out to be right. The alternative was a short drop and a sudden stop, but Aimes wasn't worried about her career. She knew O'Brien was unstable. She knew he was off the rails.

And she had to know what he might be hiding.

"Can you get the email?" Aimes asked.

"The email?" Roberto whispered, the phone rattling against his ear.

"Right. The one O'Dell mentioned."

"Uh . . . I mean . . ."

"Roberto," Aimes put an edge in her voice.

"Y-yeah. I can get it."

"Let's see it, then."

Aimes leaned back in her chair, not quite sure she could comprehend how quickly Victor O'Brien had cracked. Or maybe he'd always been cracked, and the fault lines were just now shining through. She knew he hated Trousdale. She knew he hated women in general. But this was bigger. This was the cost of too long a career spent manipulating too many people. It gave you a god complex.

"I . . . really don't feel comfortable . . . you know . . ." Roberto trailed off.

"How's the family, Roberto?" Aimes asked.

Dead silence.

"Any luck on the citizenship?" Aimes pressed.

Roberto sighed. "Okay, okay. You haven't gotta . . . be that way. Check your email."

Aimes did check. There was a message—a forward from Roberto, containing a single, secured attachment. A PDF. Probably a screenshot.

"Thank you, Roberto. Not a word of this to anyone."

Roberto snorted. "No worries about that."

Aimes hung up. She double-clicked the secure attachment and used the biometric reader on her desk to authorize the file to open, knowing that her fingerprints were now smeared all over this thing. Literally.

The file loaded. The message displayed. A screenshot indeed, of a message from James O'Dell to Victor O'Brien, itself forwarded from one Reed Montgomery.

The contents? One single photograph. An unmistakable face.

Aimes's stomach tightened, and she lifted her phone. "Get Director Purcell, ASAP."

56

Hamid located a member of Haiti's G9 gang on the outskirts of an obliterated Port-au-Prince suburb, guarding the roadway with an AK-47 underfolder hung over his chest. The man spoke broken English and was easy enough to negotiate with. A hundred bucks American purchased his mercenary services, and Hamid could tell by the glow in the gangster's eyes that he thought he was ripping off an ignorant international.

Hamid passed him the bank note without complaint, reinforcing his instructions: *Nobody* was to leave the airfield after he and his friends took off. Especially any men dressed in black aboard the little twin engine plane.

At the top of the mountain, Hamid rendezvoused with Ibrahim and Kadeem at the airstrip, which was now almost deserted as darkness closed in. There were only a handful of planes remaining, along with a squawking German woman who seemed to think she owned the place. Kadeem drove his knife into her heart before positioning her body on a bench just outside the mobile office building that served as a makeshift control tower.

The next order of business was to locate a pilot. Hamid found a skinny Spaniard dressed in UN garb who would suffice. The guy was friendly at first, but when Ibrahim offered cash for a flight to America, he was flatly turned down. The pilot didn't own the Cessna Citation parked in the rain at the side of the runway. He worked for some segment of the Spanish government, deployed here as part of the UN relief effort. The UN owned the jet, using it to transport visiting officials in and out of disaster zones. He wasn't even allowed to fly alone—he needed a co-pilot, and the co-pilot had food poisoning, besides which all flights out of Haiti were being temporarily suspended until the weather cleared.

Hamid put a gun in his face, and the Spaniard's objections melted like butter under the blazing desert sun. The twin-engine jet was fueled and ready to go. Without the German to bark into her bullhorn, there was nobody to prevent takeoff. Hamid rode in the co-pilot's seat, his pistol pointed across the cockpit, fully ready to commit an act of heroic *shahada* should the pilot change his mind.

The guy sweated bullets, but he got the plane off the ground. He spoke calmly into his headset as they rose through the weather. He asked where the trio of men wanted to go.

"Georgia," Ibrahim said. "Take us to Savannah."

57

Haiti

The UN Humvee was bullet-ridden, but somehow still drove. Turk piloted the heavy vehicle away from the port and back into the shattered city while the sky faded to black, and Reed phoned Corbyn. He wanted the plane on the tarmac, fueled and ready to go. They were headed to Savannah, where Reed would take a look inside the cargo ships churning north out of the Caribbean.

Corbyn was sleeping when he called, and acknowledged his request with a groggy curse. He hung up and braced himself against the Humvee's dash as Turk crashed through a rut with all the grace of a bulldozer. The headlights bounced and Reed was nearly ejected from the seat. He shot a glare toward his driver.

Any threats of violence boiling in Reed's gut melted as his gaze fell across Turk's face. His battle buddy glared straight ahead, face ashen. Lips pressed tightly closed.

A part of Reed wanted to voice it, to mention the fallen Haitian boy with the AK and tell Turk it wasn't his fault. That he'd done what he had to do. That Port-au-Prince was a war zone, and Turk hadn't put a rifle in that kid's hands.

But he didn't, because he knew it wouldn't make a difference. The lead in the bottom of Turk's stomach was a feeling Reed knew well. A brutal reality that couldn't be erased with simple words. The only path forward was through.

"When we get to Savannah, we'll reconnect with O'Dell," Reed said. "He should answer his phone now."

Turk didn't answer. Reed ignored the jolting ride and pressed himself deep into the seat, minimizing the bone-jarring ruts and potholes the best he could. In his mind, he saw the man on the security tape again. The same man he'd seen on the terrorist video two days prior. The man who had called him *Prosecutor*.

He might still be in Haiti. He might be hiding even now amid the rubble and the chaos, watching Reed slip by in the gathering dark. But the Italian security tape was more than twenty hours old, and a lot of ships had left port since then. The terrorist could be on any one of them, hidden among the containers.

And what else could be hidden among those containers? A dirty bomb? A plague-spreading pathogen? A lung-scorching compressed gas, ready to be unleashed in a crowded transit station?

Reed tried to fixate on the problem at hand, but his focus didn't last long. When fatigue descended over his mind, other images took the place of the terrorist and his container ships. Images of his wife collapsing in a heap. His daughter shredded before the light of day ever spilled across her infant face.

Reed felt the fire when he pictured the scene. But he'd been angry for so long, the intensity of this new heat barely touched him. A larger part of him felt very numb, as though he should be burning up inside, but couldn't turn himself on. He was in killer mode now. A state he had spent almost all of his adult life in—shoot or be shot.

It felt like a drug. Like something he'd missed for a very long time. Something that energized him like no gym or quiet life every could. Why was living the good life so hard? Why did *this*—the jarring Humvee, and the sopping wet clothes, and gunfire still ringing in his ears—why did all these things feel more...

Like home.

The reality struck him in the chest like a Mack truck, and his eyes snapped open. Rain sprayed against the bulletproof windshield of the Humvee, the road through the mountains muddy and slick. The hefty tires on the all-terrain beast slipped around, but Turk didn't let up on the gas. The diesel chugged, and Reed blocked out all further mental exploration for the duration of the trip.

He just thought about the plane. He would change clothes once on board. He thought they could make it to Savannah in about five hours, arriving well before dawn. He could send Corbyn back to Leiper's Fork with the King Air while he and Turk went to work on the ships.

With or without O'Dell's help, Reed would check each and every container until his hands found the throat of the man who killed his daughter.

At last Turk rounded the corner at the top of the makeshift highway, and the headlights of the Humvee pointed down the tarmac. Reed saw the King Air positioned at the end of the strip, propped up on her landing gear, the aluminum propellers streaming with rain. He didn't see Corbyn. He figured she was sheltering inside the aircraft.

"Can we take off in this?" Turk asked.

Reed only grunted, pointing to the motor pool. Turk parked the Humvee in the same spot they had borrowed it from less than twelve hours prior. Reed ignored the rain as he bailed out, blowing water from his lips and slinging a pack over one shoulder, the Daniel Defense M4 riding in his right hand. He turned for the mobile UN headquarters building resting between them and the plane, half-expecting the German peacekeeper with the bullhorn to pop out of the mud, ready to burn them both at the stake.

He saw her sitting on a bench at the corner of the office building instead, barely sheltered by a low awning. Smoking, he thought. It made him want a cigarette, but whatever smokes remained in his pocket were ruined beyond use. Turk fell in behind him as the two of them slogged toward the plane. They would have to pass the smoking peacekeeper. Reed readied himself with an excuse and apology for taking the Humvee.

But the peacekeeper didn't move. She remained slouched against the wall of the command post, head leaned back. Reed squinted in the darkness and adjusted his pack. He took another two long strides, a vague unease edging into his stomach.

"Ma'am?" Reed called.

No response. Reed's gaze drifted down the shadowy silhouette of her face, across her saturated jacket, down to that dark patch over her chest . . .

"Hit the deck!"

58

As soon as Reed shouted, gunfire erupted from someplace behind him—at the motor pool or perhaps beyond it. The rapid clacking of automatic AK-47s, hurtling hot lead across the airfield in a different kind of rain storm. Reed launched himself to the ground, landing in a puddle ten yards from the dead peacekeeper. Turk hit the ground next to him and both men rotated, clawing rifles up and over their stomachs to return fire.

Reed could see the targets, though not as concrete silhouettes. He only saw vague, dancing shadows amid the motor pool, kneeling behind armor-plated vehicles and dumping lead across the airfield. A momentary flash of lightning illuminated the space in bright blue, and Reed saw dozens of them.

Haitian gangsters, just like those at the port. Heavily armed and closing from three hundred yards.

"Go! Off the ground!" Reed fought back to his feet and ran, rushing past the dead German as Turk hurtled along behind. Nothing about the incoming fire was aimed. Reed doubted whether it was even pointed in their general direction. The men behind them weren't soldiers. They shot like drunken rednecks at a hunting camp, but there was a *lot* of gunfire headed their way. Maybe enough to for somebody to get lucky.

"Grenades!" Reed shouted. Turk twisted to dump his pack. The two of them slid into a rut left by one of the heavy U.S. Air Force C130s. Both aircraft were gone now, as were all of the UN peacekeepers present when the King Air had landed. They'd had enough sense to clear out before sunset.

"Here—smoke and frag!"

Turk extended a hand. Reed accepted two smoke grenades and yanked the pins, then launched them as far as he could into the dark. Both grenades landed on the watery tarmac and dispensed dark gray clouds of smoke in a dull hiss. Bullets continued to race through that cloud, some striking concrete while others whizzed high overhead.

It was a maelstrom. Death on the wind.

"We'll never get off the ground," Turk called.

Reed looked over his shoulder to the King Air. It sat at the end of the strip, another three hundred yards distant. The door was open now. Corbyn's panicked face appeared in the dark, a hand held over her brow.

"We gotta try," Reed said. "You run for the plane. I'll hang back to drive them into cover. Keep the door open. I'll jump in before you get up to speed."

Turk looked to the plane. Then back down the runway. He shook his head.

"No. I'll do it."

Reed opened his mouth. Turk offered a weak smirk. "You took Carpetbag. I'll take the gangsters." Then he broke into a sprint, straight for the gunfire.

Reed muttered a curse and turned for the plane. He sprinted all the way, twirling his finger in the air for Corbyn to fire up the engines. She stood in the doorway with her hand still up to block the rain, shaking her head.

"Fire it up!" Reed shouted. "Get it spinning!"

Corbyn ducked dramatically as a bullet whizzed overhead. Reed stretched out and consumed the final hundred yards as the thunderclap of Turk's M4 carbine opened up behind him. Quick but measured shots, engaging the enemy with precision. Several of the AKs went silent, offering a brief reprieve in the fire.

"Start it up!" Reed screamed. "We're leaving!"

Corbyn remained on the steps as Reed reached the King Air and skated beneath the lefthand wing. Water exploded around his boots and he nearly fell. He met her confused faced on the other side, her gaze flicking between him and the field of smoke obscuring the runway.

"I can't—"

"*Move!*"

Reed drove her ahead of him, up the steps and into the aircraft. Something flicked behind Corbyn's eyes, like a light switch turning on. She stumbled into the cabin and crashed toward the cockpit. Reed slung his backpack ahead of him and knelt in the door, twisting the rifle around to point over the lefthand wing. He couldn't see Turk. He couldn't see the muzzle flash of the AKs anymore. The airfield was pitch-black, save for a security light mounted to the command center. Even that was wreathed in grenade smoke.

From the cockpit Corbyn raced through her pre-flight, her voice calm but clipped as she worked down the checklist. Something about the routine procedure pushed Reed over the edge. He wrenched his head inside and shouted at the cockpit.

"Get us off the ground before we're all dead!"

Corbyn didn't argue. The left engine coughed and turned. Then the right. A surged of rain-saturated rotor wash blasted across his face, and then Reed saw muzzle flash again somewhere near the motor pool. Turk's M4 barked to his left, beyond the smoke. Not visible, but he had a bearing on it.

"Where's Turk?" Corbyn shouted.

"Inbound. Get us moving!"

The brakes released, and the King Air's nose dropped. The concrete began to move, and Reed flicked his safety off. He aimed over the lefthand propeller as a fresh storm of gunfire raced toward them. A bullet pinged off an aluminum blade and whined overhead. Reed engaged the muzzle flash with four quick pulls of his trigger finger, spraying bullets blindly in return.

The engines wound up. The plane was shaking now. They bumped over a rut and gained speed. The King Air moved at a fast jog for a man, approaching a sprint. Reed looked left and saw the command post racing toward them. He didn't see Turk, but he still heard the clap of his M4 some-place amid the thinning grenade smoke.

Bending back into the cabin, he found the frag grenades—two of them. The rifle hung from his sling, and he put a finger in a grenade pin.

Come on, Turk . . .

The King Air reached the command post. The propellers sounded like a hurricane now. Smoke enveloped them, choking off Reed's throat. He blinked, eyes burning. The airplane's nose bounced.

Then he saw two things at once. He saw Turk fifty yards ahead, dug in behind a battered deuce-and-a-half with a shattered windshield. And then he saw the motor pool, crawling with gangsters—more than a dozen, all heavily armed.

Crushing dread descended like an anvil over Reed's shoulders. He ignored it, screaming over the propeller hurricane.

"Let's go!"

Turk left cover and sprinted dead for the King Air—not circling wide to circumvent the wing. There wasn't time. The plane was moving too quickly now. He would never cut in to reach the door before the King Air raced by.

He had to go under the wing, just left of the nose gear in the gap between rushing tires and a whirring propeller. It was a narrow slot for man of Turk's size, but there wasn't time to question it.

Turk wasn't questioning. He threw the rifle to the ground and dumped his backpack, slowing as the King Air approached.

"What's he doing?" Corbyn shouted from the cockpit.

Reed ignored her, clinging to the inside of the doorframe with one hand, prepared to lean wide with his free arm to catch Turk.

The King Air roared and skipped, the front wheel bouncing. Then Turk dropped.

The nose gear raced by his torso with mere inches to spare, the proper blade shredding air just above his face. Then the wing was over him. Turk's arm shot up. He caught the end of the King Air's boarding steps as they raced by, and his arm yanked tight with a snap. Turk screamed as raw concrete tore into his exposed ribcage and hip. Reed grabbed his free arm as the gunfire redoubled from the motor pool. Bullets pinged off the fuse-lage and one zipped through the open door.

Reed dug his fingers into Turk's free arm and hauled up just as the King Air's nose left the tarmac. He felt his own hand slipping from the door, feet grinding into expensive carpet. Turk's muscles bulged as he wrenched upward on the stairs. His body skipped over the airstrip, face alive with pain.

Reed pulled, and the King Air left the ground. Turk's body fell over the end of the steps, legs dangling as he clawed his way upward. Reed braced both feet against the doorframe and heaved backward. His oversized battle buddy fell through the door with a meaty thud, and Reed crashed against a leather clad seat. His head spun, temporary dizziness overcoming him as the plane's nose rose another few degrees. Already the ground was racing away. Thunderclaps of wind beat against the open door, and an emergency light flashed a warning of compromised cabin pressure.

Reed hauled himself to his knees and grabbed the aft door cable. Wrenching upward he dragged the door toward the fuselage. Already several hundred feet below he could see the orange starlight of muzzle flash, still firing on the fleeing plane. A bullet whistled through the open door and struck the ceiling. Reed yanked the cable, slamming the door pins against the fuselage before his right hand found the latch handle. A quick turn counterclockwise to fully withdraw the pins into the door, then a hard twist to the right to lock them into place.

The carpet was sticky with blood as Reed's knees crashed into it. The plane continued to throb, the emergency light still blinking. Turk lay jammed between the rear seats and the tail, lying on his back with his right hand wrapping around his left shoulder. Total agony consumed his face, worse than any pain Reed had ever seen displayed there. Tears slipped down his cheeks, and clinched teeth ground as Turk fought back a cry. Beneath his ribcage Reed saw blood seeping out over the carpet. He didn't need to roll Turk over to know what had happened.

It was road rash from being dragged along the airstrip. Turk's rear armor plate had taken the brunt of it, but his shoulders and hips still made contact with the tarmac.

Reed found his backpack and tore past fresh clothes and MREs to locate his med kit. He tossed aside the tourniquet resting on top before digging into the aluminum packages of medication and first aid equipment beneath. Turk wasn't bleeding badly, but the wounds still needed to be sealed.

"Lie still," Reed said.

"Why does it always have to be me," Turk's voice whimpered through clinched teeth. Reed knew Turk was trying to be funny, but he wasn't in the mood to indulge him. From the cockpit Corbyn was cursing up a storm as the aircraft leveled off. Lights still flashed, and an alarm buzzer wouldn't stop squawking from someplace in the ceiling.

"Will you turn that thing off!" Reed shouted.

Corbyn appeared in the cabin, the plane apparently relegated to autopilot. Bright eyes were flush with rage, soon softening as her gaze fell across Turk.

"What happened?"

Reed ignored her, forcing Turk onto his right side to expose his back.

It was bad. Turk still had an ass, but the seat of his pants was scrubbed away and both cheeks were raw and red. His left shoulder had taken a beating, also, and the nylon webbing housing his rear armor plate was almost completely scrubbed away.

"Shut up already," Reed said. "I haven't heard you whine this bad since you took it up the ass in Venezuela."

"It's not my ass," Turk choked. "It's my . . . my arm. I think it's dislo—"

He never finished. Reed swiped raw alcohol over the exposed flesh. Turk's muscles spasmed and he shook like a branch in a storm.

From the cockpit, a new alarm went off. Outside the plane Reed heard a mechanical cough, followed by a shrill grinding sound. Corbyn's face washed pale and she raced forward again as the King Air shuddered.

"What was that?" Reed shouted.

Corbyn took the pilot's seat, fingers flying over the digital control panel. The new alarm chimed in sequence with the old one.

"What the hell was that?" Reed repeated.

"Uhm . . . no big deal . . . I think . . ."

A momentary pause, followed by a shudder. The grinding sound stopped, as did the low roar from the portside wing. Reed's stomach dropped.

"I think we just lost an engine," Corbyn said, her voice suddenly very calm.

"Lost an engine? What do you mean we just *lost an engine*?"

"Must have taken a bullet. I've got no oil pressure at all. We're going to have to land."

Reed lowered Turk to the floor and crashed into the cockpit. Corbyn was now strapped into the pilot's chair. The dash was alive with lights. Corbyn had pulled a headset on and was calling into the mic. Nobody seemed to be answering.

"What's happening?" Reed demanded.

"Portside engine gone, losing fuel from multiple tanks. Turns out it's not such a bloody good idea to take off in the middle of a firefight."

Reed looked back to Turk. The big man had already hauled himself into a seated position and was fighting to climb into a chair with his good arm. His left arm still hung limp. Reed returned to help him, pulling a strap across his waist and cinching it tight.

"I'm done," Turk growled. "I'm so freaking done with this. *No more jobs!* Isn't that what we said?"

Reed squeezed his shoulder. "But don't you want an *authentic experience*?"

Turk glared knives at him, and Reed found his own chair. He cinched the seatbelt tight over his waist. Ahead, Corbyn called into the radio. The plane was now drifting left. Reed could feel it. He could see the altimeter bleeding slowly, like Turk's ass.

"Hang on to your knickers, boys!" Corbyn shouted. "This one's gonna get rough."

59

Wolfgang called Reed four times before giving up. Every call went straight to voicemail, as did his calls to Turk.

Then Wolfgang was out of numbers. He didn't have contact information for anybody at the CIA or the White House. Not even for the quasi-body-guard guy that the president kept so near to her side. Short of phoning the public access line for the FBI, Homeland Security, or the TSA, he had nothing.

And none of those numbers would work. Not quickly enough. From the moment he read the emails and understood what they meant, he knew they were already out of time. Behind the eight ball. Racing to catch a speeding train even as it screamed out the station.

He also knew that Oleksiy Melnyk deserved to die. He almost wished he had gutted the man himself.

A quick conference with Ivan produced the next logical step in a desperate attempt to turn back the clock. They had to get to shore, quickly. Without communication and with nobody to contact in Washington, the next order of business would be to fly back to the States and break down doors in person.

But first, there was the small matter of Melnyk, his two dead goons, and his bloody yacht. Ivan decided that was an easy problem to bury—or, rather, to sink. While Wolfgang packed as much of Melnyk's electronic gear as he could find into a backpack, Ivan descended into the engine compartment. Wolfgang heard a loud thud followed by the pound of Ivan's feet coming up the stairs.

"What about the bodies?" Wolfgang asked.

"Leave them for the crabs. It's no less than they deserve."

The powerboat was smashed, a gaping hole opened in its bow from where Ivan had rammed it aboard the yacht's stern. It might float away as the larger boat sank, but before long that hole would bring it down also.

The next best option was the yacht's launch boat—not much fancier than a rubber raft with a Yamaha outboard hanging off the back. They used the crane mounted to the yacht's bow to maneuver the launch over the side, then Ivan pulled the cord to start the outboard as the yacht's stern settled slowly into the water.

"I opened all the seacocks," Ivan said, catching Wolfgang staring at the yacht. "Don't worry, I have done this before."

Wolfgang had no doubt Ivan was telling the truth, but it wasn't the yacht or the bodies he was concerned about. Already his mind had traveled back to America. His home that never felt like a home.

How many thousands were at risk? Tens of thousands, maybe. Depending on weapon deployment. His heart rate accelerated just thinking about it, and he jerked his head to signal Ivan onward. The big Russian gunned the throttle on the Yamaha, and the launch raced westward toward the nearest Greek coast.

They had crossed the midpoint of the Thermaic Gulf and were now closer to the Greek mainland than to Angelochori behind. Fortunately, only a couple miles away was a place called Makrygialos, according to the map on Wolfgang's phone. They would hide the launch on the beach and go into town. Find transportation back to Thessaloniki, and then get a ticket straight back to America.

Wolfgang would keep calling the entire time, ringing every number he could think of off the hook as long as it took. Because this was on him now. The blast outside of Nashville was nothing but a prelude.

ICA's next strike would drive the body count off the charts.

60

The Dominican Republic

"We're going down! Lock in, chaps!"

The easygoing calm in Corbyn's voice did little to assuage the thundering blast of adrenaline coursing through Reed's veins. He was already locked in, hands and feet braced against the seatback ahead of him, belt cinched down around his waist as tight as he could make it. Across the aisle Turk had assumed a similar position, albeit with only one arm. His left arm still lay in his lap, his face creased with pain.

With every flash of lightning, Reed could see the dead propeller of the portside engine turning slowly under the force of a headwind. Rain blasted against the fuselage, and the aircraft shuddered like a helicopter skipping into a rough landing—sometimes dropping three or four feet at a time as Corbyn negotiated through a pocket of turbulence.

She put the landing gear down. Dim landing lights marked each wheel as they descended from beneath the wings. The righthand gear locked into place, but the lefthand gear made it only halfway down before stalling out. The next flash of lightning exposed something thick and oily running across the tire.

Hydraulic fluid, Reed thought. Not good. Not good at all.

"You got an airstrip?" Reed shouted.

Corbyn actually laughed. "You got an extra engine in your back pocket?"

I'll take that as a no.

Reed focused on his breathing, forcing his heart rate to calm. Of all the crummy situations he'd found himself in over the past decade, an airplane crash had never made the list. This would be something to cross off his bucket list, assuming it didn't *kick* his bucket.

Without an airstrip, running under only one engine, with fuel and hydraulic fluid streaming from two dozen bullet holes, that possibility seemed likely. It also brought another thought to mind—a more ironic one.

I owe some asshole eight million dollars.

"I've got a clearing!" Corbyn shouted. "It's not very long. I'm gonna need to take her down hard."

Another flash of lightning illuminated an expanse of jungle foliage, stretching as far as Reed could see only a couple thousand feet below, and closing fast. He saw mountain ridges and deep gullies. Towering mahogany trees and snaking dirt roads.

He didn't see any civilization. And he didn't see a clearing.

The King Air shuddered, and the righthand engine coughed. Reed's heart rate spiked and he dug both hands into the armrests.

"Corbyn . . ."

"Losing fuel pressure," Corbyn said. "It's all good."

Corbyn's words came in clipped, shotgun blasts, but no fear tainted her tone. She sounded like a Marine sergeant calling orders as mortar shells detonated on all sides. A calm professional, trained for the occasion.

From the seat next to him Reed heard a dull whisper. He looked that way to see Turk bent over, his forehead pressed against the seatback ahead of him, his eyes closed. Lips moving softly.

Reed had never seen Turk pray before. Not in fifty gunfights. He wanted to put a hand on his shoulder, but the next lightning flash exposed treetops barely fifty feet down. The King Air was still hurtling along like a rocket, shaking and dropping as the righthand engine quit altogether. Rain blurred the windows. Reed's chest tightened. He clamped his eyes closed and thought about Banks. About Davy.

About his daughter.

"Brace for impact!" Corbyn screamed.

A clipping, rushing sound ground from beneath the plane. Like a broom scrubbing against the sheet metal—treetops. A clash of thunder shook the air, and Reed's stomach flew into his throat. The nose of the aircraft dropped. The tail snatched sideways. Corbyn whooped from the cockpit like a crazed cowboy flung from a bucking bronco. Reed's fingers sank into the leather seatback. The aircraft dropped another dozen feet like a rock from a balcony.

And then they hit.

61

The White House
Washington, DC

The phone calls began just after eight p.m. on the West Coast. Eleven in DC. At first they came in a trickle, reports of cryptic messages ringing into FBI field offices in Los Angeles, San Francisco, and Seattle, where FBI analysts initially suspected a wave of pranksters capitalizing on the Nashville bombing and the fear it had birthed.

But then the clock struck midnight in Washington, and the floodgates opened. 911 emergency services from San Diego to Chicago exploded with tens of thousands of panicked reports. The cryptic messages were streaming in to cell phones in two dozen states. The smooth-talking man with the Arabic accent was back, and he had a very clear message for the nation: Doom was coming. Very shortly. The righteous hand of Allah would soon level judgment against the infidels like never before experienced, a bloodbath that would dwarf 9/11.

There would be no place to hide. No chance of escape. The end was near.

The phones in the presidential residence woke Maggie from a fitful sleep thirty minutes into the new day. Dropping her feet to the carpeted floor, she scrubbed blurry eyes and mumbled into the receiver.

"What is it?"

"The robocalls are back, ma'am." It was Easterling. She sounded as though she'd never gone to bed. "I just got off the phone with Director Purcell. The FBI is receiving thousands of reports. I thought you should know."

"Has there been an attack?" Maggie's hands turned cold even as she voiced the words. She was awake now, the vague nightmares she'd been sweating through only moments prior feeling like a fairytale compared to the real world.

"No," Easterling said. "Not yet."

Maggie thought quickly, wincing as another lance of pain shot through her abdomen. She could have Easterling put a deputy on watch. Ring her again if there was a new development. Leave this problem to the FBI.

But no. That wasn't the type of leader she was. She needed to be on deck.

"Are you still in the West Wing?" Maggie asked.

"Yes, ma'am."

"Meet me in the Oval in fifteen. Order some coffee and soup."

Maggie hung up and stood. No sooner had her weight descended onto her knees than a blinding flash of pain raced through her gut and into her chest. Maggie's vision went black and she collapsed like a skyscraper imploding. The floor struck her forehead and blackness closed around her vision. She gasped, but couldn't breathe. The pain was unbelievable, and it kept radiating in waves, tearing through her body with angry vengeance. She tried to call for help but managed only a half-hearted gurgle.

The door opened anyway, and O'Dell hurtled in. Had he been waiting outside? The big man hit the carpet next to her, one hand taking her wrist.

"Are you okay? Can you hear me?"

Maggie gasped. As quickly as it had struck, the pain was subsiding. It faded into the back of her mind, leaving her with a dull headache and O'Dell's voice someplace on the other side of a fish tank.

"Maggie?"

She blinked, her vision slowly returning. Salty sweat slipped into her mouth, and Maggie panted. Her shoulders loosened, and she collapsed onto the floor.

"I'll call the doctor," O'Dell said.

"No!" Maggie's voice was dry. Her fingers dug into O'Dell's arm, and she hauled herself into a seated position with an agonized grunt. Her entire torso throbbed. Her stomach felt like it was loaded with a pound of white-hot nails. But the racing, overwhelming pain relaxed a little. She could see now.

Maggie sat up and caught her breath. She pushed tangled, sweaty hair out of her face and suddenly realized she wasn't wearing any underwear—just a thin nightgown.

Maybe it should have bothered her, but it didn't. She was glad O'Dell was close. His strong arm felt like a rock to lean on.

"What happened?" O'Dell's voice was soft, but carried a forceful edge.

"I just . . . I just fell. Got up too quickly, I guess."

She held her stomach with one arm. O'Dell squeezed her hand, and she looked up. His eyes were kind, but buried in their dark depths she saw pain even worse than the lightning bolt that had torn through her body. A personal misery.

She didn't know what to do with that, so she looked away. "Help me up?"

O'Dell's tree-trunk arm lifted, and she followed it. Back on her feet, her head swam, but she didn't fall. Her gut had returned to the same vague ache it had tortured her with ever since being shot. Not an unbearable thing, but impossible to forget.

"I need to get dressed. We're going to the Oval."

O'Dell hesitated awkwardly. Maggie forced a smile to break the tension.

"Just stand by. It's . . . nothing you haven't seen before."

He forced a laugh. Maggie staggered toward her closet.

Why were things still so awkward between them?

She was pulling the nightgown over her head when O'Dell's phone rang. He muttered a hello, and Maggie reached for underwear and a sweat-suit. Something comfortable for the long night ahead.

"Who is this?" O'Dell barked.

Maggie's blood ran cold. She returned to the door, clasping the clothes over her bare chest. O'Dell pivoted toward her, dark eyes blazing. He hit the speaker button, and the last of the robocall rumbled across the room.

A smooth voice. An Arabic accent.

"... the wrath of judgment is coming for you, infidel. When your streets run with blood, there will be no escape. Allahu Akbar!"

62

Vanderbilt University Medical Center
Nashville, Tennessee

Lucy's favorite part of her new faith was prayer. Maybe because she was typically such an internal person, or because she found it difficult to truly trust anyone. She never liked to share her feelings, her fears. Those innermost parts of her soul that she had barricaded behind sky-high walls for most of her life.

But in prayer, she was safe. There was no judgment. No misunderstanding. No interruption or condescension or exploitation. Brother Matthew used to tell her to "pray without ceasing," which she thought might be hyperbole, but the longer she practiced the more ceaseless her silent communication felt, and the more it soothed the brokenness in her chest.

Lucy prayed for Banks from the moment she learned of the blast, and when she arrived at the hospital, after sweet-talking the nurse into letting her visit Banks's private ICU room, she hit her knees alongside the bed and prayed a while longer.

Bible close to her left hand. SIG SAUER P365XL and KA-BAR BK7 Becker close to her right. Lucy wasn't really sure how to reconcile the idea of taking life with her newfound redemption, but it was a question she would be willing to suspend if anyone laid a finger on Banks.

She owed Reed that much.

As the clock reached the wee hours of the morning, exhaustion tugged at Lucy's mind. She hadn't left Banks's side for more than a visit to the ladies' room in nearly twenty-four hours, only cat-napping during the day. The nurses had asked her to leave, of course, when visiting hours were exhausted. Lucy turned on the charm again, one of her favored weapons of old, but now less sexy and more sweet. She won them over. She told stories and made them laugh. She talked about how badly she needed Banks to pull through.

Eventually they left her alone again, and the clock dragged on. Lucy tired of reading her Bible and sat staring at the wall a while, trying to avoid her reflection in the reinforced glass of the window. It was still difficult to face the lines in her cheeks or the gray beneath her eyes. Still tough to accept that she would never again be who and what she used to be.

Lucy's stomach growled, loud enough to startle her. She glanced sideways at Banks, and saw her sleeping peacefully to the beep of the heart monitor and the hiss of the ventilator. Lucy stretched both arms and contemplated the row of vending machines down the hall. A snack would help keep her awake. Then maybe she would see what was on TV.

Tucking the SIG into her backpack, she took the KA-BAR instead and slipped it into her waistband at the small of her back, dropping her loose sweater over it. Then she padded out of the room on soft feet, thighs stinging as her burn scars chafed.

Another new reality.

The hospital was quiet, the nurse's station silent save for the occasional murmur of a laugh track—some sitcom, played on an iPad. Lucy reached the vending machines and thumbed quarters into the slot. A bag of chips and an energy drink. The fuel of champions, or at least the fuel of battered ex-assassins struggling to stay awake.

Back in the hallway she cracked the drink open. Took a sip of supercharged caffeine and sugar, immediately relieved by the burst of artificial energy. And then she stopped cold.

Banks's door was open—just ten inches. Lucy was certain she had shut it. A nurse might have stuck her head in for a quick bedside check, but the floor nurse had already passed by barely twenty minutes prior.

And the nurse had flipped the light on.

Lucy bent in the hallway and deposited the chips and drink on the floor. She prowled forward like a cat, her legs tingling from the burn scars as she moved on the balls of her feet. Her right hand dipped beneath her sweater and reached her waistline. She found the handle of the KA-BAR— hard rubber and abrasive grip texture. It filled her palm, but she didn't draw. She glided without a sound all the way to the door, pressing one shoulder against the drywall. Easing up to the doorjamb. Holding her breath.

And listening to somebody else's. Not loud, but impossible to miss. A man's breathing, matched by soft footsteps. Lucy crept close to the door and slipped the knife from its sheath. She held it alongside her right thigh, the glistening blade razor-sharp and at the ready.

She saw the man. Tall, not overly broad. Wearing a tight T-shirt over muscled arms. Not medical—he wore jeans instead of scrubs, with no visible ID clipped to his belt. He stood alongside Banks's bed, a hand reached out. Bending over.

Lucy moved like a snake. She flashed around the corner and into the room, slipping through the narrow gap in the door. Blade rising. She reached the bed in a flash. The man stiffened, and started to turn.

Lucy was too quick. Her left hand grabbed his shirt collar, yanking back hard enough to constrict it around his throat, jeopardizing his airflow while also pulling him off balance. The tip of the blade found his kidney, pressing just hard enough to break skin, only a quick flick from laying him open like a gutted deer.

It wasn't a complex hold, or even a very strong one. But it did the job. The guy felt the knife and went rigid.

"You freaking flinch and I'll filet your ass," Lucy hissed. She pressed with the knife, just hard enough to reinforce her point. He inhaled, sharply. Then his head twisted toward her.

"I said don't move!" Lucy snapped, jabbing again. His hands flew up.

"Lucy! Chill out. It's me."

Lucy squinted. The voice was familiar. She cocked her head.

"*Wolf?*"

She didn't mean to prod with the blade as the question left her lips, but she must have. Her prisoner yelped and jumped, pulling against her hand. His face twisted, offering a side profile of high cheekbones and a bold chin —a profile she recognized.

"Wolfgang! You idiot. I almost killed you." Lucy withdrew the knife and wrapped Wolfgang in an automatic hug, petite arms enclosing his neck. Wolfgang stumbled under her unexpected weight. He began to push her back. Lucy squeezed tighter.

"How long has it been?" she squealed. "Wait, don't tell me. Venezuela, right? Reed and Banks's wedding? I didn't know where you'd—"

"*Lucy,*" Wolfgang snapped, cutting her short. One of his large hands closed around her shoulder and pushed her back. Light from the hallway fell across his face as he took a step forward.

The look in his eye wasn't what she expected. It had been years since she'd seen Wolfgang. A lot had happened to her in that time. By the look of him, a lot had happened to Wolfgang, too. His face was pale. There was a new scar above one ear. His hair was long and disheveled.

But it was the gleam in his eye that threw her off the most. Total earnestness. Almost desperation.

"Where is Reed?" Wolfgang said.

63

Somewhere in the Dominican Republic

The King Air's tail struck first, hard enough to send the aircraft bouncing off the dirt and hurling Reed upward toward the ceiling. His waist snatched against the lap belt, and then they were down again. The aircraft slid sideways. The front right landing gear caught the ground while the lefthand gear collapsed. Shrieking metal met rock and mud exploded over the windows. A rip opened right down the middle of the cabin, and dirt erupted over Reed's feet.

And the plane kept moving. Hurtling along, hopping and scrubbing, Corbyn still whooping from the cockpit. The King Air completed a complete spin and Reed's shoulder slammed into the wall. A window cracked. Metal crunched.

And then, suddenly, it all stopped. The airplane lay motionless on the ground and Reed's head spun. He released the seatback ahead of him and gasped, his entire body shaking. His vision blurred.

His heart was still—somehow—thumping along.

"*Ace!*" Corbyn screamed from the cockpit, and her headset struck the floor. She cut loose with another whoop, her voice trembling with naked

energy. Reed collapsed against his seatback and gasped, taking a moment
to collect himself

He was still alive.

The interior of the plane was dark. All the power was gone. Reed
fumbled with his seatbelt and found the latch. It fell away from his waist
and he coughed, reaching across the aisle for Turk. Instead of touching
flesh, he felt rough bark and damp wood. He dug into his pocket for a flashlight, and dumped light across the aisle.

Sometime during the landing a tree had broken through the bottom of
the King Air. A giant limb remained jammed through the fuselage, splintered and sharp, only inches from his right leg.

Reed blinked, realizing he would have been impaled if Corbyn had
flown only a little to the right. For that matter, eighteen inches to the left
and Turk would have met the same fate. As it was, the big man sat groaning
just beyond the limb, doubled over and holding his dislocated shoulder.

"Turk. You all right?"

Turk lifted his head, and blood streamed down his face. He was alive,
but he wasn't exactly all right. Unable to brace himself with both arms, he'd
collided with the seatback in front of him, and Reed thought his nose
looked broken.

For a split second, a flash of sympathy ignited in Reed's gut. Then Turk
opened his mouth with a guttural, whining groan, and that sympathy
evaporated.

"Why does it always have to be me?" Turk said.

Reed shook his head with a dull smile and climbed out of the seat. The
floor creaked under his boots, but it didn't sway. They had reached solid
ground. As he straightened, his back ignited in pain, but his arms, legs, and
ribcage all seemed intact. No broken bones that he could feel, anyway.

Another miracle.

Reed shone the light forward. "Corbyn? You good?"

Corbyn wriggled her way out of the pilot's chair. The flashlight beam
illuminated a spiderweb of cracks running through the plane's windshield.
All the lights and display panels in the cockpit were dead.

Eight million dollars, Reed thought again. *I owe some hairy asshole eight
million dollars.*

"We make it to the ground?" Reed asked.

Corbyn nodded. "Just barely. The treetops broke our speed."

"I can see that," Reed put a hand on the mahogany limb jutting through the floor. It wasn't moving.

He turned to the door and fought with the latch, but it wouldn't open. Sometime during their descent the plane must have warped, or a portion of the fuselage folded inward. The door was jammed tight and wouldn't budge.

"Here," Corbyn said. "Emergency exit."

She fiddled with a latch forward of the wing, then tugged. A square section of the fuselage popped out, admitting a light spray of rain and opening a hole large enough to pass through. Reed had to fight his way over a chair and worm beneath the jutting mahogany limb to reach it. Turk's situation was worse. He required assistance to climb forward, his head and shoulders ramming into the ceiling along the way. Getting him through the emergency exit was another trick altogether. Even with regular workouts that bulked Reed's chest and arms into corded bundles of muscle, it took all of his strength to haul Turk through the gap and onto the wing, boots sliding against wet metal as the rain continued to beat down.

Outside it was pitch dark, but a quick sweep of the flashlight told Reed all he needed to know. They had landed in a narrow clearing no more than fifty yards wide and maybe two hundred long. The plane had struck just inside the tree line and ripped across the muddy ground all the way to the end . . .

Where a cliff dropped off into pitch-black nothingness, less than a yard from the fuselage. The King Air's righthand wing hung over the void, rainwater dripping off a mutilated propeller and falling into the black. Even with the powerful flashlight beam, Reed couldn't see the bottom.

He shot Corbyn a look, raising one eyebrow.

The Brit shrugged innocently. "Did you die?"

No, Reed thought. *But I'm probably going to jail.*

Reed dropped off the wing and his boots sank a couple of inches into the mud, but he barely noticed as he helped Turk down. Blood still ran from Turk's nose, and he trembled as he reached the ground.

"How's the arm?" Reed asked.

"Out of commission," Turk said.

It was a simple statement, but it told Reed a lot. Turk wasn't the kind of guy to take anything out of commission until it was completely destroyed. The shoulder was bad.

"Hopefully you lads bought the insurance package," Corbyn said, popping out of the emergency exit. "If anybody asks, it was the autopilot's fault."

Reed ignored her, helping Turk into a seated position partially sheltered by the broken starboard wing. It was enough to hold back the rain while Reed regrouped.

Digging into his pocket, Reed fished until he found his phone. He didn't expect to have any signal, but it was at least worth checking. A quick inspection of the device produced a different problem—the phone was dead. He hadn't charged it since arriving in Haiti.

"What about yours?" He asked.

"I lost it at the airfield," Turk said. "You know, while I was busy playing Rambo."

"Right. Corbyn?"

"No signal," the pilot said. "But there may be an emergency radio in the plane. I'll look."

She disappeared back inside the fuselage, and Reed stared out over the cliff into the night. A distant lightning strike cast a weak glow over rolling mountain ridges, as far as the eye could see.

No visible roads. No visible cities. There might not be a cell signal for fifty miles.

Great.

"Montgomery . . . what the *hell?*" Corbyn called from the inside of the shattered plane, her tone dropping into an angry growl.

"What?"

Corbyn emerged from the emergency exit, black hair running with water, eyes laced with rage. She produced a folded piece of colorful paper. High gloss. Reed thought he recognized the logo of a popular vacation resort company.

"What?" he said again.

"You said you hired this plane," Corbyn said.

Reed didn't answer.

Corbyn threw the folded paper at him. It landed in the mud, and Reed flipped it open with the toe of his boot. It was one of those folders you get at a tourist attraction. The kind that house a photograph the tourism company printed for twenty cents and sold for twenty bucks.

The photograph was of Richie Barclay and his family.

"What have you got me into?" Corbyn shouted. "I freaking trusted you, asshole. Am I the accessory of grand larceny? I quit me job for this nonsense! I let you goad me into it. I must have lost the bloody plot!"

Reed lifted a hand to defend himself. It was no use. Corbyn was just getting started. Face flushing, her British accent growing rapidly thicker as her expressions of disgust grew rapidly more vile.

Taking a few steps away, Reed ran a hand through his hair and checked his watch. It was just after midnight. Hours until sunrise, and he couldn't afford to wait that long. What happened at the airfield might have been bad luck. The wrong place at the wrong time. But something deep in his gut said otherwise.

And that meant the man in the video tape—the butcher who had slain his daughter—was still one step ahead.

Wrecked plane or no wrecked plane, he had to get off this island. He needed a new contact. Somebody who would listen to him. Somebody with pull. That wouldn't be O'Dell, and he still didn't have direct access to the CIA. He needed something else.

Reed turned back to Corbyn. She was still shouting. Still red-faced as a beet. He waited nearly five minutes for her to finish. When she finally drew breath, his voice was perfectly calm.

"Are you done?"

Corbyn's eyes bulged. She looked down to Turk, his head only half sheltered by the broken wing. He offered no support.

"Well I guess I better be," she snapped.

"Terrific. Did you find a radio?"

"No."

"Okay then. So now we're gonna hike out of here until we can find a cell signal."

"And then what?" Corbyn quipped. "Call Uber? Freaking Yankee tossers."

"Actually, Jane Bond, I think we need a British solution this time."

64

The Citation touched down at Savannah International Airport an hour before dawn. Hamid directed the Spaniard to taxi into a parking spot allocated for the use of private jets, and then he shot him in the back of the head.

The dead guy bled out even as the engines wound down. Ibrahim led Hamid and Kadeem down the jet's steps, pulling the Cardinals hat low over his ears. Across the tarmac sat a charcoal gray Chevrolet Suburban. It was hot in Georgia, the air sticky with humidity. But at least the rain had stopped.

Bahir waited behind the wheel of the Suburban while Mahmoud stepped out to greet the new arrivals.

"*Assalamu alaikum.*"

"*Wa alaikum salaam*, brother," Ibrahim replied. He piled into the back seat of the Suburban alongside Hamid and Kadeem, Mahmoud taking shotgun. The vehicle was a rental, featuring plain cloth seats. It smelled of vanilla and flowers, some cheap air freshener. Bahir shifted into gear and drove them away, leaving the Citation sitting with its door still open.

Somebody would find the dead pilot, Ibrahim knew. Somebody would call the police. An investigation would be launched. Security recordings would be pulled. Perhaps he or one of the others would be found on them.

Ibrahim didn't care. The clock was now winding ever closer to the end. The Americans were already out of time.

"All is well with the shipment," Mahmoud pronounced, smoking quietly with the window cracked. "We picked up Omar and Youssef at the Atlanta airport this evening, and they helped us secure the rental trucks. They're almost finished loading now."

"And the calls?" Ibrahim asked.

"I just got off the phone with our ally," Mahmoud said. "We were wise to place the calls at night. Many are going to voicemails. The panic will carry straight into the sunrise."

Ibrahim nodded once, watching suburban Savannah pass by alongside the highway. Tight clusters of townhomes and endless webs of concrete. A middle class neighborhood for America, but for a man from the Middle East, it looked like paradise itself.

Minus the seventy-two *houri*, of course. Beautiful young virgins. A minimum gift of Allah to the least of his servants. Ibrahim would not be among the least, according to the sheikh whose house had sheltered him these many years. His zeal for the teachings of the prophet set him apart. He was a man of conviction. A holy one. A righteous zealot who would wage jihad against the Great Satan, bringing death to the infidels and justice to the oppressed.

It was all Ibrahim could do to hold a straight face as the sheikh prattled on about it. The man was wealthy. He had connections. The fact that he actually believed any of the mystical nonsense encased in ancient texts written by hallucinating drunks made him no less useful to Ibrahim. It only meant Ibrahim had to work harder to say the right things. To appear the right way.

To be the holy jihadist the sheikh wanted him to be. So what if the man thought he was doing it in the name of Allah? So what if Hamid, Kadeem, Mahmoud, and young Bahir thought they were all doing it in the name of Allah?

Maybe there actually would be seventy-two busty *houri* waiting for them on the other side. Maybe not. Regardless, there would most definitely be something sweeter to reward their bloodshed. Something much, much more eternal.

Cold, ruthless revenge. The kind that could bring a dead man peace.

"I have prayed," Ibrahim said, voice calm. "Allah has sent me a vision."

All four men perked up, waiting. Alert. Fully enraptured by the prospect of whatever Ibrahim was about to say.

"We will not be coming back from this, my brothers. It is the will of Allah that we perish in this fight."

Kadeem, Hamid, and Bahir slumped, just a little. Barely noticeable, and quickly disguised. Mahmoud didn't so much as flinch. He was an old man. A warrior of great conviction who had battled the Americans for nearly two decades. He'd already made peace with his inevitable death.

"*Subhanallah*," Kadeem said. "May Allah's will be done."

"Have you decided our targets?" Hamid asked, rotating in the passenger seat.

Outside the suburbs were fading. A commercial district replaced them —the Port of Savannah. One of the largest ports in America. The junction of foreign aid shipments to embattled Haiti.

The next step on a chessboard, leading inevitably toward checkmate.

"You and Kadeem will take the east," Ibrahim said. "Omar and Youssef will go west. Bahir and Mahmoud will come with me."

From the driver's seat, Bahir's chin lifted. A proud glint entered his eye. No doubt he was pleased to be joining his fearless leader on this great mission, but he shouldn't have been. It was no secret to Ibrahim that Bahir was the weak link of the group—the youngest, and the least hardened by battle. He was the most likely to break, and if he did, Ibrahim wanted to be there to put a bullet in his back.

Allah's will be done.

The Suburban turned into the port of Savannah.

65

The FBI registered more than two hundred thousand reports of ICA robocalls by sunrise. Maggie remained in the Oval Office throughout the night, bouncing between conference calls with FBI Director Bill Purcell and various deputy directors at the CIA.

O'Brien was out of the office. Aimes was out of the office. Maggie couldn't find anyone at Langley.

Stratton arrived just after six a.m., bustling into the West Wing and looking as calm and collected as ever. He wore a premium black suit and red power tie, completely shaming Maggie's wrinkled sweatsuit and loose ponytail. Even so, she had to admit it was a relief to have him at her side.

"What do you need?" Stratton said, advancing directly to the coffee bar and dumping two creams and a sugar into a porcelain White House cup.

Joining the pair of them in the Oval were Easterling, O'Dell, Director of the National Security Agency General Wayne Gravitt, and Brett Porter-meyer, Maggie's White House counsel.

As Maggie's chief legal advisor, Portermeyer's duties included directing the Office of White House Counsel, keeping her advised on all legal matters pertaining to her duties as president, and vetting any executive action against possible abuse of power. In short, he was her legal safety net. He covered her ass. But in addition to his preventative skillsets, Portermeyer also possessed a uniquely creative ability to think outside the box. To bend the rules. To find loopholes.

It was why Maggie hired him. He was a good lawyer.

"We have a problem," Maggie said quietly.

Stratton took his seat on the couch next to her and glanced sideways at Portermeyer. The two men knew each other well. Stratton understood the implication of Portermeyer's presence.

"The FBI is hitting a block wall with the robocalls," Easterling said, filling in for her boss as Maggie struggled to sip tea. Her stomach still hurt. Not the lancing, blinding pain, thankfully. But the duller aches were worse today. Substantially so. It wasn't easy to talk.

"What kind of block wall?" Stratton asked.

"The legal kind," Portermeyer said.

Stratton raised an eyebrow.

"Privacy laws have them somewhat hamstrung on what avenues they can pursue to backtrack the calls," Easterling continued. "They can't obtain a mass warrant. Essentially, they need individual warrants to authorize every intrusion into personal cell phone records."

"Can't they obtain privacy waivers from the contract holders?" Stratton asked.

"Of course. But that takes time. A lot of it. And as before, they need a waiver for each individual phone number. Then they need to contact the cellular carrier and run up the corporate chain to get the records they need. They've been working that avenue all night and getting nowhere. The FBI has no idea where these calls are coming from. Whatever auto dialing system is in place, it's using hundreds of different phone numbers to dial from, most of which appear as international callers. That makes backtracking them to a source even more difficult. It's a mess."

Maggie watched as Stratton's gaze switched automatically to General Gravitt, and then to Portermeyer. It didn't take a rocket scientist to draw a connection between the two.

"I take it by the cast of characters present for today's play that something legally ambiguous is in the works," Stratton said.

The general flushed. Portermeyer actually smirked.

"The National Security Agency may have resources to assist the FBI," Gravitt said, very carefully.

"But?" Stratton said, lifting an eyebrow.

A sudden flush of frustration ignited in Maggie's chest. It was probably just the pain gnawing in her gut, or maybe it was the lack of sleep. Either way, she didn't have patience for Stratton to play chicken with the room. Everybody knew what the problem was.

"But if they lend the FBI their *resources*, they admit those resources exist," Maggie snapped. "Come on Jordan, we don't have time for this."

Stratton ducked his head apologetically.

"General, it's a simple question," Maggie said. "Can you trace these calls or not?"

Gravitt shifted in his chair. He cleared his throat and seemed to be choosing his words. It made Maggie want to punch him, but she understood why.

Everybody knew what the NSA was capable of. Edward Snowden had made sure of that. The infrastructure to intercept and survey hundreds of thousands of electronic communications was there, beyond question. Even inside the country.

But the spotlight of public ire had moved on from the NSA during the decade following Snowden's revelations. People had forgotten—or simply decided that they didn't care—about the possibility of intrusive government surveillance. Any NSA director in his right mind would be insane to welcome that spotlight to return.

"I would need to check with my staff, Madam President," Gravitt said slowly. "Whatever legal assistance we could render the FBI would, of course, be at their disposal."

Legal. That was the key word. Maggie shot a look at Portermeyer. The attorney was tall and muscular, built like a boxer. He had ample blond hair, swept back over a charming face that she had no doubt Mrs. Portermeyer regularly swooned for.

As had the previous Mrs. Portermeyer. And the one before her.

"The legalities on this issues are pretty airtight, I'm afraid," Portermeyer said. "You could claim the Patriot Act, and suppress the investigation beneath a shield of national security, but I doubt that would hold up. With this many phone numbers and so many corporate employees working in cooperation with the FBI, it would be impossible to keep any partnership with the NSA completely covert. If and when questions were raised . . . those questions might be difficult to answer."

The answer wasn't what Maggie wanted to hear, but it reflected the pragmatic perspective on governance that she appreciated about Portermeyer. The man interpreted the law as a highway sometimes mired by traffic jams. Was it time to kick the truck into four-wheel drive and carve a new path?

"What about an executive order?" Stratton said. "Emergency action. Authorize the Department of Defense to make the resources of the NSA available to the FBI."

Gravitt's shoulders tensed. Maggie didn't have to guess why. Before he could object, Portermeyer stepped in.

"Before any such emergency power could be accessed, the president would need to declare a national state of the emergency, pursuant to the National Emergencies Act. I'm not sure a direct application of armed forces emergency power could be leveraged with the NSA. Even though they operate under the jurisdiction of the DOD, a legal argument could be made that NSA analysts do not constitute service members. The language on the use of armed forces is, I'm afraid, quite specific."

"We're not armed services, ma'am," Gravitt said.

Maggie held up a hand, wincing. She drew O'Dell's eye and mouthed a silent word.

Pills.

"Are you okay, ma'am?" Stratton asked.

Maggie shot him a glare hot enough to blister skin. He looked away.

"I'll ask a direct question, General," Maggie said. "Does the NSA have the ability to trace these calls or not?"

Gravitt fixated on the carpet, choosing his words again. Maggie wanted to come out of her chair. Growing up in Louisiana not far from the sprawling mass of Fort Polk, she was used to military people. She liked them. She appreciated their blunt approach to life and work.

But none of that prepared her for the reality of senior military leadership. Most of these generals and admirals had more in common with the politicians they served alongside than the soldiers they commanded. They hemmed and hawed. Guarded their words.

Covered their asses.

"*General*," Maggie snapped. "I've got dead civilians in Tennessee, dead soldiers in Syria, and a quarter million phone calls prophesying Armageddon by the end of the week. I don't have *time* for your politics. Answer my question or I'll find somebody who will."

Gravitt's chin lifted. Maggie saw the outrage boiling behind his eyes. She didn't care.

"Yes," Gravitt said at last, his voice perfectly flat.

"Thank you." Maggie pivoted to Portermeyer. "Brett, how can we make it happen?"

Portrayer scratched his cheek, his brow scrunched into a frown. O'Dell returned with the painkillers held discretely in a folded napkin. Maggie flipped them out and knocked them back without any care for who saw her. She could feel her mind fraying again. Her nerves pushing her toward the edge.

She needed the physical torment, at least, to fade into the background.

"As I said before, we shouldn't use armed forces code," Portermeyer said. "It's too specific. You need something vague . . ."

Portermeyer trailed off. Maggie waited. She'd never seen the man break off a sentence. Never seen him hesitate. It made her uneasy, but as with General Gravitt, she was too impatient to indulge him.

"*What*, Brett?"

"I hesitate to recommend this, ma'am. It's dicey at best. But there is a possible loophole in the Communications Act."

"Explain."

"It was passed in 1934. Under a national emergency, or the threat of war, it authorizes the president to regulate or even seize control of radio stations."

"*Radio stations?*"

Portermeyer held up a hand. "The language is inclusive. A modern interpretation could cover internet servers. Or, perhaps . . . cellular providers."

The room became very still. Both Stratton and Easterling looked to Maggie.

"That's a big step," Stratton said.

Maggie didn't need to be told. Just hearing it suggested sent a strange chill through her blood.

"I don't know if I like that idea," she said.

"It would face immediate legal challenge," Portermeyer admitted. "I certainly wouldn't recommend initiating a full takeover of the telecommunications sector. But . . . you could leverage it to authorize federal intrusion. Surveillance, essentially. Bypass the court orders and privacy waivers. Temporarily, of course."

Maggie looked at her tea. She was conscious of all eyes in the room fixed on her. A part of her wondered what Stratton and Easterling were thinking. If they were ready to throw themselves across the tracks to stop Portermeyer's train before it even left the station.

A greater part of her knew she couldn't afford to worry about what they thought. Even if it was sound advice. This burden was on her alone.

Maggie walked to the window. She looked out over the rose garden, remembering a day not long ago when she had enjoyed this view only hours after sidestepping nuclear war. It seemed to always be her view when crisis struck.

And crisis seemed to always be striking.

"Would that strategy survive a lawsuit?" Maggie asked.

Portermeyer grunted. "Difficult to say. Possibly not. But any lawsuit would take weeks, and by then, if the threat is brought to heel, you could relinquish the powers voluntarily. Then it's a political problem, not a legal one. I'm not a political expert, but with the country secured, I imagine you would land on top."

Nobody else spoke. Maggie finished the tea, knowing the crux of the question was in the threat.

Was it a bluff? Did the smooth voice from Arabia actually have a plan, or was he just working to stir the pot? Spread the terror?

She closed her eyes and breathed deep. Blocked out the throbbing pain. And knew.

Even if it were a bluff, it was a bridge too far. There was only so much fear a country could take before it came apart at the seams. Before the terror itself became the ultimate weapon of mass destruction.

"Draft the order," she said. "I'm declaring a state of emergency."

66

The Dominican Republic

The eastern sky brightened over the island of Hispaniola before Reed and his battered crew found cell phone service.

After binding Turk's arm in a sling and soothing his road-rashed hindquarters with salve—both from Reed's med kit—he was able to walk while leaning on a cut branch as a makeshift hiking stick. On a level playing field with solid ground underfoot, he might still have moved as well as Reed or Corbyn. But the mountains surrounding them were anything save level, and the ground anything save solid. Rain left everything muddy, washing out the rough dirt track they found two miles from the airplane. Even in the darkened hours of early morning, the insects were brutal. Mosquitos and biting flies swarmed by the thousands, an endless nuisance that plagued their every step.

Despite all the challenges, Turk refused to sit down or be left behind. He popped painkillers to manage the agony of his shredded shoulder and leaned heavily on his stick, but even when Corbyn tried to take his pack, he flatly refused.

Reed led the way, eventually locating a winding dirt road that led slowly upward from the crash site, praying for a passing truck to rumble along and pick them up. Corbyn was pretty sure that they had crossed the border between Haiti and the Dominican Republic sometime before crashing, leaving them lost in the rural southwestern corner of the country dozens of miles removed from any major city, but Reed couldn't believe that the region was completely desolate. The road was rutted and appeared at least semi-frequently used. Somebody would pass by eventually.

In the meantime, there was nothing to do but hike on, with Corbyn checking her phone every few hundred yards for a signal. It wasn't until they reached a ridge line overlooking a brilliant tropical lake, glimmering in the sunlight a few thousand feet below, that she finally cut loose with a triumphant whoop.

"Jackpot! I have bars."

Reed placed a hand against a gnarled mahogany tree, heaving as sweat dripped from his face in a torrent. It was baking hot on the island. The rain had cranked the humidity factor up somewhere close to hades level. What little water supply they had taken from the plane was nearly exhausted.

Corbyn extended the phone toward Reed. Reed shot a glance at Turk, but the big man wasn't paying any attention. He'd settled onto a fallen log, heaving just as hard. The agony in his face was impossible to miss.

"Well, go on. Call somebody!"

Reed swallowed water from a bottle and wiped his lips. He shook his head.

"I need you to do that."

"Come again?"

"We don't . . . have anybody to call, at the moment."

Corbyn's brow wrinkled. She looked to Turk, momentary confusion taking over. Then her face flushed something darker than scarlet. The shade edged closer to maroon.

"You tossers! You want me to call London, don't you?"

Reed didn't answer immediately. That was all the confirmation Corbyn needed. Her fist tightened around the phone and he thought she might throw it. Eyes bulging, jaw clenched, she rammed her hand into the tree.

"I must be dead from the neck up! You had me steal a bloody plane. Now you want me to turn myself in? I'll be done! They'll take everything. The job's the least of my worries. I'll be under the jail for this cock-up."

"Corbyn . . ."

"Don't you even start with me, you knob. I went out on a limb for you. I believed you. I—"

"Corbyn!" Reed's voice cracked with exhaustion and dehydration. He threw the bottle down, his own face flushing.

Corbyn stopped midsentence. She raised a finger, sweat gleaming from her face. Waiting.

Reed opened his mouth, a long speech about terrorism and innocent lives cocked and loaded. It fell flat in his throat. He wasn't arguing with a politician or a civilian. Corbyn was a proud service member, and the source of her anger was the depth of his betrayal. It was as simple as that.

Reed's let out a sigh, but didn't look away. "I did what I had to do," he said simply.

Corbyn's finger curled slowly inward until her hand made a fist. That fist trembled. Her smooth brown cheeks tightened as dark eyes flashed.

Then she let out a growl through her teeth, as though there was a wild animal inside of her and it was fighting to get out. "I'm gonna have your balls for this. Freaking Yanks."

She punched on the phone, still muttering vitriol. She switched the phone to speaker mode and it dialed slowly. It was an international, roaming connection, Reed thought. It would take time. When nobody picked up, Corbyn dialed again.

"SIS, Office of International—"

"Sally, it's Kirsten. Where's Dick?"

"Kirsten! Where the 'ell are you? We've been—"

"Not now, Sally. Really haven't got the time. Put Dick on the line."

A long pause. Clicking and electronic beeps. Corbyn shot Reed another glower.

"Corbyn. Bloody 'ell. Where have you been?"

"Looky here, Dick. I need you to connect me with somebody at the CIA. Somebody with swagger. And no muckin' about, this is serious."

"Say what? You impudent little chav. I ought to toss your ass out on the street. If you're not in this office in the next half hour I swear to—"

"If you don't connect me with the CIA in the next five minutes, the blood is on your hands. How about that?"

Pause.

"I'm in the DR," Corbyn said. "That terrorist who bombed Nashville is headed back to the States with another weapon. It's all on film. Now are you gonna put me on the line with the Americans, or do I have to put your peanut balls in a vice first?"

"You yanking my chain, Corbyn?"

"Nope."

Another long pause. "Hold on."

Corbyn looked over her shoulder again, still fuming. She pointed a finger at Reed.

"You're gonna owe me."

67

Langley, Virginia

There were three trucks—or vans, rather. The small kind with ten-foot enclosed beds. Deputy Director Aimes recognized the logo of a popular moving company on all three even through the pixilated, black-and-white footage of the security camera.

The angle was imperfect. The view limited. Only one license plate was visible, but that proved meaningless. The Georgia plate was registered to a Chevrolet Corvette, and the owner had already reported the plate as stolen.

The trio of trucks were visible from the rear wheels forward as they backed into a slot in front of a single shipping container. She saw silhouettes of men passing near the trucks now and then. The trucks shifted as something heavy was loaded on board.

She couldn't see what.

After two hours, all three vehicles drove out in a cloud of dust. Aimes couldn't make out faces behind the curving windshields, but she saw two men in each of the first two trucks, and three in the third.

Seven men in total. The loading had taken time, but the trucks didn't appear squatted over their rear axles. They weren't weighed down.

What?

Aimes punched the hold button on her phone and cradled the receiver.

"Okay, Bill. I saw it."

"That what you needed?" FBI Director Bill Purcell's voice was clipped and strained. He was overloaded. He didn't want to make time for this conversation. But when the Central Intelligence Agency's deputy director made a special request during the heat of an anti-terrorist operation, somebody was going to take that call.

"I don't know," Aimes said. "You sure there weren't any other cameras? Something auxiliary, perhaps? A doorbell camera?"

"Nothing," Purcell said. "I've got people on the ground in Savannah making inquiries. The shipping container was owned by a Spanish company. We're still waiting for the shipping history . . . it's a mess down there, Sarah. Complete chaos."

The terrorist's wet dream, Aimes thought.

"Look, Sarah. I gotta run," Purcell said. "We're moving ahead with the executive order. I'll keep you posted."

Aimes thanked him and hung up. She went back to the video and watched it a third time. Her burning eyes fixated on the screen, the gnawing sensation in her gut building into edgy nausea. Across the floor, O'Brien was still meeting with his chief deputies. A task force was being developed to assist a joint NSA–FBI investigation of the storm of robocalls that had swept through the country early that same morning, leaving voicemails by the tens of thousands.

Aimes saw it all on the TV. She saw President Trousdale's press conference, declaring a state of national emergency and announcing her intentions to exercise dramatic emergency powers granted to her under the Communications Act. The media storm following that announcement would be spectacular, Aimes knew, but she wouldn't be watching.

She wouldn't be assisting in the assembly of the CIA's task force, either. O'Brien had ostracized her, running all operational functions via Mitch Costner, Director of Analysis. Costner was an arrogant prick who had been gunning for Aimes's job since she landed it, and she had no doubt that he would willingly support O'Brien's efforts to sideline her.

Problems for another day. Aimes had bigger fish to fry. If anything she was looking at was what it appeared, Costner and O'Brien were the least of America's concerns.

Returning to the video, Aimes replayed it for the fourth time, focusing on every detail. Squinting bloodshot and burning eyes. When the phone on her desk rang again, she punched the answer button without checking the ID.

"Yes?"

"Ma'am, I have SIS Deputy Director Arnold for you."

Aimes's face pivoted toward the phone. "Say what?"

"He just rang through, ma'am."

"Put him on."

The phone chirped. Aimes opened her mouth to offer a greeting, but Arnold beat her to it.

"What are you up to, Aimes?"

Deputy Director John Arnold's usually cheery, sometimes playful tone was lost in an uncustomary burst of anger. Aimes was taken off guard.

"Excuse me?"

"Oh don't play clever with me, old girl. You get to do that with your toys. You don't get to steal mine and then pretend otherwise!"

Aimes turned away from the computer, completely lost. "John, I literally have no idea what you're talking about."

"*Corbyn!* I'm talking about Kirsten bloody Corbyn, Sarah. I thought we reached an understanding about my agents. I looked the other way in Venezuela. I can't allow you to recklessly recruit my people for your own operations—"

"John," Aimes snapped. "I'm not running *any* operation."

"You sure? Because that's not what Corbyn says. I've got her on the bell right now, and she says she's standing alongside two of your people in the DR. She just hiked out of the jungle. She just *wrecked* a bloody plane!"

Aimes's mind spun. She lifted the phone away from her ear far enough to minimize the bulk of Arnold's wrath.

The DR. Dominican. Directly adjacent to Haiti . . .

Reed Montgomery. Aimes's mind raced back to the call between James O'Dell and Victor O'Brien. *Of course.*

"John, put her on the line."

"Say what?" Arnold's voice popped.

"Transfer the call. I swear, I'll iron this out. I just need to speak with her."

More muttered grumblings and threats from Arnold. More placations from Aimes.

Then Kirsten bloody Corbyn was brought on the line.

68

"Officer Corbyn, this Deputy Director Sarah Aimes with the Central Intelligence Agency. Am I to understand this is an unsecured line?"

Reed extended a hand. Corbyn appeared only too happy to pass the phone off.

"Deputy Director, this is Reed Montgomery."

Long pause. Reed looked down to check the battery life on the phone. It had dwindled to under ten percent. This call had to work.

"Since you're taking my call, I assume you received my tip," Reed said.

"We did." Aimes's voice was clear but reserved. As though she was thinking quickly, and choosing her words. "Where are you?"

Reed squinted. It wasn't the question he expected.

"Someplace in the DR. In the mountains."

"Can you get to an airport?"

Reed looked to Turk. His battle buddy was leaned over, holding his left shoulder. Turk was pale, but he nodded once.

"Yes," Reed said. "We'll figure it out."

"Find the nearest airfield and email us the location. I'm sending a plane."

Again, Reed paused. This wasn't the reaction he expected. Something about it felt wrong. Where was the "Thank you very much, we'll take it from here" line? The blatant dismissal?

Why was he speaking to the deputy director at all? If what he had to say was important enough to run to the top, shouldn't he be speaking with Victor O'Brien?

"The CIA doesn't hand out favors," Reed said. "There's no such thing as a free plane ride."

Aimes didn't answer. Reed waited.

"What do you need?" Reed pressed.

"You know that picture you sent?" Aimes said. "Our friend in Haiti?"

"Right."

"I think he's here. And I need him found."

Reed's body tensed. Then his mind grew cold—that perfect, icy chill that alerted his body of a switch being flipped. The transition from angry soldier up to his knees in Dominican mud to cold-blooded killer.

"Send the plane," Reed said.

69

The three trucks split as they left Savannah. Kadeem and Hamid took I-16 to Macon before turning west. Omar and Youssef took I-95 across rural South Carolina and up the East Coast.

Mahmoud piloted the final truck, with Ibrahim riding shotgun and young Bahir sandwiched between them. As they routed up I-75 toward Atlanta, the kid was alive with nervous tension, sweaty hands scrubbing against his American jeans, his eyes glossed over, his mouth held in a subdued smile as though he were dreaming.

In a way, maybe he was. Dreaming of virgins, Ibrahim thought. Of an eternity in paradise.

A true believer.

With every bump on the rough American highway Ibrahim winced and tried not to ratchet his head toward the back of the truck. The barrel was well secured. They had placed it all the way in the front of the cargo space, tied to a pallet with half a dozen heavy straps, then pinned against the truck's interior wall with more of the same.

It shouldn't move. And even if it did, why should he worry? Death would be brutally painful, but this close to the spill it wouldn't take long.

Ibrahim wasn't afraid of death. He just needed to know that his enemies died with him.

The sun rose over north Georgia, and Ibrahim's truck lost a couple of hours fighting through a series of metro-Atlanta wrecks. As the city faded into the rearview, Ibrahim checked his watch to determine the time. He calculated again how many hours remained between each of his trucks and their individual destinations, and then assumed another two or three hours for deployment of the barrels.

Adding all that time together, and subtracting backward, the number matched that on his watch. Give or take thirty minutes.

Ibrahim breathed deeply, rolling his head to loosen his neck. Embracing the weight of the moment, and what it meant. Savoring the terror he had dammed up like a river at the top of a mountain.

One flick of a switch, and the dam broke. The river surged out. The whole valley was flooded in fear.

Yes . . . the time had come. He could feel it in his gut.

Drawing his cell phone, Ibrahim placed a single call. Outbound, and international. Ringing up a phone buried in a basement on the other side of the globe.

The sweaty, bearded man who called himself Ibrahim's ally answered almost immediately.

"Yes?"

"It is time," Ibrahim said. "Start the clock."

70

American Mobile Corporate Headquarters
Dallas, Texas

Federal agents arrived at the front door of the 37-story office tower fifteen minutes before noon. A half dozen black SUVs and two fifteen passenger vans, carrying a total of nearly fifty men in black suits and bulletproof vests. Not just FBI agents, but federal marshals, also. NSA officers. Even a pair of analysts from homeland security.

Exactly the sort of mismatched circus group special agent in charge John Mitchener would expect for a half-cocked act of desperation like this.

Stepping out of the lead vehicle, Mitchener allowed most of the task force to assemble on the curb while he took two federal marshals and advanced to the top of the steps. American Mobile corporate security waited just outside the front doors, arms folded. Glock 17 handguns riding their hips. Across the street, Mitchener was conscious of a CNN news van screeching to a stop after blowing through a red light.

MSNBC and CBS were right on its heels. Fox wouldn't be long behind.

Long before Mitchener reached the top of the steps, the guards at the doors parted, and a trio of men in dark blue business suits stepped out.

Their leader was gray-haired, walking with his chin up. A Rolex watch rode his wrists. His shoes probably cost more than Mitchener's pickup truck.

The man extended a hand. "Special Agent Mitchener?"

The handshake was firm, but not friendly.

"That's right," Mitchener said.

"Daniel Cook, CEO of American Mobile Industries. What can I do for you, son?"

Mitchener indulged in a dry smile. In place of an answer, he simply reached into his jacket and produced the warrant.

Or order.

Or directive.

Or whatever it was called. Who could say? There was no precedent for this.

Cook accepted the document and scanned it with squinted eyes. Neither of the bullish men who flanked him, or any of the muscular security behind so much as blinked. Mitchener checked his watch.

"I'm afraid I can't comply with this, Agent," Cook said, offering the document back. "Per the advice of my attorneys, I am closing all American Mobile corporate offices and data centers until further notice and sending my staff home while our legal department reviews the president's order and determines how we can best assist."

Cook offered a smile. It was hollow, and didn't meet his eyes. Mitchener ignored the proffered document.

"We don't need your assistance, Mr. Cook. We just need your building."

Cook's smile faded. "This building is private property. I'm afraid I'm going to have to ask you to leave, now, before I contact the Dallas County Sheriff's De—"

"I've already spoken with the sheriff, Mr. Cook. Per the directive of the president's order, the FBI and the NSA are granted immediate access to all your facilities, corporate holdings, data centers, and computer systems. Anyone standing in our way is subject to immediate arrest by the Federal Marshals Service."

Cook's jaw twitched. His teeth locked together, and he glanced across the street at the news vans.

"You sure you want to go that route, Agent?"

Mitchener was also conscious of the news vans. The cameras. The eyes of a panicked nation, fixated on him and the hundreds of other agents descending on telecommunications companies around the country. The gravity of the moment wasn't lost on him for a moment.

"No," he said. "I'm really not. But I don't have a choice."

Cook nodded slowly. Then he extended his hands.

"Then you'd better arrest me. The trust of American Mobile customers and their data security is my obligation. I can't allow you to invade upon that without a fight."

Mitchener took a slow breath. Then he pushed past Cook and headed for the door while the marshals went to work arresting all three men on national TV. As Mitchener reached the entrance of the tower and the private security melted back, he thought again of the storm of calls. The bomb in Nashville. The promise of another attack.

And he couldn't help but wonder who the real enemy was.

71

J. Edgar Hoover Building
Washington, DC

FBI Director Bill Purcell had never been so busy in his life. The phone on his desk hadn't stopped ringing for nearly four hours—calls from coordinated offices in Dallas, Seattle, San Francisco, Chicago, New York, freaking Topeka . . . anyplace where a major telecommunications provider held a corporate office or a data center.

Purcell's agents were in the field now. Hundreds of them. The mission was brutally simple—back trace the calls, whatever it took. Find the source. Comply with the president's order.

Of course, there had been resistance. Only one of the major cellular providers granted access to their data centers without stipulation or pushback. Congressmen, governors, and political pundits from both sides of the aisle were flipping out all over national TV. In Kentucky, the governor deployed detachments of the National Guard to barricade access to a T-Mobile server farm, proclaiming the gross tyranny of the president.

In his gut, Purcell wondered if the governor had a point. But Purcell wasn't paid to think, or to question. He was paid to run the largest federal law enforcement agency in the nation.

He was paid to find the terrorists before they struck again.

"Yes?" Purcell punched the answer button on his phone. The caller ID notified him of the Special Agent in Charge at Dallas. Some guy named Mitchener that Purcell had never heard of. He'd demanded to be put in touch with all his SAICs taking over corporate headquarters. He expected them to meet the most ardent resistance.

Purcell wasn't wrong. He listened while Mitchener described the takeover of American Mobile's headquarters. Arresting the CEO, COO, and CDO. More theatrics.

"Have you found anything?" Purcell barked, cutting Mitchener off.

"We're just setting up, sir."

"Call me with results."

Purcell ended the call and ran a hand over his balding head. The water bottle on his desk was nearly empty. Already the phone rang again. Before he could answer it, the door opened and his personal assistant stuck her head in.

"Mr. Director?"

"Not now, Jada."

"I'm sorry, sir. I've got Assistant Director Swank on the line . . . he's called nonstop. I—"

"I'll take it," Purcell snapped. He waited for Jada to push him the call, then smacked the button. Swank wasn't his second-in-command. He wasn't even somebody Purcell spoke to on a regular basis, normally. But as the assistant director in charge of the FBI's Counterterrorism Division, Dylan Swank had been thrust into the limelight over the past forty-eight hours. Purcell was growing tired of taking his calls.

"What is it?" Purcell demanded.

"Mr. Director, I've just received an update from IT. There's been activity on the ICA site. You . . ." Swank hesitated. "You should probably see it yourself, sir."

The internal messaging system on Purcell's computer blipped. A link popped through from Swank. Purcell followed it, shifting the phone against his shoulder.

"Is there another video?" he demanded.

"No . . . well. Yes. But that's not the point."

"What's . . ." Purcell trailed off. The page had loaded—plain black, as before. The video of the man thought to be Fakir Ibrahim taking credit for the Nashville bombing was gone, now replaced by a new video featuring the same face. Ibrahim again, but the title of the video was different.

Your time has come.

Purcell saw it all in a split second, but what drew his eye was neither the video nor the title. It was the series of six bright red numerals spread across the top of the screen, separated into pairs by colons. The first pair read 06. The next, 42. And the last, 19.

Then 18. Then 17.

It was a *clock*.

"What the hell is this?" Purcell said, his voice turning dry.

"It's . . . it's a death clock, sir. That's what he calls it in the video. It's the time remaining until the next strike."

72

45,000 feet over the North Atlantic

Deputy Director Aimes was as good as her word. When Reed and his battered crew reached the Maria Montez International Airport just outside the Dominican town of Barahona after nearly four hours of brutal slogging and hitchhiking, a brand new Gulfstream G550 waited to pick them up. It was an SAC jet—property of the CIA's Special Activities Center. Reed recognized one of the pilots from a flight to Japan eighteen months prior, but made no comment as he collapsed into a leather-clad chair.

They were all starving. All exhausted. All teetering on the edge of critical dehydration. But of the three of them, Turk's condition was the worst. Racing pain shot across his face as he manipulated his shoulder. His skin had washed pale despite the heat, and the torn blanket wrapped around his ass still oozed blood from the road rash.

He needed a hospital.

"We were directed to fly you north," the captain said, an undertone of uncertainty in his voice. Reed could guess why. The man had probably not been told why he was plucking three random strangers out of the jungles of the DR.

Then again, Reed imagined most days in the life of an SAC pilot were unexpected ones.

"Fine," Reed said. "Water?"

The captain pointed to the tail of the plane, where a case of water bottles jiggled under the howl of the running engines. Corbyn tore into the packaging as the captain closed the door, then the plane began to taxi.

Reed was so relieved to be sitting inside air-conditioned safety that he barely gave time to consider whether the prospect of another takeoff triggered any PTSD. If he never visited Haiti again, it would be too soon.

"We'll get you to an ER," Reed said. "Get that shoulder looked at. Put some lotion on your back. Get you a Hello Kitty pillow to cuddle with."

Turk offered the dullest of smiles. "Can I watch cartoons, too?"

Reed reclined the seat, sore muscles barking at him. The plane's engines raced louder and the fuselage rumbled as they started down the tarmac. He thought again of Aimes, and how readily she had offered free transportation.

He still wondered what that meant. He still didn't trust it. But he wasn't looking a gift horse in the mouth, either. The moment they were back in the States, he was headed straight to Vanderbilt to see Banks. Maybe he would phone Lucy from the airport.

Phone.

Reed fished his dead phone from his pocket. He found a charger in the seatback ahead of him and plugged into a USB port next to his armrest. The black screen flashed the charging symbol, and he guzzled more water.

Corbyn's muddy shoes crunched across the expensive carpet as she made her way to the cockpit. She'd washed her hair in the little sink built in the tail of the plane and stripped down to jeans and a tank top. Toned arms glistened with water as she poked her head in between the pilots and offered a cheery greeting.

"Howdy, Yanks. Whatcha flying?"

Reed couldn't resist a grin. His phone beeped and he checked the screen. There were missed calls . . .

A lot of missed calls.

He unlocked the device and scanned the contact list, heart racing as his mind fixated on Banks. The hospital. Lucy.

But the calls weren't from Nashville. They were international calls. Satellite phone calls. Nearly two dozen of them, all from the same number.

Wolfgang?

Reed pivoted to his voicemail. There were six messages, still from that same number. He tapped one and waited for it to load. The icon spun, but nothing happened.

The Gulfstream had already risen out of cell signal.

"Captain!" Reed shouted.

"Sir?"

"You got a sat phone?"

"Under your seat."

Reed fished the device out and powered it on. It was built out of chunky plastic with thick, rubbery buttons and an extendable antenna. It reminded him of early 2000s devices. Simple, and indestructible.

Reed dialed Wolfgang's number and waited. The connection was slow. The device buzzed.

"Hello?"

"Wolf, it's Reed. I'm calling from a new number."

"Where have you *been?*" Wolfgang's voice cracked with uncharacteristic impatience. Static clouded the line. It was difficult for Reed to hear.

"Haiti. Dominican," Reed said. "I'm heading back now."

"You in the air?"

"Right. CIA. What's going on? You called me like forty times."

"We found Melnyk," Wolfgang said.

"Who?"

"The arms dealer we were looking for in Bulgaria. The guy who sold ICA the land mines."

Reed sat forward. "You have him?"

"No. Not anymore. That's not the point. We got inside his laptop. There were emails with a buyer—the *same* buyer who purchased the land mines."

"Okay . . ."

"There was another purchase," Wolfgang said. "A big one."

A dull chill ran up Reed's spine. He wasn't sure why. Maybe it was the tone of Wolfgang's voice, or the sudden quiet that had fallen over the cabin as both Corbyn and Turk pivoted to listen in.

"What was it?" Reed said.

"Nerve agent," Wolfgang said. "VX, specifically. Russian-made, I think. Enough to kill ... thousands."

Now the chill turned to ice. The hair on Reed's arm stood on end.

VX. He knew the name. Any service member anywhere in the world knew the name—knew about nerve agents. The worst of the worst when it came to chemical warfare. Compounds that could shut down the body in mere seconds with only minimal contact. Far more deadly than poison. More lethal than gas.

So brutal they were illegal.

"Where are you?" Reed snapped.

"Nashville. I've been looking for you. Did you find the terrorists?"

"No. We were just behind them. Have you called the FBI?"

"I can't get through. They're being absolutely flooded right now. All I can get is an answering machine. The same with the CIA, Homeland Security, the freaking White House. I can't get anyone to answer! I need a direct line—"

"I've got one," Reed snapped. "I'll make the call. Do you have proof?"

"Just the emails," Wolfgang said. "I'd rather not discuss where I found them."

"That's fine. Stand by. Don't leave your phone."

Reed hung up and shouted toward the cockpit. "Captain! I need your emergency resource line, ASAP."

The captain twisted out of the lefthand seat, his face appearing next to Corbyn. "I'm sorry, sir. That's a classified phone number—"

"VX, captain! That mean anything to you? Give me a number somebody will answer."

The captain nodded once, and the first officer handed Corbyn a laminated emergency action reference guide—some bundled thing housed beneath his seat. Corbyn read off the number, and Reed punched it in.

"Special Activities Center emergency resource line. Please state your ID number and authorization code."

"Reed Montgomery," Reed snapped. "Connect me with Deputy Director Aimes. *Right now.*"

73

The White House

Chaos ruled the Situation Room.

Seated halfway down the stretching conference table, Maggie fought back a growing pain in her gut as she endured the gathering storm around her. The room was clogged with people—members of her cabinet, plus their deputies, aides, and advisors. Phones rang and people clamped their hands over their ears as they answered them. On the screen across from her, Director O'Brien's bobbing bald head was visible as he operated his own phone—checked into the emergency cabinet meeting, but not really.

General Yellin was there. SecDef Steven Kline. National Security Advisor Nick West. Easterling and Stratton.

And displayed across the screen at the end of the table, glowing for all to see and amplifying the tension, was the terrorist's website. The clock, steadily counting down.

Four hours. Twenty-eight minutes. Fifteen seconds.

A flash of new pain raced through Maggie's torso. Her arm dropped over it and she squeezed, biting back a groan. The handful of pills she had consumed throughout the morning and into the afternoon had dulled the pain, but it wouldn't go away. Her mind buzzed as she pivoted toward the clock. Her vision blurred, and she blinked to drive it back into focus.

Be sharp now. You have to be sharp.

"I've got Mayor Kingsley on the line from Chicago," somebody shouted. "He's calling for the governor of Illinois to deploy the National Guard and Springfield is shutting him down. He's asking for federal assistance."

"For *what?*" another voice demanded.

"What do you think? For the freaking attack."

"There hasn't *been* an attack," Easterling's voice cracked like a gunshot. She was out of her chair, jabbing a finger at the aide with the phone. "You tell the idiot to *calm down*. We're handling this."

"Madam President, I've put all our domestic military installations on full alert," Yellin said. "They're escalating readiness as we speak."

"I recommend we advance to DEFCON 3," Kline said. "Put our overseas assets on full alert also."

"What about public transit?" That was Stacey Pilcher, Secretary of Transportation. "We've got to think about the airlines. We could temporarily close our airspace and . . ."

The din faded in Maggie's mind, her own heartbeat escalating in her head like the slow beat of a bass drum. A steady thump, overpowering everything else. Her vision tunneled, and she fumbled for her glass of water. The glass slipped out of her hand and sloshed across the table. Barely anyone noticed.

Stratton noticed. He put a hand on her arm, leaning close.

"Are you all right?"

The voice sounded distant. Maggie's head clouded.

"I . . . I can't hear . . ."

Stratton's jaw closed. He stood from his chair and pounded once on the table. "All right!"

Sudden calm fell across the room. Stratton pointed to the door. "Aides and advisors. Out! Let's go."

A slow column moved for the door. Stratton straightened his tie and resumed his seat. "Everybody else—one at a time. And somebody get that clock off the wall."

The terrorist's clock vanished. Stratton turned to Maggie, nodding once as if to say *You have to step in, now.*

Maggie's head cleared a little. In the sudden calm, the bass drum relaxed. But all eyes pivoted on her.

Be sharp now.

"Has anyone assembled a report on our vulnerabilities?" Maggie asked.

Kline raised a hand. "I had my department generate a list of all public events in the country involving more than five thousand people. We've cataloged over a hundred so far, including four NFL preseason games. Many events are already self-canceling. People are afraid to leave their homes. They're calling out of work and pulling kids out of school by the hundreds of thousands."

Maggie visualized panicked mothers collecting their children from school lines. College kids packing into economy cars and racing home. Fathers canceling work. Businesses closing.

The terror was working. America was diving for the trenches.

"Director O'Brien, do you have *any* leads?" Maggie addressed the comment to the screen. A slight delay allowed her voice to jump the eight miles to Langley. O'Brien's lips pinched together.

"We're following leads in Syria, ma'am. We may have—"

"*Syria?* This asshole isn't *in* Syria, Mr. Director. He's *here*. Do you have anything *here?*"

O'Brien opened his mouth. Hesitated. Looked suddenly flushed and irate.

FBI Director Bill Purcell cut in from an adjacent screen. "Madam President, my agents are collecting tips of suspicious activity all across the country. We've activated the Emergency Alert System and broadcasted an open tip line. The calls are coming in. Our investigations inside telecommunications centers are already producing leads overseas, but we've found nothing concrete yet. Given ICA's publication of the countdown clock, I'm focusing most of our energy on domestic investigation."

"Is there *any* way to turn that thing off?" Maggie demanded.

The room remained awkwardly quiet. Maggie's shoulders slumped. "Okay. Steven, move us to DEFCON 3 and send a bulletin to the governors.

I want the National Guard in all fifty states placed on standby. Any nonemergency public gathering should be immediately suspended. Recommend people to shelter at home, but *kill the panic*. Nothing has happened yet. We're in control. Understood?"

Kline reached for the phone. The buzz returned to the room, but it was calmer now. The door opened and O'Dell stepped in, bringing Maggie a steaming cup of herbal tea. It was bitter and unpleasant, but the White House physician had said it would aid in her liver recovery.

Maggie accepted the mug with a grateful nod as Easterling picked up her phone. The White House chief of staff's squeaky voice chirped into the handset.

"*Who?* I've got him here—he's on video," Easterling gestured absently toward O'Brien, her mousy brow wrinkled into a frown. "Say *what?* Hold on."

Easterling cupped her hand over the phone's mic. "Ma'am, I've got CIA Deputy Director Aimes on the line. She'd like to speak with you."

"About what?"

"She has a tip. About an attack."

The room went dead quiet. Maggie's gaze snapped up to the screen displaying O'Brien's face, confirming that he'd heard the comment. He was staring dead into the camera, not blinking.

"Speaker," Maggie said.

Easterling pushed the button. "Deputy Director, you're on with the room."

"What is it?" Maggie demanded.

"Madam President, I've just received a tip from one of my field teams. We've recently obtained documentation detailing an arms deal out of Eastern Europe. The purchaser is believed to be the same party who recently bought a number of Russian anti-personnel land mines. The same kind we believe to have been used in Nashville. The destination was Haiti."

"Haiti? Why Haiti?" That was Stratton.

"International aid shipments are being coordinated via the Port of Savannah," Aimes said. "After offloading in Haiti, freighters bring empty containers back to Georgia."

Maggie's chest went rigid. It was suddenly difficult to breathe. She placed both hands on the table.

"Deputy . . . what was sold in that arms deal?"

"VX nerve agent," Aimes said. "Enough to kill a hundred thousand people."

74

Langley

O'Brien's office door exploded open. Sweat streamed down his face, burning his eyes as he thundered across the executive floor. Deputy directors and strategists appeared in the doorways of glass office cubes. His secretary stood next to the coffee station, pale-faced as he rushed by.

He reached the heavy oak door labeled *Deputy Director of Operations*. The light was just blinking out as he touched the handle. Aimes was up from her desk, jacket folded over one arm, briefcase in one hand. Headed for the exit.

O'Brian rammed the door open, standing in the gap. "What are you doing?"

Aimes stood straight-backed, chin up. In two-inch heels, she was just a touch taller than him. He'd always hated that. Always wished he could mandate flats. Their gazes met, and Aimes didn't blink. She didn't even flush.

"My job," she said.

O'Brien bristled. He glanced over his shoulder to the silenced room, then pushed inside the narrow office and slammed the door shut. He turned on Aimes.

"Where did you get this? Why wasn't I informed? Do you know what you just did to me? You just supplanted me in front of the *president*."

Aimes shook her head softly, an ironic smirk touching her lips. "Really, Mr. Director? You just learned that a lethal chemical weapon may be in the hands of a terrorist on the *inside* of our borders . . . and you're worried about being supplanted?"

O'Brien lifted a finger. "Don't you dare gaslight me, Deputy! You know exactly what you were doing. *Where* did this intel come from?"

"Montgomery," Aimes said. "He went rogue. Found the terrorist in Haiti. Then one of his sources uncovered the arms deal. He ran circles around you, Mr. Director. And thank God for that."

Aimes shoved past O'Brien, throwing the door open. O'Brien spluttered, confusion and rage melding into something of a cyclone in his chest. He wanted to rip something apart. He didn't even care what.

"I haven't dismissed you, Deputy!"

Aimes was halfway across the room, already reaching for her ID card to access the elevator.

"You don't have to, Mr. Director. The president has requested me to join her in the Situation Room."

"You can't do that!" O'Brien marched to the elevator, no longer caring who watched him. No longer conscious of the raw heat cascading down his body. "You're fired, Deputy. I want your credentials and I want you out of the building!"

Aimes actually smiled. "Whatever, man."

The elevator dinged. Aimes stepped inside. She reached for the button.

O'Brien put a foot in front of the door.

"He's not agency," O'Brien snapped. "You're deliberately feeding the president unverified intelligence."

"So call her when you verify something. In the meantime, I'm going to assume the worst case scenario."

O'Brien's lips lifted into a sneer. "God save you if you're wrong."

Aimes mashed the button. "If I'm wrong, God saved a lot of people. I'll take that deal in a heartbeat."

O'Brien swallowed, shifting his foot back. A sudden chill ran down his spine as Aimes met his gaze and refused to blink.

Then the elevator door closed, and she was gone.

75

Aimes called back within the half hour. Reed placed the sat phone on speaker.

"Yes ma'am?"

"I'm en route to the White House, Mr. Montgomery. Where are you?"

"Someplace south of Atlanta."

"Okay. Here's the deal. Early this morning, security footage at the Port of Savannah tracked three rental trucks exiting a dock where empty aid containers had just been offloaded. Each truck was occupied by at least two passengers. We weren't able to obtain the license plates, and the trucks were lost from there. The documentation of the arms sale your contact found details three units, so it's safe to assume each truck is carrying a barrel." Aimes's voice dropped a notch. "Or . . . a pallet of barrels."

"What do you need?" Reed asked.

"I've just spoken to one of our chemical weapons experts," Aimes said. "VX is a liquid, lethal on contact. Even a drop is enough to kill an adult. A barrel, or a couple of barrels, could easily kill a hundred thousand. The difficulty is in the delivery. Ideally, you'd convert the liquid into a gas and pump it into a crowd."

"Sports venue?" Reed said. "NFL preseason?"

"There were four games, but they've all been canceled. I'm sure you heard about the clock?"

Reed hadn't. Aimes briefed him, and the chill returned to his spine.

This guy has balls.

"That's an odd move for a terrorist wanting to target a crowd," Corbyn said.

"I presume by your accent that I'm speaking with SIS Officer Corbyn?" Aimes said.

"That's right, ma'am."

"You've got me in a heap of trouble with my friends in London, officer. They say you're incorrigible."

"I try my best, ma'am."

A slight pause. When Aimes next spoke, Reed thought he detected a smile in her voice.

"Well done. And you're right about the crowd. VX is a direct contact agent, and results are instantaneous. You'd need a way to hit a lot of people quickly, before they knew what was happening. A crowd would make the most sense."

Reed ran a hand through grimy hair, thinking quickly. Across the aisle Turk leaned against the wall, still cradling his arm. Sipping from a bottle of water.

Water.

"Is it deadly when it's ingested?" Reed said.

"Like how?"

"If I put a drop in a bottle of water, could it kill you?"

"Absolutely. It would dilute, but probably not enough. Ingesting it could actually magnify the effects."

"That's how," Reed said, shaking his head in part disbelief, part morbid respect.

"How what?"

"How's they're going to weaponize it," Reed said. "The clock was strategic. He *wants* people in their homes. Off the streets. Drinking tap water and taking showers. He's going to dump this stuff straight into the water supply."

"No . . ." Corbyn breathed.

"I'll call you back." Aimes terminated the call.

Reed crumpled into the seat, imagining fifty gallons of a nerve agent strong enough to drop a grown man with a drop. Diluted by the water supply, its potency would be reduced. But not enough. And the spread would be massive. Uncontainable. VX would find its way into homes and office buildings, toilets and showers for miles.

And how easy would it be to access a city's water system? As easy as cutting a lock on a fence, probably. Backing the truck in. Upending the barrel into a main line.

Done.

"He's going to kill thousands," Corbyn said.

"Tens of thousands," Reed corrected. "Maybe more, spread across three cities. Is there any way to treat VX poisoning?"

The sat phone rang before anyone could answer. Reed mashed the button.

"It could work," Aimes said. "Much of the weapon would be diluted, but my analysts estimate thousands could still die."

"Right in their own homes," Corbyn said. "That amplifies the terror factor."

Reed nodded in agreement. "You need boots on the ground. It's reasonable to assume he would still target cities. More chance of maximum contamination before the weapon dilutes. Any idea what cities are vulnerable?"

The phone shifted and clicked. Reed thought he heard the shrill whine of a helicopter in the background. Aimes was in the air, also.

"The truck left Savannah at five am. Fourteen hours, calculating for traffic . . . by now they could be in range of DC, New York, Detroit, Chicago, Dallas, Kansas City . . ."

An undertone of defeat crept into Aimes's voice. Reed's mind spun into gear again. Narrowing down targets. They couldn't field them all. There were thousands of cities in that scope with populations north of fifty thousand. It was too many to manage.

They had to think strategically.

"You should focus on major and mid-major cities," Reed said. "Have the president coordinate with the governors to supply state police forces and

National Guard with NBC gear, then split them into teams. I'll spearpoint one of them. Get the utilities department of each city on the phone and identify vulnerabilities. Water towers, water treatment facilities, junctions. Any place where the nerve agent could be easily added under minimal security. Is there any way to treat contact?"

"Immediate injection of atropine using a hypodermic needle."

"So we need plenty of that for all the strike teams. We have to assume exposure, even with NBC gear."

"I'm touching down at the White House now. What city do you want?"

Reed hesitated. He almost said Nashville, thinking about Banks. Sinju. The family.

But then another thought occurred to him. He saw the terrorist in the black-and-white photo again. Bent low, leaning down. Wearing a baseball cap.

There was something familiar about the logo on the cap. He hadn't really considered it at first, but in hindsight it stuck out. It didn't feel right— not for an America-hating radical. But it was there.

"St. Louis," he said, looking toward the cockpit. The pilot shot him a thumbs up, and the jet banked almost immediately. "We're forty minutes out."

"Fine. That should give us just enough time to coordinate a unit on the ground and locate vulnerabilities. Expect a team at the airport. And Montgomery?"

"Yes ma'am?"

"You work for me now."

"Copy that."

Reed hung up. Looked to Turk.

"I guess you can stay on the plane . . ."

"Screw you, Montgomery. Tell them I wear a triple XL."

76

The air conditioner had broken again. In the blockhouse on the outskirts of the city, the baking wrath of the desert sun heated the interior to nearly a hundred degrees. All the windows were open, and a fan blew.

Nothing was sufficient to dry the sweat coursing down Abdel Ibrahim's skin. He stood shirtless alongside the lengthy kitchen table, grinding his thumb across a cigarette lighter and not even noting the heat of the flame dancing only inches from his face.

It was no hotter than the air.

Across the room a baseball bat cracked against a ball—as loud and sudden as a gunshot. Ibrahim's twin brother, Fakir, exploded into a rowdy cheer.

"It's *outta there!*"

Ibrahim rolled his eyes, guzzling water as he navigated around souring takeout containers and frozen pizza boxes. Empty soda cans littered the floor alongside crinkled Reese's Peanut Butter Cup wrappers. The place looked like one of those fraternity houses in the American movies. A complete disaster zone.

Reaching the living room, Ibrahim found Fakir sitting on the edge of a sagging leather couch, bent over the coffee table. Another can of Pepsi sat on the tabletop, glistening with condensation. A soldering iron smoldered from Fakir's steady hand as he fixed a component to a circuit board, the sweat held out of his face by a St. Louis Cardinals hat, worn backward.

A five-gallon bucket packed with American C4 explosives rested alongside his leg.

Ibrahim reached for the TV remote with a disgusted snort. The baseball broadcast had switched to an American beer commercial. Whorish white women dressed in bikinis on a beach. An abomination.

"If the brotherhood caught you watching this, they would behead you in the yard," Ibrahim said.

Fakir laughed. "And kill their golden, explosive-egg-laying goose? In your dreams, Abdel."

Ibrahim circled the couch, leaning against one arm while Fakir focused, biting the tip of his tongue. A sure sign that whatever portion of the bomb-crafting process he was now engaged in was a critical one. Ibrahim waited patiently for his brother to finish, not rushing him. Not breaking his focus.

At last, Fakir swept the hat off and mopped sweat from his face. A boyish grin spread across a wide mouth. "*Hasta la vista*, infidels!"

"What's new?" Ibrahim asked.

"I disguised the detonator as an auxiliary fuse. There's this new bomb specialist the Americans have been using. He's good. Got four of mine last week alone."

"So?"

"So when he finds this, and pulls the wrong wire . . . lights out."

Another flashing grin from Fakir. Ibrahim couldn't resist a subdued, semi-judgmental shake of his head. Fakir was an enigma to him. To everybody who knew Fakir he was an enigma, actually. It was impossible to reconcile Fakir's habits and interests with his brilliance as a bomb maker— or his dedication to the craft. It wasn't just his obsession with American baseball, or American food and colloquialisms. It wasn't just the clean-shaven face and the consistent apathy for the teachings of the Prophet.

It was Fakir's entire persona. The way he disassociated the brutal bloodshed of his homemade weapons with the actual act of making them. He joked about killing people. He spent hours poring over textbooks and experimenting with different compounds and detonators, always searching for a weapon sufficient to outsmart the American-trained anti-bomb squads.

But he never wanted to discuss the actual effects of his weapons. He didn't want to see videos. He didn't want to know body counts. He didn't seem to enjoy associating with any of Ibrahim's contacts inside of the Islamic State.

For Fakir, the art of bomb making almost seemed to be a game. One played against himself, where the only real goal was to make bigger and better blasts.

Ibrahim often wondered what Fakir did with his money. ISIL paid well for *Mawt Khabir*'s talents. Some of those American dollars went to the purchase of imported American foods—Pepsi and frozen pizzas. Some went to the purchase of satellite internet via which Fakir streamed Cardinals games.

But that accounted for only a fraction. Was Fakir saving? Did he have plans that extended beyond the desolation of Syria?

"I'm headed out," Ibrahim said. "Try not to blow yourself up."

Fakir flipped the TV on again. The broadcast displayed a post-game interview between a player and a petite American woman dressed in a revealing blouse. Fakir smacked his lips and winked at Ibrahim.

"You're going to be the death of me," Ibrahim sighed. Leaning down, he wrapped his baby brother—the younger by two minutes—in a one-armed hug.

Fakir slapped him on the back. "Have fun with the rag heads."

"Have fun with the prostitutes," Ibrahim retorted.

Fakir settled onto the couch, slurping Pepsi, and Ibrahim made his way through a cluttered and smelly kitchen into the home's garage. He slid sunglasses and an imamah on before settling in behind the wheel of a Toyota Land Cruiser. The engine rumbled to life, a wash of welcome air conditioning blasting his face, and Ibrahim rocketed out down the long desert road. He turned east, away from Damascus. He made it to the top of the ridge.

He was almost out of sight of the house in the desert when the glint caught his eye. When he looked into the mirror to see the black SUV rushing in.

Ibrahim stopped the Land Cruiser at the top of the ridge and fumbled for binoculars. The house was nearly a mile away now. Barely visible. The men in black appeared as dots, like ants swarming the house. The gunshots popped so far away they sounded like clicks. Ibrahim's heart lurched. He adjusted the binoculars.

And then they brought out his brother. Hauling him by his arms and legs like a dead animal. Throwing him to the ground in front of the house, baking under the desert sun.

The St. Louis ball cap still cocked on his head.

77

"Venomous Agent X—colloquially known as *VX*. First synthesized in the early nineteen-fifties by British scientists developing pesticides. Weaponized shortly thereafter by the United States, the Soviet Union, and numerous other militaries. First used in open combat by the Iraqi army during the Iraq-Iran war, when artillery shells containing nerve agents— VX among them—killed as many as twenty thousand Iranians."

The Situation Room was both dark and silent. The awkward little man standing in front of the screen tapped his iPad from time to time, shifting between slides as he mumbled through his presentation. He wouldn't meet anyone's gaze.

Certainly not Maggie's.

"VX is an odorless, tasteless chemical compound with the consistency of motor oil. It works by disrupting the body's neurotransmitters, causing muscles to spasm and contract uncontrollably. Death can occur within as little as fifteen minutes after minimal contact. A drop on the skin is more than enough. Early onset symptoms include coughing, headaches, diarrhea, vomiting, runny nose, drooling, confusion—"

"We get the point," Maggie said. "Where is it?"

Deputy Director Aimes rose from the end of the table, dismissing her analyst with a subtle tilt of her head. The lights clicked back on, and she took the podium.

"VX was outlawed by the Chemical Weapons Convention in 1997. American stockpiles have since been destroyed, as have international stockpiles. Or so we were told. The weapon is incredibly dangerous to handle, but not all that complex to produce. According to email communications by the CIA, a Ukrainian arms dealer named Oleksiy Melnyk recently arranged the sale of three units of VX to an unidentified party who had the weapon shipped to Haiti. This same party arranged the purchase of Russian anti-personnel land mines only a few weeks prior."

Maggie's stomach tightened. She thought of the Nashville video again. That horrible blast. The raking fire.

"The agency believes that both the land mines and the VX may have been smuggled into the States via international aid freighters returning to Savannah. This picture was recorded this morning by a security camera at the port."

Aimes tapped the iPad. A grainy black-and-white image flashed across the screen. Three small moving trucks were displayed—the van kind, with ten-foot box beds built on the back. Racing away from the port.

"God save us . . ." Easterling whispered.

"How much is 'three units'?" Stratton made air quotes.

"We don't know," Aimes said. "While being stockpiled during the Cold War, VX was typically stored in fifty-gallon drums. Assuming a forgotten stockpile was discovered by Melnyk and sold to ICA, three units could mean three barrels. One hundred and fifty gallons."

"Which is enough to kill how many?" Stratton said. His voice was clipped and direct. No time for emotion.

"I'm not an expert on that," Aimes said. "But according to our analysts, that would depend entirely on how the weapon was deployed. Its most effective form is as an aerosol. Artillery shells were the intended method of delivery during the Cold War. The CIA has developed an alternative theory, however. One that pairs perfectly with the attack clock posted on the ICA website."

Aimes tapped the iPad again. A map of the United States displayed, cutting off just west of Dallas. A dot appeared over Savannah, with red trails snaking across the country along highway routes, landing in cities ranging in size from Asheville, North Carolina, to Chicago, Illinois. In places the red lines turned to yellow but continued to run. Up to Minneapolis, Boston, and Denver.

"The red lines mark all the cities the terrorists could have reached by now, based on the timestamp on the security camera that recorded them leaving Savannah. The yellow lines mark additional cities they could reach prior to the clock expiring."

"And?" Maggie pressed.

"And VX is deadly not only by contact, but also by ingestion. With so many Americans canceling social events and staying home, we believe our water supply could be vulnerable. If dumped directly into the mainlines of a major water network, the nerve agent could poison thousands of people via drinking water, hand washing, and showers before anyone knew what was happening. Even diluted, fifty gallons of VX could be . . . catastrophic."

Maggie's chest tightened. Her gut still hurt, but she wasn't thinking about it anymore. The dense crowd of men and women packed into the room all pivoted toward her. Waiting.

"Recommended action?" Maggie asked.

"I've already spoke with Director Purcell about the use of the FBI's Chemical Countermeasures Unit. I defer to him."

Purcell was onscreen. He stepped right in.

"I've already pushed a nationwide memo to all our field offices, notifying them of a potential chemical weapons scenario. The CCU is trained and equipped to respond quickly to any such situation, but we simply don't have the manpower to protect the entire nation. We're going to have to partner directly with local and municipal law enforcement and lean on their teams. If Deputy Director Aimes's theories about the water supply are correct, we'll need to secure water treatment plants, water towers, mainlines . . . it's a lot of ground to cover. Our best option is to select key cities and focus our efforts there. I've already got teams prepping to hit the ground alongside whatever specialized response forces larger police departments may have on hand."

Maggie nodded. "Do it. Whatever you need—you have my full authorization. Get to work."

Purcell left the call. Aimes took the lead again.

"I already have a small team en route to St. Louis. Obviously we need to focus our efforts on major cities. DC, Baltimore, New York, Chicago, Atlanta. But we can't forget mid-majors either. In smaller town, say Louisville, Kentucky, the water supply would reach less people but the dose would be more concentrated."

"Steven, can you put together a threat assessment based on the DOD's existing defense plans?"

Maggie directed the question at the SecDef.

"Of course, ma'am."

"I want everyone to make the full use of their departments available to the FBI and any other agency working to counter this threat," Maggie continued. "I will accept absolutely zero territorial nonsense. Understood?"

A universal nod.

"Get to work," Maggie said. "We're on the clock . . . literally."

Maggie slumped into her chair. The sweatshirt she wore clung to her skin, even under the unusually icy blast of the Situation Room AC unit. She lifted her water glass and moved to take a sip.

Then she stopped. Thought about the nation. How many water glasses could be lethally contaminated before the sun set. She turned to Stratton.

"I don't want a panic. Let's try to keep a lid on this . . . the best we can."

Stratton nodded, stepping away. Already at work on his cell phone. He was instantly replaced by Secret Service agent Julio Ramirez, the head of Maggie's detail. Ramirez was born in the United States, but his skin tone and gentle voice still carried the traces of his Honduran ancestry. She liked both. There was something calming about Ramirez. She'd never heard him shout.

"Ma'am, we'd like to move you to the bunker now," Ramirez offered a smile. "Can't be too cautious."

"Okay, Julio. Right behind you."

Maggie stood, still wincing. O'Dell put a hand on her arm and gave it a confident squeeze.

"Deputy Director," Maggie said. "A word."

Aimes met her just outside the Situation Room.

"Why did you call me, and not O'Brien?" Maggie demanded.

Long pause. Aimes opened her mouth, then closed it. She said nothing.

"So it's like that, is it?" Maggie asked. Still no answer.

"Okay, Deputy. You work for me now. You don't go home. You don't sleep. You don't do *anything* but hunt these people. Understood?"

"Absolutely, Madam President."

78

Somewhere in the United States

Ibrahim arrived just past four p.m., local time. The drive had gone surprising well, once he made it out of Atlanta. There was a little traffic around some of the bigger cities, but that thinned very quickly after news of the clock broke. He heard it on the moving truck's radio. An Emergency Alert, they called it. A request for all non-essential social gatherings and events to be canceled.

Businessmen left work. Mothers collected children from daycares and schools. The highways thinned to little more than those persistent truckers, still hauling their loads of American clutter from one city to the next, apparently unconcerned about any mass attack on the open road.

They were smart, Ibrahim thought. But most of America was very dumb. Gathered in workplaces and scattered around social events, he would have killed thousands. But clustered in homes, showering and drinking water? Washing hands and dishes? Nervously bathing pets and children? He might kill a quarter million.

By the time the headaches started, it would be too late. America wouldn't even know what had happened until they analyzed the bodies, and by then there would be no turning back the clock. No time to inject life-saving drugs.

People would die slowly. In a lot of pain and terror. Just the way his people had died for decades.

The poetry was magnificent.

As Mahmoud drove them across the river the sun was still high in the sky, the cabin of the truck baking hot despite the blast of the AC. Through the bug-splattered windshield Ibrahim could see the city spilling out to his left, stretching west toward the horizon. Tall buildings and gleaming glass. Miles upon miles of suburbs built almost to the riverbank, leaving just a narrow spit of land where the plant lay, all by itself.

The navigation on Mahmoud's phone led them right to the main gate. It was locked, of course. A guardhouse sat pinned between two automated, rolling chain-link gates, both of which were closed. The guardhouse was empty, and there were no vehicles in sight.

The security staff had been sent home, Ibrahim concluded. To take care of their families. To hunker down and play it safe.

To take a nice, hot shower.

Mohammad parked the truck and got out without comment. He pulled the bolt cutters from beneath his seat. Ibrahim and Bahir watched the two-lane road for incoming cars or police. The kid was alive with nervous tension, now. He wouldn't stop grinning. He was champing at the bit.

The road remained dead quiet, the suburbs nearby sheltered by a thick strip of trees. Everybody was at home, the police fixated on places of public gathering, no doubt monitoring the clock on his website.

The plant lay completely unprotected.

Mahmoud cut the chain that operated the gate, then simply pushed it open far enough for the truck to pass through. Bahir slid into the driver's seat to oblige him. Mahmoud shut the gate again, then climbed back into the truck.

By the time Ibrahim finally saw a car topping the hill half a mile away, they were inside the facility. Pulling past a giant brick building with an empty parking lot. Turning down the main utility road that led between massive, unprotected pools of river water in the process of being purified.

Headed straight for the giant clear well situated at the end of the plant. Like a water tower without legs, set directly on the ground.

Filled to the brim with clean water, ready for consumption.

79

St. Louis Lambert International Airport
St. Louis, Missouri

By the time the Gulfstream reached the city, the FBI was waiting on the tarmac. Or some of the FBI, anyway. And the Missouri state troopers. And the metropolitan police.

Even a couple of sheriff's deputies from nearby Madison and St. Clair counties, just across the river in Illinois. Essentially, whoever the authorities could find on short notice. The Gulfstream stopped, and the stairs went down. Reed dropped into the baking Missouri heat and was immediately accosted by an FBI agent dressed in full tactical gear, a drop holster on one thigh and a plate carrier covering his chest.

"Mr. Montgomery?"

"That's right."

"Special Agent Zach Hale, FBI Chemical Countermeasures Unit. I'm told you're with the CIA . . ."

Hale trailed off, maybe fishing for Reed to fill the gap. Reed simply nodded.

"You guys got a target?"

Hale motioned to a table sitting beneath the shelter of a pop-up tent. A

Bell JetRanger sat alongside it, painted with the logo and colors of the Missouri State Highway Patrol. There were a pair of Dodge Charger patrol cars from Illinois. A black van marked with yellow letters that read *FBI*. Three squad cars from the Metropolitan Police Department.

And nothing else.

Turk and Corbyn joined them beneath the tent, Turk's arm cradled in a makeshift sling, his road-rashed shoulders burning in the sun. Reed thought his whole torso must be alive with pain, but Turk didn't show it. His face remained iron cold, shooting death the moment Reed opened his mouth.

Have it your way, buddy.

Reed turned back to the table, where Special Agent Hale was leaned across a large tablet computer displaying a map of St. Louis.

"I'm told we're dealing with VX," Hale said, his tone indicating a question.

"Right," Reed said simply.

"Okay. Well. We don't have a lot of experience with that."

Reed glanced around the small knot of cops—four sheriff's deputies, three metro police officers. No other FBI. One guy in black slacks and a sweaty white shirt who kept scratching a balding head.

"Where are your people?" Reed demanded. "Don't you have a St. Louis field office?"

"Sure," Hale said, gaze dropping. "They're deployed around the city . . . apartment towers and hospitals. Key vulnerabilities."

Reed bit back a curse. "Didn't you get the memo? This stuff isn't going to rain from the sky. It's going into the water. You need your people at treatment facilities. Water towers. Anywhere with access to a pipe—"

Hale held up a hand. Reed stopped.

"I know," Hale said. "This is what we've got."

Freaking bureaucracy.

Reed gestured to the map. "Okay then. Walk me through it."

"Two freshwater treatment facilities in St. Louis. The Howard Bend Treatment Facility, fifteen miles west of downtown along the Missouri River, and the Falling Rocks facility . . . here. Just north of downtown, along the Mississippi River. Both facilities supply fresh water directly into the city."

"Which one is least protected?" Reed asked.

Hale turned to the balding man, still scratching his head. Still sweating like a pig in a slaughterhouse.

"Mr. Weiss?"

The guy looked up, seeming to remember where he was. He nodded a couple times.

"R-right. Okay. So . . . I don't actually work at either plant. I'm just an inspector."

"So tell us what you *inspect*," Reed growled.

"Neither facility is really, uhm, protected. Just a fence and a guardhouse. Easy enough to circumvent. The best way to add a toxin to the water supply would be either in the treatment facility, or just outside the clear well where last-minute chlorine adjustments are made. Both buildings are locked but . . . not really that hard to get into."

Weiss used his fingers to zoom the map until it converted to a satellite image display. He pointed to a long building just inside the guardhouse, and a series of large, round tanklike objects a few hundred yards farther down the riverbank.

"What do we need to get in?" Reed asked.

Weiss fished into his pocket and produced a key card. He handed it over. "This will get you into any building."

"Do you have a map of the interiors?" Reed asked.

Weiss swallowed hard. Shook his head. "It's not . . . an amusement park."

Reed looked back to the map, weighing his options between the two plants—one on the banks of the Missouri, the other on the banks of the Mississippi. A fifty-fifty chance. Or was it?

"Falling Rocks," he said. "I'll take my people and secure it. Send everybody else to Howard Bend."

"Why Falling Rocks?" Hale said.

"Because that's what I would do. It's closer to the city. Less dilution. Where's your NBC?"

Hale led Reed to the back of the FBI van. It was loaded down with heavy black NBC suits—nuclear, biological, and chemical protection for use in combat. Reed had trained with plenty of them in the Marine Corps, although it had been a while. He remembered the suffocating heat of all that rubber, locking in humidity and sweat. Airtight protection that failed completely the moment a bullet cut it.

But it was better than nothing.

"Just . . . hold one." Hale raised a hand. "I don't . . ."

Hale lowered his voice, checking over his shoulder to make sure nobody was within earshot. "Look. I don't know who you are. But . . . I'm kinda . . . I don't really know what I'm doing here."

"No kidding," Reed said, kicking his boots off.

"I just finished training last month," Hale said. "I mean, I know all about chemical weapons. But I'm not supposed to be in charge. They just put me out here—"

"You know about VX?" Reed said.

"Enough not to touch it."

"Then you know enough. Can you shoot?"

"Sure."

"So here's the plan. We'll take the chopper—"

"We don't even have a pilot! We can't get him on the phone."

"I have a pilot. We'll take the chopper to Falling Rocks while the rest of your people drive to Howard Bend. We'll secure the facility. Ideally, we'll kill a few terrorists. Then we'll all go out for beers. Fair enough?"

Hale's response was cut short by a gut-wrenching scream. Reed looked back to see Turk bent over a table, one of the cops wrenching his arm backward. The joint popped into place with a gunshot snap. Turk growled like a maniac and smacked his chest with his good arm.

"Hoorah!"

Hale pivoted back to Reed, his brow screwed into a frown. "Who *are* you people?"

"The monsters in the closet," Reed said, grabbing a pair of rubber pants and throwing them Hale's way. "Suit up."

80

"Chicago is clear!"

FBI Director Purcell's voice barked from the speakerphone. A low cheer rang across the confines of the White House bunker's version of a situation room. Little more than a conference room, really. Maggie sat at the end of the table, Stratton on one side and Easterling on the other. O'Dell at her shoulder. A map of the U.S. spread across the screen on the wall.

Green checkmarks covered Chicago, Detroit, and Columbus. A lot of red circles spread around the remainder of the country.

"Where are we with New York?" Maggie's called into the phone.

"Still working. There's a lot of ground to cover. Will update."

Purcell hung up, and Maggie looked to the iPad on the table next to her. It displayed the terrorist's clock, counting down inside of sixty minutes now. A part of her wondered if there was any actual relevance to the clock beyond spreading terror—and driving people inside, if Aimes's theory was accurate. Maybe the attack would strike unexpectedly thirty minutes early.

Maybe it wouldn't strike at all, and tomorrow a new clock would be posted. Maybe the game was the terror itself, at this point. An endless psychological cycle.

But no. She could feel more in her gut than just racing pain. Something was about to happen. Someplace in one of the many red circles where the FBI, National Guard, Armed Forces, and local police task forces had yet to secure the city's water supply, an attack was underway. Maybe only minutes from execution.

"I wouldn't do it this way," Stratton's voice was calm. He'd removed his suit jacket and now sat spinning an ornate pen on the tabletop. She could feel the tension radiating from his body, suppressed by years of steady practice.

"What way?" Maggie said.

"Major cities," Stratton said. "If I was gonna dump VX in a water supply, I would do it in smaller cities. There's only so many people you can kill before it dilutes, right? The terror factor doubles when jihad comes to Small Town, USA."

Maggie coaxed her mind past a fresh wave of pain. Not overthinking. But agreeing.

"Jill, contact Purcell. Have them escalate focus on smaller cities."

Easterling reached for her phone. Deputy Director Aimes stood from down the table, racing quickly to Maggie's side. She extended an iPad.

"My people just sent this."

Maggie scanned the screen. It was a black-and-white photograph. A toll booth with automated cameras. A moving truck was blazing through, two men visible behind the windshield, a Virginia plate bolted to the front bumper. The number was clearly legible.

"Where?" Maggie said, immediately bypassing the obvious question of *how* the CIA had access to toll booth cameras. It didn't matter.

"Wilmington, Delaware. Headed into Philly."

Maggie looked to Stratton. "Small cities?"

"It makes sense," he said again.

"I've already advised the FBI," Aimes said. "We'll run the license plate number through our databases and find what we can."

"Stay on it," Maggie said.

She checked the screen. Two more cities bore green checkmarks—Raleigh and Richmond.

On the iPad screen, thirty-nine minutes, twenty-seven seconds remained.

81

"Let's go! Get it spinning!"

Reed stood outside the FBI van, fully dressed in an inky black NCB suit. Already sweat pooled in the bottoms of his rubber boots. His shoulders hung heavy with the plate carrier he'd strapped on over the suit, mag pouches stuffed with 30-round MP5 magazines.

He would have preferred his Daniel Defense M4, but Hale hadn't brought any compatible magazines or ammunition, and the M4 was still caked with Haitian mud anyway. Better to settle for the 9mm MP5 and know that it would work.

Across the tarmac, Corbyn was already strapped into the JetRanger. She'd refused an NBC suit, insisting that she'd rather risk the VX than drive the chopper into the ground compliments of a bulky sleeve. Reed didn't argue.

Next to him Turk struggled to get his plate carrier on, teeth gritting every time he moved his left arm. The joint had been relocated, but God only knew how many tendons and muscles were torn. It was amazing that Turk could stand at all.

"Hey," Reed put a hand on his arm. "No BS. Do you—"

"*Move it or lose it,*" Turk growled, punctuating each word. Reed removed his hand, then helped Turk adjust the plate carrier. It was too small, but it would have to suffice. Turk selected an FBI-issued MP5 equipped with a C-MORE Railway red dot optic, a matched pair alongside Reed's. He filled his plate carrier with mags, then affixed a chest-mounted holster loaded with a Glock-19. Last of all, Turk slid a wired earpiece into his right ear. Reed and Hale wore identical earpieces, linked not only to each other but also to Corbyn's aviation headset, allowing free communication even after they departed the chopper.

"You ready or what?" Turk barked.

Across the tarmac, the JetRanger howled like a caged animal. The cops had already dispersed—headed to the treatment facility on the Missouri River. Hale remained, encased in an NBC suit with an MP5 slung over his chest and a plastic case cradled in one arm. Approaching Reed, he set the case on the bumper of the FBI van and cracked it open.

Inside lay three large syringes, each filled with a clear liquid and fit with two-inch hypodermic needles.

"Atropine," Hale said. "In event of contact, inject directly into the thigh or heart."

"We only have three?" Turk questioned.

Hale shrugged apologetically. "We weren't really ready for this."

"We never are," Reed muttered. He advanced to the JetRanger, throwing the side door open and finding a single bench seat bolted to a metal floor. The interior was a lot tighter than a Black Hawk, especially with Turk jammed in beside him. Hale shoved the plastic case beneath the seat and sat just inside the doorjamb, legs riding the skid.

"Let's roll, Corbyn!" Reed shouted.

Corbyn grabbed the center-mounted collective and added power. The little chopper screamed under the weight of four bodies, but skipped off the ground. Hale snatched a sharp breath as the tarmac vanished beneath him, and Reed put a hand on his shoulder.

"You got a family, Hale?"

"Just married," Hale said. "Baby on the way."

Reed nodded slowly, the testosterone-charged encouragement he'd primed in his mind falling suddenly flat.

Baby on the way. He thought of Banks. The hospital. The blast. Their daughter. Suddenly his throat felt very thick, but his blood pressure spiked.

"You're gonna be a great father," Reed said. "Lock and load!"

He smacked the charging lever on his MP5, ramming in a fresh round of 9mm. The JetRanger now raced high above the city, hot wind thundering through the open cabin as Corbyn banked northward. Reed saw the Gateway Arch gleaming in the afternoon sunlight. A portal to a new world inside the New World. A beacon of freedom and opportunity and promise, yet again under attack.

The JetRanger nosed down, and Corbyn shouted over her shoulder. "Coming in hot, chaps! Where do you want it?"

Reed looked out the window. He saw the river—the wide, muddy Mississippi. He saw a highway bridge stretching across it, offering passage for I-270.

And just beneath that, he saw the treatment plant. A sprawling, fenced facility populated by giant pools of water and multistory brick buildings.

"Just inside the fence," Reed shouted.

And then he reached for his mask.

82

Falling Rocks Treatment Plant
St. Louis, Missouri

Ibrahim heard the chopper ripping in from the south. He spotted the gleam of sunlight across its windshield, the brim of his Cardinals hat blocking only a little of the glare.

He couldn't read the markings on the side. He couldn't discern the logo, or even identify the color of the stripes. But he knew it wasn't a civilian aircraft. This wasn't a pleasure cruise.

The Americans were coming.

Ibrahim snapped at Bahir to hurry with the hand truck. Mahmoud was already racing back from the sheltered side of the clear well. He discarded a pair of bolt cutters next to the truck and heaved his aging body into the cargo box next to Bahir.

While the men slid the barrel of VX onto the hand truck, Ibrahim unzipped a heavy nylon case to expose a trio of spruce-stocked AK-47s. Fully automatic, smuggled into the country alongside the VX. Just in case.

Behind them, the clear well door was open, the lock lying on the ground. Bahir and Mahmoud ran the barrel down the moving truck's

LOGAN RYLES

loading ramp and pivoted toward the door. Ibrahim cradled the rifles and spare magazines in his arms. He looked toward the sky and smiled.

The Americans were already too late.

83

Reed hit the treatment plant's parking lot before the JetRanger had even settled onto its skids. Turk bailed from the left side, and Hale fell into step on Reed's right. Their MP5s rode muzzle-up, safety-off. A finger's flick away from delivering thirteen rounds of death per second.

Behind them Corbyn was already spinning up again, the JetRanger howling into the sky as her calm voice chirped in Reed's ear.

"I have overwatch. Moving toward the clear well."

Reed broke into a sprint down a long line of empty parking spaces. On his left a lake-sized basin of bluish water gleamed under the sun, suspended someplace along the treatment process. A brick building lay directly ahead, running alongside the lake. Not an office. This would be the primary treatment facility that Weiss had told them about—one of the two places the terrorists were most likely to insert the toxin.

Reed moved instinctively toward it, breathing evenly through the NBC mask. With the hood pulled low, every sound was muted. His vision was blocked at the peripherals. Each stride felt hampered and sloppy, as though he was running through ten inches of mud. Sweat gushed into his boots and burned in his eyes.

Sliding to a stop next to the door, Reed brandished the MP5.

"Turk, take point!"

Turk slid automatically up to the door, covering Reed while Reed swiped the keycard. The reader chirped, and the lock clicked. Turk yanked the door open. Blackness greeted them beyond—a wide, empty space. Turk swept his muzzle across it, then ducked inside without hesitation. It was an imperfect breach on a good day. Rushed and risky, but there was no point in holding back.

"Clear!" Turk called. Reed and Hale followed. The inside the of the building was pitch-black and thick with humidity. Reed hit the weapon light on the MP5 and shot a high-powered LED beam across tangles of iron pipes and filtering machinery. It all looked the same to him, stretching a hundred yards to his left. The weapon light cast a harsh beam against the wall, illuminating dust and damp bricks. A single skylight in the roof failed to offer full illumination.

"Clear it, clear it!" Reed called. Turk took left by default, looking like something out of a fifties science fiction flick—all swishing black suit and bulky hood. Reed swung right, and Hale followed as though by default. They skirted to the back corner of the building and turned down the length of it. Turk called the all clear from the end. Reed's heart thundered, fresh sweat obscuring his vision. Already he could barely see. His chest felt heavy, and the full-face lens on his mask misted with condensation.

He reached the back corner of the building in a full sprint, sweeping each corridor and gap between pipes and tanks along his way. Each space was empty. The dust on the floor undisturbed. The doors shut and locked.

Reed and Hale rendezvoused with Turk at the end of the room. Already the bigger man was lifting his mask, gasping for fresh air. Reed followed suit, scrubbing away sweat and sucking down unfiltered oxygen.

Maybe he'd been wrong about St. Louis. About the hat.

Then Corbyn's voice crackled through his earpiece, and the doubt vanished.

"I have a moving truck matching suspect description parked beneath equipment shed at far end of facility near clear well. No persons visible. Rear cargo door open."

Reed yanked the mask down and turned for the nearest door. Turk was quicker, ramming it open and sprinting into the sunlight. From high above, the JetRanger beat a path through a cloudless sky, but Reed couldn't see it beyond the constrained view of the mask's lens.

"Which way?" Reed called.

"Dead ahead, six hundred yards. Don't move—I'll get you!"

The thunder of the rotor blades magnified into a hurricane. The JetRanger screamed out of nowhere, rotating in midair before slamming down on the concrete barely twenty yards ahead. This time Corbyn didn't spin the engines down. The helicopter continued to roar, skids skipping across the narrow concrete road that ran between the wide-open lakes of treatment water.

Reed sprinted. He reached the righthand side of the bird as Turk circled left. The doors were still open. He put both feet on the skid and bent over to keep his head well beneath the rotor, one hand clamped to the doorframe. Hale found a similar position next to him, with Turk on the other side. Already Corbyn was lunging off the ground, the JetRanger leaping up and nosing down. Concrete and treatment reservoirs raced by in a blur. Six hundred yards and then some, evaporated in seconds. Reed saw the clear wells—not one, but three. Another wide metal building stood next to them, a rusting roof baking in the summer sun.

And then he saw the truck. Parked beneath a mechanical shed across from the metal building. The back door open. Limp straps lying across the empty floor of the vehicle. A built-in ramp leading down from the bumper to the gravel below.

Twin hand-truck tire tracks marking a path to the clear well building.

"As soon as you put us down, radio St. Louis!" Reed shouted. "Have them terminate the water supply and issue a no-use bulletin."

Corbyn nodded once as she cut altitude, dropping the helicopter like a rock. The runners hit the gravel with the aggression of a Navy pilot making an emergency landing. Reed's boots hit the ground. His chest heaved for air, body alive with adrenaline. The tire tracks led directly to a door in the side of the clear well building.

The door stood open.

84

Falling Rocks Treatment Plant
St. Louis, Missouri

Ibrahim heard the helicopter return. The metal roof of the clear well building rattled as though a hurricane was making landfall, cracks of light dancing across the concrete floor and the network of thick iron pipes feeding the trio of clear wells adjacent to the building. Through the door that Bahir had foolishly left open, Ibrahim could see dust exploding from the dirty parking lot. The roar of the chopper grew louder, its jet engines shrieking.

It was streaking in for a landing—fast.

Behind the heavy folds of a Russian-made chemical warfare suit, Ibrahim could barely breathe. The mask was fit tightly to his face, the hood cinched down around it blocking any air from cooling his sweating face. His rubber boots splashed through shallow puddles on the concrete floor as he turned from the door and raced to the back of the room.

There was a twelve-inch iron pipe there, rising out of the concrete and striking across the concrete floor before diving into the clear well furthest to the left—the first clear well to service the city. Atop the iron pipe were a number of valves, hoses, and gauges, each used to selectively add last-minute treatment chemicals to the water on its way into homes and office buildings across the region.

Chlorine, usually. Or fluoride. Favored treatment products in America. But today those injection systems would be used for something far more potent.

Bahir had the barrel in place. Mahmoud had tapped into a chlorine line and attached a hose and vacuum pump which would be used to transfer the VX. The entire process would be closed and contained—no open barrel gushing into an open pipe with precious nerve agent splashing around.

Every drop would go into the water system, making the attack much safer for the three jihadists while also ensuring that every deadly drop reached St. Louis. But pumping it that way required time.

By the sound of the JetRanger, that time was fast running out.

"Mahmoud, start the pump!" Ibrahim hissed. "Bahir, take a rifle."

The air outside the open door clouded with dust. Ibrahim could barely see. But he heard the helicopter make impact, and maybe it was his mind playing tricks on him, but he thought he heard the heavy footfalls of American soldiers jumping to the ground.

Hauling the AK around by its strap, Ibrahim snatched the charging handle to load a fresh round of lead-core Russian ammunition. The selector lever was already switched to fully automatic.

He aimed for the door.

85

Reed reached the door first. He approached from the righthand side, MP5 at his shoulder, finger over the trigger. Behind him Turk fanned out automatically to the left, ready to draw a line of fire on the righthand side of the building beyond the door. The air was thick with a cloud of dust from the JetRanger. Corbyn was taking off again, rising above them and spinning ninety degrees to provide a token amount of overwatch.

Though without guns, the chopper was now next to useless.

As Reed closed on the door, the mask pressed against his face felt like a wet blanket. Each breath was labored and thick. His whole body was saturated in sweat. His boots sloshed with it. Dizziness swept his head.

Turk fell into a crouch, ready to cover. Reed took two more strides to the right, ready to enter at an angle that would provide him the greatest field of fire during that harrowing moment when he was most vulnerable—right as he entered the door.

He should have briefed Hale. Should have voiced what he was doing. He and Turk had completed this maneuver so many times they didn't need to talk, but Hale was new, and he immediately misunderstood.

"I've got point!" Hale called. He rushed dead ahead, straight for the door.

"Hale! Wait—"

It was too late. Hale reached the open door amid an immediate thunderclap of automatic gunfire. Loud, slow, and clacking. The unmistakable voice of an AK-47. From inside the building, muzzle flash lit the darkness like lightning, and Hale went down with a shriek. Blood splashed from the legs of his NBC suit and a chunk of his face mask exploded into plastic shards. Even as he fell the AK continued to blare, holes opening in the metal walls of the building as hot lead sprayed in every direction.

Both Reed and Turk hit the deck the moment the first shot cracked. Concrete and gravel bit into Reed's chest and he fumbled for the MP5. He couldn't see the muzzle flash anymore—not directly. But in that split second before he fell, he'd located the source of the gunfire as orange starlight off to his left.

"Ten o'clock!" Reed shouted. "Cover fire!"

Turk hit the switch on the side of his MP5, locking the gun into full auto mode. The muzzle of the submachine gun spat fire, smoke, and a hail of whistling rounds straight into the side of the metal building, ventilating the sheet metal with thirty holes in just over two seconds. The AK fell silent and Reed was back on his feet, leaping across the fallen Hale and heading for the door. He clamped down on the trigger as he hurtled through the opening, aiming left and spraying a dozen rounds in the general direction of the AK. Sparks exploded as copper-jacketed bullets pinged off iron pipes and steel superstructure.

Reed gasped for air but couldn't get a full breath through the mask. It had shifted on his face when he hit the dirt, and now sweat drained directly into his eyes, blurring his vision. His peripherals were still blind. He was fully exposed from half a dozen angles.

But he saw the shadows. At least three of them, working at the far end of the building from where the AK had fired, maybe fifty yards away beyond a tangle of pipes and a stack of plastic barrels marked CL. Chlorine. A mountain of it.

Reed dove for cover behind a trio of twelve-inch iron pipes all stacked on top of each other. Behind him, Turk had reloaded and reached the door.

His weapon light blazed and his MP5 barked. The AK clacked and thundered, now joined by a twin. Reed saw the silhouette of a skinny man dressed in a black NBC suit huddled behind the chlorine barrels. Thirty yards.

He rotated the MP5 to bring the red dot to hover over the spot. A quick press of the trigger delivered a three-round burst. A barrel exploded, a cascade of chlorine treatment crystals gushing over the floor. Somebody shouted and one of the AKs fell silent. Almost immediately the whole building smelled like a pool house. Reed could taste it even as he breathed through the mask. Turk found cover five yards to his left and focused on the second AK. The air was alive with the thunder of gunshots. Bullets pinged and zipped through metal walls. A ricochet whined and spun past Reed's head. He could barely see. The mask was fogging quickly, the imperfect seal allowing chlorine fumes to leak inside. His eyes burned and watered. His head went light.

And then he saw another barrel. Strapped to a hand truck, resting on the concrete alongside a thick iron pipe. A hose ran from the pipe to an electric pump mounted to the top of the barrel. Reed saw it all through a narrow slot between the chlorine barrels, sixty yards away at the very end of the building.

And he also saw the third shadowy figure dressed in a pitch-black NBC suit—moving for the pump.

86

The White House Bunker

"Contact! We have contact in Philadelphia. Baxter Water Treatment Plant."

The aide shouted from the end of a table, ripping a headset off and standing bolt upright. But he didn't look toward Maggie—he remained fixated on his laptop, fingers rattling over the keys as he communicated directly with the FBI operations management center via secure messaging software.

Maggie's heart lurched with temporary thrill, dampened almost immediately by a crushing sense of dread.

Philadelphia *wasn't* Small Town, USA. Not even close. Stratton had been at least partially wrong.

"Who's on the ground?" she demanded.

"A full detachment of the FBI's Chemical Countermeasures Unit," the aide responded. "They're taking the plant now. We've got one KIA for sure."

Another lance of pain shot through Maggie's gut, but she blocked it completely from her mind. Only the screen at the end of the room mattered —all those red circles slowly replaced by green checkmarks. But not in Philly—the City of Brotherly Love was now circled by a pulsating red X. Marking the site of an invisible battle.

God be with them, Maggie thought.

At the end of the table, Aimes put down a phone. "Contact in St. Louis," she said.

Maggie's head snapped in her direction. "What do we know?"

"Almost nothing. We just heard from the pilot who dropped a three-man team at the Falling Rocks Treatment Plant. She's requesting immediate backup—there's heavy gunfire."

"Get her whatever you can," Maggie said. "Are these CCU?"

"One of them is," Aimes said. "The others are mine."

Aimes was already back on the phone, punching numbers and snapping commands. Two chairs down, Easterling was also on the phone, directing her staff to reach out to municipal authorities in Philadelphia and St. Louis to immediately shut off all water services and notify the public of possible contamination. It was a step the FBI had probably already taken, but Maggie appreciated the effort.

It was better than being forced to sit and watch this thing unfold like a horror movie.

In the chair next to her, Stratton was doing literally that, tabbing across the screen of the iPad to map out the rest of the country. Gone was the terrorist's clock. That no longer mattered. This thing was happening—for real.

"We still haven't heard any updates from the southwest," Stratton said. "Where are we with Texas?"

"Working on it, sir!" an aide called. "Lot of ground to cover."

Maggie's gaze dropped to the screen. She gulped water and inspected the circles and checkmarks. The pair of pulsating X's.

One more truck. Headed in which direction?

One to the northeast. One to the Midwest...

Maggie's gaze settled by default over Louisiana. Her home state. The wild, swampy, forever-hot homeland she loved more than any other corner of America. By now the third truck could have reached far beyond Louisiana. It could have reached Houston, Austin, Dallas, San Antonio. Maybe even Oklahoma City.

But what if it had stopped short? What if deadly VX was even now poisoning thousands of Louisianans?

"Where are we with Baton Rouge and New Orleans?" Maggie said. The question was directed at nobody in particular, but the aide who announced the Philadelphia strike was the first to answer.

"Local police moving to secure the treatment facilities, ma'am," he said. "There's a lot of them."

Maggie knew. It was hard work purifying muddy Mississippi water. Nearly five million people depended on it.

"FBI?" she asked.

"They're moving a team in from Mobile via helicopter," the aide said. "Six members of CCU. They were headed to New Orleans first, but if you want me to redirect them . . ."

The aide trailed off. The room was suddenly very quiet as everybody pretended not to listen in. They all knew where Maggie was from. They all knew about her college days in Baton Rouge and party days in New Orleans.

Maggie trembled despite herself. She shot a sideways glance at O'Dell. He sat to her left, keeping her water glass full. Not speaking. Just remaining close.

Baton Rouge. Or New Orleans.

Two obvious targets, with New Orleans being the default priority. More people. But something in her mind gnawed at her. A sort of raw uneasiness. An instinct, maybe. Or was it just good college memories, clouding her judgment? Her days as governor obscuring her ability to think rationally?

"Ma'am?" The aide's voice broke through.

"Keep them on track to New Orleans," she said. "Secure bigger cities first, then move down the chain."

The aide went back to work. The buzz of preoccupied business returned to the room. Stratton spoke softly enough that only Maggie could hear.

"Perhaps we should consider posting a national bulletin. Advise all at-risk cities to avoid using any water. Just in case."

Maggie had already considered that option. A phone call to municipal authorities in cities like Baton Rouge and Houston could cut the taps off quickly. Better yet, a pulse notification via the Emergency Alert System could notify millions of smartphone users in seconds.

Avoid the water.

But how long could that last? An entire nation cut off from life's greatest essential?

And—a better question—how much terror would that spread? The panic would shoot off the charts. There would be no possible way to scale it down.

"No," Maggie said. "We stay the course. Clear New Orleans, then move to Baton Rouge."

Stratton returned to his iPad. Maggie looked to the map on the screen. More green checkmarks had appeared across a swath of midwestern and southeastern states.

But Maggie wasn't looking at them anymore. She only looked at Louisiana.

87

St. Louis

"Barrel! Back wall!" Reed shouted into his mic as a fresh burst of AK fire forced both him and Turk to press low against the concrete floor. The temperature inside the clear well room was ten or twenty degrees hotter than outside, the metal roof turning the interior into a baking inferno. Reed's suit was now heavy with sweat, audibly sloshing as he moved. The mask misted and every breath required focused effort. The plate carrier dragged him down. The world around him tilted and rocked, like the deck of a ship in the midst of a squall.

"I see it!" Turk's reply crackled over Reed's sweat-logged earpiece. The thunder of the AK pounded on, an endless hellish din. It consumed the narrow building, pounding off the walls. Dust exploded from the concrete as rounds made impact, skipping off metal superstructure and pinging against the pipes that the superstructure supported. One round made direct impact. An iron pipe burst under pressure, spraying clean water across the room in a geyser.

And still, they couldn't move. Every time Reed raised his head, the storm of gunfire turned directly on him. At least two guns, firing as though they ran on ammo belts.

Reed saw through the crack between the chlorine barrels. The shadow of a terrorist had reached the VX barrel. A wire was uncoiling from around the electric pump. The man was moving for a wall outlet, fifteen feet away.

"Cover me!" Reed said. "I'm gonna move."

"Hold one!" Turk called back. Reed pivoted his way. His vision was obscured now by the fog of the face mask. He saw Turk crammed into cover behind the trio of iron pipes, fishing with one hand across the floor. Finding an aerosol can of lubricant left next to a toolbox. Turk lifted his mask with his left hand and screamed across the room.

"*Frag out!*"

The can arced over the pipes and hurtled toward the pair of blaring AKs. It wasn't a grenade, but the fake worked. Both AKs went momentarily silent as the can struck. Reed seized the opportunity and found his feet, turning immediately right. Deeper into the building. He lunged down a narrow channel between the pipes, pivoting left toward the tower of chlorine barrels and opening fire just as the shadow reached the outlet box. A snarling storm of 9mm exploded from the MP5 and sprayed the far metal wall. Two rounds caught the shadow across the shoulder blades. The guy shouted and stumbled, his black NBC suit swishing as he pitched toward the floor.

The AKs were back on Reed. Hot lead zinged past his face and sprayed holes through the far wall. Reed ducked behind the chlorine barrels, but the fire didn't stop. Raw chlorine rained from the containers, generating a rising cloud of dusty white particles that closed around Reed, coating the NBC suit and burning his mouth even through the mask. The air tasted suddenly acidic. Reed fought back a cough and focused on his breathing.

In. Out. Don't freaking die.

From the back of the room Turk's MP5 snarled again. A dozen or more 9mm slugs drew fire from the AKs, and Reed twisted around the end of the chlorine barrel stack.

The shadow wasn't dead. He moved now, back on his knees. Obscured by the same trio of pipes Turk now sheltered behind as they twisted toward the clear well. Reed saw the guy crawling toward the wall, dragging the pump's power cable with him. Leave a trail of blood behind.

Reed leveled the MP5 over his target. His finger dropped to the trigger, but then he froze.

He couldn't fire. The window between the pipes was barely two inches wide, and the shadow now moved alongside the VX barrel. One stray round would puncture the barrel, unleashing deadly nerve agent straight into the room.

NBC suit or no NBC suit, it wasn't a move Reed was ready to risk. But the shadow was nearing the wall, the cable clutched in one hand.

Reed returned to his feet. "Moving right! They're about to turn on the pump."

"I got you!" Turk's reply was immediate, accompanied by the snarl of his MP5. Reed lunged out of the cloud of chlorine, sprinting directly across an open three-yard gap. His next position of cover would be a ten-foot-tall, multi-thousand-gallon tank standing right alongside the pipe the VX was set to pump into. Thick iron walls were coated in peeling blue paint. From behind it, Reed could open up on the both the shadow and his friends with their AKs.

He just had to cross those final three yards.

Reed made it halfway before the AKs switched fire. Time itself seemed to stand still as he hurtled for the tank. The rapid *clack-clack-clack* of the AKs paused, just for a brief second. The amount of time it takes a man to detect movement out of his peripheral vision, and pivot in that direction. Reed's foot slammed into the concrete, sweat sloshing up his calf, boots heavy and stiff. He reached both rubber-coated arms forward, lunging for the tank.

Then the gunfire came as a storm, pinging off the concrete and ricocheting off pipes. Thirty yards away. Impossible to miss.

The first round cut through his sleeve just above his shoulder. The next tore through his leg, so close to his skin that he could feel the hot passage of the bullet like a blade. Two more ripped along his back and shoulder blades. Reed toppled to the ground behind the tank in a rubber heap and thrashed onto his back. There was blood on the floor—his blood. He couldn't find the bullet wound, but a quick inspection of his torso revealed shredded rubber and gaping holes. He thought the blood was streaming from his left leg, but he couldn't be sure. He couldn't feel the wound.

Adrenaline had masked everything out, and what was worse, the clunky NBC suit was effectively worthless now.

The shadow.

Reed fought to his knees and scrambled to the other end of the tank. He leaned left, looking down a narrow gap between the tank and the wall—just wide enough for the pipe to pass through. He saw the VX barrel as a silhouette. He couldn't see the pump.

But he saw the shadow, reaching toward the wall, lying on the floor. Wounded from Reed's last rounds, draining blood across the concrete. But not dead. Not yet given up.

The man wormed across the floor, trailing the cable. Reed lifted his MP5 and trained the red dot on his arm. Clamped down.

The MP5 spat hellfire and the man thrashed. Two rounds cut his arm, but he didn't retract it. He made one final shove.

The next round caught him right in the temple, and he lay flat. A moment of dull stillness fell across the room—all guns silent as if by temporary ceasefire. Reed's ears rang. His vision was still obscured by the fog of his face mask.

But as the gunshots faded, two things broke through the fog of war to enter his mind.

First, the pump was running. He heard it as a dull whine, shrill at first, then dropping in pitch as air left the lines and a thick stream of nerve agent took its place.

And second, he saw the pool on the floor. Too bright to be blood. Too slow to be water.

One of his bullets had punctured the barrel.

The VX had been unleashed.

88

Reed had experienced moments before when the world stood still.

The moment he first saw his wife in a grungy Atlanta nightclub.

The moment they married atop a Venezuelan mountain, on the run for their freedom.

The moment he first held his newborn son.

The moment he learned he would never hold his daughter.

Almost never had he experienced that feeling during open combat. Time slowed, often. A blend of adrenaline and raw, animal instinct accelerated his mind to the point where all else unfolded in slow motion. But never did the world actually seem to stop.

Not like it did now. Reed saw the VX. He heard the pump. And for what felt like a full minute, everything else vanished. He didn't hear the AKs anymore. He didn't hear Turk's MP5 or know whether his friend was calling to him over the radio. He only heard his own heartbeat.

And then he saw Banks's face. In the nightclub.

He saw her in a wedding dress in Venezuela.

He saw Davy in his arms.

He saw the medical paperwork in his hands. His daughter's effective death certificate.

He saw a city spread across rolling Midwestern fields, hallmarked by a

Gateway Arch famous the world around. A baseball team on a hot summer day. Children in the stands, sweaty and smiling. Fathers cheering on their favorite players. Bats cracking against ninety-mile-per-hour fastballs.

And he knew. Every second that pump churned, one less face appeared in that dream.

Reed clawed the mask off and yanked it to the floor. It was useless now. The earpiece wiggled against his face but the mic was still there.

"I punctured the barrel," Reed said calmly. "Cover me the best you can. Tell Banks I'm sorry."

"Wait. What—"

Reed yanked the earpiece out. He dropped it alongside the now useless face mask, eyes burning from the chlorine in the air. But he could see. He could breathe. He led with the MP5 and spun around the tank. Toward the AKs. Toward the barrel.

Both men opened up. Hot lead zipped toward him. Reed sprinted, clamping down on the trigger and spraying a full magazine toward the dug-in terrorists across the room. Somebody screamed. Reed reached the fallen body and nearly stumbled over it. The voice of Turk's MP5 chattered like a soundtrack on repeat. AK rounds zipped over Reed's head and between his legs. Another cut his suit, right next to his side. He thought it tore through flesh but he couldn't feel anymore.

He reached the barrel. He reached the pump. A yank of the cable tore it free of the pump's body. The barrel shuddered and raw VX sloshed out. Some of it splashed against the torn rubber of Reed's NBC suit. He stumbled back, catching himself against the wall, sliding down before he could regain his balance. Bullets skipped over his head, followed by the harsh snap of an AK's hammer dropping over an empty chamber. Reed fought to his feet, vision blurring. Skull pounding with a sudden headache.

He saw the man hurtling toward him out of the darkness like a pouncing jungle cat, wielding an AK-47 like a club. A young man, his eyes alive with crazed fire. Crashing through the puddle of VX like it didn't exist. Reed hit the floor and jerked the MP5 upright, clamping on the trigger. He shot the guy in the leg and then the submachine gun locked back over an empty chamber.

Reed's heart thundered. He could feel the poison in his blood now. Not just the headache and the sudden wash of brain fog. His stomach convulsed, and bile exploded from his mouth. He sucked in a desperate breath and it burned all the way down into his lungs, like boiling water.

The man in the suit crashed onward. The AK came arcing downward, butt-first. From someplace far away, Reed detected MP5 shots—quick and precise. Semi-automatic, now. Kill shots. He tried to pivot out of the way of the AK but it was too late to avoid. It glanced off his head and struck his shoulder. Reed barely felt the pain. He toppled over sideways, crashing against the floor.

He saw the puddle of VX, only inches from his face. He couldn't move his arms. They felt suddenly rigid, his hips locking up. His chest tight. His eyes burning. Everything was burning.

"Reed! *Reed!*"

The voice was familiar, but so far away. Reed's eyes flickered shut. He was in pain. *So* much pain. He felt it in every part of his chest. Down to his legs. He suddenly realized he wasn't breathing, and he tried.

His chest wouldn't move. His lungs wouldn't move. He thought his arms and legs were jerking, but he couldn't control them. The headache redoubled, and panic set in.

From beyond the realm of his consciousness, Reed heard a final stream of gunshots. Snappier than an MP5. The voice of a Glock handgun. A strangely clear, crisp thought.

And then Reed let go.

89

Joshua Schaefer was afraid for his daughter.

From the cramped confines of his two-bedroom apartment on the wrong side of the tracks, he and his wife, Ashley, huddled in the living room to watch the news unfold on the tiny flatscreen. The TV sat on moving boxes full of books. The furniture was hand-me-down and faded. Little Louise's toys lay scattered across the carpet.

The eighteen-month-old slept in her mother's arms, face pudgy with leftover baby fat. Ashley fixated on the screen while she held their daughter. Every change of the channel displayed a new talking head—local news and national. Experts and random citizens with a microphone stuck in their faces.

They all wanted to know the same thing: Where would the terrorists strike? How could anyone be safe?

Even as the dreaded death clock struck zero and no news of carnage or bloodshed exploded across the nation, the fear remained. The panic redoubled. It was as though the whole of America stood on the edge of a cliff. Teetering on the edge. Clinging to life by a thread.

And over that thread hung an invisible knife that might drop at any second.

Joshua gave up watching the TV an hour after the clock expired. He poured himself a glass of tap water and returned to the Bible spread across the rickety kitchen table.

He read. He drank. He prayed.

What kind of world would Louise grow up in? A world of fear and rage?

Joshua's throat turned tight as he surveyed the stacks of textbooks piled next to the door. The summation of six years of dedication and sacrifice. Undergrad, and then seminary. The dream of pastoring a local church. Of guiding a local flock.

Of being a light on a hill.

His family had scraped and scrabbled to survive during those six years. Ashley had miscarried once. Louise was born by a miracle. Joshua had interviewed with three churches over the past month.

Suddenly, all of that felt very far away.

Rocking the glass back, he finished the water, wiping droplets from his lips. His chest felt heavy. A headache played at the edges of his worn mind.

His throat was still dry.

Taking the glass, Joshua returned to the kitchen. He filled it halfway, then fumbled in the cabinet. His chest was more than tight, now. It felt constricted, as if a belt were cinching around it. The headache reached a crescendo, and his vision wavered.

Too much stress. Not enough sleep.

He fumbled in the cabinet again, but couldn't find what he was looking for.

"Honey?" Joshua's voice came out as a rasp. Sweat popped out over his lips. The headache was blinding now. Every few seconds it seemed to double in intensity. His chest was so tight it was difficult to breathe.

"What is it, Josh?" Ashley sounded distracted from the living room. Joshua could barely hear her over the TV.

"Ad-Advil?" he choked.

The world spun. The cabinet fell away from his grasp.

No. It was him falling. His head struck the countertop and the ceiling spun. Ashley screamed and rushed into the kitchen. He could barely see her face. He felt her hand on his cheek, but couldn't move his arms. He was covered in sweat. His legs jerked, and he couldn't make them stop.

All he saw was Ashley, mouth wide. Red eyes laced with fear. Screaming his name.

But Joshua couldn't answer. He couldn't even breathe.

90

Reed saw light.

Not a lamp. Not the harsh LED beam of his weapon light. Not even the sun.

This was something else. Clear and somehow very clean, coming from nowhere and headed nowhere. It just ... was.

He didn't feel the ground. He didn't feel himself. He looked at his hands and he saw blood dripping off them. Tattered clothes and rubber boots full of sweat.

Where was his gun? A shot of panic rushed through his chest. His right hand dropped to his side, searching for his SIG. It wasn't there. The MP5 wasn't there. The NBC suit wasn't there.

Reed gasped. He'd been holding his breath. Fresh oxygen flooded his lungs, but no matter how greedily he sucked it down it never felt like enough. His whole body shook.

He opened his mouth—he couldn't speak.

"Daddy?"

Reed's chest went rigid. His eyes blinked slowly, as though he were no longer in control of them. The light was still there, but now he saw a vague shape, also. A silhouette, at first. A small person who drew steadily nearer.

"D-Davy?" Reed rasped. He didn't recognize his own voice.

It wasn't Davy. The child didn't toddle. It walked smoothly, like someone much older than Davy. As the figure neared he detected the outline of a little blue dress. Curly blonde hair. A round, smiling face.

Reed stopped breathing. His knees buckled beneath him as though they were made of paper. He hit the ground, hands falling open. Suddenly his vision blurred.

The child remained. She stepped nearer until her body was silhouetted by the light.

She was beautiful. Five or six. A smile both broad and deeply familiar. Bright, shining blue eyes.

Like her mother's.

"It's okay, Daddy," the girl didn't stop smiling. "You're loved. You're not finished."

Reed raised a hand. Lightning pain exploded in his chest. The light pulsated, and a dull beeping joined it.

The child began to fade.

"Wait!" Reed's voice was raw and ragged. He fell forward.

The girl stepped back. Still smiling. Her body melded with the light. Her silhouette faded.

The beeping grew louder.

"Don't!" Reed screamed. The lancing pain in his chest returned. His body went rigid.

"I love you, Daddy," the girl said.

And then she disappeared.

"Another!"

"He can't take another! He's BP is 195 over 115. He's pushing cardiac arrest."

The voices pounded in Reed's ears. His eyes snapped open and light glared in his face—harsh and fluorescent. His arms were restrained. Lancing pain shot from his chest. His vision clouded and his body shook.

His head felt ready to explode.

"If you don't neutralize the VX it won't matter what his blood pressure is! Give him another!"

The voice was vaguely familiar. Alarmed and urgent.

It was Zach Hale. The downed FBI CCU agent.

An arm flashed. Silver gleamed. A needle the size of a telephone pole. It pivoted over Reed's chest.

Then rocketed down.

The stabbing sensation erupted right through Reed's heart. He shook and screamed. Strong hands constricted around his arm, holding him down. The light shifted, and Reed saw open sky.

And then he saw Turk.

Wide eyes, a half-open mouth. The needle was removed and Reed gasped. The thunder in his head didn't relax for a moment. It rolled and clapped like a marching band, pounding so hard he could barely see. A migraine, and then some.

But slowly his body relaxed. His next breath came deeper. His head slumped against cold concrete. He heard sirens and noted flashing lights. Boots pounding, and a helicopter roaring someplace far ahead.

And Turk, eyes rimmed red, strong hand gripped around Reed's arm.

"You're okay," Turk said. "We got you, brother."

Reed closed his eyes. Something hot and wet slipped down his cheek, and he didn't fight it.

When he blocked out the Missouri summer glare, he saw the child again. Small and beautiful. Looking more like her mother than him. He heard her voice.

I love you, Daddy.

91

Nobody spoke. The conference room was as silent as a crypt, all eyes fixed on Maggie as she sat at the end of the table, a black plastic phone pressed to her ear. Body growing cold, throat turning dry.

Not talking. Just listening. FBI Director Bill Purcell spoke quickly on the other end, his voice clinical and direct. An update on both Philadelphia and St. Louis. *Mission accomplished.* Mostly. Some of the VX toxin had made its way into the water supply in St. Louis, but authorities were moving quickly to isolate it. One terrorist was believed to have escaped in St. Louis, but four more were dead.

The good news fell flat on Maggie's ears. Her heart accelerated. She knew what was coming. She'd already been briefed.

New Orleans was clear. The FBI CCU team had reached Baton Rouge . .
.

Just a little too late.

"Thank you, Director." Maggie's voice rasped. "Keep us posted."

She hung up, hand trembling. Next to her the iPad that had displayed the terrorist's clock now displayed a stream of live secure-message updates from the joint counterterrorism task forces descending on Louisiana's capital.

Thousands of 911 calls. Millions of gallons of fresh water infected.

And bodies . . .

Bodies already stacking.

"Can . . . can I have just a minute?" Maggie's voice didn't sound like her own. It was dry and lifeless.

Stratton rose and opened the door for the others. The members of her emergency cabinet who hesitated to leave were driven out by his iron glare.

Only O'Dell remained. He descended to his knees alongside Maggie as the door closed. Her face fell against his shoulder. His hand rested on her back. Maggie's vision fogged and her breath caught in her throat. All the things that had clouded her mind for so many months—her sudden ascent into power, her work to stabilize the country, the campaign for office, the attempted assassination, even the Cunningham investigation—it all faded away. It just evaporated, like mist in the morning. It no longer mattered.

She only saw the bodies. Thousands of faces staring at her in haunted desperation, now out of reach forever.

Americans she had *failed*.

Their death cries echoed in her brain, and Maggie sobbed.

92

Ibrahim made it out of St. Louis without trouble. The little beater car loaded with fresh clothes, a roll of American cash, and a convincing Canadian passport waited in a storage unit two miles from the Falling Rocks treatment plant—right where it was supposed to be. He stripped out of his NBC suit and faded into the shadows while watching Bahir fight the American alongside the barrel of VX.

Ibrahim had been wrong about his young soldier. Bahir had never faltered. He flung himself straight into the heart of the battle, wielding his AK like a club when his magazine ran dry. Willingly surrendering his life for the cause. A true believer.

Of course, Bahir had thought Ibrahim was right behind him. Ibrahim had promised he would be. Just like he'd promised Mahmoud that not everyone would die. That they would leave Bahir's body to grow cold while they drove the battered Nissan Sentra across the Canadian border and deep into the wilderness, there to wait until the time was right to return to their homeland. He told Mahmoud that two passports waited in the Sentra's glovebox.

It didn't matter to him that Mahmoud's body would now be defiled by the Infidels, probably burned to ash before being washed down the drain. Hamid and Kadeem would meet a similar fate, now that they ran without aid or support across southern Texas. The American bloodhounds would find them eventually, chewing them to shreds the way they had already devoured Omar and Youssef.

For Abdel Ibrahim, this was always the first step in a greater mission. The radio of the Sentra informed him that the VX strikes in Philadelphia and St. Louis had been largely foiled, with only a couple dozen deaths in Missouri. But Baton Rouge had been brought to its knees. Thousands of people infected. Bodies stacking like bricks.

A one-third success rate. Not bad at all. Hamid and Kadeem would die in glory.

In America's motor city, Ibrahim stopped at a Starbucks and parked in the back of the lot near a tree. He wore a disguise now. A fake mustache, contact lenses that turned his eyes gray instead of rich brown, and streaks of dye that turned his brown hair dirty blond. Enough of a transformation to match the photo on his fake passport and get him across the border into Ontario.

But first he had an administrative task to attend to. An update to send to his ally, on the far side of the world. He used a laptop from the Sentra's trunk and the Starbucks's complimentary Wi-Fi to access the internet. He clicked on the *Favorites* menu and selected a weblink midway down. The page loaded slowly, and when it did he clicked quickly past a greeting page and into a forum—a discussion page dedicated to American baseball. He navigated to the correct message thread. He input a simple line of text under a pre-designated user name.

CardsManiac2019: Prayers for America during this difficult time. Hope we get baseball back soon.

Ibrahim reviewed the message carefully, one word at a time. Then he hit *post.*

On the other side of the world, the bearded man in the small, dark room was still sweaty. A stack of empty liquor bottles littered the floor around him—mostly good vodka, with some gin mixed in for good measure.

The alcohol kept him relaxed and helped the endless hours to pass while he reclined in a sagging desk chair, surveying half a dozen computer monitors. A pedestal fan squeaked in the corner, blowing hot air across his naked upper torso. His stomach growled and he considered breaking for dinner. It was nearly midnight in America, and the news cycle had descended into a predictable pattern of repeated facts.

Bodies stacking in Baton Rouge. Terrorists still on the loose. Fear blanketing the country.

All good news for the bearded man. But not the news he was looking for.

He refreshed the sports forum one more time, and rocked a gin bottle back. The liquor burned his throat and pooled in his belly. He suppressed a burp and hit refresh again, ready to head to the kitchen and warm a meal in the microwave. Something quick. Probably more braised lamb and rice.

The food in this place was such a drag.

The computer screen loaded slowly. The bearded man drank from the bottle again, thinking about next steps. His work with the website was finished, at present, as was his work with the complex robocalling software that had blanketed America with so much panic in recent days. His bosses would probably want his computers to be demolished in order to scrub away any breadcrumbs for the CIA or the FBI to follow. They'd probably want him to relocate, also. With any luck, his deployment to this hellhole might finally be drawing to a close. There was just one more matter to resolve.

The page finally reloaded when the bearded man was already halfway out of his seat. Ready for dinner. Then he stopped.

There was a new message—finally. *CardsManiac2019* had posted. Just two clipped sentences.

The bearded man returned to the seat to consult his notes, translating the encoded message quickly. The prayers for America bit meant *CardsManiac* had evaded capture. The word *difficult* versus *tragic* meant he had successfully reached Detroit and was preparing to cross the border into

Canada. The comment about baseball returning meant he was on schedule to rendezvous with a Liberian flagged container ship in Montréal—his ticket back to the Middle East.

The bearded man selected the *thumbs up* button on the post, then closed out of the message board. Ibrahim would know his message had been read. That his allies still had his back.

At least until they were finished with him.

93

Aimes didn't make it back to the George Bush Center for Intelligence until nearly three a.m. The executive transport helicopter set her down at Langley's helipad, and she marched inside carrying a briefcase and enough crushing defeat to drive her to her knees.

Fifteen hundred dead, so far. And the body count in Louisiana continued to rise.

America's intelligence capital was still buzzing with activity as she navigated to the executive floor. She guessed that wouldn't change for the foreseeable future. And per the president's direction, she would be caught right in the heart of it.

The elevator doors rolled open, and Aimes stepped out into strange calm. She stopped just inside the sprawling room lined by offices, and looked from one end to the other.

The secretaries were gone. Most of the directors and deputies were gone. A light shone here or there, and a couple of faces peered at her silently. Nobody spoke or moved to greet her.

Aimes held her chin up and marched for her office. Her keycard chirped in the reader. The door unlocked. She pushed inside . . . and then stopped.

Victor O'Brien sat in her high-backed leather chair behind the computer desk laden with wide-screen monitors and notes. The dull glow of a desk lamp cast eerie, semi-illumination over his face. Gone were the round glasses, suit jacket, and tie. His shirt was stained with sweat. His eyes bloodshot. Resting on the desktop next to him was a bottle of medication. Aimes couldn't read the label, but she didn't care what the bottle contained. She stood in the doorway a moment, shoulders stiff, blood turning hot.

Then she calmly stepped inside and closed the door.

"Congratulations, *Madam Director*."

O'Brien's voice was thick with venom, that animalistic glow in his eyes so sharp it almost threw Aimes off guard. But nothing could shake her after today. She'd numbed her mind to everything, so that only cold calculation and focused leadership took precedence.

It was a skillset she actually learned from her boss. Back before whatever complete mental breakdown she was now witnessing had taken him by storm.

"I'm not the director, Victor."

O'Brien nodded slowly, standing from the chair. Rocking the bottle and palming two little white pills into his mouth.

"But you will be," he said. "Or didn't you get the memo?"

For the first time, Maggie noticed the sheet of paper lying across her desk. She couldn't read it from so far away, but she recognized the heading printed across the top.

From the Office of Jillian Easterling—Chief of Staff to the President.

O'Brien stepped around the desk. Still sweaty, his eyes so bloodshot he looked drunk. Aimes smelled liquor on his breath, and realized he probably was. But he didn't lash out. He closed to within inches of her, so close his chest almost touched hers, their eyes locked. He didn't say a word, but she saw the raw hatred behind his gaze, as angry and violent as the glare of the ICA terrorist.

Aimes didn't blink. She didn't budge. O'Brien smiled.

"It's too bad she's finished with me," O'Brien said. "Because I'm not even close to finished with her."

Then he pushed past Aimes and marched through the door without another word. The elevator dinged, and Victor O'Brien left Langley.

94

Nashville, Tennessee
One week later

The little room where Banks recovered had quickly become a sort of makeshift mausoleum to her exploding fame. Nobody knew for sure who started it. Somebody from the concert, probably. One of the survivors. Maybe the anonymous attendee who was filming Banks when the bomb went off.

Whoever it was, once Banks's name had been associated with her story, there was no stopping that story from running viral across social media. Her website exploded with traffic. Her social media exploded with followers. The trio of songs Reed had paid for her to record at a studio in Nashville and uploaded to Spotify raked in streams by the hundreds of thousands.

It was like the ending of a Disney movie, but maybe that was what the country needed. Mainstream media was mired in death and despair at the moment. The body count in Baton Rouge had reached over two thousand, and was still growing by the day as infected residents succumbed to the brutal poison their water was still laced with. From Haiti to Tennessee and across the nation, the fear was palpable. The terror and heartache absolute.

Maybe people needed something positive to break the tempo of doom. Maybe Banks was just a tool. Whatever the case, Reed couldn't turn on a television or pass a newsstand without seeing his wife's face. Flowers and gift baskets poured in until Vanderbilt was forced to refuse them. Sinju set up a donation page to fund Banks's recovery, and it struck six figures within hours. Talk show hosts were calling. Agents and record label reps arrived at the hospital.

Turk drove them all away, one arm wrapped in a sling, the other rising from time to time like a warning shot when somebody pushed too hard. He sat outside the hospital and chain-smoked, making friends with the security guards and raising a middle finger to anyone who attempted to take his picture.

Leaving Reed in peace in Banks's room, waiting day and night by his wife's side as she cycled in and out of consciousness and grew stronger only by fractions. Lucy came and went, and Wolfgang visited several times. Sharon was there every day, Davy propped up on one hip while she buzzed around like a distraught mother hen. The nurses doted on Reed and the hospital meals blurred into one endless stream of tasteless monotony.

And Reed didn't leave. He remained by his wife's side while the doctors labored on. Their prognosis was generally positive—they now believed that Banks would live. But the wounds inflicted by the land mines would take months to fully heal. Maybe a couple of years. Her liver would have to heal, and her body would need to adjust to sustaining itself on only one kidney. The perforations in her intestines and stomach would require time to seal, after which intensive physical therapy lay in her future. She would need therapy for the trauma, also. Medication for the pain.

And she would never be pregnant again. The doctors were fatally absolute about that. The baby she lost on stage would be her last.

"Some guy called today," Reed whispered. He sat alongside Banks, spoon-feeding her pudding and rubbing her hand. The feeding tube had been removed earlier that same day, but the doctors had warned Reed that if he couldn't get his wife to eat, they would have to replace it. Banks didn't want to eat. She didn't want to talk.

One of the nurses had let slip about the baby. About the end of her ability to carry a child. The effect was predictable.

"I forget his name," Reed said, keeping his tone light. "He said he was from some place on Music Row. He wants to talk about a record deal."

Banks ran a swollen tongue over puffy lips. Reed eased a straw into her mouth and waited for her to suck down a swallow of clean water—from a bottle. He squeezed her hand.

"Isn't that great?"

Banks didn't answer. Her blue eyes misted, and a knife shot through Reed's stomach as hot and as sharp as the hypodermic needles the wounded Zach Hale had used to bring him back from the dead. As he withdrew the spoon, racing pain shot through his chest. It still hurt to breathe. He still felt a little unstable on his feet. Regular treatments of pralidoxime were easing the effects of the nerve agent. According to first responders who joined Turk and Hale at the scene, Reed had contacted very little of the toxin. Enough that he could be yanked back from the precipice thanks to Hale's quick thinking.

The FBI agent had been shot twice in the leg and had his face mask blown off. He was bleeding as he dragged the atropine case to Reed's side, risking his own contact with the puddle of VX on the floor.

Reed owed Hale his life, but Reed's own recovery would still take weeks. Maybe longer. The muscle pain would stick around for a while. As would the headaches.

A soft knock rang on the door just as Banks was drifting off again. Lucy entered, cotton pants swishing, a loose T-shirt dropping over her shoulder. She carried a soda and a little black Bible—something Reed hadn't seen her without since he'd returned to Nashville. He knew there was a story. One day he would ask.

"How is she?" Lucy whispered.

"Resting," Reed said. His voice was flat. His chest felt tight. As much as he focused on Banks and her recovery, it felt like only a shield to ward off other trains of thought. If he ever closed his eyes and returned to the dream and the child . . .

It was like raw nuclear radiation exploding in his chest. Beyond anger. Beyond pain. Even worse than the blinding rage he'd felt when Banks hit the stage. Whether he'd been right about his unborn child being a girl or whether his mind had simply displayed what he wanted to see, he didn't know and he didn't care.

What he did know was that two corpses had been dragged from the clear well room in St. Louis. Two more in Philadelphia. The terrorists in Baton Rouge had escaped, but didn't make it far. They were run down in east Texas, where one of them was shot and the other taken prisoner.

But none of those six faces matched the face of the man in the videos. The man who had murdered his child.

"I'm gonna get a smoke," Reed said.

Lucy took his seat next to Banks's bed. The soda bottle hissed and her Bible fell open as he left the room. In the same courtyard he and Turk had planned the Haitian mission in, he cupped his hand around a cigarette and lit up, barely tasting the nicotine. Every part of him felt numb. He settled onto a bench and rotated a Bluetooth earbud in one ear. Tabbing to the call log on his phone, he tapped on a number he had twice sent to voicemail over the past two days. Area code 571. Northern Virginia, just south of DC. He didn't listen to the voicemails. He already knew who was calling.

Reed sucked on his smoke while the phone dialed.

"Hello, Mr. Montgomery. Thank you for calling me back."

The voice was clear and crisp. Female. Confident.

Dr. Sarah Aimes, of the CIA.

Reed didn't answer right away. Aimes filled the silence.

"How is your wife?"

Reed almost made a quip about Aimes already knowing. Like she knew everything. Instead he only exhaled and leaned against the wall. "Better. Slowly."

"I'm glad to hear it. And you?"

Reed rolled the smoke in his hand. "I'm fine."

There was no conviction in his voice, but he was too tired to worry about that. He knew Aimes wasn't calling as a courtesy. This was business.

"Have you found him?" he said. He didn't have to clarify who he meant.

"No," Aimes said. "We're still working leads. At this point, we have to assume he escaped the country."

"But you found the hat," Reed said.

"Yes. On the floor inside the clear well room in St. Louis. The FBI was able to obtain a DNA sample from a hair found inside the sweatband. We contrasted it against a target the CIA eliminated in 2019, a bomb maker named Fakir Ibrahim. The DNA was quite similar. Our working theory now is that Fakir had a twin. The twin is our target."

Reed thought of the smooth-talking man who left him the voicemail. The man who appeared in the ICA video, then again on the Haitian security tape, wearing the Cardinals hat.

The thought of his face poured just enough fire into Reed's gut to cut to the chase. "What can I do for you, Deputy Director?"

"It's Director now, actually. There's been a bit of a . . . restructuring, here at the agency. None of which is public information, just yet. I appreciate your discretion. Suffice it to say that things will be functioning differently than before. I understand you had a somewhat tumultuous relationship with Mr. O'Brien. He wasn't a man who valued talent apart from the right gender and pedigree. We're moving now to a more pragmatic approach on recruitment—whoever is best for the job. Which is why I'm calling. I need you back."

Reed was neither surprised nor flattered by the invite. He simply dragged on his second cigarette, trying to relax. Trying to block out a fresh headache.

"I'm still retired," he said simply.

"Is that what you call it? Could have fooled me. I'm between a rock and a hard place, Reed. I've got a truckload of problems and a short list of dependable people to help me solve them. I need Fakir Ibrahim's brother on ice. Yesterday. I need people I can trust who know how to bend the rules and get away with it. That's you. And your team."

"I don't know who you're talking about," Reed said coyly.

"I'm talking about Rufus Turkman, Wolfgang Pierce, Ivan Sidorov, and Lucy Byrne. Yes, I know about Sidorov and Byrne. Oh, and Corbyn, also. The Brit. She's caused me a world of trouble with my contact at the SIS. I owe him some favors now. I might have to sleep with him, frankly. But he's agreed to loan us Ms. Corbyn indefinitely. I understand she has a passion for field work and coloring outside the lines. My kind of girl."

Reed flicked the cigarette butt onto the concrete and stamped it out, wondering how many members of his "team" Aimes had already contacted. Or who she would contact next, if he refused her.

And then he knew it didn't matter. His claims of retirement didn't matter, and neither did the nagging feeling deep in his gut that no amount of bloodshed could extinguish the pain ripping through him. He knew he wasn't going to deny Aimes. She had him on the hook from the moment she called.

From the moment that Fakir Ibrahim's twin brother escaped St. Louis.

"I'm not cheap," Reed said.

"But you are in debt," Aimes retorted. "Or maybe you forgot about Mr. Richard Barclay and the illegal use of a certain King Air 360. He filed a report with the sheriff's office. He was ready to burn the world down. I had one of my people advise him of his aircraft's participation in a matter of national emergency, and we furnished him with a suitable replacement. He's agreed to let the matter go. Your slate is clean—with him, anyway. Now you owe me."

"How much?" Reed said.

"Oh, I don't know. Why don't you bring me a dead terrorist, then we'll go from there?"

Reed stood from the bench. Stretched his aching body until most of his muscles loosened. His still ached.

"I talk to my team," he said. "Nobody else. They work on a strictly volunteer basis."

"Fair enough."

"Anybody who does work is compensated. Well."

"Of course."

"And I operate on my own terms. No leash. No rules."

"I'd certainly hope so."

"I'll call you."

Reed hung up, rubbing a thumb across his screen. He barely recognized his own reflection. He needed a shower. A shave. A haircut. A change of clothes.

And a target.

WHITE ALERT
THE PROSECUTION FORCE THRILLERS Book 6

As America bleeds, one man's relentless chase for the world's deadliest terrorist begins.

In the wake of gut-wrenching terrorist attacks across the American heartland, the Prosecution Force—led by relentless black ops specialist Reed Montgomery—is entrusted with one objective: capturing Abdel Ibrahim. Known as the world's number one terrorist, Ibrahim has eluded them before.

Following leads to Beirut, a city mired in chaos and distrust, the stakes are raised. Every alley hides danger, and every contact could be a potential traitor. Just when Reed believes they have their man cornered, Ibrahim vanishes, leaving behind a chilling clue—a weapon, more devastating than anything they've ever encountered.

Tracing him to London's shadowy streets, Reed and his team must navigate a web of deception, betrayal, and looming threats. With time running out and Ibrahim's next strike imminent, the Prosecution Force finds themselves in a deadly race against a ticking clock.

Terror knows no boundaries. But neither does the determination of the Prosecution Force.

Get your copy today at
severnriverbooks.com

ABOUT THE AUTHOR

Logan Ryles was born in small town USA and knew from an early age he wanted to be a writer. After working as a pizza delivery driver, sawmill operator, and banker, he finally embraced the dream and has been writing ever since. With a passion for action-packed and mystery-laced stories, Logan's work has ranged from global-scale political thrillers to small town vigilante hero fiction.

Beyond writing, Logan enjoys saltwater fishing, road trips, sports, and fast cars. He lives with his wife and three fun-loving dogs in Alabama.

Sign up for Logan Ryles's reader list at
severnriverbooks.com

Printed in the United States
by Baker & Taylor Publisher Services